# Spinifex

A North Queensland Cadet Adventure

C.R. Cummings

## *Also By*
## CHRISTOPHER CUMMINGS

| | |
|---|---|
| *Kylie & Skip* | *Coast of Cape York* |
| *The Boy and the Battleship* | *Kylie and the Kelly Gang* |
| *The Green Idol of Kanaka Creek* | *Beyond the Barrier Reef* |
| *Ross River Fever* | *Behind Mt. Baldy* |
| *Train to Kuranda* | *The Cadet Sergeant Major* |
| *The Mudskipper Cup* | *Cooktown Christmas* |
| *Davey Jones's Locker* | *Secret in the Clouds* |
| *Fourteen* | *Mischief at Mingela* |
| *Air Cadet* | *The Word of God* |
| *Below Bartle Frere* | *The Cadet Under-Officer* |
| *Bowling Green Bay* | *Through the Devil's Eye* |
| *Airship Over Atherton* | *Barbara in the Bush* |
| *Cockatoo* | *The Smiley People* |
| *The Cadet Corporal* | *Barbara at her Best* |
| *Stannary Hills* | *Barbara's Bivouac* |
| *Sugar & Spice* | *\*Spinifex* |

# Spinifex

A North Queensland Cadet Adventure

C.R. Cummings

DoctorZed
Publishing
www.doctorzed.com

This First Edition published 2024 by DoctorZed Publishing

DoctorZed Publishing books may be ordered through booksellers or by contacting:

DoctorZed Publishing
10 Vista Ave
Skye, south Australia 5072
www.doctorzed.com

ISBN: 978-0-9756145-7-0 (sc)
ISBN: 978-0-9756145-8-7 (ebk)

A Cataloguing-in-Publication entry can be found at the National Library of Australia
www.nla.gov.au

Cover design © Scott Zarcinas

Printed in Australia, UK & USA

DoctorZed Publishing rev. date: 18/03/2024

# Dedication
# and
# Special Thanks

This story is dedicated, with love, to my wife Cheryl.

Good Friend
Excellent Travel Companion
Officer of Cadets
and
An equal partner in life's battle
and
Always hard-working, careful, and supportive
and
A good dressmaker, costume maker and administrator
and
Great Field Exercise Control Group commander.

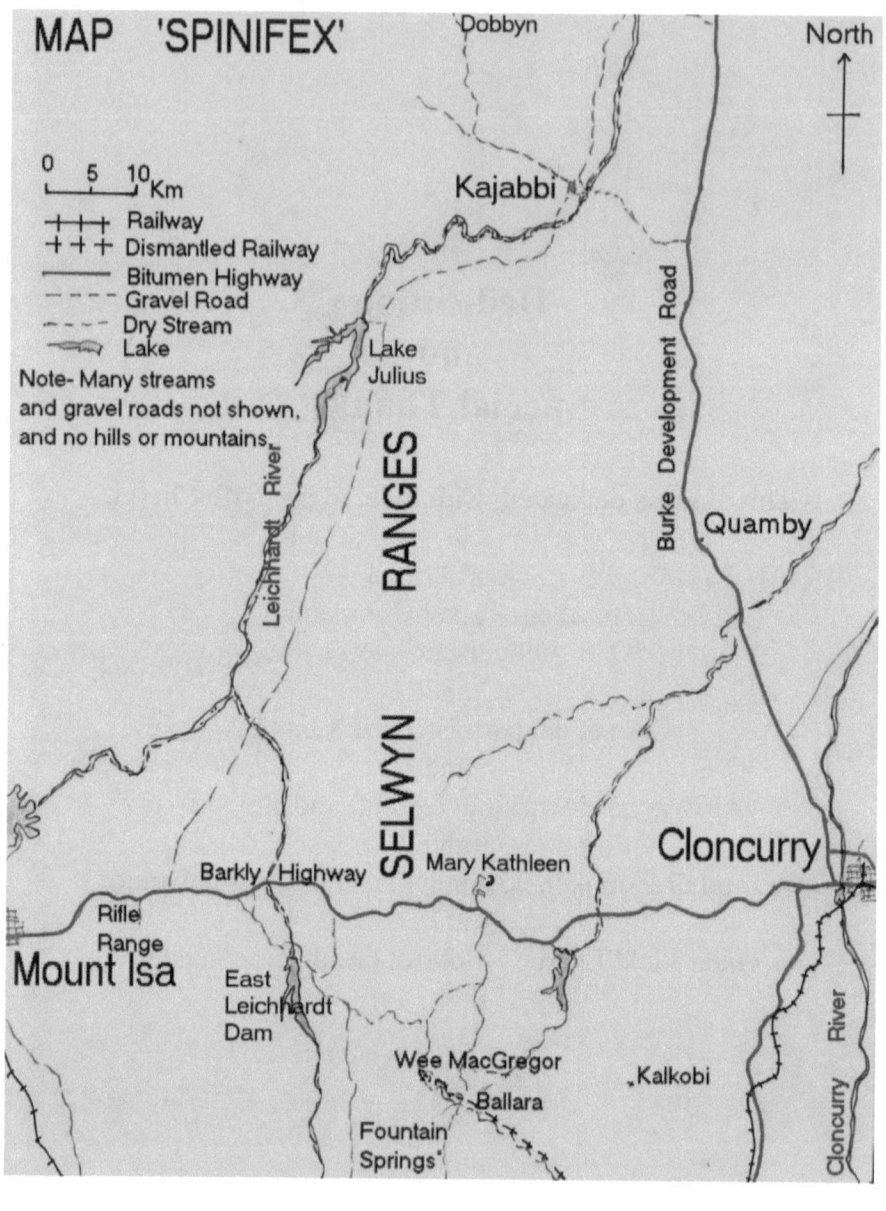

MAP 'SPINIFEX'

Dobbyn

North

0  5  10 Km

┼┼┼ Railway
+ + + Dismantled Railway
─── Bitumen Highway
- - - Gravel Road
- - - Dry Stream
～～～ Lake

Note- Many streams
and gravel roads not shown,
and no hills or mountains.

Kajabbi

Lake Julius

Leichhardt River

SELWYN RANGES

Burke Development Road

Quamby

Barkly Highway

Mary Kathleen

Cloncurry

Rifle Range

Mount Isa

East Leichhardt Dam

Wee MacGregor

Ballara

Kalkobi

Fountain Springs

Cloncurry River

# Chapter 1

## ROSE

In the Spinifex country of north west Queensland.
Mid-morning; Day 3 of the September school holidays.
In a small depression at an old mine site.

Fourteen-year-old Rose MacGregor smiled as the watched her baby sister Belinda try to catch a small lizard. The tiny reptile easily avoided the fumbling grasp of the eighteen-month-old toddler by scuttling into a clump of spinifex. Belinda, also nicknamed by her mother 'The Ball of Busyness', had already learned from painful experience that the tough, spikey grass could cause painful jabs so she gave up the attempt.

"It's alright Bee Bee," Rose said as Belinda's mouth puckered in disappointment.

Belinda made a fierce face. "My name ith Belinda, not Bee Bee. I not a bee!"

"No, but mum thinks you are very busy and dad says you are a ball of mischief," Rose agreed, softening this with another smile.

"I not a ball!" Belinda insisted.

Rose nodded and held her tongue. *But you are a bit of a ball,* she thought. Which made her sigh. Belinda was very chubby, with fat little arms and legs and that worried Rose. It seemed to be a family trait and she feared it was one she was doomed to copy. *Mum is pretty chubby,* she told herself, glancing at where her mother was busy digging beside her father. Then she sighed again. *And so am I!*

That she was not slim was one of her mental and emotional burdens and something that gave her rivals and personal enemies among her peers ammunition to bully her with.

That got Rose thinking about school for a moment and left her unsure if she was glad or sad about the school she was attending. She was attending Northern Goldfield College, a co-ed boarding school in Charters Towers and was in Year 9. The school choice was something Rose knew that her parents had really battled over but now her mother seemed to be reconciled to the decision. This was despite the fact that it was 1500 kilometres from the family home in Sydney to Charters Towers, a small town on the edge of 'Outback' North Queensland.

At the heart of the argument was the fact that Rose's parents were among the richest people in Australia, billionaires, not mere millionaires! Her father was a mining engineer by profession but was also the owner and director of MacGregor Enterprises which had a portfolio of mines and associated industries spread across half the world, but concentrated in NW Queensland. And the family home was a mansion on the North Shore of Sydney.

Her mother, Corinda, was a product of that Sydney social environment and a product of an elite and very expensive private college in the same area. She had wanted Rose to have all the benefits and favours of growing up in such an environment with its life-long social and financial connections. It was an environment that her mother revelled in. Which made it surprising to Rose that she had agreed to the two-week holiday here in the blazing 35 degree heat of the harsh and rugged country south of Cloncurry.

The selection of her school had been one of the few things Rose was aware of that her father had opposed her mother on. Usually he gave in to her on most things. But he had insisted that Rose would be a better person with a more rounded personality and with more self-confidence and self-respect if she went to a 'normal' school and grew up just a 'normal' teenager. He had also insisted, and so far it seemed to have worked, that no-body at the school, except the principal, knew who she was. Rose had been carefully instructed to keep her family links and history private and the result was that she had been accepted by most of the other girls as just another kid from western Queensland.

*And I have made some really good friends,* Rose thought, her mind conjuring up images of school friends. *I suppose it is a good school and I am enjoying myself really,* she told herself. She was also aware that NGC, as the school was nicknamed, was also her father's and her grandfather's old school.

Her father had been particularly pleased when she had joined the army cadet unit based in the school the previous year. He had explained that when his grandfather had attended the college it had its own very strong cadet unit but it had gone by the time he had gone there. Now there was a small detachment of a regional AAC unit based there. Cadets was only a part-time, volunteer activity with 2 hour 'Home Training' parades on Mondays after school and weekend camps or activities at least once a term.

"Do you good," her father had commented, although her mother had been less enthusiastic.

*And it has done me good,* Rose mused.

That cast her mind back a few days to the last week of school before the school holidays. For 6 days she and some of her friends had been in the bush at Macrossan doing their Annual Field Exercise. Rose was now a 2nd Year cadet with the rank of Cadet Corporal. It was her second AFX and during it she been a section commander with four younger cadets to look after. It had been stressful and testing, but she had coped and she was proud of that.

*And most of my best friends are also army cadets,* she thought.

For a minute or so she did some half-hearted digging and even held up a few shiny stones to check them. The family were having a day of looking at more old mining sites and doing a bit of fossicking. In this case they were looking for amethysts but Rose was neither very interested nor very hopeful. She was very well aware that the family fortune was founded on fossicking and mining but it was not the direction she felt her life was moving in.

She straightened up and looked into the distance to where the huge steel chimneys of the derelict Kalkobi Smelter showed through the heat shimmer. That had been one of those giant mineral enterprises the region's wealth was based on but the smelter had only functioned for a few years back in the first two decades of the 20th Century and was now just a massive ruin in the semi-desert spinifex country.

*Hard to imagine that once there were thousands of people here, a town and railway sidings and all,* she mused.

Belinda stood up and began toddling down the bank into the sandy bed of the nearby creek bed, picking up stone after stone and then tossing them down. Rose held up another small stone to the light and noted it was a pinky-coloured crystal.

*That might be a gem,* she decided.

But it could be looked at later so she reached into her backpack and took out a screw-top plastic bottle (That had once held honey) and placed the find in it with two others. After screwing the lid back on she slid the plastic container back into her backpack and hesitated over taking out her water bottle for a drink but then made a face and heaved herself to her feet.

*I'd better keep up with little sister,* she told herself.

Groaning at stiff muscles she picked up her bag and followed The Ball of Busyness down into the shade of the trees along the dry creek bed. She did not expect to find any water there, knowing well that it was the tropical 'Dry Season', that period of 4 months of dry summer from September to December. Not until the 'Wet' was any water likely to flow in most of the streams in this part of the world.

Rose did not know NW Queensland well but she had been there for three holidays. Her father insisted that they keep in touch with their heritage, with when Great Great Grandfather had come out from Scotland in 1910 to drive trains on the mining railways, before making his first big find at Mt Egbert.

Four days before this the family had flown from Charters Towers in a company aircraft after picking Rose up from school the day after her cadet camp had finished. They had gone to the Mt Egbert mine. From there they had toured as ordinary tourists (albeit in a well-supplied company 4WD) to stay at the bush 'pub' in the tiny town of Kajabbi. More family history was covered while they visited more old historical mines and railways in the Dobbyn area, now just bush and a few small mines and some old ones. Yesterday they had visited the Ballara area, where a long dismantled 3'6" gauge railway had linked with a 2' gauge light railway from the Wee MacGregor Mine.

Rose and her father had walked 4.5km in 37-degree heat along the line of the old railway to walk through the only railway tunnel in NW Queensland. Her mother and The Ball of Busyness had stayed at the vehicle. It had been the 4.5km back Rose had found more testing, even though it was mostly downhill. Even now she could feel her sore muscles and feet but had to smile at her father teasing here about it.

"Oh come on!" he had cried with a grin. "You just did a week of cadet camp in the bush. You should be fit!"

Rose had actually really enjoyed the little expedition, despite the heat and sore feet, partly because she saw how much pleasure it gave her dad, but also because it gave her a better appreciation of how determined and tough her own ancestors must have been. To her own surprise she did not resent having to walk around the spinifex country and bush in the blazing heat when she could have been on the beach at Manly or in an air-conditioned cinema.

Belinda bent and picked up another stone that sparkled in the sunlight. Turning to Rose she held it up. "Is this a diamond?" she queried.

Rose smiled but shook her head, only glancing at the stone. "No, it's not a diamond. It might be mica or a quartz crystal. There are no diamonds in this part of the world."

Belinda frowned. "But Daddy said he was going to find Mummy a great big diamond," she replied.

"Daddy was just joking," Rose replied, being very familiar with her father's sense of humour. "He said it because he really loves Mummy and likes to give her nice things."

"I love Mummy too," Belinda replied, tossing the stone aside and bending to pick up a much smaller one. "This is a nice diamond. I will give it to Mummy. Is it a diamond, Rosie?"

Rose walked over and took the tiny stone the size of a small pee from Belinda and then held it up between her finger and thumb against the light. To her surprise, it showed almost clear with a lovely pink tinge. "This very well might be; well, not a diamond, but possibly an amethyst," she answered.

"Mine keep it!" Belinda insisted, sticking out a grubby hand to claim it.

"Put it in your sample bottle," Rose insisted.

She handed the gem over and then knelt to help Belinda extract her plastic screw top bottle, this time one that had originally contained instant coffee. She unscrewed the top and Belinda dropped the gem inside where it rattled around, being the only thing in it. Rose screwed the top back on and struggled to put the bottle back in Belinda's little carry bag, had to struggle as the Ball of Busyness was busy again bending to pick up another shiny rock.

Rose took off her brown 'stockman's hat' and wiped sweat from her face with her sleeve. As she put the hat back on she glanced to check Belinda's was still secure. It wasn't. In her busyness the little girl had pushed her cloth hat back so that brown curls protruded at the front and her face looked red. Only the cotton chinstrap held the hat on.

Another glance showed Rose that Belinda's face and wrists were looking very red. "Come here Chubby Cheeks and let me fix that hat and put some suncream on you," she said.

"I not Chubby Chips!" Belinda replied. "I Ball of Bossiness."

Rose laughed and had to smile. "You certainly can be," she agreed.

She remembered her dad making that comment and was surprised that Belinda had remembered it. Still chuckling she adjusted the hat, not without difficulty as its wearer kept bobbing up and down as she picked up more shiny stones. Rose knelt and took a tube of suncream from her bag and squirted some on her fingers.

"Hold still you little wriggler!" she cried.

She gripped Belinda by one sleeve and proceeded to smear and rub the cream on the toddler's face and hands, a procedure the baby mostly ignored. That done, Rose returned the tube to her bag and wiped her hands on her work trousers.

Looking around to keep track of Belinda's movements distracted her from her own fossicking but she did note a small area where a past flood had eroded the creek bank to expose layers of soil and gravel.

*That looks like it might be a good area to search,* she thought.

By then Belinda was digging near a big overhanging clump of grass at the end of a small washout which led down from the old mine site.

*There might be snakes there,* Rose thought, remembering the safety brief on her cadet camp. *We were warned that the snakes come out of winter hibernation in September and slide around looking for a mate.*

She had only ever seen two snakes in the bush in her life, which was quite different to seeing them at a zoo. Both had been during the recent camp. They had been a small brown tree snake which had caused some minor drama during one night; and a large golden coloured snake Captain Ross had said might be a Western Taipan, and therefore very deadly.

Moving quickly to join Belinda she anxiously scanned the dry grass; not Spinifex this time, but some of the spear grass that covers much of inland Queensland. "Just watch that spiky grass, Bee Bee," she cautioned.

"I not a bee!" Belinda replied as she bent to pick up another shiny stone. "I a busy little person."

"You are too!" Rose agreed, smiling at her little sister's response.

At that, moment she heard her father say quite loudly: "Yes, what do you want?"

Curious to know who he was talking to Rose stood up and looked over the top of the creek bank. She got a glimpse of her mother's white hat with its wide, floppy brim, and then, beyond her, of her father. He was standing facing towards the road where the vehicle was parked and was leaning on the shovel he had been using. Then movement beyond her father brought two men into her view. She had never seen either before. Both looked to be in their thirties or forties, but one was lean and suntanned and wore a dark blue baseball cap while the other was more square of face and build and wore a felt hat with what looked like a hatband made of plaited leather.

Then she saw that both men carried guns and she experienced the first stab of alarm. This shot up a notch when the man with the hat lifted his gun, some sort of sporting rifle with a telescopic sight, and pointed it at her father.

"Are you Mister MacGregor?" the man queried.

"What if I am? Who the hell are you? And point that gun somewhere else," her father retorted angrily.

"You are Mister MacGregor?"

"Yes, now stop pointing that gun at me," her father snapped. "What do you want?"

"Only money, and lots of it," the man with the hat replied, bringing a snigger from the thin man wearing the cap. Rose now saw he had some sort of automatic rifle and that bothered her because she had a notion that such weapons were illegal for civilians to have.

Rose's father shook his head and then said, "So are you threatening us? Is this a robbery or something?"

The man with the hat shook his head. He had now stopped only a few paces from her father. "No Mister Big Boss Man. We've been put on a contract to kill you."

There was a moment of silence during which Rose's heart filled with dread. Then her father spoke, his voice still sounding quite calm. "What about my family?" he asked.

The man with the hat shook his head. "Sorry man, it's a package deal."

To Roses's admiration and amazement her father again spoke in a quiet and calm voice. "Are you open to negotiation?"

The hat man shook his head but the thin man raised an eyebrow. Hat man replied, "If we don't do the job the people who hired us will have a contract out on us."

Rose's father nodded but then spoke more clearly. "Now, I don't want to sound like I am making threats but you can be sure that if something like this happens to me certain business associates of mine will follow up and you might find it even harder to avoid them."

Hat Man shrugged but still looked impassive. "Occupational risk, I guess."

"But I am sure I am far richer than whoever has hired you and my agreement will include your escape package; a new identity and so on with a cover clause," Rose's father said.

For the first time thin man glanced at Hat Man and said, "Maybe worth listening to what Mr MacGregor has to offer Lucas?"

"No names dumbo!" Lucas, Hat Man, snapped back but a frown crossed his face. His rifle stayed steady but Rose saw his mouth go tight. By now her heart was starting to palpitate with terror as the reality of what she was seeing and hearing began to sink in.

*He's thinking about it,* she thought, experiencing a glimmer of hope.

Several times in the past there had been death threats against her father or the family, so she always had a background nagging fear of such a thing from people with a grudge or radical political views and she had heard her mother several times suggest they have bodyguards or at least increased security. But so far her father had preferred to live as a normal person in Australia.

Then Lucas nodded. "Okay man, what can you offer?"

"Name a figure. Be a bit realistic but if it saves my family at least I really have no upper limit," Rose's father suggested.

"This includes a no-comeback clause to protect us?" Lucas queried, raising both eyebrows as he did.

Rose's father nodded. "Of course. The deal has to satisfy both parties."

Thin man now nodded. "Sounds good to me Lucas. Let's do a deal."

"No names you dumbshit!" Lucas retorted. "Okay Mr MacGregor, how much and how will a deal like that work?"

Now Rose really did feel a glimmer of hope and she realised she had been holding her breath and hyperventilating as the fear had built. She glanced down to check on Belinda and saw she was still happily oblivious to all of this and was scooping sand and stones into a small pile.

"How does ten million sound? Five million each, in whatever form you want," Rose's father suggested.

To Rose's dismay Lucas shook his head. "Nah! Five million for each family member," he countered. "Twenty million, half in used bank notes and half in gold."

Rose expected her father to bargain but to her surprise he just nodded. "If that is satisfactory; and as I said, a cover clause to get you and your … er… your associate here future security."

"So how will you organise this?" Lucas asked.

Rose's father shrugged and gestured at the bush with his left hand. "I can't do much here. I need to get to one of my offices where I can use the communication facilities, and it will take some time," he replied.

"How long?" Lucas said. For the first time he looked plainly anxious.

"Two or three days at least, probably a week," Rose's father answered.

Lucas frowned and chewed at his lip and then swung the rifle to point it at Rose's mother. "Okay, but we will keep your family as security against any sort of double cross," he snarled.

"As hostages?" Rose's father commented.

"That's right. Any trouble and they start to die," Lucas replied.

Thin Man now snickered and pointed at Rose's mother and snickered. "And only after they have enjoyed a bit of special treatment," he said.

It took a moment for the meaning of what the man was implying to sink in. Rose wasn't exactly innocent; there had been plenty of 'girl talk' in the girl's dorm, along with stories she had read, not to mention a few suggestions by grubby boys. But this was real evil and only then did it hit her that she might also be subjected to disgusting outrages.

*Rape, he means,* she thought with growing horror.

At that, her father shook his head. "If you harm my wife and daughters in any way the whole deal is off, even if you shoot me. And you can be sure that retribution will follow you."

Lucas curled his lip. "We call the shots, Mr Boss Man. Now let's just agree that they are going to be held as security against any sort of double cross."

"Yeah," Thin Man added. "Now where are the two little girls?"

Rose's father shrugged and gestured away from the creek. "Around here somewhere. They are digging in the old mullock heaps like we are, looking for gems."

Only when she saw her father pointing in the opposite direction did it dawn on Rose that her father was trying to give her a chance. *Daddy knows we are just here in the creek! He watched us a few minutes ago. Does he mean I should try to hide from the men?* she wondered.

Now fear was hammering in her mind and heart and she was nearly gasping from hyperventilating as the horrible thoughts pounded at her sense of unreality. The men were just there, both looking away towards the overgrown piles of mullock. Rose began to shake.

*Of what should I do?*

# Chapter 2

## WHICH WAY?

Her fear was now so great that Rose was feeling paralysed. Her vision seemed to blur and she realised she was taking huge gulps of air.

*Oh my God! These men mean to kill us!* she thought.

Through eyes that were misting and blinking in the heat she saw the man named Lucas turn to the thin man.

"Marvin, you cover this pair while I round up the two girls," Lucas ordered.

Thin Man, Marvin, gave a sour grin. "I thought you said no names."

"Just do what you are told!" Lucas snarled. He then looked all around.

As he did, it dawned on Rose that he had not seen her. *There is long grass and that little bush between us and him,* she reasoned. Then another thought seemed to pop into her head like the light bulb coming on. *Dad knows we are here. He just looked at us. Maybe he wants us to try to hide?*

Even as the idea formed she acted on it, dropping to her knees in the soft sand so that she was well below the level of the washed out creek bank. And next to her was Belinda, which presented another problem.

*Does he mean both of us to hide?*

And that was a real problem. *How do you hide with a busy-bee toddler!*

But she knew she had to try so she grabbed her backpack and Belinda's carry bag and scurried over to where her little sister was digging industriously in the soft sand nearby. As she did, Rose looked frantically around for a place to hide. To her dismay, there was no obvious hiding places in the creek bed. There were no large rocks or logs and the trees mostly had fairly thin trunks. And a glance showed her she had no chance to hurry across to the far bank. It was at least 25 paces and there were almost no grass or bushes there. And beyond was a long, gently rising slope almost bare of even spinifex.

The only possible place was the tiny washout among the overhanging grass next to Belinda. Then into her mind came the cadet fieldcraft lesson she had watched as a 1<sup>st</sup> Year cadet, 'Why things are seen'. During it a demonstration squad of corporals had been positioned for the cadets to observe or locate. One corporal had been lying in very short grass only ten paces in front of the squad and she had only seen him when Captain Ross had told the corporal to stand up.

*Must be here,* she told herself.

It was obvious there was no time to go anywhere else. But what to do about Belinda. Desperation seemed to make her mind go faster and she crouched down beside Belinda and reached out to grab her arm. "Stop digging Bee Bee. Daddy wants us to play hidey seekey."

"I dig up diamonds," Belinda replied, still digging.

"Please Busy Bee. Play hidey seekey with me so Daddy can't find us," Rose pleaded. She knew she was getting desperate but sheer terror was making her shake and gasp as the ghastly reality sank in.

To her immense relief, Belinda stopped digging and looked at her. "Okay, where we hide?" she asked, a mischievous grin dimpling her chubby cheeks.

"Just under this grass," Rose whispered back, gesturing. "Here, you lie here, and I will keep the grass and leaves off you. Quick now, and please don't talk."

"Why not?" Belinda queried as she began moving over next to the sandy bank.

"Because Daddy will hear us. Please be quiet," Rose whispered back.

With what seemed like a huge amount of effort she forced a face that felt like it was made of hard plastic to form a smile. Again she felt a surge of relief when Belinda crawled hard against the bank just in the little washout, but this turned to instant alarm as she heard Lucas speaking, his voice getting louder.

"There's nobody out there," he snarled. "Where are they?"

Rose's father's voice came back, "That's where I saw them last. They were digging in an old mullock heap looking for amethysts."

"Well I can't see them."

Thin Man, Marvin, now spoke. "Maybe they're in the creek just there?"

"Yeah, I'll look," Lucas agreed.

The sound of his movement through the long grass and spinifex came to Rose and she hunched in under the grass, clutching both bags and

Belinda tightly to her. She began to pray as the terror coursed through her system.

The sound of footsteps stopped nearby, and Lucas spoke from directly above her. "I can see what look like footprints in the sand," he said. "But I can't see them."

At that, comment, Rose nearly wet herself and her gaze flicked out to the sandy creek bed. She could clearly see indentations that she and Belinda had made while moving about but the dry sand was so soft there were no obvious tracks which showed which way they had moved.

But the man was just there. She could hear him breathing! The man moved his boots and a few trickles of sand fell off the bank beside her. She looked down and found herself looking into Belinda's eyes at a range of a few centimetres. Belinda's were dancing with excitement and amusement. *She thinks it is a game,* Rose thought. But then another worrying idea came to her: What if Belinda made a noise or called out?

She knew that would lead to instant discovery, so she risked being seen and moved her right hand so as to be able to cover Belinda's mouth. As she planned what to do a horrible scene from a movie she had once seen came to her. It had been a war movie and a man and woman with a baby had been hiding behind a door when German soldiers came to the doorway and looked in. The baby had started to make a noise and the man had covered its mouth and nose with his huge hand and held it there. Then the Germans had gone away but the baby was dead, smothered by his grip!

*Oh, I couldn't do that. But I must keep her quiet,* she told herself.

To help she moved her hand in front of both their faces and put it to her lips in the 'Sssh!' gesture. To her relief, Belinda nodded and gave a little silent chuckle.

Lucas suddenly stamped his boots and then called loudly, "Okay Mister Boss Man, where are they?"

Rose's father replied in an irritable tone, "I don't know! They were around here a few minutes ago. Maybe they've wandered further away?"

"They better be here bloody damn quick! Call them," Lucas ordered.

As he did, Rose heard his footsteps moving away back towards her parents.

Rose's father suddenly called loudly, "Rose! Belinda! Come here girls."

At that, Belinda looked startled and then anxious but Rose gripped her tightly and shook her head while smiling.

"Daddy can't find us. We will keep hiding," she whispered.

To her relief, Belinda accepted this and she even chuckled when their father and mother both called loudly. But Rose was worried.

*I think Daddy wanted me to hide us both,* she told herself.

Lucas also called loudly and then said, "Marvin, go and get Norris and then do a walk around among these mullock heaps. They must be just here somewhere."

Marvin obviously wasn't happy with this. "Bloody hell!" he grumbled. "It's too bloody hot to be walking around in the sun. It must be forty degrees out there."

"Just do it! They can't be far away. They are only little girls," Lucas snarled.

*Oh are we!* Rose thought, even as Belinda opened her mouth to speak.

For an instant Rose feared she was going to make a noise but instead Belinda hissed softly, "Naughty man use bad language."

Rose nodded and went, "Yes, Ssssh!" But she knew this couldn't last.

*If they walk around the creek bed they must see us,* she told herself. *So I need to risk moving now, while that Marvin is moving away and the other one is guarding mum and dad.*

Or at least she thought he was. Not knowing made it harder to plan and to act. But she now took several deep breaths and nerved herself to act. Trembling with anxiety, she let go of Belinda and crouched. Then she hauled her backpack on and risked a peek through the tuft of grass.

*Yes, Lucas is half watching mum and dad and half watching that creep Marvin,* she noted. *Now, which way?*

She looked both ways along the dry creek bed. It was obvious she could not cross to the other bank unseen, so it had to be either way along the bed. Behind her the creek went towards the gravel road. The other way went away from it, east, she thought. But the bank was slightly higher in that direction and seemed to have more grass, so she opted for that.

Gasping as though she had already run a race Rose knelt and picked Belinda up, holding her tightly against her front. Bent double she was just below the bank. She realised she could not stand upright for at least 50 metres. But there was nothing for it so she started shuffling on her knees and one hand and then crab walking along right next to the bank.

That was hard to do as she had to hold Belinda up at the same time. And the fear made her muscles seem like rubber that wouldn't properly obey her mind.

*I don't think they will just shoot if they see me,* she thought. But the fear was real, and her flesh began to cringe in anticipation.

Rose had only gone about ten paces when she had to detour out into the open bed of the creek to get around a tree growing up out of the sand. To do that she went down to a low crouch but that was very awkward, and she had trouble moving and keeping a grip on Belinda.

Belinda obviously wasn't comfortable either as she twitched and said, "This hurting, Rosie!"

"Ssssh! Just a bit more," Rose replied softly.

"Where we go?" Belinda asked, pushing with one hand to break free.

"Ssssh! To a better hiding place."

"I not want to go," Belinda replied. She began to squirm strongly, trying to get out of Rose's grasp.

Rose felt her anxiety level shoot right up as she knew from many episodes that if Belinda got it into her head to really resist there would be a screaming tantrum.

"Oh please, Bee Bee, just be still. Mummy will not be happy if the bad men find us," she whispered.

"Bad men say bad words," Belinda replied, but to Rose's relief, she seemed to accept the idea.

Rose continued crawling and once beyond the tree trunk she again risked a look over the bank. What she saw emboldened her. Lucas, her father and her mother were all standing with their backs to the creek, and she glimpsed Marvin's head among the hummocks a good 50 metres out in the spinifex. He was moving away from her and seemed to be searching in a semi-circle to her left around the area. A brief glimpse showed the head of a third man further out.

*Now! Move now!* Rose told herself.

Experience from games of Hide and Seek and also cadet exercises like 'Mr Wolf' helped her make the decision. So she stood up and clutched Belinda to her front and began hurrying away, even though that meant her head was above the level of the bank.

By now she was gasping from walking in the soft sand in the heat. Sweat was pouring from her. To her concern, Belinda pushed at her.

"Yuk! You all sweaty, Rosie," she muttered.

"Ssssh! We are nearly away from the bad men," Rose replied.

She was so winded and gasping by this that she just wanted to stop but fear kept her forcing legs that felt like lead to keep functioning. Another glance back showed that she was now at least 50 metres from her parents and Lucas and Marvin had vanished among the small dips and hollows of the old diggings.

*But he and that third man will come around to the creek behind us and will be able to see right along it,* Rose reasoned.

The creek looked to be annoyingly straight for at least a hundred metres in both directions, lovely white, bare sand studded with the even lovelier white-trunked gum trees that made the region so beautiful.

By now the creek bank was higher and Rose felt safer from Lucas but knew she had to get out of the bed to avoid Marvin seeing her. There was also the fear that the men might just follow her tracks, but a glance back eased that somewhat. Most of the bed of the creek was dimpled with little hollows from cattle and other animals and her tracks did not look all that clear. And when she walked across areas of dead leaves and pebbles, they were even less obvious.

But which way to get out of the creek bed? Up onto the open spinifex country on her left? Or take the risk of being seen crossing the creek and getting so far away that the trees and bushes hid them?

Rose came to a patch of creek bed which included several sheets of bare bedrock. The plan at once came to her. *Go right, go across the creek and put as much distance between the men and us as I can, as quickly as I can,* she told herself.

She was painfully aware she could not carry a wriggling Belinda much further and also that Belinda was not going to stay silent much longer. The novelty of the game was clearly wearing off!

"Be a koala please Bee Bee," Rose croaked, the words coming out with a quaver that she was ashamed of.

But she was really scared and admitted it to herself. To her relief, Belinda co-operated, clinging to her front with both arms and legs. Rose did not wait. She set off across the sand as fast as she could push herself.

As she did, she kept glancing back over her right shoulder. For the first time what she was wearing became a concern to her. Remembering the cadet camouflage lesson she was glad she was wearing a long-sleeved khaki work shirt and jeans, but Belinda had a bright pink hat. And she was wearing a pink and red floral shirt under her red 'overalls' pant suit! That got Rose making sure she kept Belinda tight against her front on the side away from the men.

Those fifty running paces almost brought her to an exhausted standstill. By the time Rose reached the steep little climb at the far side of the creek, she was gasping and her legs felt like lead. But fear kept her going and she found a cattle pad that led up the metre high bank and hurried up it.

There she had to stop. Chest heaving, she scurried behind the first tree she reached and stopped. Leaning back against the rough bark, she gulped in great deep breaths. A fit of trembling coursed through her and for a few moments all she could do was stand there, still gripping Belinda.

Then the terror returned with redoubled force, and she moved to peek back around the trunk, oblivious to the rough bark scraping her cheek. It took her a few moments to focus her eyes, but she was relieved there had been no shouts to stop or cries of alarm. Even better she found that there were now so many tree trunks between her and her parents and Lucas that she could only just glimpse her mother's bright floral green shirt in the distance. Of the other men there was no sign.

*But they will be at the creek soon,* she told herself, her gaze flicking west along the creek for any glimpse of them. *I must keep moving. I have to get away from here.*

But which way? Rose now looked around more carefully on her side of the creek. Directly in front of her was the long, gentle rise studded with spinifex and a few small bushes but almost no trees. To her left front, the slope grew to become a small hill with a few exposed rocks and a couple of white-trunked trees.

*There is no way I can walk straight up that without being seen,* she realised.

So that meant continuing along beside the creek away from the men. After another quick glance to check if they could see her, she pushed herself away from the tree and resumed walking.

Belinda was now squirming restlessly. "Mine want to stop playing," she cried. "Me want to go back to Mummy."

"Those bad men are there, Bee Bee," Rose replied, fearful lest Belinda cry out loud enough to be heard by the men.

"I not Bee Bee! I Blinda. Want Mummy!"

"Okay, we will go to her," Rose lied, feeling bad about it as she did.

Belinda jerked and squirmed, then pointed back over her shoulder. "Mummy back that way!" she said. Her face began to take on the determined look that usually presaged a temper tantrum.

"Oh no please Belinda," Rose pleaded, gasping still as she was hurrying along. "Daddy wants us to stay away from the bad men. We will go back to Mummy when they are gone."

To her relief, Belinda frowned and peered back over her shoulder. "What bad men?" she asked.

"You heard them saying naughty words," Rose replied, casting another fearful glance back over her left shoulder. She was having trouble making her way along the top of the bank because the spinifex stems were so long and the spiny leaves were continually sticking through her trousers. It was painful but she forced herself to ignore it. With every step she felt safer and was sure that she was invisible from anyone on the other bank of the creek back where her parents were.

*And probably from anyone in the creek,* she reasoned.

But what if they crossed to the same bank she was on? That caused her to pause and look back and she was appalled. She found she could see for many hundreds of metres.

*All the way back to the road!*

Which left her with very stressful decisions to make. *Do I just keep on going along this side of the creek and try to get away before they work out what we have done?* she wondered.

The other option was to get away from the creek. But that meant going out across that long rising slope. A look to her right dismayed her even more. She saw that the low hill was now almost directly on her right.

*I can't go up over that,* she reasoned, again remembering her fieldcraft lessons. The word 'silhouette' flitted across her mind. *Captain Ross said to stay off skylines,* she remembered.

So that meant going around the lower slopes. But to do that required her to angle away from the trees along the creek and out onto those almost bare slopes. It was a fearful choice, and she walked another twenty-five paces while making her mind up. Reasoning she was now at least a hundred and fifty metres away from the point where she had crossed the creek, she took a deep breath and forced herself to direct her footsteps to her right front.

*East, or southeast,* she told herself as she was now out in the open and walking into the morning sun.

And Belinda was complaining again and getting heavy and hard to hold. Luckily, she grizzled fairly quietly and kept hanging on but Rose knew she could not keep it up much longer.

Picking the easiest route between the clumps of spinifex took up much of Rose's attention and she feared her legs were getting badly scratched. They were certainly hurting, and hurt even more when she walked into a spiky little bush whose thorns ripped straight through the cloth.

"Yah! Ouch!" she cried, then felt a stab of guilt at having cried out.

Belinda looked concerned. "What matter, Rosie?" she asked.

"Just a prickly bush Bub-O," Rose replied.

"I not bub anymore. I big girl now!" Belinda insisted.

"You certainly are," Rose agreed.

She took the opportunity to halt and change her arms to ease the muscles that were starting to cramp and fail. Now she was right out in the open, a hundred paces from the cover along the creek line and it still looked several hundred until she reached the far slope of the hill. Another fearful glance behind showed her no sign of the men so she glanced down to pick the easiest path between the spinifex clumps and resumed walking.

She would have run if she had been able, but she was a normal teenage girl, healthy but not fit.

*I'm no athlete,* she thought ruefully but did hope that the cadet camp had toughened her up a little bit. *At least I've had some experience at walking cross-country,* she told herself.

But the sun was in her eyes and so was her sweat and she knew she was weakening. A feeling of apprehension almost amounting to dread began to build and she felt that panic was close. It became a real effort just to keep walking and several times she stumbled as her feet caught in clumps of spinifex.

*Oh God give me strength!* she prayed.

The rising ground just seemed to be as far away as ever. Gritting her teeth she persevered, plodding steadily across the gentle slope and now gasping for breath and struggling to find arguments to pacify Belinda.

*God it's hot!* Rose thought, wiping a trickle of perspiration from her eyes.

The salt in the sweat stung and she found her vision going blurry and she began blinking and then sobbing.

*Oh I can't do it!* she thought.

Despair began to build and dread began to compress her chest and heart. Sobbing and gasping she stumbled to a standstill and looked back.

To her astonishment, she saw that all she could see behind her was a gentle slope of spinifex and a clear, blue sky. To her left, the trees along the creek were still visible but they looked a long way away. Then it came to her.

*I am over the crest. I am in dead ground,* she told herself, again remembering a lesson by Captain Ross on 'Lines of Advance'.

Knowing that she was temporarily hidden from view brought Rose to a gasping halt. She stood and shuddered and then looked around for a patch of bare ground to put Belinda down on. She let her little sister slip down and then slumped onto the ground, sobbing and shivering with reaction.

But the respite was much briefer than she wanted. The bare earth existed because it was an ant's nest. Belinda let out a loud howl of pain had jumped up, hitting and brushing at her left ankle. Rose looked down and at once saw the area was crawling with red meat ants. Springing up she snatched Belinda up under her armpits and held her tight while she plucked off the ant that was biting Belinda. Then she brushed at her shoes and legs to get rid of any other ants. Belinda began to cry loudly.

*Bloody hell! I can't stay here,* Rose thought. *But which way should we go?*

# Chapter 3

## REGRET

R ose looked around almost frantic with anxiety. Belinda's wail grew louder, and Rose's first reaction was to plead with her. Her second was to start walking directly away from where she thought the men were. This took her down a long, open slope eastwards, parallel to the creek line.

"Please don't cry, Baby Bee!" Rose pleaded.

But Belinda was not to be pacified so easily. The ant bite had obviously hurt and also caught her by surprise and tears began to course down her red face. Belinda also squirmed and scratched at her ankle.

"Want Mummy!" she cried.

By this time Rose was almost running through the spinifex, heedless of the sharp stings and stabs from the spiky stems. But it was a stumble over a termite mound that stopped her panicked flight. She just managed to stop herself and Belinda from tumbling headlong into the long grass and spinifex. As she regained her balance, she realised that the shock had temporarily silenced Belinda.

Steadying herself she managed a weak smile. "Sorry Buby-O, I nearly tripped," she explained.

For a few moments she stood there gasping, wondering if she could hear her parents calling in the distance. But she decided that it was just the normal bush noises she could hear, cicadas and so on. Then she realised her mouth was very dry. Finding another patch of bare earth that was not crawling with ants she lowered Belinda carefully and then knelt beside her. Quickly she took off her backpack and extracted her water bottle.

As she unscrewed the cap, Belinda reached out. "Mine want dwink!' she called.

*That will help keep her quiet,* Rose reasoned.

So she handed the bottle to Belinda and carefully controlled it while her little sister gulped a big drink, some of the water trickling down the side of her mouth.

"That's enough Bee Bee," she said.

She took the bottle away from a reluctant Belinda and had a big drink herself. Then a dismaying thought came to her. Not only was it very hot but if she was to hide with Belinda in this semi-desert country water would become a critical factor in their ability to stay hidden.

*I must conserve the water and I need to give it to Belinda or she will get heat exhaustion and then heat stroke and die.*

She looked at her little sister affectionately but with dread in her heart. *This might be harder than I thought,* Rose reflected.

She knew that the air temperature was probably already in the mid-30s and would go higher during the afternoon. From comments she had overheard adults making she dimly understood that the actual air temperature was not the critical factor, but that humidity was also very important. Images of the Officers of Cadets using a gadget to measure the relative temperature on cadet activities came to her.

But it was also obvious they could not stay where they were. They were out on a long gentle slope where the only way to hide was to lie down in the spinifex, which would obviously be very unpleasant!

*And with the sun blazing down we couldn't do that for long,* she understood. That got her looking around while she allowed Belinda a few more sips.

*Do I go back to the creek?* she wondered. It was very obvious that if one of the men climbed to the top of the low hill behind her he would be able to see her. That got Rose studying the ground in all directions. *Which way should we go to get to safety?* she thought.

As she puzzled over this, a stab of real regret made her bite her lip. *I wish I'd studied the map a bit better!* she told herself.

As a mining engineer and geologist her father had a passion for maps and always carried them and showed the family where they were and where they were going. This had gone on all Rose's life but until now it had never really been important. Her father had always done the navigating.

But now Rose realised that such knowledge was going to be vital if she and Belinda were to escape. Looking around in the growing heat shimmer revealed distant lines of rugged hills in all directions and it came to Rose that she was a very long way from any civilization or settlement. The nearest town she could think of was Cloncurry and she thought she had heard her father say it was about 50 kilometres away.

*Fifty kilometres, and in this heat! How can I walk that?* she thought with growing dismay. It was obvious that Belinda could not and that she would have to carry her little sister. *Can I do that? Am I strong enough?* she worried.

And she knew she could not spend long making up her mind. She was sure that the men must be looking and could appear along the creek line or on the hill at any time. She knew she had to get further away quickly but was loath to walk in the wrong direction when she was so anxious about her own strength.

Nearly whimpering with anxiety, Rose tried to recall what she could of the map she had seen several times during the last three days. She was dismayed at how little was clear in her mind and she felt another stab of regret. So she went back over the morning's expedition in her memory.

*We drove south along a bitumen road from near Cloncurry,* she told herself. *And it was a very pretty drive.*

There had been lots of very rugged and impressive hills and at one point the road had curved through a spectacular little pass or gorge.

*Then we drove in along this side road through lots of hills to follow the creek,* she remembered. *Coppermine Cree? No, Copperlode Creek,* she corrected. That got her looking in the direction she knew from cadets was east. *At least I paid attention during the lesson on Navigation by the Sun and Stars.*

Lifting her eyes she looked out across several kilometres of spinifex and bush covered terrain to where a line of very rugged hills extended right across the whole eastern skyline.

*That bitumen road is the other side of those hills then,* she reasoned. Which was a depressing thought. It looked a long way and very hard going. *Especially in this heat and carrying little Ball of Busyness!*

Squeezing her eyes shut, Rose tried again to visualise the map. That helped and she remembered that the main highway between the towns of Mount Isa and Cloncurry ran east -west somewhere to her north.

*And it is closer, only twenty or thirty kilometres,* she thought.

But having travelled that road several times she was also very aware that it was lined by ranges of very rugged hills, mountains even. Looking that way she was confronted with dismaying glimpses of higher mountains in the far distance, beyond the stony hills ringing the wide valley that Copperlode Creek ran along.

And the problem with going to either road, she suddenly realised, was that there was the risk the bad men would be driving along them.

*With my luck the first car I flag down will be them!*

And long before she reached either road, she realised that she would need to find water. Again she was assailed by regret at not having studied the map better as she now remembered seeing various waterholes and windmills marked on it. But she could not remember any details so had no idea where the closest one was. She knew that this was cattle country and that the station owners erected windmills to pump water from underground into drinking troughs for the cattle. She had often seen them while travelling but up until now they had meant very little, just a curiosity of the Australian landscape.

But where might the nearest be?

*If I go north to the Mount Isa Road, the Barkly Highway, I have to walk back and cross the creek and then that open country beyond to the gravel road. That takes me back where the men might see us,* she reasoned.

But going east did not look like a good option either. From where she was she could see for several kilometres as the country to the east was very open, just a plain covered with spinifex and a few bushes and the occasional tree.

Going west was no choice either as that was back over the low hill and towards the men. *So that only leaves south,* Rose told herself.

Looking that way she was heartened to note that a few hundred metres away the trees thickened up and that there were an increasing number of patches of long grass and thickets of bushes.

*That way then,* she decided.

She knew it was the most obvious direction so the one the men might search but it still seemed the best option. Knowing that time was critical she did not hesitate but put her drink bottle back in her backpack, quickly slung it on her back and then picked up Belinda.

"Come on Bub-O, we have to move," she said.

"Mine want to go back to Mummy!" Belinda replied loudly.

"Sssh! Please don't call out Belinda. The bad men might hear you."

"Mummy! Want Mummy!" Belinda screamed. By now she was red in the face and began to hammer at Rose with her little fists and tiny sandshoes.

Terrified the men would hear, Rose pleaded with her as she walked, but to no avail. Belinda kept wailing and screaming and then real tears began. All Rose could do was grip her tightly and stride on down a long, open slope towards the first clump of bushes.

*Oh I hope the hill blocks the sound,* she thought.

Anxiety kept her moving, walking as quickly as she could across the spinifex. The heat was now getting very oppressive, and she guessed it must be nearly midday. But she could not loosen her grip on Belinda to check her watch. All she could do was keep walking, gasping with the effort and perspiring copiously.

As she got closer to the thicket of bushes, Rose's hopes crept up a notch. But two minutes and a hundred or so paces later she received an unpleasant shock. Yes, the bushes were thick and tall and did offer good cover, but they were horrible to walk through. She had been expecting them to have thorns or prickles, the usual sort of semi-desert vegetation, but instead they were covered with thousands of seed pods three to five centimetres long. And the seed pods had all opened and were secreting some sort of sticky sap. As soon as she brushed against the first ones, Rose felt the unpleasant sensation of things sticking to her and she looked down and saw that the sticky stuff was adhering to her skin and clothing, along with hundreds of tiny seeds.

*Oh yuk!* she thought.

But they did not seem to hurt so she pushed on into the thicket. Now she had to slow down to keep her hat from being swept off by branches and she tried to keep Belinda from being covered with the sticky seeds. In this she failed, and Belinda quickly noticed and then plucked at them, getting sticky seeds on her hands and then on her face and in her hair. This led to more tears and wails and Rose could only shake her head and hope that the sap was not poisonous or going to burn their delicate skin.

A glance back showed that she could hardly see the low hill through the bushes and that the creek had completely vanished from her view. She became even more hopeful, but was painfully aware that she was tiring fast. Gritting her teeth with determination she pushed on for another hundred paces or so, taking as much care as she could to weave her way between the sticky buses to avoid as many as possible. She then stopped in the shade of a big gum tree and lowered Belinda onto an area of dry grass and leaf litter.

"Dwink!" Belinda demanded.

Reluctantly Rose gave her another drink, this time from her own small drink bottle. She badly wanted a drink herself and was anxiously aware that both water bottles were more than half empty. To add to her concern she was conscious that her tongue felt dry.

*I need to conserve water,* she thought as she lowered herself to sit on the ground. A careful look around assured her there were only a few of the usual little black ants so she tried to relax and think.

Then reaction set in and she began to tremble uncontrollably. Belinda saw this and looked anxious, which didn't help. Tears came and that got Belinda even more concerned.

"What matter, Rosie? Why you cry?" she asked.

That steadied Rose and she managed a smile as she wiped away her tears. "Just happy the bad men haven't seen us," she replied.

Belinda seemed to have forgotten her tantrum and just nodded. "You will be or'right," Belinda assured her. "We good at hidey seeky."

"We are," Rose agreed, forcing another smile.

"What we do now?" Belinda asked.

*Yes, what do we do now?* Rose wondered.

# Chapter 4

## HARD DECISIONS

Once again it was the ants that got them moving. Belinda let out a little yelp and brushed at her left hand. Rose saw that one of the tiny black ants was nipping her so she quickly reached forward and grabbed Belinda's wrist with her left hand while plucking the offending ant off with her right finger and thumb.

"Only a little ant Bub-O," she said, hoping to defuse the situation.

"Not little! And I not bubbie anymore. I growed up. I toddles," Belinda cried.

"You certainly can toddle," Rose agreed.

She brushed off a few more ants and then found a couple crawling on her own clothes and wrists. She was also aware that the ground they were sitting on was uncomfortably hot.

*Eucalypts don't cast much shade,* she noted ruefully.

Deciding she could move a bit longer she stood and then picked up Belinda, placing her on her right hip. After a long searching look back at the hill she turned her back on it and began to thread a wandering path through the spinifex and the sticky bushes.

*Bloody hell! If I have to walk all the way like this it won't be twenty kilometres to somewhere but thirty or forty!* she thought.

She managed another five minutes, maybe 200 metres, before Belinda's weight was too much for her. She came to a panting halt at another dry creek line. This one was tiny, only a couple of paces wide and with a depth of less than half a metre. But it was clean sand with a few dead leaves and with plenty of shade as the trees grew thicker here. Looking back Rose had trouble seeing the hill and decided to rest again.

*I need to think this out,* she told herself.

After carefully lowering Belinda she again took off her backpack and settled herself on the warm sand. The heat was now really worrying. In the sunlight it had seemed to burn thought the cloth of her shirt and even in the shade the air felt heavy and hot to breathe. There was no breeze. A glance at her watch showed it was 1140 .

Rose badly wanted a drink and she licked lips that were starting to dry and crack. That got her to check Belinda's and she dug out a lip salve and with some difficulty applied a smear to Belinda's lips. Belinda submitted meekly, with only a few grimaces at the taste.

"There be diamonds in this creek Rose?" she asked, starting to sift the sand with her fingers.

Rose shook her head. "I don't think so. No pebbles," she replied.

By now the adrenalin had drained from her system and reaction set in, leaving her feeling exhausted and dejected. She began to worry that it was all a terrible mistake.

*Is this all real?* she asked herself. Doubts about what she had heard and what was actually going on began to assail her.

In her mind she replayed the scene as it had unfolded. And as she did the terror returned. There was no doubt the man named Lucas had told her father he was there to kill him.

*And us!* Rose told herself, clearly remembering the man's comment that it was a 'package deal'.

The calm conversation between her father and the men which had followed increased her certainty that she had not misunderstood the situation. It also immensely increased her admiration for her parents, especially her father.

*Dad was willing to let them kill him to save us!* she marvelled. It made her determined to carry out what she saw as his wishes.

Her father was only 40 and her mother five years younger but she now understood that her mother had not gone into hysterics or started to scream or plead for mercy.

*Good old Mum!* Rose thought. But what was happening now?

Rose had seen movies and crime shows on TV which included contract killings, so she believed that the situation was real, and potentially deadly.

Even as she thought this the reality was reinforced by a glimpse of movement through the trees. Way off in the distance, now at least half a kilometre away, she spotted movement on top of the low hill. The sight sent her heart into her mouth and she held her breath with anxiety while she lowered herself into the grass and squinted against the glare. It was a man in a dark shirt and cap and he had a rifle or shotgun.

Seeing the man stand on the very top and look around made Rose shake her head. *Just like Captain Ross said. Don't silhouette yourself on the skyline,* she thought. The sight of the man had dramatically increased her apprehension but also gave her confidence. *These guys must be city men,* she decided.

Luckily, Belinda was happily digging and oblivious to the drama so Rose could kneel behind a tree trunk and watch. To her relief, the man looked in all directions, then vanished back towards the main creek.

Rose was just thinking she needed to move them further away when the sound of a vehicle came to her. That sent the heart racing again and she crouched to look. It came from her left, from the northwest, and, to her dismay, a white 4WD appeared through the trees. It was racing south along the dirt road, leaving a long trail of dust. What bothered Rose was that the road looked to be only about a hundred metres away. She had thought it was much further.

The vehicle went roaring past, bouncing across the small dip where the road crossed the tiny creek and then went on to vanish up a long rise in the distance.

*Are they looking for us? Or going to get more men? Or was it someone just passing who has nothing to do with the men?* Rose wondered.

And that brought her back to her original dilemma: which way to go? She was now certain that her father wanted her to hide with Belinda so the men could not harm them or use them as hostages. But where?

*Does he mean hide out here in the bush or to try to get to some place where I can contact the police?* Which led her to thinking about whether she and Belinda could actually survive out in such a wilderness. *Water will be the problem,* Rose decided.

One of her weekend cadet activities had been Bush Survival and Captain Ross had emphasised that food was not worth the effort.

"It takes a person weeks and weeks to die of starvation, between forty and seventy days. Don't waste one minute looking for food," he had said. "If you want food go to the shop!"

He had said it sarcastically but had qualified it by pointing out that even in the more remote parts of Queensland, if they just walked for a few days they would come to a fence or road and then could follow it to a homestead. Then they could go to the shop.

"What he actually meant was that it was a waste of energy looking for food, especially trying to trap or hunt animals or reptiles," Rose murmured. "He said use your energy to get to water and then to help."

He had told the cadets to walk downhill to a creek, then to study which way the trees were bent and any flood debris to work out which way was downstream and then to walk along it until they found water, or a farmer's pump. "It is only people like commandos or pilots who are doing escape and evasion behind enemy lines who need to try to find food," he had said.

That was a worrying idea to Rose. *This is a bit like being behind enemy lines,* she told herself. *But he is still right about the food. I need to find more water, or we will be in a serious situation by tomorrow.*

The lesson had made it plain that without water in tropical heat a person could be dead within one or two days. During that cadet activity, the cadets had been taught to dig in dry creek beds and were shown how to make solar stills and how to collect water from the leaves of trees by tying large plastic bags over them so that the sunlight drew the water out of the tree and evaporated it and then condensed it in the bag. But that knowledge was no help.

*I don't have any big plastic bags; and I can't tie them up on trees or the men would see them,* Rose thought.

She studied the tiny creek and shook her head. It was most unlikely she could dig and find water in it, and she knew, from that one short lesson, that digging in sand with bare hands soon wore the skin off. Nor did she think that she would find much water in any of the creeks in the region. She had never really bothered with knowing about the weather or seasons, but she did understand that the last three months of the year were the very hot, dry summer in Northwest Queensland. She bit her lip and again licked them. Noting that they were starting to crack, she renewed her lip salve.

*We can't stay here. I need to find water,* Rose told herself.

She thought it would also be good to put more distance between herself and the men. She was anxious lest a more systematic search by them would find her tracks and then follow them. This notion was reinforced when she heard the vehicle returning. It came from south of her and was going slower this time.

So as not to be seen she checked that Belinda was safely down in the dip and then lay down herself. Peering through a bush she watched as the vehicle came into view.

*Definitely searching,* she decided.

There was a moment of anxiety when the vehicle went even slower to cross the creek, but Rose decided that was probably because they had hit it too hard the first time. Then she realised she was holding her breath, and as the vehicle went out of sight northwards away from her she gave a huge sigh of relief and resumed breathing normally.

But which way to go? *Where can I find water?* she fretted. The idea of walking through the bush in the hope of finding a windmill and water trough she rejected. *I would just be blundering around in the heat,* she decided.

That left natural water. But the only natural water she knew of was a waterhole the family had visited the day before when they had gone to a lovely place called Fountain Springs. It was a delightful pool 25 metres across set against the base of a cliff and in among a grove of big trees, cool and shady. They had even had a swim in it, a real pleasure in the heat of yesterday morning.

*But that was a long way away, on that road past Ballara where dad and I walked along the old railway,* Rose thought. But then a memory came to her, a casual comment by her father as they had stood around their vehicle preparing to fossick this morning. *Dad pointed at those hills to the west and said that Ballara was on the other side of them, or rather he said that that was where we were yesterday.*

Rose experienced a surge of hope and again tried to visualise the map. This wasn't helped by the fact that her father had used a 1:250 000 scale map when driving, the one that had both Cloncurry and Mount Isa on it; and a 1:100 000 scale map when they were walking. The 1:100 000 scale had many more creeks and contours and other details, and the pattern was not as clear to Rose. But what was clear was the memory that the hills and mountains, the Selwyn Ranges she knew they were named, mostly ran in parallel ridges in a north-south alignment.

*Something to do with the earth's crust faulting and folding in the old days,* Rose remembered.

It was hearing many mining and prospecting stories which suggested the fact that the tectonic movement had brought the valuable minerals to the surface. As that was the basis of the family fortune, and of the extensive mining industry in the region she had absorbed that sort of knowledge without realising it. Now it made sense. But how far was it to Fountain Springs?

*More than ten and possibly as many as twenty kilometres,* Rose decided. *So, should I just try to reach the bitumen road to the east or the road, the Barkly Highway she remembered, to the north, and run the risk of being caught? Or do I try to reach the only water I know about?*

Once again cadets came to her aid. A group of lessons on her Corporals Course had covered the 'Military Appreciation', that system of logical thinking and problem solving that helps commanders come up with the best plan.

Rose vividly remembered the lessons by Major Wickham, the OC of their unit in Townsville. He had covered both the Military Appreciation and the simpler Cadet Appreciation. He had explained the military one as he assumed that because they were in the army cadets they were interested in the army. "And if you who are thinking of joining the army you need to understand it is a war fighting organisation, ready to do battle; not just a cushy career in peacetime. And the appreciation is the very heart of the military art. This is how commanders earn their pay. This is the most important thing commanders do and what decides if battles are won or lost. So I will give you an example," he had said.

And now the headings came to Rose. In school she rarely studied or worked in class, being too busy drawing pictures or writing notes to her friends and even in many cadet lessons she had not paid attention as she was still writing notes or flirting with the boys (She was just reaching that age!). But some of the lessons had really interested her. Appreciations had been one.

"So," she said to herself, "What is the Aim?"

Screwing up her face with concentration she thought hard. *Is it to escape? Or is it to hide? Or is it to get to the police to save mum and dad?*

It all seemed suddenly complicated until one of Captain Ross's sayings came to her. "Keep it simple stupid! This is army, big pictures, little words."

*So it is to get to safety,* Rose decided.

That meant to escape, to hide and to get adult help (Police). The next heading had been FACTORS and the first was TOPOGRAPHY. That got her puzzling over the map problem again and that helped too as she now remembered that her father had pointed to the map and indicated that Ballara was roughly west of where they were in Copperlode Creek.

*So I go west, one or two ranges of hills,* Rose decided. *Now enemy. Major Wickham was careful about that as cadets aren't taught that, but in reality, he said we all have enemies. even if it is just the weather or the terrain, or our life situation,* Rose thought. Now she listed her enemies: Lucas, Marvin and ... and who? She couldn't remember his name. *It doesn't matter, there are three of them. No, there must be four. Someone has hired these men, and he is the real enemy,* she decided.

The more detailed questions of what are the enemy doing? What are they likely to do? and so on she could only speculate about but she decided they would make a determined effort to find her and Belinda.

*Us being free and likely to contact the police are a real threat to them,* she told herself.

That got her worrying that her actions might have upset the deal her father was trying to make with the men. *Maybe mum and dad have just been murdered now?* she worried.

But she could not see what else she could do other than go on with her plan. Just surrendering to the men might just result in her and Belinda being murdered and the sheer dread of that, and of any degrading and disgusting things the men might do to her beforehand, made her clench her jaw in determination.

*If they have harmed mum or dad then I will make sure they are brought to justice,* she vowed.

So she went back to her 'appreciation'. The weather, heat she really thought was a major enemy and that made her think that she probably should not move in the heat of the day. *But can we afford to wait?* she fretted.

Then it was on to Options or 'Courses Open'. *We can go east to the Cloncurry Road; or we can go north to the Barkly Highway; or maybe I go west to try to find Fountain Springs? Going south doesn't seem like an option,* she thought. *But water is the priority so I will go west and try to find Fountain Springs. They won't expect that and will have a lot of ground to search if we do.*

Having decided that Rose pulled on her backpack again and looked around to check there were none of the men visible. She particularly studied the crest of the hill but there was no sign of anyone there. *So, go now while we can!* she told herself.

"Going again Bee," she said.

To her relief, Belinda just nodded and allowed herself to be picked up. She still looked hot but had stopped sweating and was obviously tired. It took Rose an effort to hoist her up to get a firm grip and then even more effort to use her boots to brush out their tracks in the soft sand.

Rose stepped up out of the creek on the south side and turned right. She had decided to go west and that meant crossing the vehicle track. One relief was that the vegetation under the trees was more grass than spinifex and there were extensive areas of almost bare sandy soil scattered with leaf litter. That got her worrying about leaving clear boot prints, so she was careful to step on grass and leaves as much as possible. She moved away from the creek but kept looking ahead for place to hide if the vehicle appeared again.

Belinda was so heavy that Rose had to stop twice and rest in the hundred or so metres to the vehicle track. Near the track she rested among a clump of trees while she picked her route and listened carefully. Hearing nothing she took several deep breaths and then picked Belinda up and hurried forward.

When she got to the vehicle track, here just two wheel ruts with grass and spinifex between them, she glanced anxiously to the right and was then careful not to step on the sand of the wheel ruts. As quickly as she could she hurried on into a thicket of stunted little trees and bushes (More of those b… sticky bushes!).

Within two minutes she was puffing and sweating, and she had to detour over towards a small dip with some rocks on the lip. She hurried into this and put Belinda down. Unfortunately she had picked a poor spot and there was very little shade. Belinda immediately began to complain it was too hot so Rose took a few deep breaths and picked her up again and continued walking.

She managed another fifty paces before slumping down behind a clump of bushes on grass in a good patch of shade. Belinda at once made a face.

"Hungry!" she cried.

"Drink first," Rose replied.

She dug out her water bottle and gave Belinda a drink, noting with dismay that it was now about three quarters empty. Another of her father's laughing comments came to her and she shuddered.

"This is the country Burke and Wills passed through," he had said.

*And they died out here somewhere!* Rose thought anxiously. She now understood that she and Belinda were probably in as much peril from the environment as from the men.

Belinda had some small sandwiches in her lunch box and Rose took these out one at a time, careful to keep them wrapped in plastic as long as possible lest they dry out in the fierce heat. The sandwiches kept Belinda happy for a few minutes and Rose could only look on. She had already decided that all the food and most of the water were going to her little sister.

*I can afford to go without food for a day or so,* she told herself.

She actually meant that because she was tubby she could well afford to live off her fat but didn't want to word it that way.

Rose still wasn't happy with the distance she had put between them and the men, so she again picked Belinda and her bag up and resumed walking. Ahead of her was a wide plain covered with trees and bushes and waist high grass. She knew she would still be visible from the vehicle track for quite a distance and was dismayed to find she had trouble pushing through some of the long grass.

She was also scared. The clumps of grass and spinifex were so close together she had to stand on them and she could not see where she was putting her boots. Fear of snakes welled up to almost paralyse her. For a few seconds she just stood and whimpered, too afraid to go on, but terrified of what was behind her!

By an effort of will power she pushed herself to walk and managed to go another hundred paces. She found that she was now having trouble keeping direction except by selecting a distinctive tree in the distance and aiming for it. The problem was that in among this savannah woodland she could see very little of the distant hills so could not navigate by them and the sun was now overhead, making it difficult to work out east and west.

And the sun was fierce! The heat seemed to scorch through her clothes and the air was hot to breathe. Belinda looked very sunburnt, but Rose hoped her ruddy complexion was just from being hot. On three occasions Rose had been taught lessons on Heat and Cold as part of her safety training and now bits of information came to bother her.

"If they are red in the face and sweating that is okay," Captain Ross had said. "But if they go pale and clammy they are moving into heat exhaustion. You need to stop what they are doing and treat that at once as very serious." He had then explained the best way to cool people down as well as hydrating them.

*He also warned us that drinking too much water could be potentially fatal,* Rose remembered.

The excess water leaches out the body salts and that leads to cramps, including cramps of the heart muscles. "So you must eat as well as drink. You must replace the lost salt," he had cautioned.

It was the same problem with Heat Stroke, though deadly serious, Rose remembered. Then the skin was hot and dry, and the heart rate increased dramatically as the body tried to keep cooling liquid to the important organs.

*That can cause the strokes in the brain and death from heart attack as there isn't enough blood and it thickens,* Rose thought.

It was all very scary and got her looking out at the heat shimmer on the plain with real anxiety. *Do I dare keep walking in this heat?* she wondered.

She understood that if she became a heat casualty then Belinda would also die.

To add to her anxiety was the notion that she was still much too close to the area where she had last seen the men. This worry was almost at once reinforced when she heard the vehicle engine again. Looking back towards where the vehicle track was, she saw it appear in the distance. This time it was going very slowly, and she felt sure the man (or men) in it were deliberately searching. All she could do was crouch low and check that Belinda was also keeping down.

Her anxiety kept building until the vehicle passed the point where she thought they had crossed the road. She did not think she had left any obvious tracks and when the vehicle drove on south and vanished from view she again sighed with relief.

"But we are still too close to the area," she told herself. "We need to keep going."

With a groan she hoisted Belinda up and started walking.

# Chapter 5

## HEAT

Rose managed another couple of hundred paces before her aching muscles and laboured breathing brought her to a standstill. Having sought out a patch of shade without too many ants she again put Belinda down and gave her a drink.

*I don't know if I can do this!* she thought, dread clutching at her heart. *I don't think I am strong enough.*

But even that effort had paid off. She was now able to get glimpses of the hills in the direction she had been walking.

*West, I'm sure,* she told herself as she noted the shadows cast by the trees.

Having given Belinda a drink, she held the open water bottle and argued with herself. The temptation was strong and so was the argument that if she collapsed then Belinda was doomed as well. So she compromised and had a mouthful. That was good, even though the water was now warm and not very palatable.

She got another boost when she heard the vehicle returning from the south. It went past in the distance and was so far away that it was barely visible.

*If I go a few more hundred metres the men will not see us from the road,* she reasoned.

So, despite feeling wrung out she turned to pick Belinda up and found she was lying on the grass with her hat as a pillow. It took a real effort to get the sleepy little girl up on her hip and her hat back on and that got Rose anxious that her strength would give out. Biting her lip with anxiety she set off walking towards the distant hills despite the searing heat.

But she could not keep it up long. She had to stop every fifty paces or so to move Belinda to her other hip. Each time Rose leaned on a tree to keep her balance and to provide cover. And then Belinda nodded off to sleep and while that was also a relief it meant Rose had to hoist her up and put her head on her shoulder. That was much harder, and she found she was puffing with the exertion all the time.

And another dilemma was opening up ahead of her. The forested area was coming to an end and ahead of her was half a kilometre of almost open grassland and then the hills. The big hill in front of her was almost devoid of trees, being covered by spinifex and clumps of rocks. It looked quite forbidding.

*And I will stand out like a fly on a ceiling if I go up it,* she reasoned.

So go around it. But which way? Looking to her right she realised that the trees along Copperlode Creek were again visible. That made sense as she knew from the map that the creeks all came out of the hills. And the small creek she had rested in earlier was still nearby on her right, but she saw it angled out of a small re-entrant in the hill.

*I'm not going over the hill. I will go round it. There must be another creek on the south side,* she told herself. Indeed she could see how the hill was sloping down in that direction.

So she summoned up her strength again and set off across the grassy plain, walking as fast as she could to get to cover before the vehicle re-appeared. She found in fact that the ground favoured her. It had a slight rise to it so that when she had crossed over it that put her in dead ground from Copperlode Creek and, after another hundred puffing paces, from where she thought the vehicle track was.

For a moment Rose stopped and looked back, hugging her hot little sister to her front, and got a horrible shock! Walking up the very gentle slope had put her in full view of the low hill she had skirted around earlier.

*Oh my God! If there is one of those men there he will see us.*

There was nothing for it but to turn and hurry on, staggering and stumbling across the clumps of spinifex and grass. As she did, she angled to the left and that took her down off the gentle rise and out of sight of the hill, hidden by the tree canopies behind her. It also led her into another small creek. This was also dry and had many more rocks in its bed.

Gasping and sweating she halted in the shade of a spindly tree in the creek bed and sat down to get her breath back. *I can't rest long,* she thought. *If those men saw me, they will be on their way.*

So, as soon as she could, Rose hoisted herself to her feet with the aid of the tree and set off west up the rocky creek bed. And that gave her another decision to make: walk beside the creek in the spinifex, or along the stony bed?

*I've had enough of spinifex for a while,* Rose told herself, hotly aware that her lower legs were tingling and stinging from the jabs of the needle leaves.

So she made her way into the creek bed. Almost at once she considered changing her mind. To walk along it she had to step from rock to rock and use one hand to steady herself and as soon as she reached out to grab a rock she cried out in pain. The rock was so hot from the sun she felt it had burnt her skin.

"Ow! Bloody hell! You could fry an egg on that," she grumbled, teetering while she looked for another hand hold to keep her balance.

With Belinda on her shoulder it was both difficult and dangerous, particularly when she had to step up as the slope steepened. There was no help for it. She had to touch the hot rocks for safety. She realised that if she fell Belinda could be killed or injured if her head struck the rocks. It was a horrifying image that made Rose become extra careful.

So she laboured on for another fifteen sweaty minutes, scrambling awkwardly up the ever-steepening creek bed. As she did, the sides of the creek became more and more nearly vertical and she found herself in a steep-sided re-entrant that resembled a gorge. There was no breeze, and the steep-sided little valley trapped the sun so that the heat reflected off the rocks. To Rose it felt like she was walking in an oven. The situation began to resemble a nightmare.

She came to another gasping stop and leaned on the heated rocks, perspiration dripping from her face and arms.

"Bloody hell it's hot!" she muttered.

She blinked sweat from her eyes and looked around, wondering if she had made a serious mistake. The glare and heat caused her to squint.

*This is killing heat,* she thought. *We can't go on in this. I will drop from ordinary exhaustion soon, never mind heat exhaustion.*

So she looked around for some shade to shelter in. The nearest was a tiny patch in under an overhanging rock on her right. Edging awkwardly up into the shade Rose carefully lowered Belinda and laid her on her back on a small patch of bare soil. A few balls of dung suggested it was probably a place where wallabies sheltered. Then Rose squeezed up as far as she could into the shade.

But this did not work as the space was too small and her lower legs and boots were left out in the direct sunlight. This was soon a cause of some discomfort and she tried to curl them up under the rock. And the air was stifling and hot. It felt unpleasant to breathe and the whole situation seemed to be rapidly becoming untenable.

Then Belinda woke up and began to grizzle. "Want Mummy!" she cried. Rose tried to pacify her with another drink and a biscuit from her bag. Belinda became more and more upset. "Mummy! Want Mummy!" she screamed.

"Please baby, please don't yell," Rose pleaded, but to no avail.

All she could do was hold Belinda to stop her wriggling out into the sunlight and to prevent her falling on the hot rocks. Belinda screamed louder but then gasped and began to cough. That got Rose even more worried. But then Belinda broke down into sobs and Rose held her tight and patted her back.

"I want Mummy too," she said, "But the bad men have taken Mummy and Daddy away."

"Want Daddy!" Belinda sobbed.

There was nothing to be done but hold her and pat her back and shoulders. As she did, Rose became aware that Belinda felt very hot and she eased her away from her front and felt her forehead. That was cool and clammy and that was worrying too.

*Is she going into heat exhaustion?* she worried.

Just in case she gave Belinda another drink, almost draining her own bottle. As the little girl took gulps Rose had to resist the urge to grab at it and drink.

*God I'm thirsty,* she thought. Which led to a crisis of conscience. She realised that she had to have the water and take a risk by denying her little sister. *If I drop, we both die!* she told herself.

So she waited until Belinda was not looking and had another mouthful. That sneaky and apparently selfish act did not make her feel good.

Then she became very conscious of the heated air. It seemed to be like a hot liquid and she began gasping, wondering if she was having trouble breathing. Panic started to take over and she found she was panting as though she had run a race.

*I'm hyperventilating,* she thought.

With an effort she slowed her breathing, aware that her vision was blurry and that black dots were dancing in her eyes.

An expression she had read in a story flitted across her mind: *Fear*

C.R. Cummings

*is clutching me by the throat and squeezing my chest,* she thought. She closed her eyes to cut out the glare and then had to open them as she found it hard to stay calm. *We might die in this place,* she thought.

Still holding Belinda Rose struggled to her feet and looked back the way she had come, wondering if she should go back down to the shade of a tree out in the open somewhere. Shielding her eyes from the brightness she studied the view. She saw that she was just above the height of the tree canopies out on the plain and that she could see lines of very rugged hills in the far distance. They were distorted by the heat shimmer, but she realised they were the ones between her and the Cloncurry Road.

For a few minutes she was again tempted to go that way. But then she shook her head. *We might not find any water and we will die if we don't,* she reasoned. The only water she knew of was the pool at Fountain Springs and she was sure that was closer. *We must go there,* she decided.

But then she became aware of the blazing sun burning through her clothes and she realised she was standing out in the full sun and holding Belinda who had no hat on.

*Shade! We need shade and quickly,* she thought.

With that driving her she turned and groped in under the rock ledge to get Belinda's hat. With some difficulty she managed to fit it on, Belinda not helping by continually turning her head and calling for Mummy. Then Rose reached out and grabbed the backpacks and began making her way up the creek bed.

*There must be a better patch of shade,* she told herself hopefully.

And there was. Only about 50 metres further up, where the creek did a sharp turn to the left, there was a bigger rock overhang and the afternoon sun was now beyond so that there was a strip of shade several metres wide with a rock ledge and patch of clean sand. With a sigh of relief Rose made her way into the shade and cast the backpacks down. Thankfully she eased Belinda down to sit on the sand.

"Sand hot!" Belinda wailed as she put her hands down.

Rose had found it a huge relief to be in that piece of shade but knew Belinda was right. But the only thing she could give her to sit on was her own backpack so first she emptied it of the digging tools, her sample bottle, the now almost empty water bottle and the packet of sandwiches. Belinda still wasn't happy but did accept a drink, which emptied the water bottle, and calmed down to just grizzling.

By then it was nearly 2pm and Rose was close to despair. *We must sit here until it is cool,* she told herself, knowing that was at least four or five hours away.

Belinda at last stopped making noises and Rose tried to distract her by pointing out the coloured and curved strata in the rocks they were sheltering under.

"Is it diamonds?" Belinda asked.

"No mate," Rose replied. "Just rock. It might have minerals in it."

"Daddy find minerals," Belinda replied. "Want Daddy."

"We will get to him as quickly as we can but we can't walk in the sun in this heat," Rose explained.

"Hot! Want cold dwink!"

"Yes, it is hot but I'm sorry Baby, but I don't have any cold water."

"Cold water in car!"

All Rose could do was shake her head. "The car is back there with the bad men," she explained. The thought of those bottles of cordial and cold water in the small refrigerator in the back of the 4WD made her salivate for a few seconds before her mouth went dry again.

She squeezed her eyes and tried to make them water and then lay back and tried to relax. Then a distant sound made her sit up and look out.

*Is that a vehicle?* she wondered. But there was no longer a view out over the country to the east so she could not check, and she did not have the energy to walk back to look.

Luckily, Belinda also lay down and began playing with small pebbles. Rose lay and watched her, panting slightly in the heated air. There was still no breeze and the sun was reflecting off the opposite side of the gully. But she knew she had to endure and that she was unlikely to find anywhere better, so she pursed her lips and tried to relax.

Time began to drag. As she sat there, Rose began to brood. *Mum and Dad must be worrying about us,* she thought. In fact she was sure her mother would be desperately worried. *And what if none of it is true? What if I misunderstood what I heard?* That got her fretting that she might have made a huge mistake. One of the things that bothered her most was the quiet and calm voices of the men's conversation with her dad. *I've dragged poor little Busyness out her into the heat and she could die. Poor Mum will be really upset,* Rose worried.

It came to her that her parents (If they are still alive!) would be worried that she and Belinda were lost in the desert, but that notion made her shake her head.

*I'm not lost. I know roughly where we are and I can work out which way to go,* she told herself. *Cadets has given me that much knowledge.*

The confidence that came from that helped her to calm down. But it didn't help make the time go any faster, or with keeping Belinda calm. The next challenge was soon up on. Belinda stood up and looked anxious.

"Want pee pee," she muttered.

Rose had forgotten about such bodily issues, but the moment Belinda mentioned it she found she needed to go as well.

"So do I Busy Bee. Let's go along the creek a bit."

She took Belinda's hand and led her a few metres along to where there was another patch of sand. It was in the sun, but she did not have time to be fussy. As quickly as she could, she unbuttoned and unzipped Belinda's pant suit and then lifted her up to take it off, forgetting that the shoes would make that difficult. She managed it and took off the panties then lowered Belinda down.

"Okay Belinda, you do pee pee," she said.

But Belinda looked around askance. "Want toilet!" she cried.

"We are in the bush, Bub. Just do it here."

"No! Want toilet!"

"Please, Bub. There is no toilet. We are being prospectors and they just do it in the bush," Rose pleaded.

Belinda still looked unhappy. "Want toilet," she muttered. "Want Mummy."

"Sorry mate, but there is no toilet. Now you just do it there and I will go a bit further along the creek," Rose replied, now feeling an urgent need herself.

She quickly walked away, at which Belinda began to call out and then wail loudly. "Don't leave me! Rosie, don't go!"

"I'm just here Belinda," Rose cried in exasperation as she crouched half behind a rock. She found it very embarrassing to relieve herself with her little sister nearby. But she had to and then she had to hastily dress and hurry back. By then Belinda was standing with tears running down her cheeks, nearly hysterical.

"Hush! Hush Baby!" Rose cried, patting and trying to sooth here. "Just do what I did, and you will be alright," she explained.

Belinda looked around and then, to Rose's great relief, squatted to relieve herself. It was all an exhausting drama that had them both in the sun for more than ten minutes and Rose found it an enormous relief to carry Belinda back into their patch of shade where she dressed her.

More time dragged by. Belinda then wanted a drink and Rose found herself torn. All they had was the small water bottle of Belinda's, a 500ml bottle that was already half empty. But after thinking about it she shrugged.

*I have to keep Belinda hydrated,* she reasoned. *The water is better in her than in the bottle.*

So she allowed her another small drink and then put the bottle out of sight. By then it was after 3pm and she was really feeling dry and thirsty herself. She was also worried about what she had seen when she relieved herself. A cadet lesson on Heat had cautioned that urine should be a pale yellow, straw colour, but hers had been dark yellow. *I need to get water soon,* she thought.

But she also knew there was no hope of that. Her mind told her it would not cool down until the sun began to set, but she had not paid attention as to when that was. She was not in the habit of watching the TV news or weather.

*I think it is about six?* she thought.

But then she frowned as she had a vague memory from a geography lesson that sunset was different at different times of the year. Only after real thought did she remember that sunset times also varied with where in the world a person was.

*So it could be another three or four hours,* she reasoned.

In fact it was nearer five, as she had not known that sunset in the east of the state, Townsville and Charters Towers, was an hour or so ahead of when it set in western Queensland. They were hot, wearing and fretful hours with frequent need to pacify or entertain Belinda until she just felt exhausted.

During that time Belinda not only demanded more water but also food. "Hungry!" she wailed. "Want morning tea!"

That at least made Rose smile. Ever since Belinda had realised that morning and afternoon teas were a daily thing she had latched onto Morning Tea as a great time for a cup of cordial and a cream biscuit.

"I don't have any biscuits, Bub-O, but I do have some sandwiches,"

Rose explained. She unwrapped a triangle of sandwich and passed it over. Belinda took one look at it and then frowned.

"What this?" she demanded.

"Corned beef with pickles," Rose replied.

"Don't like pwickles! Want wedgemite!"

"Sorry," Rose answered. She hastily took the sandwich back and wrapped it up, conscious that the bread had begun to dry out even in those few minutes. Then she unwrapped another. "Here, this is a honey sandwich," she said.

Belinda took the offered triangle and subjected it to a critical examination before gingerly tasting the honey. Then she nodded and took a bite out of it and began munching happily. Rose silently thanked her mother's foresight by having two different sandwiches for their lunch.

*Good on you Mum!* she thought. And then she began to cry.

"What matter, Rosie?" Belinda queried.

"Just glad you like the sandwich," Rose answered.

There was no way she was going to mention her fears of what might have happened to their mother. *Oh poor Mum! Please God may she be alright!*

Belinda slowly ate all four of the small triangles of bread and honey. As she handed Belinda the last one Rose tossed the used plastic wrap aside. A fly at once landed on it and sunlight glinted on it, attracting her eye. Hastily she reached out and picked it up.

*Oh no! No litter. If those men find it they will know for sure we have gone this way,* she told herself. The plastic wrap was placed in her backpack. Then Rose sat and brooded. She decided she did not need to carry the small pick and trowel. *They are just extra weight,* she reasoned. So she carefully buried them, smoothing the sand. *We can always come back and get them after this is over,* she told herself.

And then at last a faint breeze began up the gully and Rose sighed with relief. She looked around and also noted that the shade had crept right across the gully and well up the slope beyond.

"Won't be long now," she muttered, glancing at her watch to check the time. It was just before 5pm, 1700hrs she told herself, wanting to be a good cadet.

"Still too hot," she muttered. But then another worrying thought came to her.

*It will get dark soon and it might be too dark to safely walk, particularly if we are up on a rocky hill.*

That got her mentally berating herself for not paying attention in school and in the real world. Into her mind flashed snippets from the 'Patrol Orders' she had received and then given to her little section on the recent cadet field exercise.

*Captain Ross always includes the phases of the moon and the time of moonrise or moonset,* she thought.

So, was there a moon tonight? And if there was, when did it come up or was it already up? She remembered not believing that the moon could be up during the day until taught about moon phases in the lesson on Navigation by the Sun and Stars. The next day she had looked up and had seen the moon clearly visible in the bright blue sky. So now she looked up and scanned the sky. Not seeing the moon she stood and moved a few paces to take in more of the sky to both east and west.

Belinda also stood up. "What you look for Rosie?" she queried.

"The moon," Rose explained.

"Hey diddle diddle, the cow and the spoon!" Belinda sang.

"No Bub, it goes, 'Hey diddle diddle, the cat and the fiddle, the cow jumped over the moon'," Rose said, glad of a way to distract the little girl for a few minutes. So they sat and sang nursery rhymes for fifteen minutes.

But as they did, knowing that she lacked vital knowledge gnawed at Rose and she bit her lip and decided she must take the risk and start walking in daylight. Packing Belinda's bag and bottle into her own backpack she pulled it on and stood up.

Reaching out she said, "Okay Busy Bee, let's start walking."

# Chapter 6

## UPHILL

Belinda stood and took her hand and began walking without complaint. That was part of Rose's plan.

*I can't carry her all the way,* she reasoned. So she planned to have Belinda walk as much as she could.

But the plan barely lasted ten paces before she had to start helping Belinda up over rocks. She had decided the easiest and safest route to begin with was to go up the gully and only move out onto the spinifex-covered hillside when they had to. It was also part of her plan to stay in the shade of the hill as much as possible while the sun set on the other side.

But it was a bit too soon and the sun was above the skyline and stabs of light kept stinging her eyes when she glanced up. Belinda also had problems and muttered a few times. But the little girl gamely tried to clamber up over the rocks, despite complaining that they were too hot.

But the rocks were too hot. Belinda began to baulk so Rose reluctantly scooped her up and then continued clambering up the gully. It was hard going and she was soon puffing and sweating. Within minutes she began to wonder if she was strong enough. And the gully was quickly becoming narrower with overhanging grass and spinifex she had to brush through.

Belinda began to complain so Rose stopped and studied the hillsides. They were steeper than she liked and looked difficult to get up onto. But she saw she needed to and she spent a couple of minutes finding the easiest way up. The effort left her gasping and she stood up on the slope with perspiration dripping off her.

From there she could see out to the east and the line of Copperlode Creek stood out clearly in the distance. She stared hard to see if any vehicles or people were visible but saw nothing.

*If those men are watching they might see us, particularly if they have binoculars,* she thought.

But she felt she was committed so she turned and began plodding upwards, directly into the last of the sunlight. Bending her head to avoid the sun she gripped Belinda tighter and gritted her teeth and pushed herself to keep going. Ignoring the spinifex she found the hardest as it kept jabbing through her trousers.

The only good thing was that she now had a fair breeze at her back, and she found that a real relief. After a couple of minutes hard going, she had to stop to get her breath. She eased Belinda down to stand on a big rock. Belinda liked that and stood there looking around.

"Oooh look!" she said. "Can see lots."

Rose smiled and agreed. Then she smiled again. The sun had sunk below the skyline, and they were in shadow! Heartened she picked Belinda up and resumed her upward slog. Now she wished she had a map and had studied the hill more carefully when she was out on the flat. Looking up she wondered how far it was to the top.

Then she shook her head. *Fieldcraft! I'm not trying to get to the top. I want to go to the lowest point between it and the next hill to save effort and to keep off the skyline,* she reasoned.

She decided that was to her left, so she slowly angled that way. She soon saw the next hill over to the south, and was relieved to find that if she continued up the spur she was on it took her to just beside the saddle between them. She also noted that the gully she had been in ended just below that but was very steep, small and rocky.

It took until nearly 6pm to puff her way up to that saddle, stopping every 50 paces or so to get her breath back and allow her aching arm and back muscles a rest. The effort of carrying Belinda was starting to tell!

And then she was there, squinting into the setting sun as it went down behind a range of very rugged mountains in the distance. She crossed over the crest line and found an area of bare rock to sit on and arranged her pack so Belinda could sit on it. She then lowered herself onto the hot rock, her leg muscles trembling from overexertion.

Now she more carefully studied the view. Her first impressions were of great beauty, extreme ruggedness and huge distances. Then she focused. Her eye was drawn to where the last of the sun, a huge ball of orange and red, was sinking behind a very jagged mountain peak to the west. The sun now silhouetted a whole range of steep and sharp-pointed peaks and ridges. Beyond these she had glimpses of yet more mountains, the impression being of vast distances. The feeling of extreme isolation this engendered struck fear into Rose's very being.

*God that looks rough!* she thought. *And we are a long way from anywhere.*

Feeling quite daunted she looked to both sides of the setting sun. Out to her left her eye was drawn to an isolated but very jagged peak that looked like a huge castle on a rock. It was most impressive, even if it was ten or more kilometres away. And then, beyond the 'castle', she saw the sharp outline of a long, very steep line of cliffs extending off to the south.

"That is the Foutain Range!" she muttered, recognising it from the previous day.

Then her eye caught a pronounced 'dip' in the range through which a bar of sunlight was streaming. At once her heart leapt. Her father had pointed out the nick in the escarpment the day before. It was where a stream had cut through to become a waterfall which fell into the pool at Fountain Springs.

"Yes!" she cried.

All afternoon she had been picturing that shady pool among its grove of lovely trees and the image had glowed as a beacon of hope. It was almost as though God was showing her the way! And now she could actually see it. But it looked a dismayingly long way away!

That got her studying the intervening ground. To her satisfaction there was no great range of hills. Most of the land appeared to be flat or undulating with a scattering of rocky outcrops and hills. All of it was covered with either savannah woodland or grassland.

*I shouldn't have too much trouble crossing that,* she thought hopefully. *Particularly if there is a moon.*

It was her plan to walk cross-country in the dark so as to avoid doing it in the heat the following morning. She was already feeling so dehydrated she was worried that she might collapse before she got there.

By the time she had come to this decision the sun had sunk completely below the distant mountains, leaving a wonderful gold, red glow which bathed the entire scene in a ruddy tint.

And then another thought came to her which brought her back to reality with a mental jolt. *I need to get down off these hills while it is still light!*

And the dusk was setting in fast! Rose got quickly to her feet and stood an obviously tired Belinda up. Picking up the backpack she pulled it on and then hoisted Belinda to her front.

"Be a koala, Bub. I need to walk downhill quickly."

"Why?"

"We need to get down onto the flat ground before it gets dark," Rose answered, starting to take careful steps as she did.

"Want Mummy!" Belinda whispered.

"So do I Bub. I love you," Rose replied, patting her back.

And within ten paces she wished she had Belinda on her back somehow as she had trouble seeing her own feet and had to keep leaning over to check that she wasn't stepping on the football-sized rocks that littered the hillside in among the grass and spinifex.

That she needed to was quickly made evident as she seemed to stumble at every second step. She wished she had a walking stick to help her keep balance. As she staggered along, aiming for a long spur to her left that went in the direction she wanted, she tried to work out how she might use the backpack or Belinda's to make a carrier the toddler could fit in.

"Yaah!" she cried.

A rock rolled under her feet and she fell hard on her bum. Belinda's head smacked up into her nose and that really hurt as well. For a few moments she just lay there, hurting all over because the spinifex was digging in right along her body. To ease the pain and discomfort, she held Belinda up and then placed her on her feet while she struggled to get up.

By then Belinda was crying as well as she had hit her head. Rose tried to comfort her while rubbing her bum.

"It's alright, Bub-O," she said. "You just got a fright. But I hurt my bum."

"You... sniff... you say naughty... sniff... word!" Belinda retorted.

"I did too, and I'll say a few more if I trip again," Rose replied grimly, thinking of words she heard at school every day.

She found tears in her eyes and for a couple of minutes was unable to move. Then she took a grip on her emotions.

*That daylight is going fast!* she noted.

It took her an effort to pick Belinda up, this time placing her on her left hip, the uphill side, then start walking again. By then the evening gloom was very obvious and to her eyes she looked to be only a small way down the slope. The trees on the flat ground at the bottom looked to be a long way away.

It was all less than satisfactory as Belinda was both uncomfortable and anxious and kept squirming, even after being asked to stay still.

"Just concentrate. One foot in front of the other," Rose told herself, very careful now to feel where her boot was going before putting any weight on it.

She was hotly anxious that a bad fall could break a bone or sprain an ankle and strand them both on that hillside. *Nobody would ever find us in time,* she thought, *not unless they had a helicopter or aircraft.*

And that introduced a whole new range of worries: Would the men have the use of a helicopter when the sun came up? *And do they have any night vision or night shooting sights?* she thought.

Her cadet unit had Infra-Red monoculars that they used on sentry duties and night patrols and she knew such rifle sights existed. Certainly she had seen them at army displays and in the Night Training facility at Lavarack barracks.

*Even civilian hunters can buy things like that,* she told herself. And where were the men? And what had they done with her parents?

It was all very distressing, and she found it hard to think straight beyond being reasonably sure the men were not in the low ground ahead of her. So she kept plodding down, having to repeatedly take awkward steps over rocks or down from one rock to a lower one.

Darkness set in but she kept slowly moving, using the dim red glow behind the distant spikey peak as a guide. Now she thanked her cadet experience as she was not terrified of moving through the bush in the dark.

"And it is dark," she noted aloud.

Then she realised that Belinda was slumping loose. *She is asleep,* she thought, heaving the toddler up onto her left shoulder.

By this time her arm and back muscles were getting so weak and overstrained from carrying the unaccustomed weight that she had to call a halt after another hundred paces. Carefully she scanned to find a clump of grass, not wanting to sit in spinifex. With several groans and gasps she lowered herself to a sitting position and then lifted Belinda down to hold her across her lap.

"I must be more than halfway down," she told herself, more to lift her own spirits than for any other reason.

But she did not think it was a good place to rest. The image of a sandy creek bed came to mind, but she had no idea how far one might be. So all she could do was sit there, tired and drained and very thirsty.

Rose rested on the hillside, exhausted and shivering, for over half an hour. Then, perversely, she realised she felt cold. And she knew it could be. She had enough experience of inland Australia to know that away from the coast the night temperatures often drop dramatically. She remembered her mother commenting two nights before, at Kajabbi, that the night temperature was only 17 degrees Celsius, even though during the day it had gone up to 36.

Carefully she felt Belinda's wrist and decided she was greeting a bit cool as well. *I'd better keep moving,* she decided. Her plan now was to find a more sheltered place to rest until either the moon came up or dawn the next day. *Although I really need to be at water by then!*

She managed another couple of hundred steps in the next quarter of an hour. But then she tripped again and this time she fell forward, Belinda sprawling into the long grass. That woke her and started her howling with fright and pain. She had suffered several small scratches and bruises and so had Rose. She sat there hugging Belinda with one hand while rubbing sore knees with the other.

*This will have to do. It is too dark and rough for safety,* she decided.

Looking around she saw that she appeared to be much lower down the hill, the dark masses of the tree canopies on the flat just showing in the starlight. And at least it was grass and not spinifex. The ground had a distinct slope so she had to brace her boots against a rock. With her boot she flattened the grass some more to make a bed for Belinda. "Hope there aren't any ticks," she muttered as she persuaded the little girl to lie down with the backpack as a pillow.

During her first cadet camp several small ticks, so tiny they were pinhead size, had burrowed into Rose's skin around her waist and back of her neck. Luckily, she had been noticed scratching at them by one of the lady OOCs, Lieutenant Ross. Closer examination had revealed the problem, and the ticks were dealt with by liquid soap, which persuaded them to back out.

"Never use tweezers if you can help it," the Officer of Cadets had explained. "You risk leaving the head in to fester and when you squeeze them you often pump the fluid into you as a poison."

*I must check Bub in the morning,* Rose resolved.

Carefully she lay down beside her, hoping there were no snakes slithering around the hillside. Sighing with relief she stretched out and tried to relax. Instead she experienced the agony of a cramp in her left calf muscle. That left her gasping, and she knew she would have been in tears, if she had enough water in her system.

Then mosquitos began to buzz and nip. "Bloody hell! Mozzies in the desert!" Rose cried.

She slapped at them and then began to pat at Belinda, guessing that from the way she was muttering and twitching, that the mosquitos were attacking her as well. There was a breeze but not strong enough to ground the annoying little insects.

And the breeze was cool. Rose began to shiver, both from reaction and over-exertion and from the cold. She was left feeling wide awake and utterly miserable. Between the terror induced by the situation and her own desperate efforts to escape she felt drained and afraid. Noises by various nightbirds did not help. The flap of wings or squarks and screeches all made her start with fright. Worst of all was the mournful call of some curlews somewhere out to the east.

With no chance of sleep, Rose sat and tried to keep the mosquitos off Belinda, who thankfully had gone into a deep sleep, and with massaging and trying to ease her own sore muscles. Then her stomach grumbled, and she knew she was hungry.

Thinking that Belinda would not eat the corned beef and pickle sandwiches, she unwrapped one and began to eat it. To her dismay, she found that her mouth felt like it was not functioning normally. Her sense of taste seemed to have gone and she felt as though her tongue was too big for her mouth. And the bread was dry and stale.

For a few minutes she sat with the half-eaten sandwich in her hand. Then she forced herself to resume chewing. *I need to the energy and if I leave them any longer in this heat the meat will go off,* she reasoned.

So she sat and ate all four triangles during the next hour. After that she went to throw the plastic wrap away but then reached out and pricked it up.

*No litter!* she reprimanded herself. *Don't leave a trail.*

The food helped but what she really wanted was a drink. Images of Fountain Springs kept forming in her mind and she determined to reach it. Time dragged but the mosquitos went away. Then Belinda began to shiver so Rose lay down and gently cuddled her against herself. That helped warm them both and Belinda settled again, with the occasional twitch or murmur as she dreamt.

Rose dropped off to sleep at about 10pm, the air still and cold and a million stars in the sky, as only inland skies can be. She also began to murmur and twitch. It was a cramp in her other calf that woke her. The pain was so intense and sudden that Rose woke with a cry that also woke Belinda.

"Mummy! Mummy!" Belinda cried and then she began to sob. Rose held her close and tried to soothe her while massaging her leg.

"It's alright Baby, Rosie's got you," she said.

As she did, she looked around, sleep fuddled and puzzled. Everything looked different. *What is it? What am I looking at?* Rose puzzled.

And then it came to her, the moon was coming up! Now she could see distinct shadows and a lot of detail. A check of her watch showed it was 0115hrs.

*Zero dark hundred as the OC says,* she said. But her spirits had lifted with the moonlight. *I need to get moving. With ten kilometres to go I need to get as far as I can before daylight and then find somewhere to hide,* she reasoned.

She did some calculations that cheered her. *If it is daylight in say five hours and I have ten kilometres to go I need to go about half a kilometre every half hour. That should be possible. That is a hundred metres in... er... in...*

The maths defeated her but she was still confident. So she made sure she had everything and then picked up a still sleepy Belinda and started carefully putting one foot in front of another.

As she walked slowly down the rocky slope her mind completed the maths. *If I rest for ten minutes every hour that leaves 50 minutes to walk. Fifty into 500 equals 10 minutes to walk 100 metres. I should be able to do that. That is just a toddle.* She knew from Drill lessons on her Corporals Course that a person marching in 'Quick Time' covered 100 metres in one minute. *Surely I can do it in ten?*

But she soon had doubts as she stumbled frequently and paused to ensure she had a firm footing before each step.

The real doubt came as her arms quickly weakened and her back began to ache. *I don't think I can carry Bub that far!*

That got her thinking again about how to carry her. She considered sitting her on her shoulders but decided that was too unsafe on the rough ground.

*If I trip, she will be dashed hard to the ground,* she thought.

That only left the backpack, but it was too small. So she persevered with carrying her little sister, changing arms and position every minute or so. And during all this deliberation she reached the bottom of the hill. Here she paused for a minute and put Belinda down. But it was spinifex, so she quickly picked her up again and kept moving.

Now direction keeping became the priority. Knowing that she had to go about southwest Rose put the moon at her back and did a 'Left Incline'. That put the moon behind her left shoulder. Off to her left front she could also see the Southern Cross and its Pointers, but it was low in the trees and would obviously set in the next hour or so. She knew how to find south by it but shrugged.

*The moon will do.*

Satisfied she was going the right way she resumed a slow walk through the long grass and spinifex.

Her watch now registered 0200hrs, so Rose stopped and allowed herself the 10-minute rest. In fact she was up and moving after seven as Belinda was shivering and complaining of being cold. Now Rose set herself to keep to her timetable, counting her paces and stopping every 50 to check if it had taken 5 minutes. Luckily, the ground was fairly free of stones but there were a few logs and ant hills. The logs were mostly easy to see and so were the small gullies as the moon, a half-moon she noted, was bright enough to cast strong shadows.

*Thud! Thud! Thud! Thud!*

Rose let out a little shriek of fear and then shook her head and grinned. For a moment she stood there shaking before starting to laugh. Belinda was awake enough to be scared.

"What that, Rosie?" she asked.

"Only a kangaroo," Rose replied.

"I want to see!" Belinda cried.

"Sssh! It's gone. You go back to sleep and I will keep walking," Rose replied.

Despite her aching muscles and sore back she wanted to keep moving to stay warm! So she pressed on for another 5 minutes before coming to a panting halt. She wanted to keep going but had to put Belinda down and rest.

*Oh my God! If I have to stop for five minutes after walking only five minutes it will take twice as long!* she fretted.

Thirst and images of the pool among the trees filled her mind to torment her. To her dismay, she found she was having trouble salivating and her eyes felt dry and scratchy. Her skin felt hot and dry.

*That's if I don't collapse from heat exhaustion!*

Once again anxiety clutched at her heart. She sat and sobbed but then began to shiver again.

*I must get on!* she told herself.

By sheer willpower she made herself get up. She took her hat off and shoved it into her backpack and slung the backpack on her front. Then she hoisted Belinda to her shoulders, taking a calculated risk in carrying her that way. After getting her little sister settled, she started her sore and tired muscles into motion.

It was better but Belinda was an awkward load as she was half asleep and slumped and had to be held tightly by the ankles. The little girl objected, but Rose was determined so she kept walking as fast as she could go, until she came to a puffing standstill after about ten minutes. Reasoning she must have covered her hundred metres, she paused to get her breath, leaning on a tree as she did.

"Yah! Oh bloody ants!" she muttered as she felt the tiny creatures running around on her hand and wrist.

Slapping and brushing at them she resumed walking. In this way, often with gritted teeth, she kept going for another twenty minutes before coming to a halt as a creek line was now evident ahead of her.

She rested for a few minutes and then scouted the creek line for an easy place to cross. Luckily, it was only a few metres across and she was able to follow a cattle pad down into its sandy bed and then up out again. That sand was tempting as a safe place to sleep but the urgent need for water drove her to keep pushing herself.

"Bub-O is depending on me! I must keep moving," she told herself.

# Chapter 7

## GRIT

By 0300hrs Rose was feeling utterly exhausted. She was stumbling at every second step and was feeling giddy and lightheaded. Her feet felt like they were encased in lead, and they hurt! The soles were hot and sharp pains in both heels and little toes came with each painful step. And Belinda was just hanging in both her arms, asleep or comatose, she could not tell which. But at least she was breathing. Rose kept blinking and was having difficulty focusing her eyes and knew she was suffering from dehydration and heat illness. But she was buoyed up by the belief that she had covered at least 4 or 5 kilometres, more than half the distance to her now magical goal of the water in the pool at Fountain Springs.

She flopped down for a rest, shuddering and cramping and knowing that her fingers were also starting to cramp. Whenever she tried to do something with them, they just curled up into the shape of claws. For at least a quarter of an hour she just lay in the spinifex, her pain wracked body almost oblivious to the tiny pin-pricks of the coarse grass.

Then Belinda stirred and that roused her. "I must save Bubby," Rose muttered. "Must get to water!"

By an effort of will power she had not known she possessed Rose forced herself to her feet and used her claws to scoop up Belinda. Then she stood there, swaying and disoriented until her brain started to function. *Where is the moon?* she queried. She found it higher in the sky and turned herself until it was behind her left shoulder. Satisfied she was pointing in the correct direction she pushed herself to start walking.

Ten minutes later she realised she was starting to go uphill. In her fuddled state she had not noticed the hill rising ahead of her, silver in the moonlight. The idea brought her to a standstill; and she lowered Belinda and knelt to relax while she thought the problem out. Her memory of the country she had seen at sunset helped her. From that she decided to go left around the hill.

Easier said than done, but by alternately walking for five minutes and resting for another five for about half an hour she reached a point where her tired brain told her she was now south of the hill. In fact she was now looking at a second hill, one studded with dark clumps of rocks, out to her left front.

*I need to go between these hills,* she told herself.

So she walked until that hill was beside her. Then she turned away from having the moon almost on her right back to her southwest heading.

It worked. An hour of steady slogging, stumbling, and resting had both hills behind her. Then it was down a long, gentle slope through waist-high spear grass to another creek line. This one had steep, eroded banks lined with trees and long grass and a bed studded with stones and pebbles. It took her ten minutes to get down into the bed and then a very awkward five minutes of stumbling to get across, only to discover she could not climb out. It was just too high and steep.

That reduced her to a weeping, huddled mess, hugging a shivering Belinda, or rather, she was sobbing but dry as she had no moisture for her eyes. Belinda kept waking and giving fretful little cries and twitches. When Rose eventually calmed down and summoned up her willpower again, she took five more minutes of painful effort to find a way up out of the creek.

Then another problem arose. The moon was now so high, almost directly overhead it seemed, that she had trouble orientating herself by it. She managed to work out which direction she wanted eventually but it was not by the moon. By chance, as she looked around for the Southern Cross, her gaze detected three bright stars close together and in line. They were just above the skyline behind her.

*There's those three stars Captain Ross showed us!* she thought.

It took a bit of mental effort to remember the name and then how to use the information. "That is Orion," she said aloud. "Those three stars are his belt; and the three nearby pointing away are his sword. Now, where are his head and shoulders? Captain Ross said Orion was a pinhead. Ah, yes!"

Rose detected a small star in the right area of sky and then two that she was sure were Orion's shoulders. Lowering Belinda to allow her hands to be free she turned and stood with both arms out until she was facing the same way as Orion's head. Then she aligned her arms with his shoulders.

"Roughly east-west," she told herself.

A feeling of real achievement surged through her and she quickly did an about turn.

"So south is that way." Putting her arms out again in the east-west line she brought her left arm to face south and then brought both hands together. "Southwest!" she cried in triumph.

But how to use the knowledge? She opted for the method of selecting a tree and walking to it and then re-orientating herself again. It was slow going but she plodded slowly up a long slope, confident she was heading the right way.

And then she encountered a wide belt of the sticky bushes. "Oh bugger!" she muttered.

"Naughty girl!" Belinda said loudly.

"Shh! Yes. You just go back to sleep Bub," Rose replied.

But it did cause her a tired grin. But pushing through the bushes didn't. She was far too worn out to waste time and effort detouring around them as they looked to extend for a long way either side. Luckily, they did not turn out to be very sticky.

And then she stopped and gaped. She had come to the crest of a gentle rise and there ahead of her was a line of mountains that extend right across her front from horizon to horizon. With a shock she realised that it was dawn. A glance at her watch confirmed this. It was nearly 0500hrs.

Finding a clear area she lowered Belinda and then stood and stared at the mountains. They looked to be only a few kilometres away, and as her gaze moved over them she felt a real surge of triumph. There, only a kilometre or so away, was a great jagged mass of rock that went up to mark the end of a massive wall of cliffs that extended off southwards as far as she could see.

"The Fountain Range!" she cried. That meant she was only three or four kilometres from the pool. "Five at the most!"

She looked to her right front and nodded. *Those mountains are the ones dad and I walked into yesterday, no, the day before to go to that railway tunnel. I know where I am.* But it took her a few minutes to remember the name of the area. *Ballara, a little town built at the junction of two railways to move copper ore to that smelter at Kuridala.*

For the next five minutes she just sat there, hugging Belinda and feeling happy, if very sore. Until a horrible thought came to her. It would be full daylight soon, and if those men were looking for them they would be moving about.

*We need to get to Fountain Springs and get water before those men even think about looking in this area,* she told herself.

That worry got her on her feet and moving, Belinda again clutched to her side. The going was easy, mostly knee-high grass but with a few clumps of spinifex and some of the horrible sticky bushes.

A vehicle track brought her to a stumbling standstill. It was only two wheel ruts in the grass and it went east-west across her route.

*Where does this go?* she wondered.

To her right she realised it must connect with the good, graded gravel road that came south for the Barkly Highway. But it was the other direction she was worried about.

*Does it connect to the road we were on yesterday? Is it the same road?* She didn't know but it seemed logical if it went east. Suddenly it became a sinister thing. *Those men might come driving along it,* she thought.

That got her looking and listening. As she did, she realised that there was already the ruddy glow of sunrise off to her left. "The sun will be up soon," she murmured. With that came the notion of the men searching and then the even more worrying truth that with the sun would come heat.

*We won't survive another day like yesterday without water,* Rose realised. That got her trying to lick dry and cracked lips with a tongue that seemed to fill her mouth and felt like cardboard. *But can we make it? I must!* she thought.

So she stepped carefully across the vehicle track and hurried on towards a line of white ghost gums that appeared to line a creek. They did and when she reached them, she found a way down into the sandy bed of the large creek and slumped down.

Rose wanted to rest but Belinda got her moving. "Dwink! Want dwink!" she cried.

"Okay Bub-O, but we have to walk there. I will get up," Rose answered.

She did, but it hurt. She was now chafed under her armpits and in her groin and her feet felt like they were on fire. She knew she was starting to stumble from dehydration and began to worry that she would make silly decisions or hallucinate.

*I need to get us to water before I pass out,* she told herself.

At least navigation was no longer a problem. There in front of her was the big hill with a mass of black rocks that looked like a castle and to her right, towering up and starting to glow in the dawn, were the cliffs of the Fountain Range. When she had first seen them in the morning two days before Rose had thought them both impressive and beautiful: the rocks all red and white strata tilted to the sky, the lower slopes all bright green spinifex or grass and patches of red earth. In lovely contrast were the bright white trunks and branches of the ghost gums. Even in this state of exhaustion she still thought the range beautiful but was focused on reaching that dip she could now see.

It took real grit and determination to get up and keep walking, but she did it. She plodded up a long slope through some woodland and sandy soil and came to the graded gravel road.

*Just on six o'clock,* she noted. Where did the time go!

That road brought her to standstill. She found she was faced by another dilemma, a situation where the wrong decision could be potentially fatal.

*Walking along the road will be much easier, but can we get off the road to hide in time if we hear a vehicle?*

While trying to decide, she lowered Belinda. Her little sister looked at the road and then made her mind up for her.

"I walk!" she said.

"Yes, okay," Rose agreed.

She found she was panting and had been dreading the effort of picking her up again. Taking Belinda's right hand she walked slowly out onto the road and turned left.

That went well for ten minutes, during which they covered perhaps half a kilometre. Belinda happily chirped away for most of this time but then began to slow.

"Where we go, Rosie?" she asked.

"To that nice pool of water where we had the swim a couple of days ago," Rose answered.

"Oh goody!"

That kept her going for another hundred metres or so but on the next upslope (the road went up and down over small rises), she stopped and began to drag her feet.

"I want Mummy!"

"So do I, Bub," Rose replied with conviction.

She tried to urge Belinda to keep walking, very aware that sunlight was now striking the tops of the mountains to her right and that the air was already quite warm. She was anxious that time was hurrying along and that every minute they were out on the road they were at great risk.

Then she metaphorically slapped her forehead. *We are not only walking along out in the open but we are leaving tracks!*

Appalled she looked behind and saw a clear line of dusty boot prints. She conceded that they could have been made by anybody, but she also knew that if the men came along and saw the prints they would be very suspicious and might then concentrate on that area.

So she took the hard decision and bent to scoop up Belinda and turned right and walked off the road into the scrub. The mental effort was almost as much as the physical as she knew she was near the end of her endurance. But there seemed no other option, so she gritted her teeth and plodded on through spinifex and head-high shrubs.

*To be so close!* she thought bitterly as her sore and overtaxed muscles complained on the next upslope.

Somehow she made it, and on the crest received a little boost. There, ahead of her, all lit up by the rising sun, was the section of the Fountain Range where there was an obvious dip.

"That is where that creek has eroded a slit in the rocks," Rose told herself, picturing the narrow rocky cleft and almost dry waterfall she had seen two days before. It looked to be only a kilometre away.

"I must make it!" Rose told herself, again forcing tired legs to move.

"What you say?" Belinda queried.

"Nearly at the pool," Rose answered and then she sniffed. *Oh no!* she thought. "Bub-O, have you done a poo?"

Belinda snuggled into her and hid her face, so Rose was quite sure from the smell that she had. *Oh bugger! Another thing to deal with!*

But on the scale of problems it was a trivial one, so she just ignored the fact that her arms and hands were squashing her little sister's poo all over the inside of her pants. Walking became a sheer effort of willpower and love.

Down a long slope beside the road she plodded and then around a bend and up another, steeper slope, which she realised halfway up she didn't have to climb if she detoured right. She did this, annoyed by the continual prickling of spinifex. Black dots began to dance in her vision and she several times stumbled. The line of cliffs now towered over them.

It took her nearly half an hour to walk those few hundred metres and by the time she came to a barbed wire fence Rose was staggering. Down to her left was a road junction and the road going to the right went through the fence via a cattle grid. Beyond that was an open area of bare gravel which she knew was a car park. From there several vehicle tracks wound in among the tall trees in the creek bed. Rose sobbed with relief as she knew she was at Fountain Springs.

"Only a hundred metres to go!" she gasped.

After a careful look to check that there were no cars there, she walked slowly down beside the fence to the cattle grid. For a moment she stopped to listen, aware that she was now virtually trapped against the mountain if the men arrived. Hearing nothing she carefully stepped over the grid and onto the gravel area.

As she did, Belinda began to squirm. "Want!" she cried.

Rose lowered her thankfully to the ground and Belinda at once began running towards where the pool was hidden among the trees.

"Wait Bub, wait!" Rose called. But Belinda didn't and Rose had to force her cramping leg muscles to work to follow.

Belinda trotted down among the trees where several areas of bare sand showed where vehicles drove or parked. *That is where dad parked our vehicle,* Rose remembered as she hurried painfully past the first big trees.

As she did, she noted that there was rubbish that had not been there two days before. Obviously other people had been there.

Seeing a litter of empty beer bottles and food wrappers, Rose wrinkled her nose. This changed to disgust a bit further along when she encountered several unburied turds and a mess of used toilet paper. The smell was enough to hurry her on. To her relief, Belinda did not step in any of it.

The pool was now just visible through the trees and shrubs. Towering up beyond were the steep cliffs that actually overhung the site. Rose knew from listening to her father that the whole Fountain Range was a massive layer of rock strata that had been pushed into a vertical wall by some massive tectonic force millions of years ago. Now she paused to glance up, again impressed and in awe of the natural forces involved.

*And it is very pretty!* she thought as she noted the bright colours of the rocks as they were lit by the morning sun.

The narrow foot track curved left just before the pool and at that point a small stream escaped to flow into the creek beyond, before soaking into a patch of reeds and sand. Several flat stepping stones allowed easy access across the water. Seeing that water made Rose gasp with relief.

But then she realised she had another problem. Belinda was stopped on one of the stepping stones and was staring down at something. Rose stopped and opened her mouth to ask what when she saw it. It was a snake!

"Snake! Oh stand still Belinda!" Rose cried.

For a moment her eyes went out of focus and her heart leapt and hammered. By then she had seen it was quite a small snake, an indeterminate brown. The snake heard her and now curled around to sway its head. Its tongue flickered, blue and forked. That got Rose all anxious but then it suddenly slithered off into the reeds and grass in the creek bed.

At once Rose grabbed hold of Belinda and lifted her up. "It's okay Bub," she said as she hurried on past to the small sandy beach on the edge of the pool.

"Snake," Belinda replied, twisting around to look back.

"It's alright. It's gone now. You did the right thing by stopping and standing still," Rose told her. "That's why I want you to stay with me and not run on ahead."

Belinda made no reply to this but pointed to the water. "Swim! Swim!" she cried.

"Yes Bub-O," Rose said, nodding with sheer relief.

She lowered Belinda and then knelt with her. For a few seconds she was quite unable to move, just trembled. A few glances back at the reeds assured her the snake was gone. She looked around to make sure there no other dangers and again made sour face. Nearby were more empty beer bottles, several of them broken.

But there was no other obvious danger, so she turned her attention to the unpleasant job of undressing and cleaning Belinda and then her clothes. It was a chore she had often done at home but during the last few months it had been rare as Belinda had been 'potty trained' and rarely pooed her pants.

Belinda was helpful, being used to such treatment. Wrinkling her face against the sight and smell, Rose carefully peeled off Belinda's clothes and then panties and placed them carefully aside.

"Don't go in deep," Rose ordered. "You wait for me."

Belinda ignored her and just rushed in until the water was almost over her head. Then she came spluttering back into shallower water. Here she put her head down and began to drink. Rose was about to tell her not to when she realised there was no point.

*That is all we are going to drink anyway!*

There was also a hygiene aspect. She understood she should be collecting their drinking water before Belinda washed herself, but she could see there was no way she could stop the little girl from wading in and splashing around, other than by physically restraining her. And she just did not have the inclination or the energy.

So, while Belinda began splashing around Rose took off the backpack and extracted the two drink bottles. It took self-control not to just plunge her face in and drink but instead she filled the small bottle and carefully screwed the lid back on before filling the large bottle. When it was full, she used it to drink from. The water was cool but a bit murky, but she was so thirsty she did not care.

*This might upset my stomach,* she thought. But then she shrugged. *You have to be alive to be sick!*

Having drunk a whole bottle, Rose refilled it and then placed it in the backpack. As she did, she found Belinda's little plastic sample bottle. It was only small but Rose decided that every mouthful would be helpful. She unscrewed the lid and went and dipped it in the water. Only then did she realise that Belinda's little 'diamond' was in the bottom. She shrugged and screwed the lid back on. Time to worry about things like that later. There was also her own sample bottle. This time she took the three small stones out and slipped them into her shirt pocket. Then she filled the bottle and put it in her pack.

Rose now faced the prospect of stripping in front of her little sister. They had shared baths when Belinda was a small baby but not recently. There was also a degree of anxiety in case the men turned up.

*Or anyone else,* she thought, blushing at the idea.

Only then did she sit and take off her boots and socks. She was tempted to wash in her clothes but then shook her head. Wet clothes could chafe, and she knew she had to keep walking. So she took off her trousers and then stripped, blushing with embarrassment. For a few seconds she looked down at her body and was appalled at all the red blotches, scratches, and bruises. Then shame at standing in the open nude made her hurry into the water.

But Belinda was too happily playing in the water to notice. She was pushing a floating stick around in a game her father had played with her when they had swum there two days before. She was so busy she did not even glance as Rose waded in and lowered herself to neck deep. Which was a shock. The water was cold! Rose gasped and then shook her head at how perverse the human race was.

And the water stung. All her chafing and scratches started stinging and tingling. Sighing with a mixture of pleasure and relief she splashed water on her face and head. What relief! Just getting the dry salt off her skin and out of her eyes was wonderful! Then she gingerly rubbed her sore places. That was bliss. Her vision of Fountain Springs was all she had thought.

*This is great!* she thought. But nagging at her was the knowledge that they must be gone quickly. The men could turn up at any moment.

So she reluctantly stopped washing herself and turned to grab Belinda.

"Come here Miss Ball of Busyness!" she said.

Belinda did not object to being rubbed and washed but did complain about her name. "I not Ball of Busyness. I Busy Bee!"

Rose managed a smile. "You are little monster," she agreed.

Quickly she made sure Belinda was clean and then turned to the more distasteful task of washing and scrubbing her soiled clothes. That done she waded ashore and looked around for a patch of sunlight to dry them in. But there wasn't any, not there beside the pool. The sun was still too low. There was no way Rose was going to walk all the way out to the open car park area naked, so she draped the wet clothes over some bushes at the back of the beach and then quickly dressed herself. Not having a towel she had to tug the clothes on over her wet skin.

But she did dry her feet. As she pulled on her socks, she puzzled over what to do next.

*Do we hide somewhere near here where we have water, coming down to get it when it is safe; or do we try to get to where we can contact the police?*

# Chapter 8

As she puzzled over this, Rose felt her stomach gurgle. That embarrassed her but also clarified her thoughts.

*I am really hungry. So, we can't stay here. We have nothing to eat and will get quickly weaker every day. That means we must walk to safety.* A glance at her watch told her it was already 0710hrs. *And we had better move soon.*

She began thinking through what she needed to do. *Water was our problem yesterday. So we need to carry more water.* But how?

Then her gaze settled on the empty beer bottles. She was reluctant to use them as she had a distinct aversion to touching their necks, not knowing what germs might be on them from the drinkers. But she knew she must. So she quickly picked one up and waded in to wash it as thoroughly as she could.

While she did, Belinda came splashing around. Rose shook her head. "Don't put your head underwater Bub. You could get germs in your ears and get sick," she said.

Belinda made a face at that and then knelt to suck up a mouthful of water. Rose was about to tell her not to and then shrugged. *That is what we are drinking anyway, and I need her to drink as much as possible.*

So Rose continued washing till she had six of the small 750ml bottles cleaned. Then she walked as far along the beach as she could to get away from the area where she had washed Belinda and her pants. Carefully she filled the six bottles and then carried them back and stood them carefully beside the backpacks.

*Now, how do I stop the water spilling out?* she thought.

Several ideas flitted across her mind, using a mud stopper, or a stick jammed in like a cork? But she could not find any that suited. Those that fitted were too long and she had no knife or tool to shape any wood.

*Oh what can I use?* she fretted, very aware that minutes were flying by, each one possibly adding to their danger.

Seeking ideas, she knelt and rummaged in her backpack hoping to find something. And she did. *The plastic wrap the sandwiches were in,* she thought.

Quickly she tested the concept and then, as quickly and carefully as she could she tore the plastic into six pieces and carefully wrapped each one over the neck of a bottle. But the result was less than satisfactory. It was obvious it would quickly come loose and leak when they were moved.

*How can I secure it?* she puzzled. *I need something to tie them. Ah! Ties! Hair ties.*

In Belinda's bag there was a packet of elastic hair ties, Bub being prone to pulling them off or losing them. Working fast Rose soon had all the necks of the bottles secure, having to twice stop to rescue Belinda as she floundered out of her depth. The bottles were then placed carefully in the backpack with a tea towel between them to stop glass on glass.

*Okay, nearly seven thirty. Time to get going.*

She knew this could be a battle and had put it off, hoping Belinda would tire of being in the pool. But now she was tossing sticks and splashing at them.

"Okay Bub-O, out you get!" she called.

Belinda ignored this and only replied after Rose called again, and louder. "I not Bub-O! I Belinda Busy Bee," she said.

"Yes, Busy Bee. Out you get so we can get you dressed," Rose said.

But it was a battle before she had her little sister up on the beach. Then the real struggle began. Belinda did not want to put on the damp panties. It took quite a bit of persuading, and it was 0740hrs by the time she had them on. The top was easier as is dry and there was less resistance to the damp trousers. Socks and shoes were added, despite protests that she did not want to wear them.

"You have to, please Belinda Babe, in case you have to walk on rough ground," Rose tried to reason.

"Want Bwekfast!" was the response.

"Sorry little bub but we do not have any food."

"Want bwekfast! Hungry!" Belinda wailed, "and I not little bub, I big girl now. Mummy say so. Want Mummy!"

Rose was at a loss on how to persuade or console, the result being that Belinda began to scream and then threw herself into a full-blown bout of hysterics. She threw herself to the ground and kicked with her hands and feet and sobbed. As she did, this her clothes began to soak up water from the wet sand. Smears of mud appeared on her clothing.

With difficulty Rose restrained her, being very upset and crying herself by then. In the process Belinda twice kicked her in the face, resulting in a split lip and bruised eye socket. Her hat was knocked off.

"Ow! Please Belinda, that hurt me. Please stop!" Rose wailed.

Angry and upset she resisted the temptation to hit her sister. Instead she put her hat back on and pushed it firmly into place.

Belinda looked at her and at least stopped her furious twitching and kicking. Rose knelt and lifted her onto her left knee and began to pat her while trying to brush off the wet sand and mud with her other hand. There was quite a smear of grey mud on the left knee of Belinda's pants and as Rose scraped at it with her fingernails Belinda looked down to see what she was doing, then burst into tears again.

"Want Mummy!" she sobbed, tears again streaking down her face.

Rose looked at those tears through her own and then bit her lip. *Bub is losing a lot of liquid in those tears. I need to keep her as hydrated as I can if we are to survive another day,* she thought. She had no idea where she might next find water. *Even walking to the highway might be beyond me,* she decided, remembering how long it took her father to drive the distance, half an hour or more.

"I want Mummy too mate, but we have to walk to see her. Please don't cry. Here, have a drink."

She held out her own water bottle and, to her relief, Belinda did stop crying and began to drink in big gulps. As soon as she had stopped, Rose drank the remainder of the bottle.

*I need to carry as much water in me as I can,* she reasoned.

So she put Belinda down and waded in to refill the bottle. Then she drank again and refilled it. By the time she placed the bottle back in her backpack she felt bloated but sure she would last the day.

*Okay, let's go,* she told herself.

It was now five to eight. Pulling on the backpack, with Belinda's pack stuffed inside it, she then picked up a protesting Belinda.

"Want to stay here!" Belinda cried, squirming again.

Rose stopped and held her firmly. "It would be nice," she said, her gaze roving up the steep cliffs and jagged rocks.

For a moment she contemplated that life-saving slick of water that was trickling from the narrow cleft up in the cliff. Then she turned and began walking back along the walking track towards the car park area.

There was a pause at the stepping stones to check there was no snake there, then she hurried on.

She was nearly at the line of big rocks that barred vehicle access when she realised Belinda did not have her hat on.

"Oh Bubsie! Where's your hat?" she cried.

Belinda's response was to give a sulky look and then hide her face. Rose sighed and put her down beside the last big rock.

"You stay here. Don't walk around. There might be snakes," she ordered.

At that, Belinda looked anxiously around. Then, as Rose turned to hurry back along the walking path, she let out a loud cry.

"Rosie! Rosie, don't leave me!"

"Sssh! I'm just going to get your hat. Be quiet please," Rose replied.

But Belinda wouldn't be quiet so Rose reluctantly picked her up and walked back to the pool again. She found the hat halfway, lying just among the reeds. Gasping with effort and exasperation she bent and snatched it up, the bottles in her backpack giving a warning clink as she did.

*Oops! Careful,* she told herself.

Clapping the hat on Belinda's head she again turned and made her way back out. As they made their way along the walking track, Belinda snatched the hat off and leaned right away before dropping it. All Rose could do was swear and crouch to pick it up. This time she held the hat in her other hand while carrying her little sister with her other arm.

They reached the shady car park area a minute later and Rose stopped in the shade where her father had parked their car. The air was already hot and the glare of the morning sun was unpleasant.

*Oh I hope Mum and Dad are alright!* she thought.

At that moment, she was feeling very stressed and very alone. But at least Belinda had stopped her game. She allowed Rose to stand her in the shade and place her hat on. While Rose was tying a nice bow under Belinda's chin with the cloth tapes, she noted an empty clear plastic water bottle lying with other rubbish at the base of the next tree. It was one of those 'Spring Water' bottles that her father despised. He thought it ridiculous that people would pay more for a bottle of water than for a bottle of fruit juice or a soft drink.

"Council water will be fine," he had said. "Anyway, the human race did not evolve drinking clean water, so it is probably bad for you, like white bread."

Memory of those words added to Rose's misery, but she also had an idea. It was a 1 litre bottle.

*We need all the water we can get,* she told herself. An extra litre could be the difference between life and death. She walked over to it and picked it up. It had no lid but looked clean. *I will just carry it and we will drink it first,* she decided.

"Wait here Bub. You look for diamonds while I fill this," she said.

To her relief, Belinda crouched and began picking up small stones. Rose did not wait.

*Quarter past eight!* she noted as she began to run.

The clinking of the glass bottles in her backpack immediately stopped that but she still walked as fast as she could. A minute later she was back at the pool and two minutes later she was on her way back with the bottle full. She was afraid Belinda would wander off or start screaming.

*Or find another snake!*

But she was happily playing. Rose held her new water bottle in her left hand and bent to scoop Belinda up with her other hand. To her relief, Belinda just clung on.

"Where we go, Rosie?"

"Looking for Mum and Dad," Rose replied.

"Want Mummy!"

"So do I, so please help," Rose replied.

She walked quickly out from under the trees and then paused to see if she had left tracks in the sand. There were indentations but the sand was too dry and loose to hold any clear impressions. With tracks in mind she was careful to walk on the gravel of the road, not the dust at the side.

But that hundred or so metres back up the open slope to the cattle grid was an anxious time. Rose felt very exposed. She also quickly grew tired and feared she lacked the strength to go far. By the time she had gingerly made her way across the steel rails of the cattle grid she was panting and sweating.

Once across she turned left. North was now her planned direction. Almost subconsciously she sensed that south was an unknown wilderness and that it was more dangerous than the men.

*We will just die in the desert like Burke and Wills,* she told herself.

And then she smiled as she had once seen a movie titled 'Wills and Burke' that was a comic send-up of that fateful expedition. The smile hurt as it cracked the scabs on her lips, but she felt better.

Her course led her up the slope beside the fence she had followed earlier. This meant dodging the sticky bushes and some sort of grey-green spindly shrub with prickles on it and dead leaves that stuck to her skin. Some got down the back of her shirt and began to irritate.

And then her hear leapt as fear flooded into it. A vehicle was coming!

Not knowing who might be in it brought back all the terror of the previous day. Worse still, she was only about 25 metres from the road and on a fairly open slope. The sound was coming from the north. She cast around for a good hiding place but there was none.

"Do hide and seek like we do at cadets," she told herself. That meant scurrying across to the nearest clump of bushes and crawling in behind it to lie flat.

As she did, the vehicle came over the rise to her right front. She quickly fell flat, hearing a distinct tinkle of glass in her backpack as she did. But a broken bottle was the least of her worries as she suddenly got a clear view of the vehicle as it went past. It was a white 4WD ute. The driver she had never seen but the other man in the cab was Lucas!

*Lucas! They must have worked out which way we went,* Rose thought.

Another pulse of paralysing fear coursed through her, and she let out a stifled sob. The vehicle went around behind her. There was the skid of tyres on gravel as the brakes were applied, and for a moment Rose feared they had been seen.

But a man's loud voice said, "Go right, damn it! We will go and check out this waterfall place."

The ute's engine roared and Rose looked back over her shoulder. With her heart hammering furiously she got a glimpse of the vehicle as it roared across the grid behind her. She was hotly aware that if either man looked up along the fence line, they would be able to see her!

But they obviously had their eyes on the spectacular cliffs and trees ahead of them as the vehicle went on down the slope and she heard it stop among the trees.

*Oh my God! We got out of there just in time,* Rose told herself.

She could feel water seeping onto her shirt and knew at least one of her improvised water bottles was broken. And the one she held in her right hand was half on its side and water was glugging out.

*Oh you idiot!* she berated herself. Holding the bottle upright she scrambled to her feet. *I need to get off this slope fast,* she reasoned.

Hoping that the focus of the men's attention was the pool area, she walked as fast as she could up the rise. It was about 50 metres to the crest and by the time she reached it she was gasping and perspiring.

As soon she was over the crest, Rose stopped and looked back, her ears trying to work out what the men we doing. She heard the vehicle engine get turned off then vehicle doors slam.

*They are going to check out the pool for sure,* she thought. Anxiety about whether there might be tracks or something she had left there caused her heart to flutter and her throat to go dry.

Then her attention was turned to Belinda. The little girl was trying to reach the water bottle she held in her hand. Thankfully Rose allowed her to drink and then had a drink herself, lowering the water level to only about a third.

"Baby Bee, that was the bad men. We have to hide from them. Daddy said so," she explained.

"Bad men!" Belinda replied. "Want Daddy! Want Mummy!"

"Yes mate, but we need to hide from the bad men. That means no noise. Please don't cry or call out," Rose said.

She glanced back and then began walking determinedly north. The spinifex pricking her legs she ignored but it was harder to ignore the sticky bushes and other prickly plants. The whole area was covered in trees and bushes but with frequent patches of bare red earth. Rose hurried across these, worried she might be leaving tracks but wanting urgently to put distance between them and the men.

As she hurried through the scrub, she kept glancing up at the long line of steep hillslopes and cliffs on her left. She was anxiously aware that she was in a narrow belt of bush between the gravel road to her right and those cliffs.

*If those men spot me, I don't think we will be able to hide,* she worried.

It was also obvious that any observer up on the steep grassy slopes would be able to see any movement along that whole strip of country. But would the men think of that?

Rose conjured up all sorts of dreadful threats and possibilities and these spurred her to keep going until she came to a gasping, staggering standstill. It was 0840hrs by then and she estimated she had covered at least a kilometre. She found a dip in the shade of a tree where they would be hidden from anyone on the road and sat down for a rest. There were ants but she beat them away and gave Belinda another drink. She had a sip herself and wiped sweat from her forehead. She understood that she had the apparently selfish duty of making sure she stayed hydrated, or they would both die. So she finished the water in that bottle. As she did, she noticed that it had a crack in the thin plastic and that water was dribbling out of the bottom corner. Reluctantly she hid it in a bush.

As she sat there getting her breath back, her mind roamed over possible options. But the plan she had decided on at the pool still seemed best.

*I will go north to the Barkly Highway and flag down a car,* she affirmed. But how far was it? She thought 25 or 30 kilometres, based on the driving time two days before. *I think I can manage that if I am careful,* she thought.

All this time she had been straining her ears for any sound of the men or their vehicle. Just once she thought she heard something but after a time the only sounds were the usual bush ones of birds, leaves, cicadas and so on. When she started walking the sound of her boots scrunching on the red earth sounded very loud.

*And I am leaving tracks,* she noted with dismay as she glanced back. The only way to avoid that was to walk only on the grass and spinifex, and the spinifex hurt too much.

After ten minutes she had to stop again. By then the sun was well up and was scorching. Sweat dripped off her and even Belinda's skin felt slippery. She became fretful and whimpered from time to time.

"Firsty!" she cried.

So Rose gave her another sip and then finished the bottle with the half mouthful remaining. At the next stop she took off her backpack, itself a relief as her back was wet with sweat, and carefully fished out some pieces of broken glass. With some difficulty she put the empty bottle in the backpack. Then it was pushing herself on again.

It quickly developed into a nightmare ordeal for Rose: walk for a few hundred paces, rest for five or ten minutes, walk some more, rest. Time quickly slid by, and the temperature climbed with every hour. 0900hrs came and went, and then 10. By then she was level with the northern end of the Fountain Range, but more rugged peaks were appearing to her left front. All the while she was wondering where the men were.

She came to a large, dry creek. *Is this the big creek near Ballara?* she wondered. For a few minutes she rested in its sandy bed and then climbed out and made herself go on.

Now, as she puffed and plodded along, continually shifting Belinda's position to ease her cramping and tired arms, her mind was focused on the visit two days before. She tried to remember the dates of when the tiny township had been set up as a railway terminal but could only remember that it was around the time of the First World War.

*The price of copper went right up because they needed copper to make rifle cartridges and so on,* she told herself. *Anyway, it doesn't matter. It's more than a hundred years ago and there is nobody there now.*

And there was almost nothing to show that a town had been there once. Her memory of the visit was of reading a sign at the road junction and going through a gate nearby and then walking up a cleared path to where the railway station had once been. All that was left now was the concrete platform among the weeds and bushes. On the crest of the nearby rise were the ruins and remains of the town: a set of concrete steps, some old fences and garden borders and post holes. It was all covered in long grass, bushes, and weeds.

And now she saw the sign and road junction, only 50 paces to her right front. Cautiously Rose crept towards it, weaving her way between the bushes. A low, concrete structure came into view among the grass and scrub only 25 metres to her front.

*Ah! Dad said that was the Goods Loading Platform,* she remembered. Then she stopped. *I shouldn't be going near any of this,* she told herself. But there was that Tourist Information sign under a small roof, and she remembered that it had on it the distances to various places. *It has a map. That might be useful.* But was it worth the risk to go out and look? What if the men came back.?

Rose strained her ears but all she could hear was the shrill shriek of cicadas and the squark of a distant crow. Temptation warred with cowardice. Then she shook her head.

*I need that information and the map will be a great help.*

So she threaded her way through the bushes and past the end of the long, low, concrete goods platform. At the edge of the scrub she paused to look and listen. Still no sound.

*Don't leave tracks,* she cautioned herself.

Very carefully she tiptoed out onto the gravel car park and turn-around area around the Tourist Sign. No sound. Good! Then Belinda saw the sign and began babbling on about their visit.

"Mummy and me stay here when you and Daddy go for walk," she said.

"We did, to an old tunnel," Rose agreed as she hastily but carefully scanned the information.

The first fact that she gleaned really lifted her hopes. The sign told her that the Barkly Highway was only 19.2 kilometres to the north. The next was that the pool at Fountain Springs was only 3.8 Kilometres.

*It seemed a lot further than that!* she thought ruefully, very aware of her aching muscles and sore feet.

And then she heard the vehicle. It was coming from the south and coming fast!

# Chapter 9

## BALLARA

*The men! They're coming!* Rose thought.

For a few seconds she froze as a surge of pure terror gripped her. Her vision went blurry and her chest constricted.

*Oh run!*

Gasping with fear she turned to run, and Belinda swung in her arms and nearly fell. In the process she knocked Rose's hat off.

"Oh no!" she cried.

Turning again, she scrabbled to pick the hat up and then decided it was a good thing. As her vision cleared, her mind started working again.

*Tracks, wipe out my tracks!* she told herself.

Using her hat, she beat at the dust as she hurried backwards across the open gravel to the edge of the bush. By then the vehicle had crossed the creek to the south. Rose glanced that way and sobbed with near despair.

"Oh, where can we hide?" she asked.

The only place she could see was behind the low concrete goods platform. There obviously wasn't time to go further away into the scrub. But the platform was right there, and it only had an overhang on either side of about 15 centimetres. The closest side was against bare gravel and with no cover and the other side only had a sticky bush at the end and then dry grass and spinifex.

Clutching a scared looking Belinda to her front Rose ran to that side and was about to push in through the sticky bush when she paused and then changed direction to run to the left side of it. Then she turned right and pushed through the bushes to get to the platform. As she did, the sound of the approaching vehicle grew rapidly louder and she got a glimpse of it through the scrub.

*I'm out of time, and options,* she told herself, sobbing in near panic. But she knew she had to hide Belinda's pink hat and red clothes!

Dropping to her knees, she tried to shield Belinda from the prickly branches and sticky seed pods as she pushed in against the base of the concrete platform.

"Oh Bub-O, please help me to play hide and seek. Please don't cry or talk. These are the bad men coming, and Daddy said to hide from them."

"I play hidey seekey!" Belinda agreed. Then she spluttered as a leaf or seed pod stuck to her lips.

"Oh Bub, no noise please," Rose begged.

As she pushed Belinda against the concrete, she half laid on her and moved her hands to be ready to cover her little sister's mouth. By then the vehicle was skidding to a stop near the tourist sign but the hammering of her own heart sounded just as loud. Fear kept causing her hearing to swash in and out with the heart beats and she found her throat constricted and eyes going unfocused. She knew she had no hope of running.

Lying flat and half covering Belinda, she made sure she could see her little sister's face. With an effort of will power, she managed a sickly smile even as the vehicle's engine was turned off and doors were opened. Rose twisted her neck to look and was appalled to note that she could see the men through the screen of grass and sticky bush! The situation looked hopeless. She braced for discovery and the horrors that might follow.

Quite clearly she saw Lucas and the other man move away from the vehicle to stand in the shade of the tourist sign's roof.

"What's this place?" queried the other man, a solid man in his thirties wearing a washed-out orange work shirt.

"Ballara," Lucas replied. "Used to be a town back in the old days."

The other man looked around. "Not much here now?" he commented.

Then he leaned forward to read the sign. Lucas joined him and Rose was relieved to see that neither man was carrying a gun. Not that she thought she had any chance of fighting off two big men!

Then the other man looked directly in her direction. "What's that thing?" he said, pointing towards her.

"Goods platform," Lucas replied, pointing to the map on the sign. "Used to be a railway here."

"Goods platform, eh?" said the other man.

To Rose's horror, he began walking towards it. Realising she was breathing very rapidly, she deliberately slowed it, and then stopped as the man's boot scrunched right there, only a metre or so from her face. Then his boots and legs appeared, and her heart leapt in dread. She saw his face as he bent to look under the overhang. Then he cried out and his face vanished.

"Oh ptooie! Yuk!" he cried, spitting and slapping. "Bloody sticky seed pods!" he cried.

To which Rose could only agree, as both her face and Belinda's and their clothes were covered with the things.

Belinda made a little noise, and Rose turned her face to look into her eyes. She managed to shake her head and hiss, "Sssh!" very softly. To her relief, Belinda nodded.

Lucas let out a coarse laugh. "Serves ya right, ya bugger!" he said.

Belinda opened her mouth to say something and Rose shook her head again, bumping it on the concrete. There was a moment of dizziness. She realised she was holding her breath and starting to black out so she slowly exhaled and then took a big, deep breath as silently as she could. The sound of boots on top of the concrete sent her heart rate shooting up again, and she trembled. Worse still, her right calf muscle began cramping and she knew she could not run even if she wanted to.

The men's voices carried clearly to here. "Can't see anything. So what do we do now?" the other man queried.

Rose understood that the men did not know they were in the area. She had feared they had found their tracks or some other clue.

Lucas answered, "Keep looking for these two little girls," he said.

"I big girl!" Belinda whispered indignantly, to Rose's horror.

"Shh! No sound!" Rose hissed, shaking her head.

"Dunno why we are wasting time looking here," the other man said. "They could be anywhere."

"Yeah, well, the boss said to look, so we look," Lucas answered.

"They'll just be lost back in the bush back over the other side of those hills," the other man said.

"Maybe," Lucas agreed.

"Well, they're just city kids from Sydney," the other man commented. "They won't last long out here in the bloody desert and with this heat."

That comment was a revelation to Rose. *These guys haven't been very well briefed,* she thought. *They don't know we do holiday trips out here, or that I am an army cadet.* And that gave her a sharp spike of hope. To this was added a frisson of fear at the next comments.

"Yeah, well, we'd better find 'em, and quickly," Lucas said. "If we can't produce their bodies then it's no money for us and somebody might then come hunting us."

The other man grunted. "Huh! Well, the boss should get a plane. That would find them in five minutes."

"Probably," Lucas agreed. "But we had better get on with looking. If word gets out that they are missing before the job is complete, then we are in trouble. And if they are alive and get to the police our goose might be cooked too. So let's go."

"Where to?"

"Where the boss said. We will drive north to the Barkly Highway and search all of that area and then search back again," Lucas answered.

There was the sound of boots moving away from just above Rose and Belinda and then the voices were less distinct.

"Why not this other road?" the other man suggested.

"Boss said to go north first. It is the most likely, if they have made their way west across the hills," Lucas replied, adding, "Where are you going?"

"There's another sign just over here on this other road. I just want to read it first," the other man answered.

"Yeah, well hurry up," Lucas snapped.

His boots also moved away and there were thuds as both men jumped down off the far side of the concrete platform. As they did, Rose shuddered with relief and took a couple of deep breaths. She knew exactly which sign. She had read it with her family two days before. It had an enlarged image of a little steam locomotive and information on the railways. Her father had made a point of reading it aloud, very proud that his great grandfather had been the locomotive driver on one of those trains.

Then Belinda provided a crisis. Quite loudly she said, "What that man cooking? I hungry."

"Sssh! He's not cooking anything. Don't make a sound," Rose hissed.

"But I hungry! He say he cooking a goose," Belinda said, even more loudly.

Luckily, it was drowned out by the sound of boots crunching on gravel and then of a vehicle door opening, followed by the usual strapping in and starting up sounds.

It was just as well because Belinda looked unhappy and kept muttering she was hungry. "He say he cooking a goose!"

Rose was scared she would suddenly start a tantrum. "It's okay Busy Bee. He did not mean he was actually cooking a goose. It is just a saying, an expression." Her mind tried to dredge up the correct name from English lessons at school. But she couldn't so she continued, "When the men are gone, we will have a drink and look for some food. You wouldn't eat goose anyway."

To her relief, Belinda nodded and then said, "I see goose in my picture book."

"You have too," Rose agreed.

Shivering with fright and from the nervous strain of trying to keep as calm as she could, she now heard the other man's boots heading for the vehicle. She knew Belinda was referring to one of her nursery rhyme picture books.

There was the sound of the other man getting into the vehicle and then the roar of its engine and wheel spin throwing up dust and gravel as it accelerated away. Rose glimpsed it briefly before it was gone from view. As the sound receded, she gasped with relief and then began to tremble and weep. For a few minutes she was quite unable to do anything but sob until Belinda's wails about the sticky pods and wanting a drink forced her to calm down.

*Get a grip girl!* Rose told herself.

Shuddering with effort she backed out from under the overhang, banging the backpack hard against it as she did. This caused another tinkle of broken glass and more precious water soaked down over her shirt.

*Oh bugger!* she thought unhappily.

With an effort that was delayed by cramps in both legs and arms she hauled Belinda out and stood her on the concrete platform.

For another five minutes she was busy calming her sister and carefully plucking off all the sticky pods she could see. Next, she dusted her clothes and only then plucked at the sticky pods on her own face, hair, and clothes. She was very thirsty again by this, battling with her conscience about drinking until she told herself that if she collapsed they both died. So she drank half of one of the beer bottles. Belinda drank the other half.

Then Rose considered what to do next. The news that the men were searching the road north to the highway had demolished her plan. Casting back in her memory to the drives in and out two days before, she realised that walking that way, even in the scrub, would be very difficult and dangerous. She remembered several ranges of hills where the road went through narrow passes, with steep, bare hillsides on both sides.

*And lots of really rough hills,* she thought. The idea of walking beside the road until she saw the vehicle or heard it, and then having to try to hide on a steep slope in spinifex, was not one she thought viable. *You can't lie down in spinifex without risking eye damage,* she told herself.

*So which way do I go?* she worried.

Remembering her Corporal's Course lessons on Appreciations, she told herself not to reject any options until she had thoroughly examined them. So she weighed the pros and cons of going back east.

*I might find out if dad and mum are still there,* she thought. But that led to other horrible thoughts: Were her parents still alive? What had happened to her father's attempts to buy the man off? What was really going on? *And who is their boss?*

Rose tried hard to remember the conversation she had just overheard and got the distinct impression that she and Belinda were in great peril. It also gave her hope.

*They don't have an aircraft. We can walk quickly in the open some of the time.* That notion got her back to thinking which way. After a bit of thought she rejected going back south, even as far as Fountain Springs for more water. *So that leaves west,* she told herself.

But could she walk over those very steep and rugged hills she knew were there? *It will have to be the road, or near it,* she reasoned. At least she had been along part of the road and knew what it was like. *And dad showed me on the map that it connects to other roads, or tracks, that come out on the highway closer to Mount Isa,* she remembered.

Her memory also helped her decide that was a good way to go at that moment. She remembered that much of that road was gravel or bare rock and that it should be possible to walk along it without leaving boot prints.

*But I have to go now,* she told herself.

A quick mental calculation told her that the men could drive to the highway in half an hour. She glanced at her watch and saw it was 1020hrs.

*So they could be back here in an hour.*

She and her father had walked up to the Wee MacGregor Railway Tunnel in a bit over an hour two days before. But that had been much earlier in the day, at 0800hrs when it was cooler.

*And I wasn't lugging baby sister,* she thought ruefully.

But it had to be done so she walked quickly around the platform and out along the side road. As she came to the sign about the railway, she glanced briefly at it to check the distance to the tunnel.

"Three point five kilometres to Hightville and the tunnel is about another kilometre," she muttered.

Then she read that the road was unsuitable for cars and caravans. 'Extreme 4 Wheel driving' it read. That comforted her.

Belinda wanted to touch the sign so Rose let her and then she began walking as fast as she could along the edge of the road, only detouring to avoid the overhanging sticky bushes. These were thick for the first hundred metres but then thinned out and after that there was only savannah, with more grass than spinifex. The big dry creek angled in on her left so that the road ran along beside it.

After a hundred paces they came out on a long straight. It was very easy walking except for carrying Belinda. Rose now took off her hat and stuffed it under the pack straps before swinging her little sister up to sit on her shoulders. It was safe enough along that stretch of road and had the added advantage of her blocking the sun from the back of Rose's neck and head.

Ahead of her Rose saw the 4-metre-high concrete wall that supported a bench cut above the line of the old railway, which was now the road along this stretch.

*That is the two foot gauge railway up there,* Rose told herself as she came to it. Her father had carefully explained how the little trains brought copper ore from the Wee MacGregor Mine and how it was shovelled and dumped down from the higher track into the wagons of the 3'6" railway below. *Amazing what they did in the old days!* she thought again.

Belinda did not take any notice of any of the high retaining wall as they walked past. Her attention was taken up by some white cockatoos that were screeching and fighting among the trees which lined the creek beside them. By the end of the straight section where the old 3' 6" railway ended and the 2' one descended they were in among the foothills and the high ground cut out most of the breeze. Rose began to sweat profusely. She knew that was good for a while but was also anxious as she was very aware she would quickly dehydrate.

Ten minutes walking had her on a section where the road was following the bench cut for the 2' gauge tramway as it curved sharp right through a rocky little gorge in the hills. The rugged end of the Fountain Range rose majestically up on her left, and steep rock and spinifex studded slopes ahead and to her right. The heat became intense as the sun's rays were reflected around the rocky slopes.

But knowing her exact location Rose found a great comfort. In her mind she visualised the road ahead and then what she could of the map. That brought back images of her father and she experienced a bout of intense anxiety.

*Are Mum and Dad alive, or dead?* she wondered.

These gloomy thoughts were startled out of her by sudden movement ahead as the road dipped down to cross a branch of the creek. Rose felt her heart leap and then she sighed and gave a little laugh.

"Only wallabies," she said to Belinda.

"Want," Belinda demanded, but not very forcefully.

Rose watched two wallabies bound away and noted their black forepaws and faces. "Rock wallabies, I think," she added.

But her attention now had to be turned to getting safely down to the dry creek. The surface of the road was potholed and eroded and studded with patches of bedrock. Much of it was loose pebbles or even quite large stones and she slipped several times. Fearing to trip and cast Belinda down hard, or to twist an ankle, she took it very slowly and carefully.

*At least I'm not likely to leave any tracks on this,* she consoled herself. A glance back revealed none.

She had been hoping to find water in the creek but it was dry so she just plodded across the stony bed and on along the gravel road. The next section was a hundred metres in the shade of trees down in the creek bed. Beside her was what she expected, the concrete abutments of a bridge. The bridge itself was long gone but the earthworks of the permanent way were clear to see as an embankment and then, after the line crossed the road, as a bench cut up on her left. A hundred paces further on the road recrossed the creek bed and there were the remains of another bridge there.

By then Rose was really puffing and she was starting to feel aches in a whole lot of different muscles. And she was feeling very tired. Her eyelids felt like they just wanted to slide down and shut. She had to blink and shake her head to stay alert. Also Belinda felt somehow loose and floppy, and she suspected she had gone to sleep. For safety she eased

Belinda down off her shoulders and found that this was indeed what had happened.

Placing Belinda on her front with her head on her shoulder, Rose replaced her own hat and set her teeth to plod up a steep fifty paces to the next level. At the top the old line merged with the road at some old mine sites, dips and mullock heaps. Rose had to stop to get her breath and then felt incredibly thirsty. It did not seem possible after all she had drunk at the pool but it was so.

The road now curved right, along the bench cut of the old railway. It followed the lower slopes of a series of steep, rugged but bare slopes. These led up to a line of rocky peaks. To her left the creek split and one branch was still beside them but angling away. The valley opened out so that she could see all the way to the very rugged range that she knew the tunnel was in. But it was all uphill and all hot!

Despite feeling exhausted Rose forced her tired legs to keep working and grimly clutched Belinda with her aching arms.

*I must keep going! We have to get out of this area quickly,* she told herself.

Several old embankments were crossed and then the earthworks deviated away from the road, curving up and to the right at the crest of a wide spur she had managed to walk up. She paused there, swaying and badly wanting to rest or lie down but there were no trees for shade and very little cover, so she shook her head and took several deep breaths and resumed walking.

A hundred metres ahead, down a shallow dip, was the Old Hightville Cemetery. *Not much of a cemetery,* she recalled.

It was just five or six lonely graves in an overgrown and fenced off area on the right of the road. But it had some shade trees and she had to stop. Reluctantly she lowered Belinda to a patch of grass, anxious she did not wake the little girl up. She didn't and Rose shrugged off her backpack and unbuckled it. Very carefully she extracted another beer bottle and drank half of it. Then she placed it aside and even more carefully used her fingers to pluck out the shards of broken glass. Reluctantly she repacked and pulled the backpack on.

A slight breeze came up the valley, but the air was hot and seemed to dry her skin rather than cool. She was painfully aware that her eyes felt scratchy and that she was badly sunburnt.

*It's bloody hot!* she thought.

At that, time of day, two days earlier, her father had said it was 37 degrees C. A check of her watch showed it was already 1125hrs. The hour was up!

Fear flooded back in. Knowing that the men could appear at any moment Rose looked around to try to pick a route that offered some cover and a chance of escape but the steep, spinifex-covered slopes up to her right were almost bare of trees and bushes and looked hopeless. To her left, the slope down to the creek was now a hundred metres or more of almost open ground.

"I'd better get off this section as quickly as I can," she muttered.

Fear lent her strength, and she scooped sleeping Belinda up and got her comfortable. Grimly she set herself to plod up the long slope ahead of her.

It was at least 500 metres of gently undulating road, predominantly up. And all the way along it she was desperately aware that anyone back at where the road came up out of the creek where the second bridge had been could see all the way up the valley to this point! She knew the men would come by vehicle and they would be able to drive that distance in a few minutes.

*Oh what will I do if they appear?* she asked herself, letting out a small sob as she did.

# Chapter 10

## THE TUNNEL

Somehow Rose found the strength to keep going. She adopted the method of plodding up the slope for fifty paces, counting, and then stopping for the count of 25. There was almost no shade and the sun beat down relentlessly. There wasn't a cloud in the sky and the only relief was from a light breeze blowing on her sweat-soaked back.

"Fifty, stop. Count," she muttered again.

It took her fifteen minutes to reach a point where the road curved around a rise to the right and was hidden from the far end of the valley. From there Rose could see all of the western side of the Fountain Range and she could only shake her head at the beauty of the scene and the contrast of her own possible fate!

Thankful to be out of sight she plodded on, and then a new set of fears crept in. *Now I can't see back down the valley and the vehicle might just arrive right behind me,* she worried. She began straining her ears to try to detect the sound of the vehicle's approach.

Then she found she urgently needed to relieve herself. For a few moments she dithered, partly out of embarrassment and partly out of fear. Not wanting to be caught by the men with her pants down in the middle of the road, she moved 20 paces into the spinifex to an area of bare earth. It looked big enough and despite the ants she put a sleepy Belinda down on another bare patch and then pulled her trousers and panties down.

Belinda watched and frowned. "What you do, Rosie?" she asked.

"A pee… Youch!" was Rose's reply, the yelp because as she squatted down several sharp spinifex prongs had dug into her bare buttocks. She swore and then quickly moved to get clear of them.

Belinda giggled. "You said naughty word!" she cried delightedly. "What happened, Rosie?"

"Bloody spinifex prickled me in the bum," Rose retorted angrily. She was nearly at the end of her self-control and knew it.

Again Belinda giggled and covered her mouth. "Oooh! You swore again, and you say bum."

"I'll give you bum!" Rose snapped. "I'll smack yours!" Then she tried to ignore her sister as she relieved herself, burning with embarrassment as she did.

And then Belinda wanted to go as well and that took another five minutes, getting her clothing out of the way and then dressing her again. As she did, Rose noted that Belinda's pudgy little arms and fat fingers were bright red from heat and sunburn.

*And so is her face.*

So another few minutes were taken up with smearing on suncream. Then Belinda wanted a drink, so Rose muttered again and dug out her little sister's water bottle and let her drink a mouthful. She badly wanted a drink herself, but she resisted.

Then, with a groan at the sore muscles and real mental and physical effort she hoisted Belinda up to her shoulders and started off again. For the next ten minutes she kept doing the walk, stop, walk, stop, forcing her gasping lungs and aching muscles to lift those boots made of lead. The road remained very rough, washouts, potholes, sharp rocks sticking out and even patches of soft sand. She tried to avoid these but did not always remember to. Several times she stumbled, and she feared she was again reaching the end of her strength.

*I need to find somewhere to hide and rest.*

But she had set her mind on the old railway tunnel, so she gritted her teeth and kept going. The road curved up and around to the right and then left to run almost along the top of an undulating crest of a ridge for half a kilometre, the higher ground just to her left. Ahead of her she could clearly see the rugged line of hills she knew the tunnel went through. To her left front she could also see a gravel road climbing up over a saddle to the left of the highest peak.

*That is the road to the Wee MacGregor Mine,* she remembered. *And it looks bloody steep!* She did not think she could manage that in her exhausted condition, so she set the old tunnel as her objective. *At least I know what it is like.*

1200hrs came and went. Every hundred metres took three or four minutes, and she became quite despondent about ever reaching even the Hightville area. But at 1223 she rounded a curve and there, a hundred paces ahead on her left, was another tourist sign.

"Oh thank God! Hightville," she murmured.

It was slightly downhill to the sign and she just walked on past it. She had read it during her previous visit and the best bit she remembered was about the extreme 4-wheel driving. There was a faint hope the men might not drive along the old railway.

But by the time she had passed the sign Rose was almost staggering and she found she had to stop and rest. She kept hold of Belinda and eased herself down behind some bushes just off the road to the right of where the old tramway came through a low cutting from her right and went on across a gully. Selecting a bare patch free of ants she lowered Belinda and then sat. As she did, she noted that among the clumps of spinifex and grass were numerous pieces of broken glass and very old rusting tin cans.

Five minutes was all she allowed herself and then she struggled to her feet, waking Belinda in the process. So unsteady was she that she had to grab at a tree to stop herself falling. After a few deep breaths and a deliberate calming of her trembling legs she pushed herself back onto the rough vehicle track and carefully made her way down the loose gravel slope to the bottom of the gully.

The track forked and on her right there were the concrete abutments of another bridge. She went between these. It all helped her as she knew exactly where she was and which way to go. But then it was uphill for 50 metres, up a slope of loose gravel and rocks that sparkled in the sun.

*Mica or pyrites or something,* she thought.

At the top of that slope was another fork in the vehicle track and she came to a gasping, staggering halt. She knew she had to go right but was so drained of energy she felt she just could not go on. And Belinda was grizzling and demanding a drink and some food!

"I haven't found any food," Rose explained.

And then she froze. Quite clearly to her ears came the sound of a vehicle's engine. *Oh no! Is it the men?*

And there they were!

Around the slope 200 metres away appeared the vehicle. It was going fairly fast and doing a lot of bouncing and banging on the rough road. Rose gasped and looked around with terror-stricken eyes for somewhere to hide. But she was on the start of the bench cut around the side of a very steep hill, so big it was really a mountain.

Thinking to just lie in the grass and bushes, she began to run on along

95

the rough track that existed on the old bench cut of the railway. And it was very rough. She felt her ankle twist and a sharp stab of pain went up her left leg. Then she fell and Belinda went tumbling.

Belinda began to cry, and Rose ignored her own bumps and bruises and scrambled to her knees, sure she had broken her kneecaps or something. She hurt but fear kept her moving. Scooping Belinda up she clapped her hand over her mouth.

"Shh! Quiet Bub-O. It is the bad men," she hissed.

Then she realised that the vehicle had stopped back on the other slope. She moved to where the track ran through a small cutting and then crouched behind what cover she could find to peer back. It was hard to see as there were a lot of trees and bushes intervening but to her surprise and relief she saw the two men, it was them, had stopped and gotten out to read the Hightville Tourist Sign.

Fear helped summon up her last reserves of energy and to clear her mind. Thinking fast she realised she still had a few minutes. *If I can get through the tunnel we might have a chance!* she told herself.

But that was still a few hundred metres away. *Will the men see us if I walk out of the cutting and on along the old railway?* she worried.

But there wasn't much choice, other than going over the side and trying to hide on the steep, grassy slope below. A quick look convinced her that there was no way she could climb the steep slope on her left, even on her own!

Knowing she had to take the risk, Rose resumed walking, having to go slow as the going was so rough. The vehicle track that had replaced the old railway was mostly two deep ruts among jagged rocks and was pitted with dips and holes and had numerous rocks sticking up.

*Extreme four-wheel drive alright!* she thought.

As she picked her way along as fast as she dared, she kept looking back. To her relief, the road curved left so that she was hidden from the vehicle.

A minute and fifty metres, two minutes, another fifty. She was gasping by then and knew she was weakening fast. Sweat trickled into her eyes and the salt stung. Belinda began to squirm and object to being held so tight and to being muzzled.

"Be quiet please mate," Rose pleaded. "The bad men are just back there, and we don't want them to know we are here."

To her relief, Belinda leaned out to stare back over her shoulder and nodded. Rose took the risk of taking her hand away as she needed both hands to hold her sister and to keep her balance. That meant reaching across to steady herself against the rock sides of the cut, and that was painful and unpleasant as the rock was so hot it seemed to burn.

"Oh how much further!" sobbed Rose, as she staggered on for another fifty paces.

The track seemed to her to be very narrow. On the left was a steep rock face, and on her right a very steep drop. She did not think it would be very easy to drive along the track. Luckily, it still curved to the left, despite the fact that the mountain side was now looming high above them.

And then she heard the vehicle coming along the track behind her. The terror was so intense she nearly wet herself. And she was on a section of the track where the only option to hide was over the side, and that looked dangerously steep!

Rose began to run but not for long. She was too tired, too winded and the going too rough. She stumbled and barely saved them from a nasty fall. Gasping and sobbing she levered herself back up and lifted Belinda to her front. Desperate ideas like throwing stones at the vehicle or the men flitted across her mind.

The engine sound grew rapidly louder, as did the banging of metal on stone. A frantic glance over Rose's shoulder showed her the bull bar and bonnet of the ute appearing around the curve behind her.

*Oh no! Caught!* she thought.

But at that moment the front wheels of the vehicle hit a large stone and there was a loud bang and then the offside front wheel bounced up and came down hard across a big rock, right on the edge of the steep drop. The vehicle's engine roared, and Rose heard men cry out in alarm and then loud swearing.

"Naughty men!" Belinda cried.

The men were certainly angry. Rose heard the engine rev and then roar but the vehicle stayed stuck. And the cab was still not visible.

*Have they seen us?* Rose wondered.

She did not think so, but she knew she had only seconds to get on further around the curve as the men were sure to get out and look at the problem.

So she summoned her last reserves and hurried on. Her breath began to come in hot, rasping gasps and a stitch began to develop in her right side. Belinda felt like she was made of lead and kept moving around so she was hard to hold. But a glance back showed Rose that she could no longer see the bonnet of the vehicle.

"Maybe!" she croaked.

She staggered on and then let out a sigh. The track curved even further left and came to a flat area which she knew was outside the eastern end of the tunnel. Now sobbing with desperation she forced her legs to keep moving. Another glance back and she had to come to a trembling stop.

*The engine noise has stopped,* she told herself.

Standing there shuddering and gasping she had trouble hearing but then quite distinctly she heard an angry man's voice call, "You bloody idiot! We will need a winch to…"

The rest was lost as a slight breeze rustled the leaves of nearby trees. That was enough for Rose. *We have a chance,* she mused, hope surging.

But she was so out of breath she could do little more than totter around onto the large flat area. Her dad had explained to her that such areas were made using the spoil excavated from the tunnel and were used by the workers to camp on and to organise tools and stores and so on.

And there, fifty paces ahead, was the start of the cutting that led into the actual tunnel! And there was the black hole of the entrance! Rose slowed and began to walk with careful steps, staggering with exhaustion.

Until she heard another sound. It wasn't one she had heard many times, but she had heard it enough to know what it was. It was that peculiar vibration through the air that indicated a helicopter.

"Helicopter!" she gasped.

She felt a wild hope it might be her father or that the helicopter might be the police or Emergency Services, but there was also the fear that it might be more of the men. Knowing she could not take the risk, Rose took a deep breath and again forced her overtaxed muscles into action.

*I must get out of sight before it arrives,* she told herself.

And that meant into the tunnel. The helicopter was coming up the valley behind her and from the sound it was only seconds away!

It was a close thing. Rose staggered into the cutting, stumbling over piles of loose rocks and earth that half blocked it. But now the fact that she been there before gave her a real advantage: she knew the layout and the problems so was expecting them. Then the helicopter swept overhead behind her and began to circle back. Rose ducked below the level of the bank and then slowed to make her way over another pile of fallen rock and down into the darkness of the tunnel.

She was just in time but at least she had been through the tunnel so knew what it was like. *It is only 77 metres long,* she thought, remembering the statistics her father had read aloud. And she could see right through it. A bright circle of light showed the other end quite clearly.

"Safe!" Rose gasped, even as Belinda began to howl in fright in the relative darkness.

And then Rose let out another sob and changed her mind. Dust billowed and the sound of the helicopter's engine changed.

*Oh no! It is going to land!*

Rose looked frantically around. Having been through the tunnel and back she knew it was impossible to hide in. It was only about 3 metres wide, and the rock walls had no recesses or side areas.

*And anyone moving in it is silhouetted,* Rose remembered, having watched her dad walk through it. That only left one option, run! *I must get out the other end before anyone gets to this end,* she reasoned, sure that the men would look in the tunnel.

Fear-fuelled adrenaline gave her strength as she turned and ran into the darkness, which was a mistake as her eyes were not yet adjusted to the semi-darkness. Almost at once she tripped on a rock, and in a frantic effort to stop them both from falling she put out her hand. Sharp pain lanced up her hand as the fingernail of her left ring finger was split.

"Yaah! Oh bugger!" she cried.

Belinda was also screaming in fear, but Rose had no time for that. All she could hope was that the noise of the helicopter's engine was drowning it out. Having recovered her balance she moved more slowly, ignoring the searing pain and using that hand to try to shield her eyes from the glare coming in from the other end of the tunnel.

"It's okay Bub-O, it's only a tunnel. It's the railway tunnel Daddy and I walked through the other day," she gasped.

"Want... sniff... Daddy... sniff... Boo hoo!" wailed Belinda.

But then she began to sob instead, her little chest giving huge heaves. Light from the other end lit her face and showed she was scared but then Rose noted her looking around and the crying dried up.

"Twains?" Belinda asked.

"Not now Bub-O," Rose croaked.

"Choo! Choo!" Belinda cried.

Rose could only give her a sickly grin and nod. And then Rose was at the other end of the tunnel. There were more fallen rocks to negotiate but for a few seconds she paused and glanced back. As she did, she saw the nose of the helicopter lower into view as it settled on the flat area.

*One of those little ones they use for mustering on cattle stations,* she noted. The name of the type eluded her, but she just shrugged. It wasn't important.

But there were men in it, half hidden by the dust and grit blown up by the rotor downdraught. Fearing to be seen against the light behind her Rose quickly crouched just inside the tunnel. Thus she saw a man wearing long khaki slacks, a long-sleeved white shirt, sunglasses and a blue baseball cap with a yellow badge or logo on it open the door and step out.

*If that man comes in here now, we are done for!* Rose told herself.

If she moved, she would be seen! So apprehensive did she feel that she felt physically ill. For a few anxious seconds she crouched there, bracing herself for discovery and tensing ready to run, and knowing what was on the other side of the tunnel gave her little hope of escaping!

But the man turned and leaned in to speak to the pilot and then closed the door and walked off back down the track towards where the vehicle was. The helicopter's engine changed note and Rose realised the pilot had switched it off.

"Now is my chance," she told herself.

Hoping that the pilot was focused on the instruments she stood and made her way quickly up over the pile of soil and rocks half blocking the far entrance. Beyond was another cutting, this one about 25 metres long and also half blocked with rocks and soil. She stumbled along this, very aware of her left fingernail smarting painfully.

She came out on another flat area, this one twice as big, at least 50 metres across. And also into a most spectacular view. She had seen this before so barely noticed it but ahead of her was a rugged valley with a range of very jagged peaks on the right and steep spinifex covered hills on the left. The hills were deeply scarred by mining and by roads which had been cut into their sides. Concrete ruins down in the valley marked the site of the long abandoned 'Wee MacGregor' copper mine.

The real problem was that the old railway, now a vehicle track, went on gradually downwards on a long bench cut in the side of the mountains on the right. It was bare of cover and fully visible all the way to the big bend about a kilometre to the west, where the railway looped back as it slowly lost gradient. But the slope on the left of the track was much too steep for Rose to hope to climb down. And the mountainside on the right was also very steep and mostly devoid of cover.

"Oh where can I go?" she cried, looking frantically in all directions.

# Chapter 11

## THE REAL ENEMY

Rose dithered for a few seconds, her gaze scanning the surrounding hillsides. There were quite a lot of trees but widely spaced and almost no bushes or undergrowth. There was a small tree growing on the outside edge of the flat area, so she hurried over to it and looked down. She had been hoping that her memory was at fault and that there might be a way down. But it was dangerously steep.

*I'd never get down that with Busy Bee,* she thought. She was also uncomfortably aware that they would have no cover from above if the helicopter flew over to this side of the hill. By now she was in a lather of sweat and indecision. *I need to get away from the tunnel,* she told herself.

So she hurried along the edge of the steep slope, eyes casting around hopefully. There was a bit of a gully a hundred metres or so ahead and beyond that a steep, rock-studded spur which offered some possibilities.

*If I can get into the dead ground beyond that we can get down to that creek at the bottom of the valley with lots of cover,* she reasoned.

So she cast an anxious glance back towards the end of the cutting leading to the tunnel and then hurried on, hotly aware that her left finger was now throbbing. At every step she expected to hear a shout to stop, or worse still, a shot.

There was a tiny dip on the left, so she hurried over to it, and then went too close to the edge. Before she realised the danger, her left boot slipped on loose gravel and she fell painfully and started to slide over the edge. At that, she screamed, and so did Belinda, who had also fallen heavily. Rose got a glimpse all the way to the bottom of the steep slope, hundreds of metres, and then scrabbled frantically for a handhold.

All she could feel were spikey spinifex bushes, so she ignored the stabbing pains and grabbed at one. To her relief, it held just as all of her body was sliding over the edge in a cascade of dust and stones. But Belinda was also sliding over. Rose made a desperate grab and got her wrist, and then got the dismaying shock of feeling her little sister's wrist slipping through her grasp!

*Sweat and suncream!* Rose thought as Belinda slid down past her, shrieking with fear.

Rose made another frantic grab and managed to catch her clothing. Desperately she clung to the spinifex with one hand and her little sister with the other. Then she heaved as hard as she could, risking going over herself. But it worked. Belinda was sent sprawling on the flat gravel of the track half a metre from the edge.

Rose scrambled back up and flopped down beside her, painfully aware that she was hurting from scratches and a lot of other small pin-pricks. A glance revealed that they were coming from various burs and prickles, 'Bindis' and other horrible little two-pronged things that were now embedded in the palms of her hands and in her clothing. Belinda had a lot stuck in her skin and clothes too and she was sobbing.

*We can't stay here!* Rose thought.

Glancing towards the tunnel she got to her knees, ignoring the pain. Then she picked Belinda up with one hand and levered herself to her feet, gasping at the pain as prickles were driven into her skin. She tried to hurry across the track to where a tiny re-entrant and bush offered a small bit of cover. To her dismay, she found herself limping, a muscle in her thigh not wanting to work at all.

A small tree was growing in a drain. The drain ran along between the hillside and the track and went into a small dip, all overgrown with spinifex and long grass. This was in a tiny recess in the side of the cutting. Rose stepped into the drain and leaned on the rocks, sobbing and gasping for breath. Her intention was just to sort out the worst of the prickles before hurrying away.

As she leaned back on the hot stones of the cutting side, Rose glanced to her left, back towards the cutting, and almost fainted with fear. The man in the white shirt and blue baseball cap had come out of the cutting! And behind him was Lucas and this time Lucas was carrying a rifle.

Luckily, Belinda was only whimpering at that moment, so Rose was able to shush her. "Sssh! Baby Bee, there are the bad men," she said. "No noise."

There was almost nowhere to hide. She was half hidden by being in the tiny recess in the rocks, but she knew that if the men kept walking towards her they must see her. The only other choice was the tiny drain. This was all overgrown with grass but was only knee deep.

But it was all there was, so Rose began lowering herself to a crouch. She moved her right foot down into the drain and then suddenly slid further, wrenching and scraping her right leg. Shock then held her still.

*A hole!* She thought, dismayed.

Belinda gave a grunt but luckily did not cry out. Instead she leaned out to look at the men. Equally luckily, both men had walked to the outside edge of the flat area and were looking down the valley.

Rose struggled to get her leg free and then discovered that she was actually in some sort of sump. By then she was sitting in the grass and preparing to lie flat but now she changed her mind and lifted Belinda down in front of her leg, pushing the grass aside to do so.

*I might be able to save her at least,* she reasoned.

Belinda slid right down so that she was standing with her head sticking up through the grass. She looked shocked and annoyed. Rose felt with her foot and then was able to get both feet in the sump. Leaning forward she pushed the long grass aside and saw that it actually led into a culvert.

*That makes sense,* she thought.

Her father had explained that railways were built on long mounds of ballast and needed plenty of drainage. He explained that, in this part of Queensland, while it didn't rain much, when it did it was from violent thunderstorms. That meant a lot of water very quickly. So, to stop the track being washed away, drains and culverts were constructed.

And here was one, about a metre in diameter and made of concrete. Pushing at Belinda, she hissed, "Get in, Bub-O, quick! Play hidey seekey."

To her relief, Belinda did and Rose was just able to slide down after her into the sump. It was a tight fit, but she got down so that only her head was sticking out. Seeing the men turning in her direction she used her hurting left hand to snatch off her hat and then pull the long grass up over her face. Then she squirmed to get lower, bumping at Belinda in the process and hoping the little girl would not cry out. She made some comment that Rose could not understand, and she hoped that there wasn't a snake living in the culvert.

Then she just had to sit still, her heart in her mouth, as the two men were walking down the track towards her. They were looking in all directions and Rose was sure they must see her. But they were mostly staring up at the hillsides and over the steep edge. And now she needed to get control of her breathing as she was sucking in great rasping gasps!

With an effort, Rose managed this just as the men arrived near the point where she had slipped over. By this time she was almost paralysed with fear and was trembling violently from reaction and fright. But even in her extremity she could not help noticing the man in the white shirt.

*He looks like 'The Boss',* she thought. And then she frowned. *I've seen him before. Now, who is he?*

The two men came to a halt only a dozen paces away and stared down at where she had slid over. Lucas pointed down.

"Looks like somebody went down here."

"Bit steep, an animal maybe," the man in the white shirt commented.

And hearing his voice brought his name to Rose's memory. *That is Cousin James!* she thought.

Cousin James was the son of her late uncle Magnus. Her great, great grandfather had two sons: her grandfather Alexander, who was her dad's father, and a younger brother, Robert. Robert had only one son: Magnus. Magnus had died in a road accident a few years before but to her he had always been a nasty and unpleasant man. James was his only son, and was in his early twenties.

*Is James a friend or an enemy?* Rose wondered.

But he was family and she was half minded to call out for his help. But his next words shocked her and quickly dispelled that idea.

He snarled, "You pair of drongos have really mucked this up. If we don't find these two girls, the whole deal might fall through and we will have to go to Plan B."

"Yes boss, sorry," Lucas replied.

*He is the boss. He's one of the bad men!* Rose thought, dismay and anxiety both gripping her. She tried to slip lower into the sump.

"So, why did you come this way?" James queried.

"Just a hunch, and then I thought I saw some clear tracks back along the road near Ballara," Lucas explained, at which Rose pursed her lips and reprimanded herself.

James sneered and shook his head. "Could have been anyone. Lots of tourists come here."

"Yeah, but I went back and found some crushed grass under the side of the goods platform there," Lucas added.

*Oh, this man is dangerous!* Rose thought.

"So? Might have been an animal," James said.

Lucas nodded. "Might have been, but there were a couple of bushes with stems broken. I think the girls hid there when we drove past."

"Well, I will soon find them in the chopper. They are just a school kid and a toddler. What are they wearing?" James asked.

"The older girl is wearing a stockman's hat, khaki work shirt, jeans and what look like brown army boots," Lucas replied.

That dismayed Rose even further as it meant that the men had been watching them for some time. But she was maliciously amused by the next comments.

James grunted and said, "That figures. She will be copying her dad, and besides, she is an army cadet."

"Army cadet! What do you mean?" Lucas asked.

"You know, she does drill and goes to cadets in army uniform once a week and so on," James answered.

Lucas swore and then replied angrily, "It would have been good to know that beforehand! How long has she been a cadet?"

"I think she's in her second year, why?" James answered.

"Any rank?"

"I heard her dad boasting she had been promoted to corporal earlier in the year," James said.

Lucas swore again. "Bloody hell! What you really mean is that she has probably been trained at fieldcraft."

"What's that?"

"Camouflage and concealment, creeping and crawling and so on; and she can probably navigate as well," Lucas snapped, obviously annoyed.

*I can too!* Rose silently gloated. She tried to squirm lower and hoped Belinda would stay quiet.

"So you know all this army shit!" James snapped back.

"Be useful if you did too!" Lucas retorted. "This puts a whole new complexion on this search." From which Rose deduced that Lucas probably had been in the army once.

"Yeah well, what do you recommend? What do you think she is trying to do?" James asked.

Lucas pointed down the valley. "I'd say she is trying to get to the highway, to the police. Somehow she knows what is going on and if she isn't stopped we are in deep trouble!"

"We certainly are!" James agreed. "What do you think we should do?"

"Water will be her problem. If she hasn't already collapsed from heat exhaustion, she must find it," Lucas said. "There isn't much around, just a few windmills for cattle and the odd waterhole. We need to watch those, and the roads to the highway."

"Bloody hell! We haven't got an army!" James expostulated. "There's only four of us. Don't count the pilot. I've fed him a line."

"So get Norris to watch the next road junction along this road in case she is going this way, and I will go back and put Marvin to watch the road junction near the Corella Creek Dam. I will drive around and you will search in the helicopter," Lucas said.

"Okay. So what is little Belinda wearing?" James asked.

"Pink!" Lucas snarled. "Bloody bright pink! Pink hat, pink shirt, bright red trousers, and even pink sandshoes. She should be pretty visible from the air. And that tells me the big sister knows we are looking for her and has been able to hide her whenever we come around."

"Yeah, well, now we know. So let's get moving with this plan, and I'll try to get you a couple more men, you know pig hunter types who might not ask too many questions," James replied.

All this time, the two men had been standing with their backs to Rose. Now they turned and walked quickly back towards the tunnel. Rose held her breath for a bit, her heart hammering with anxiety lest they look back and see the bump that was her head. Then she slumped down and broke into a shivering fit.

This only lasted for less than a minute as Belinda now spoke. "Rosie, can I talk now?" she asked.

"Softly, Bub-O," Rose replied, trying to squirm lower so she could see into the culvert.

"Come and see my friend," Belinda replied.

*Oh bloody hell! I hope she isn't making friends with a taipan!* Rose thought.

But when she was at last able to wriggle down and into the culvert she had to chuckle. The concrete pipe was not big enough for her to sit up in, but Belinda could. The bottom was just a thin layer of sand and a few pebbles that had been washed in. Belinda's friend was near the outer edge and was a lizard, one of the ones with a big head and a spikey fringe around his neck. It was shifting its head from side to side to study them.

But when Rose got her boots in and then squirmed inside, the lizard ran out the other end and vanished into the long grass.

"Aw! You scared him away, Rosie," Belinda complained.

"I did, sorry," Rose answered.

Then she slumped down, completely drained. For a couple of minutes all she could do was shiver with reaction, painfully aware that she hurt almost everywhere.

But Belinda was also hurting and could not be denied. With a sigh, Rose pushed herself across and began gently plucking burs and Bindis out of Belinda's hands and then her clothes. In the process she dislodged some of her own and drove others in deeper, breaking their heads off. The pain in her left fingernail grew worse and she had to pause to check it. With dismay, she noted that the nail was torn up and there had been some bleeding. It had snapped just past her fingertip.

"Oh drat!" she muttered. Then her stomach rumbled loudly.

Belinda heard this and at once looked anxious. "Hungry! Want food! Want morning tea," she cried.

"We haven't got any food mate, but you can have a drink," Rose replied.

With difficulty she pulled out her own water bottle and gave her a drink. Then she had one herself before screwing the cap back on. With another sigh she lay back, temporarily totally exhausted.

Within seconds sleep claimed her.

# Chapter 12

## THE AMETHYST

"Rosie! Rosie! Firsty!" Belinda cried.

Rose stirred in her sleep and tried to ignore the cries, but her little sister was tugging at her arm. Then a stab of alarm surged through her body and her mind dredged up the images and words 'Bad Men'. In the beginnings of panic she went to sit up, but cracked her forehead into the concrete of the culvert.

"Aaah!" she cried, flopping back and hitting the back of her head on the backpack she had been using as a pillow.

Very reluctantly she dragged gummed up eyes open and stared up. To her dismay, everything looked blurry and grey. Then she realised she was staring at the concrete culvert at close range. With difficulty she unstuck her cracked lips and turned her head.

"What... what is it Busy Bee?" she croaked.

Her throat felt constricted and dry and her tongue seemed to be stuck to the inside of her mouth. *Heat exhaustion?* she worried.

"Firsty. Want dwink!" Belinda demanded.

"Is it the bad men?" Rose asked, her heart still hammering.

"Dwink!"

"Okay Busyness," Rose agreed.

More carefully she raised herself and gingerly felt the top of her head. It was sore and she had a throbbing headache, but she put that down to dehydration and too much sun. A glance along the culvert showed nothing but glare.

*Are the bad men still around?* she worried.

Carefully she took out Belinda's drink bottle and allowed her another gulp. That lowered the level to about a quarter. Which was very worrying.

*We need to find more water. We are still a long way from safety,* Rose thought.

But where were the bad men? She had to know so she carefully eased herself back and by a bit of contortionist twisting was able to get her head up in the sump. Cautiously she pushed the grass up and looked out, listening as she did. Her first impression was of heat and glare. But there were no voices or vehicle sounds and she could not hear the helicopter.

*Have they gone to those places they talked about?* she wondered.

Squinting in the glare she looked both ways along the track and then out and up. All she could see were the spinifex covered hills and a brassy blue sky. The air was stifling and seemed to be much hotter out of the culvert.

"How long did I sleep?" Rose muttered.

She looked at her watch and got a shock. *Heavens! Five past five! It was about One o'clock when I went to sleep. That means I have been asleep for about four hours.* But then she shrugged. *I needed it, obviously.*

She knew she had reached the end of her strength and that she badly wanted food and water as well as more sleep. But she also knew they could not wait here much longer.

Which led her to one of those life-and-death debates about whether it was at all safe to move in daylight. *The heat will kill us, even if the men don't,* she rationalised.

She really just wanted to go back to sleep and was then tormented by images of food: steak and onions, fried eggs, crisp bread rolls with butter! As she thought this, she wormed her way back into the culvert.

"Did you see or hear the bad men, Bubby?" she asked.

"I not bubby! I big girl busyness!"

"Yes, but did you see or hear the bad men?"

Belinda shook her head. "No. I sleep. Hungry! Want food."

"So do I mate, so let's get organised and see if we can find any," Rose replied.

She had decided to move and to make as much progress in the cool of the evening as she could, knowing that they were hemmed in by the mountains. There was no chance of them crossing those in the dark. She even doubted if she could do it in daylight. The Corella Creek Dam was her chosen objective.

It took ten minutes to get organised and to crawl up out of the culvert. Rose allowed herself another sip from her own drink bottle but knew she was very dry. She also wanted another pee but there was no way she was going to expose herself to risk on that open hillside. For several more minutes she sat there in the tiny patch of shade cast by the cliff behind her, listening and trying to summon up the resolve to move.

It was still very hot, and the afternoon sun was blazing down so that the rocks, gravel and air all felt hot.

"Oh come on! You can do it!" she told herself, sighing with reluctance. Her arm and finger muscles felt so stretched and drained of energy that she doubted she had the strength to carry Belinda very far.

Fear kept her there a few more minutes. She could see the ruins and red earth scars of the old 'Wee MacGregor' Mine on the other side of the valley and was desperately worried that one of the men might just be hiding there watching. For her and Belinda to walk out into the open seemed to her to be a fearful risk.

*And where will we hide if that helicopter comes back?* she fretted. She knew it would arrive suddenly, skimming into view over the crest of a hill or ridge.

"But I can't sit here. We are drying out just doing nothing. I have to get us to water," she told herself.

She estimated she might have as far as fifteen to twenty kilometres to walk to get to the dam and that was a very daunting prospect. By her estimate she had only walked that far since the drama began.

Sobbing at the unfairness of fate, Rose stood up and pulled on the backpack, then lifted Belinda to her hip. After another anxious look around, she set off at a brisk walk westwards along the old railway. This was almost directly into the setting sun, and she realised she should have renewed Belinda's sun cream. *And my own!* Feeling her face told her it was dry and sore and definitely burnt. There was a fine powdering of dry salt on her skin.

It was the urgent need to pee in safety that got her walking fast. But she also knew that the sooner they were off that section of mountainside the safer they would be. As she strode along, she kept straining her ears and looking up and around for any hint of a helicopter. Scanning the opposite hillside where the actual road went past the remains of the mine also made her anxious.

Rose covered that half a kilometre in 7 minutes. Every step of the way she felt vulnerable and exposed. And looking up at the rugged mountains that loomed over her on her right she found a daunting experience.

*I could never get over them,* she thought. Which meant going on westwards until she was past them.

As soon as she reached some cover, Rose relieved herself, still

111

embarrassed that her little sister could see part of her while she did. What worried her most was that there wasn't much urine and it was a very dark colour, like old tea.

*I am not drinking enough,* she thought.

But there was no help for it so she continued on, coming to where the old railway looped sharply back around a small hill. As she rounded the curve Rose looked out to her right, to the west. The valley continued on in that direction, opening up as it did and the hills on either side becoming lower. The gravel road ran along on the left of the creek. The most demoralizing aspect of the view was seeing several lines of distant hills extending into the far distance. The sight made her feel very lonely.

"We are still a long way from help," she thought.

But now she opted to leave the old railway. *No point in following it back to the east. I will cut down this spur to the creek,* she reasoned.

She did but it was not easy, the ground very rough and stony and with lots of spinifex. Several times she slipped or tripped and fell on her behind in the spikey grass. Even Belinda got pricked and started to howl. And it was directly into the setting sun, which was now so low it was shining in under the brim of her hat. Along the lower slope she had to walk through several old mining sites, scrapes, mullock heaps, remains of camps, rusty corrugated iron and old bottles, mostly broken.

When she reached the shelter of the trees along the creek Rose stopped. *Time for another drink,* she thought, glad now of her forethought.

She lowered Belinda to the sand and swung off the backpack. Taking out the last surviving beer bottle she drank half and allowed Belinda to drink the other half.

"More!" Belinda asked.

Rose could only shake her head. "Later, when we camp," she replied. But her heart was heavy with dread. Now she was very dehydrated and anxious. Her eyes stung and her vision was continually going blurry. The headaches persisted and so did the aches in seemingly every muscle and the throbbing in her left finger.

*I'm a wreck!* she lamented, seeing how her jeans were ripped and tattered in several places, red scratches and pin-pricks from the spinifex showing through. Then an idea came to her, the bottles she had seen.

*I broke three so I need to replace them, so that if I find water there are containers to put it in,* she told herself.

Standing up she pointed. "You just sit here, Bub-O. I am going back up to that old mine to get some bottles."

Belinda wanted to come and began to grizzle and then to call out, but Rose shook her head and was determined. So Belinda's mouth turned down and she sat there sulking and looking unhappy. Rose was as quick as she could be, now very aware that there was probably only about an hour of daylight left. It took five minutes to walk back but it was worth it. She quickly found three big brown beer bottles, very old and much bigger than the modern 'Stubbies' she had; and also a square shaped bottle of clear glass that had 'Dewar's Finest' moulded on it.

"Whisky?" Rose muttered.

Then she shrugged. It didn't matter. It was a good strong bottle. She placed the bottles in her backpack, though with some difficulty as they over-filled it, and then she hurried back down to where Belinda was starting to call out in growing hysteria.

"It's alright mate, here I am," Rose called as she scrambled down the steep slope to her.

At once she picked Belinda up to calm her and then kept walking along the top of the creek bank until she could find an easy way down. It was in her mind to walk along the creek bed, but she quickly gave that up. The sand was very soft and while it did not retain obvious tracks it was very hard walking. So she detoured up the bank to her left and pushed through the long grass until she found the road.

The road was more dirt than gravel and was very rough. There was also the fear of what she had overheard. *Lucas said he would position one of his men to watch the road junction somewhere ahead,* she remembered. But how far? And was it Norris or Marvin? She could not remember but sensed it might be important. *Norris is the more dangerous. Marvin is just a moron,* she thought.

As she walked, she wracked her brain to recall the exact conversation. In the end she decided it was Norris. That got her thinking about how to avoid him.

*If he is watching the next road junction then I need to be off the road,* she deduced. But on which side?

She opted for the creek side and moved away to trudge through long grass. By now she had pushed fear of snakes into the background of her consciousness. They were nothing compared to the threat from the men!

113

But after ten minutes the road jinked left and crossed to the north side of the creek. Rose stayed on the creek side.

By then the road was coming out of the big hills into fairly flat country, undulating and with the hills on either side much further away, barely visible through the tree canopies. The country was mostly semi-desert savannah, but she did come to an area of very pretty trees with virtually no undergrowth. The trees had white trunks that glowed ruddy in the sunset but while it was easy country to walk through it was worrying as there was very little cover.

She found it a relief to come back into 'normal' savannah, even if it meant trudging through waist high spear grass.

"At least I can hide here," she said to herself.

By then Belinda was asleep again, her head resting on her shoulder. But Rose's arms were giving up.

"I need a rest," she mumbled.

So when they came to a small dry creek that flowed across to join the main creek she stopped in its bed and sat down. As she put Belinda down the little girl woke up.

"Where we Rosie? Where Mummy and Daddy?"

"In a creek, Bub, on our way to find them," Rose answered.

"Want dwink,"

"Okay Bub-O. So do I," Rose replied.

It was coming on to dusk by then, the sun now shining redly through the trees. *I may as well drink all the water now,* Rose told herself. She thought, but didn't want to, that if she did not find some more by early tomorrow that would be it.

She took off the backpack and extracted both her sample bottle and Belinda's. She passed Belinda hers and then picked up her own. Belinda put her bottle to her lips and gulped greedily. Then she gasped and gagged.

"Urgh! Uh! What that?" she cried.

"What Belinda? What's the problem?"

"Something in water," Belinda said, peering in through the top of her bottle.

Rose could see from the side that all that remained was a small amount of water. "Nothing there now, just some water."

Then it came to her: she had put the small gem Belinda had found in the bottle. "Did you drink a small stone, Belinda?" she asked.

Belinda nodded. "Hard, got stuck. Gone now."

"That was your gem," Rose told her, and realised she should not have even as she said it.

"My what?"

"Your amethyst you found," Rose answered. "Your diamond you want to give to Mummy."

"Want!"

"Can't kiddo, it's in your belly now," Rose explained, not thinking.

"Want diamond!"

Rose shook her head. It suddenly dawned on her that it might not have been a good idea to start this conversation. But there was no help for it.

"You will have to wait for it to come out in your poo," she said.

"Don't want a poo! Want my diamond!" Belinda almost shouted.

"Sssh! Not so loud mate. The bad men might hear you," Rose hissed.

"Don't want poo!" Belinda went on, but in a fierce whisper.

There was nothing for it, Rose thought, but to explain. So she pointed at her stomach and explained that the amethyst would move down into Belinda's stomach and then come out in her poo.

Belinda frowned. "How I get it then?"

"We have to search your poo each time," Rose explained.

Belinda looked askance. "Look in poo!" she cried.

"Yeah, well, everything in life has a price," Rose replied, using one of her father's favourite sayings. "Sometimes there needs to be a bit of dirty work to get a good result."

"Not me," Belinda answered, shaking her head.

Rose could only shrug and then try to calm Belinda down as she began to cry. She got her to finish the water and then placed both sample bottles back in the backpack. By then the sun was so low it was shining in under the trees and casting long shadows.

*I've only come two or three kilometres,* Rose calculated. *I'd better push on till it is dark.*

It took her an effort to get going again. All her muscles had stiffened up and the chafing, scratches and bumps were all hurting. She found she was blinking a lot and could not make her eyes water. They felt sore and scratchy, and the black dots were dancing again.

But she gritted her teeth and kept it up for about twenty minutes, when she thought she had covered another kilometre. They came to another small creek and were out in the middle of a large plain. It was getting dark by then and Rose had had enough. She reasoned she had 8 to 10 kilometres to go to reach the dam.

*I can do that in the moonlight. It will be easier in the cool,* she rationalised. But in her heart she knew she was exhausted and needed to rest.

She found a nice clear space that seemed to be free of ants. Belinda and the backpack were put down and Rose slumped down, only to be assailed by cramps in both forearms and legs. The pain was so sudden and so agonizing that she gasped and sobbed. Then, after each cramp eased she cringed in anticipation of another one.

She lay down and just wanted to sleep, but Belinda was wide awake and wanted to play and talk. There was nothing for it but to stand and check there were no lights or vehicles and to listen. Having heard nothing but a few night birds Rose sat and chatted to Belinda, playing various simple games and then telling her a bedtime story.

"Once upon a time there were three little pigs," she began, just as the last of the light faded. There was just enough light to see Belinda's face, all expectant.

"Go on, Rosie! Go on. I like this one."

The Three Little Pigs were followed by The Little Engine That Could. Belinda wanted to know if he had been the engine on the old railway. Rose did the best she could.

"Same sort of engine," she agreed.

It was a tiring two hours of stories and games before Belinda consented to lie down. She snuggled into Rose's arms and gave her a kiss.

"I love you, Rosie!" she said.

Which made Rose cry. She loved her little sister dearly. *Oh, I hope I can save her!* she thought.

Dark thoughts and misery followed while Belinda slept peacefully. Anxiety over the possible fate of her mother and father predominated, along with fear of the men and then of plans to thwart them. A fierce desire to win through and save her parents added to her emotional drain.

She slipped into an exhausted sleep.

# Chapter 13

## MOONLIGHT

The moon was up when Rose woke. She was shivering with cold and found Belinda snuggled right in against her. It took her a few moments to work out where she was, and then the anxiety surged in.

*I've been wasting moonlight! We need to get moving!*

She rolled over and knelt to haul on the backpack. But it wasn't as simple as that. Belinda then said, "Hungry! Want dinner."

"Sorry, Bub, haven't got any," Rose replied, still flustered and fuddled from her sleep.

"Want!" Belinda shrieked.

That scared Rose. "Don't call out Bub-O, the bad men might hear you," she snapped.

"But want food!" Belinda wailed.

"Sorry Chubby Cheeks, you will just have to live off your fat for a couple of days," Rose said, being tired and irritable.

"I not Chubby Cheeks, I Ball of Bossiness," Belinda retorted.

"You are that," Rose agreed. "I want food too but it will do me good to go without a bit longer."

As she said this she gripped the layer of fat around her waist that she wished wasn't there. *I can do without this!* she thought.

"Hungry!" Belinda persisted, but more softly.

As Rose moved so did her stomach and bowels. There was a soft *ffft!* and she hoped she was not going to have to do a 'Number 2'.

*In the dark and without toilet paper that is going to be unpleasant,* she thought.

Belinda wrinkled her nose. "You fart!" she said.

Rose blushed with embarrassment and from the odour she knew she had. "I did not!" she denied.

"Did so! I smell it," Belinda retorted, chuckling as she did.

Into Rose's mind flashed a saying of her mother's, so she used it. "Mummy said that ladies do not fart. They emit small amounts of colonic miasma."

"You not a lady, you my big sister," Belinda replied.

"Oooh! You Cheeky Chimp!" Rose cried. Scooping up Belinda she stood up and immediately started walking.

Only after about twenty paces did she calm down enough to think sensibly. *Which way am I going? The road was going north. Am I?*

A glance at the half-moon now just rising above the mountains to her right told her that she was. "Good!" she muttered and kept on, striding angrily through the long grass.

But not for long. A log nearly tripped her, so she slowed to a safer pace, her eyes now alternating between scanning ahead for dangers and searching the ground in front for obstacles.

There was no doubt the sleep had done her good. She was still stiff and sore and her finger began to hurt again, but she was able to keep going for more than ten minutes before feeling the need to slow and rest. Another small dry creek provided the opportunity. Easing Belinda onto her knee she sat on the low bank and slowed her breathing.

*That man Norris might be waiting at a road junction ahead of me,* she remembered.

But how far? And how would he do it? Rose had watched a road junction for several hours on a cadet night patrol as an Observation Post and she had found it boring and tiring.

*I kept my section back from the road in a hide among some bushes,* she remembered. *Only two of us at a time were on duty.*

So how would one man on his own do it? And was he on his own or was that Lucas with him? How would Norris be likely to do it if he wasn't army trained? It was a worrying puzzle, to which she got the answer half an hour later.

After walking for another twenty minutes with one rest stop, all the time in short grass and bushes on almost flat ground, Rose suddenly smelt smoke and came to a halt against a tree.

*Smoke! Tobacco smoke. Someone is smoking ahead of me,* she thought. Then another fieldcraft lesson came to her. She was standing in the shadow of the tree with bright moonlight lighting up the grass all around her. *It will silhouette me. Captain Ross said to try to get the moon on your front, not behind you. And don't stop in shadows.*

Rose knew that the road must be somewhere to her right as the trees marking the main creek line were a hundred paces to her left. But she could not see the road. Her cadet training persuaded her to edge away down moon. Walking slowly and with one hand ready to muffle Belinda, she went that way, angling towards the creek.

And then she saw a sudden pin-point of red and felt a surge of fear and elation simultaneously. A tiny red glow appeared again briefly about a hundred metres ahead.

*Cigarette! There he is! Good, now I will go around him,* she thought.

She made a face to express her contempt for the poor discipline and fieldcraft of the man, Norris she presumed.

Angling left took her to the creek line. It was big creek lined with big trees and it took some effort to find a way down into it. Luckily, the bed was dry sand, she knew that hoping for water was too optimistic, and she was able to cross easily. On the other side she found a cattle pad that led up through clumps of spikey bushes to the flat ground beyond. In the process, a bush scratched Belinda and she let out a little yelp.

"Quiet, Bub, there is one of those men over there," Rose whispered.

Belinda went stiff and then leaned around to look in the direction Rose was pointing. To her great credit she nodded and then snuggled her face into Rose's shoulder.

"Cold," she whispered.

"It is," Rose agreed, not having noticed as the walking had warmed her.

Still taking great care to make no noise, even though she was sure they were at least two hundred metres away from the man, she started walking north beside the creek. Now she wished she had a map.

*I wonder where this creek goes?* she thought.

She had to rest after another ten minutes, and she had difficulty finding a bare patch to sit on. In the end she sat on the long grass and held Belinda on her lap. She sighed with relief but longed for a drink. After wrestling with her conscience for a few minutes, she decided to drink the remaining water. This was only a quarter of her own bottle and about the same in Belinda's.

*We need water now. And then I need to find more water as Priority One,* she told herself.

So they both drank and Rose immediately felt better, but very anxious. The empty water bottles were carefully repacked. As she sat there her stomach gurgled. She also realised she was weakening.

*Lack of food that will be,* she reasoned.

That got her wondering how long she might be able to keep up the strenuous exertion of walking while carrying her sister.

Her mind then moved on to considering the 'Bad Men' and their plans. *If there are only four of them and Norris is here and Marvin is at the Corella Dam, where are Lucas and Cousin James?* she puzzled. Which led to more worries: Where were her parents? *If they are dead then the men will have hidden their bodies; but if they are alive, where are they and who is guarding them?* She could not imagine the men just leaving them locked up somewhere.

The swish of a bird's wings brought her back to the need to keep walking. Softly groaning and with several muttered swear words her mother would not have approved of, Rose got to her feet with Belinda and resumed walking, only to get a surprise. Within fifty paces she came to a dirt road.

It was just two wheel ruts in the spinifex and long grass but her mind immediately told her that it was the other road from the road junction. But this one was going northwest.

*I wanted the other road, to go north to the dam,* she thought.

But that must now be at least a kilometre away to her right somewhere. She hesitated, shifting Belinda from one hip to the other as she tried to decide what to do. The sheer effort of detouring back she found daunting.

But Corella Creek Dam was the only water she was aware of. "This other road must go somewhere," she reasoned.

She remembered seeing other roads on the map, a whole web of them among the hills. She deduced that it must link up with the Barkly Highway somewhere.

*Closer to Mount Isa,* she thought. *And these men can't be watching every road junction along a hundred kilometres.*

That meant her chances of flagging down a car and getting to the police without the men seeing them were much better. But what if there was no water? Despite this she decided to go northwest along the track and risk it.

*I might find a windmill,* she thought. But even if she didn't, she thought she was less than 20 kilometres from the highway.

"It is better than going back across to that other road as that Marvin is somewhere near the dam and that Lucas is probably in that area too,"

Rose said to Belinda, who did not understand at all but nodded and looked around in the moonlight.

Rose began walking beside the vehicle track, keeping close so as not to lose it in the darkness. It was awkward going as she had to continually weave among the spinifex clumps, but she was too afraid of leaving tracks on the dirt road. She remembered the comment by Lucas of seeing tracks back near Ballara.

*But I don't think they are sure,* she thought. *I don't believe they've actually had one real glimpse of us. If they had they would have been on us like a shot!*

Which was the wrong simile and she at once regretted the ghastly images it conjured up of her parents being murdered. It was all too horrible to think about. So Rose concentrated on putting one foot in front of another and on keeping direction.

*Definitely northwest,* she told herself. That cheered her as it meant every step was closer to the Barkly Highway.

High, rocky hills began appearing, lit up by the bright moonlight, the rocks looking black and forbidding. The hills were on both sides, and as Rose walked northwards they seemed to close in. After an hour and four rests she was at what was a definite pass between them. The road was still on mostly flat ground but did wind back and forth around trees and up and down over small rises and dry creeks. It was definitely not what her father would describe as a 'formed road'.

A dingo suddenly howled from the hills on the left. Belinda jerked in fright. "Rosie, what that?" she cried.

"Only a dingo howling at the moon," Rose explained.

Then the dingo howled again, a long drawn out Oooooo-OOoooooo-OOoo. Belinda twitched. Her eyes went wide and she clung to Rose.

Rose hugged her. "It's alright, Busy Bee, it is only a dog. They don't eat people," she said.

And then she got scared herself, remembering overhearing her mother and her friends talking about some incident many years ago in the Northern Territory where a dingo allegedly stole a baby and killed it.

*Oh I hope not,* she thought, worrying now whether dingos went around in packs like wolves.

Fear kept her walking when she badly wanted to rest, and the result was that they were through the gap in the hills and out in open grass country again a kilometre or so further on before she allowed herself a rest. Her watch informed her that it was nearly 0300hrs.

*Bloody hell! The night is nearly over. I've only got another couple of hours of dark. Then that helicopter will be up,* Rose thought.

That anxiety kept her rest short, only five minutes, barely time for the perspiration to chill, and she was up and going.

Now it became a determined slog. In the process, Rose lost sight of the vehicle track and had to detour back to the right to find it. Once again, she was sorely tempted to walk along it as being much easier. Resolutely she put that idea aside and went on weaving through the trees and spinifex. Despite feeling worn out she pushed herself and 0320hrs found her plodding up over the low slopes of a small hill which stuck up out of the plain. The road went around the lower slopes and in the bright moonlight she walked beside it. From up there she got a good view out and a much better idea of the lay of the land.

Off to the east a few kilometres away was a line of big hills with a very obvious pass through them. Ahead was an indecipherable maze of hills and to her left, out to the west, was a wide, mostly open plain ending in a lower range of hills with several obvious gaps.

She rested again, staring around with her sore and dry eyes while memorizing and thinking. Then she plodded on, actually ending up on the road several times. Ahead of her she could see a dark line of vegetation that she was sure marked another big creek. It was running west to east across her front.

But before she got to it there was another drama. Movement and thudding, shuffling noises brought her to a halt. Peering into the night she frowned.

*What is that noise?* she wondered.

Unsure, she resumed walking, and soon found out. Cattle. A whole herd of cattle. They had been resting and now they were alarmed and were getting to their feet. Some of them began snorting and lowing and a couple let out loud bellows.

"Oh bugger! That will alert anyone that we are here," she muttered.

Belinda had been dozing but now she twitched awake again and jerked around to look, anxiety on her face.

"What that, Rosie?" she queried in a quavering voice.

"Just cattle," Rose said, wondering if she should make a wide detour.

"Cats?"

"No cattle, moo cows," Rose replied.

Belinda's arm went up. "Cow jumped over the moon!"

"It did, Bub-O," Rose agreed, but she was scared and her heart was now hammering.

*I hope there are no bulls,* she began worrying, because she had decided to walk along the road through the herd. *If all these cattle are camped here there must be water,* she reasoned. Into her mind came images of water troughs at windmills and pumps she had seen on drives with her parents. *The cattle will blot out any tracks we make,* she reasoned.

But now the whole herd, hundreds of cattle from the amount of noise and the visual spectacle of shifting whites and greys amid a cloud of dust, were up and starting to move. Some closer cattle broke into a trot and then stopped. Others took alarm and also began to run.

*Oh bloody hell! I don't want to start a stampede,* Rose thought.

She stopped to allow the cattle to calm and to also reassure Belinda who was starting to whimper. Her rational mind told her that there was nobody in the area, certainly not any of the Bad Men.

Once the immediate shuffling and scattering had settled, she again began walking slowly forward. Now she could see individual beasts in the moonlight. They were all Brahmins or something similar and they were all standing watching her. Suddenly, a close one turned and bolted. A hundred more took fright and ran. There was a stampede, but it did not go far. The shuffling, restless herd stopped a hundred paces away and there was more snorting and bellowing.

And Rose came to a gate in a barbed wire fence. *Oh damn! I was wrong. My tracks won't get rubbed out on this side of the fence.*

But she was too exhausted to go back to try to rub them out in the dark. Instead, she walked off the road and on along the fence for about 50 paces, all the cattle shifting restlessly as she did. Finding a patch of bare earth under one of the panels she sat down and held a quivering and frightened Belinda.

"It's okay, Belinda. They only eat grass," she explained. Then she began to sing softly, "Hey diddle diddle, the cat and the fiddle…"

Belinda liked that and began to sing with her, making jumping motions towards the moon with her free hand. Having calmed her little sister, Rose shrugged off her backpack and pushed it under the fence.

"Now you wait here, Baby Bee," Rose instructed.

"What you do?"

"I am going to crawl under this fence," Rose answered. "You stay away from it. It is barbed wire, very bad. It will cut you and hurt."

Belinda tried to move away but Rose held her. "Just stand here and I will get you," she said.

Then she moved to get under the fence as she had been taught at cadets. Captain Ross had carefully instructed them on this skill as they often encountered three and four stand barbed wire fences on cadet exercises.

"Don't try to crawl under them on your front like you see in the movies," he had instructed. "They are not a low wire entanglement. Lie beside it on your back, reach up and grab the bottom strand and push it up as far as you easily can, then move yourself under at a diagonal, feet first. Once your head is under and clear you can let go and roll onto your hands and knees."

Rose had done this many times and now did it easily. Then she reached over the top strand and lifted Belinda up and over. That done she pulled on the backpack and went looking for the water. She was now so worn and thirsty that she just called angrily at the cattle to stop being silly. This precipitated another short stampede and then more bellowing and shuffling.

But it also revealed to her the windmill and water trough that had been hidden by them. Hurrying forward she noted that all the ground around it was blotched with dark cow pats and that gave her pause.

"This water won't be very clean or hygienic. It might make us sick tomorrow," she said.

*So what? You have to be alive to be sick,* she told herself, knowing that without water she would probably collapse in the heat and then both of them would die.

The water in the concrete trough looked dark in the moonlight but it was cold and felt good. Rose lowered Belinda and then took off her backpack. She cast a quick glance around to check they were safe, noting the hundreds of cattle standing watching in the moonlight and dust. The panic in the herd had subsided and the cattle were now just restless and curious.

Taking her own drink bottle Rose first drained the last drops and then filled it, placing it immediately back in the pack. Then she filled Belinda's and handed it to her. Belinda took it and began drinking with great gulps. Then she stopped.

"Erk! Not like," she complained. "Want our water."

"There isn't any, Bub-O. Just drink what you can," Rose replied.

She used her hand to test the water and found it did taste awful. And it was full of floating solids. *Oh yuk! That will be cow poo,* she thought.

But there was nothing for it. She had to have water so she took her last small beer bottle and filled it and then drank as much as she could before the smell made her gag. While trying not to breathe she swallowed and forced herself to drink some more.

Next, she filled the two small sample bottles and the three big beer bottles and the whisky bottle and spent an anxious quarter of an hour tying plastic wrap over the tops and nesting them in the backpack. It was 0415hrs by then. Taking Belinda's bottle from her she refilled it and packed it. Then she stood and used her hands to wash her face and head. That was close to bliss, after the first shock because the water was so cold. She also carefully rinsed Belinda's face, but the little girl resented this and kept pulling away. Satisfied she had enough water for another day Rose forced herself to drink another few mouthfuls.

"Time we were gone," she muttered.

# Chapter 14

## HEAT AND ROCKY HILLS

Anxiously conscious that the time was rapidly ticking away and that dawn was not far off Rose pulled on the backpack, groaning at the weight. But then she shrugged. That weight was life itself. She bent and picked up Belinda. The little girl grumbled objections, but Rose ignored that. She set off at a fast walk, wanting to be well away by daylight. The whole area around the windmill and trough was just dusty bare earth covered with hundreds of cow pats and it took her a minute or so to pick out a vehicle track. The cattle all edged around as she passed, with a lot of jostling and snorting and dust.

Belinda was frightened but Rose was too tired and stressed to worry about that. She just strode along the wheel ruts out into the spinifex plain. It was only after she had been going for about five minutes and her arms were starting to weaken that it occurred to her to check her navigation. She had to glance around to find the moon. To her surprise, it was high above and almost directly behind her.

*I am going almost west,* she thought. *I want to go north or northwest. Is this the right road?*

Unsure she slowed, thinking hard. She realised that there might be more than one road leading away from the windmill. Now she remembered seeing one coming in from the east back at the gate. That brought her to a stop and she looked around in the moonlight, vaguely conscious of a cool wind blowing against her face.

Belinda was much more aware of that wind as she began to shiver and grumble. "I cold, Rosie!" she cried.

Rose was annoyed with herself but also so tired and worn down she could not summon the energy to go back. *I will keep going. This road must lead somewhere,* she thought, although a niggling worry was that it might just lead out into the bush and end.

To warm Belinda, she lowered her to the other wheel rut and took her hand. "You walk for a bit please, Toddle Toy. I need a break," she said.

"What you break, Rosie? And I not Tobble Toy; I Ball of Busyness."

"I broke a fingernail yesterday and it hurts," Rose answered, glad that Belinda had started walking.

But it didn't last long. There were some large clumps of spinifex growing between the wheel ruts and several of these pricked Belinda, making her yelp and cry. Rose also realised, with some dismay, that they were now so far from the windmill that it was unlikely that the cattle would trample out their tracks.

"Oh blast!" she muttered, scooping up her little sister as she did.

The aches and cramps in her arms now brought tears to her eyes. But she persevered and kept walking, detouring off the track to her right. That slowed her down immediately. Now she had to weave a course around the larger clumps of spinifex and grass. It was all very wearing!

After another ten minutes she had to stop. A large area of bare earth offered an opportunity and Belinda was lowered. But only for a minute before she let out a loud cry of pain. Ants! Big, red, bull ants! Rose had begun shrugging off the backpack, but she now pulled it on again and swore. Quickly she plucked Belinda up and brushed her legs and ankles while she started walking again.

"It's not fair!" Rose sobbed, self-pity welling up. "I just want it to stop!"

Belinda helped. "You swore, Rosie," she said between sniffles.

"I did too, and don't you tell mum," Rose retorted.

"Want Mummy!"

"We are going to find her."

Belinda began to sob. Rose hugged her and patted her back and somehow managed to keep her own tired legs moving until she found another bare patch that did not seem to be crawling with ants. A ten-minute rest followed. But a check of the watch telling Rose it was 0450hrs got her scanning the eastern sky and then up and moving again.

As before, she walked close to the vehicle track so as not to lose it. As she trudged along, she noted that she was approaching the hills to her front and that they looked quite large. Of more concern was that the only really obvious gap was well down to the southwest.

*I don't want to go that way,* she reasoned.

Then a small but obviously very rocky conical hill loomed up against the skyline. The track went to the north of it but up over the lower slopes. That was a real puff and also continually painful from the spinifex prickling her ankles. As she started down the western slope Rose saw another, larger rise blocking her path. Seeing it made her reconsider going back to look for the other road, but she thought it was now about 2 kilometres and she found she could not face that.

Feeling a bit defeated Rose resumed walking, finding it quite difficult because of the stones among the grass. She was then relieved to find that the vehicle track did a sharp turn to the right.

*Going northwest again,* she told herself.

There were a few hundred metres of flat ground. While crossing it Rose saw that the bigger hill was now to her left and that she was only likely to go over a low spur at the northern end. This turned out to be the case, but the rise was so stony and difficult to negotiate in the moonlight that she decided to take to the track. She thought it looked as though it was more rock and gravel than sand and therefore unlikely to retain boot prints.

It was a steep little slope that brought her to a puffing standstill halfway up. After a few minutes rest she reverted to the walk 50, rest 50, walk 50 method. This got her to the top at 0540hrs. By then she was anxiously aware that the sky behind her was lightening and that the first pink flush of dawn was showing. The mountains behind her were outlined like jagged black cardboard cut-outs. Spurred on by this she hurried on, only to find that the vehicle track did a sharp left turn and wound its way up the spine of the spur.

This led her up onto the larger rocky hill she had been trying to avoid. It turned out to be wide and flat but studded with large rocks, so many that walking around them all was not an attractive option. So she kept to the vehicle track and hoped. Ten minutes of puffing and sweating, even though it was only about 20 degrees, had her at the west side of it. Aware that it was fast becoming daylight, she hurried down the other side, slipping several times on loose gravel as she did.

Now she could clearly see bigger hills to her left front and a large creek line down to her right. There appeared to be a gap ahead and the track wriggled that way. At 0600hrs Rose rested in a small gully beside the track. At ten past she moved on, her ears now focussed on listening for the sound of the helicopter.

As the first rays of sunlight hit the tree tops, Rose moved again, ready to run off the track at the first sound of a vehicle. The track went down across quite a big creek coming from the side and she was tempted to find a place to hide for the day. But knowing she was getting weaker from lack of food decided her to get as far as she could while she still could. Ignoring Belinda's grumbling she plodded up out of the creek.

The track now wound along a narrow flat between two rocky slopes, the creek close beside it on the left. Bush flies arrived and began to annoy. Belinda began to grizzle and brush at them. Rose tried to chase them away as well, but the flies kept coming back and clustering around Belinda's eyes and mouth, and her own.

"Bloody flies!" Rose snarled, waving a hand angrily at them.

"You swear," Belinda accused.

"I do too. Now you help me sing. Shoo flies, don't bother me; shoo flies, don't bother me...," Rose sang. Which worked until a fly flew into her mouth and she had to gag and spit to try to clear it.

Belinda laughed and then suffered the same. Rose gave a wry grin at Belinda's spitting and coughing. "You wanted something to eat, Bub-O, so you enjoy it," she said.

"Not funny! Want food!" Belinda demanded before bursting into tears again.

Rose hugged her and consoled her and kept trying to chase the flies. *Maybe it's because of the cattle?* she thought.

Another rest was called for as the road could be seen to go steeply up the end of another stony spur. Once again Rose considered hiding in the creek bed. But after some thinking she decided that up on top with a longer view might be better. So she steeled herself for the effort and spent twenty minutes plodding and gasping upwards. She arrived at the crest sweating and trembling to find big hills on her left and a quite large valley, almost a gorge, on her right.

"Big creek down there," Rose said, pointing it out to Belinda.

Further north were seemingly endless ranges of rugged hills. Rose noted that the creek appeared to flow roughly west to east out of another line of very obvious hills a few kilometres further west. That dismayed her as she appreciated that she really had little option but to continue walking along the track.

The ground between her and the hills looked to be a grassy plain, more spear grass than spinifex. It was dotted with a few trees but was more savannah grassland than savannah woodland.

*Not much cover there,* she thought. But she decided to take the risk. *I will find a hiding place in those hills,* she decided, estimating an hour to get to them.

It was 0710hrs and she was worrying about the heat. Already she was feeling uncomfortably hot, and Belinda's skin was clammy with perspiration. That called for a drink, so she extracted one of the big beer bottles. As she held it up, she could see the solids swirling in it but just grimaced and hoped Belinda wouldn't notice.

She didn't but she did notice the smell and the horrible taste. Luckily, she drank a fair bit before she screwed up her face in disgust. That led to a bit of a battle, but Rose didn't pursue it. She forced herself to have a big drink and then she resealed the bottle and returned it to the pack.

Having rested for a few more minutes, Rose picked Belinda up and walked out onto the plain. She had only gone about a hundred paces when her ears picked up a faint vibrating hum. Fear immediately lanced through her and she stopped and crouched down, her eyes scanning the sky. Her ears gave the direction before her eyes picked out a tiny object many kilometres away to the north. It was a helicopter and she noted that it was coming from the west and flying almost directly east.

*From Mount Isa Airport,* she told herself. Which made her wonder if Cousin James was in it and if he had spent the night in a hotel in Mount Isa. *His gang won't be very impressed if he did!* she thought.

But she also accepted that the helicopter might have nothing to do with her. Even so she remained crouched among the low bushes until it vanished into the haze to the east.

With that fear to spur her to move, Rose stood up and hurried on. She pushed herself to walk as quickly as she could, aware that she was panting and sweating profusely. The track was fairly straight, winding a bit between rocks and larger clumps of spinifex. As she walked Rose remembered Captain Ross's advice to select your next piece of cover before leaving the one you were in.

0800hrs came and went and by then the sun was scorching her back. She held Belinda in front to shield her and during a ten-minute break among a clump of small trees she smeared more suncream on the resisting face and hands of her little sister. Remembering how sunburnt she had become, Rose added some to her own face and the backs of her hands but she found the cream very sticky and unpleasant.

Then it was on again, getting closer to the stony hills with every step. And the closer she got the more impressive they looked. It was a range of dozens of small hills studded with big boulders and rocks among a scattering of white -trunked gum trees. With the pale green of the spinifex and the darker green or bushes and tree leaves and the red earth and white tree trunks, it made a very pretty scene. This time Rose did not stop but pushed herself across the last kilometre, now glancing back over her shoulders frequently for a glimpse of the helicopter.

*Or that vehicle,* she mused.

She knew it could just appear behind her before she heard it and that worry drove her on until she was plodding up a slope between two of the stony hills. She came to gasping stop and looked back to scan the sky to the east and the far edge of the plain. Nothing showed in the sky and there was no sound.

Then she staggered on for another couple of hundred leaden-booted steps to a crest line. Here she stopped and slumped into the shade of a big boulder beside the track. It was the view more than exhaustion that brought her to a standstill. What she saw filled her with part dismay and part admiration. In front of her was a valley running north-south and beyond that, as far as the eye could see, were range after range of stony hills, also all running north-south. By now the whole vast wilderness was being distorted by heat shimmer.

*Oh my God! How will I ever cross that?* Rose wondered. Dread clutched at her throat and chest, and she feared she had made a series of terrible mistakes. *Oh my God! We are lost in a trackless wilderness! We will die, from starvation if not thirst! I should have gone back to look for that other road.* At that moment, she felt very alone and isolated.

"And bugger off flies!" she added angrily, swishing at them.

Then she gave a wry grin. *Well, not exactly a trackless wilderness. Here is one beside me, and it must lead somewhere.*

But she decided that it was getting too hot to keep walking. So she started looking for a good place to hide, one with plenty of cover and shade and a view. She could not find all three but managed to find a creek line a hundred paces down the western slope. The creek came from the north and did a sharp bend to the west just to the right of the track. In it she found a deep cleft that offered shade for the morning as did several small trees growing in its bed. There was also some clean sand to lie on.

The backpack was carefully placed in the shade and Belinda was offered another drink. But when she saw the bottle and sniffed it, she declined. That was a worry.

"Bubie, you've got to drink. You will dehydrate," Rose explained.

"Want our water," she insisted.

And so the battle went on for quite a while, until a small skink appearing at a crack in the rocks distracted Belinda. Rose gave up the struggle, assuming her sister would drink when she was really thirsty. She had a big drink herself, confident she had enough water for the day.

She had no plans to walk any further during the heat of the day, so she made herself comfortable and stretched out. Only to be assailed by leg cramps that made her cry out in agony and then pummel at the knotted muscles until they eased. The pain left her sobbing and trembling.

Belinda watched with shock and concern but soon lost interest and began tapping small rocks together and trying to entice the curious skink to come closer. Rose closed her eyes and made herself relax. But peace of mind would not come. Instead her thoughts roamed over all the events of the last three days, which led to her castigating herself for poor decision making.

Belinda several times wandered out into the sunlight as she explored. Rose had to summon the energy to call her back. Then she had to get her to stay while she went off around the corner to relieve herself. Which led to an embarrassing scene when she came back and asked Belinda if she needed a pee.

One glance at Belinda's face and then at the crutch of her trousers told Rose that Belinda had already done that. Which led to a tantrum and tears when Belinda wanted to be washed and changed.

"Sorry Bubby Girl, I don't have water to spare, and we do not have a change of clothes," Rose explained.

After a full-blown kicking fit as she had her tantrum, Belinda subsided to a sobbing heap. Then she wanted a drink but when offered the water from the cattle trough she threw another temper tantrum. Rose began to become seriously worried.

*She will dehydrate and overheat,* she fretted. She considered undressing her but then shook her head. *The air is very hot, and if we have to move in a hurry I won't have time to dress her,* she reasoned.

At last Belinda dropped into a deep sleep and Rose lay beside her and dozed. The heat grew worse until the air was stifling. There was almost no breeze and the sun's rays were reflected off the stony sides of the gully. Rose kept shifting uncomfortably, listening from time to time for any sound of the men. But all she heard was a crow cawing in the distance, the buzz of bees or wasps and the whine of cicadas.

*Where are the men? What are they doing?* Rose worried.

Then her body demanded attention. Seeing that Belinda appeared to be sound asleep she took herself off around the corner of the gully and managed a poo, which she buried in a patch of sand. But she could only use dry grass to wipe herself and that was unpleasant and not very satisfactory. Unhappy with the result and sure she must smell Rose moved away from that spot and stood contemplating her legs and the numerous bruises and scratches. There were so many red dots from the spinifex she thought it looked like measles around her ankles.

As she pulled up her trousers, she gave another wry grin. *Could have been worse. At least there is grass here. Using spinifex would be no fun!*

Still, it was an unhappy girl who made her way back to the rock overhang, to find that the area of shadow had shrunk by half and would soon vanish altogether as the sun rose higher. That got her searching for another. The nearest suitable spot was a hundred metres down the creek and took quite a scramble on the rough slope to find and return from.

It was even more of a struggle to pick up the pack and Belinda and then make her way there. By the time she had accomplished that it was midday, and she was puffing and wheezing and perspiring so much she felt like she had run a race. During this Belinda woke and she was tired, sunburnt, and fractious. She cried and grizzled and did not want to be comforted. She just wanted her Mummy. Rose tried singing and hand clapping games and making shapes with her fingers, but Belinda stayed in a bad mood and would not be comforted.

After another big drink, which Belinda again declined, Rose lay in the small patch of shade and worried about what to do next. Despite the flies and the heat she dozed and then drifted into a deep sleep.

# Chapter 15

## THE THIRD NIGHT

The afternoon dragged on. Despite the heat, ants, flies and worries Rose managed a few hours of deep sleep. She woke at 1630hrs with a mouth that, as her dad said, tasted of old socks. She sat up and took out another big beer bottle and had another big drink. As she drank, she saw Belinda looking at her and licking her lips. Rose held out the bottle to her, but she shook her head and looked unhappy.

Now deeply worried, Rose recapped the beer bottle and put it back. Then she had an idea. Taking out Belinda's own drinking bottle she held that up. Belinda nodded and reached out for it. As Rose unscrewed the cap, she shook her head.

"It is only the water from the cattle trough Busy Bee," she warned.

But Belinda still wanted the bottle, so Rose handed it to her. Belinda put it to her mouth and took a big gulp. Then she stopped and grimaced. Rose tensed ready for a tantrum or battle but to her surprise Belinda put the bottle back to her lips and continued drinking. To Rose's great relief, she almost emptied the small bottle. And that gave her an idea. After Belinda handed it back, she waited till she wasn't looking and then used another big beer bottle to refill it. It was then slipped back into the backpack and Rose took another swig from the big beer bottle.

Almost at once she began to perspire. This was helped by a gentle breeze blowing up the gully. The air was very hot, but the humidity was very low, so the evaporation was obvious and cooling, a slight prickling sensation on her skin.

The next hour she found very wearying as she had to play with Belinda and keep her entertained. Despite not having eaten for 72 hours, Belinda seemed to have plenty of energy still.

*She's a Ball of Busyness alright!* Rose thought.

With a sigh she went back to making finger shapes. That helped. She got Belinda to copy the bunny rabbit, the dog, and the spider. The butterfly she really liked but when Rose showed her the earthworm by turning one hand upside down and bringing the fingers together with one index finger upwards and one downwards, Belinda was stumped. For ten minutes Belinda tried to get her pudgy little fingers to make the shape, but she couldn't. She became more and more frustrated and then burst into tears. Singing calmed her down and then naming animal noises.

Rose several times stood and looked out of the gully, listening as well and scanning the landscape. She neither heard nor saw any sign of a human being or a vehicle or aircraft. That got her wondering if the men had even the remotest idea where she and Belinda were.

*And remote is right! I am in the middle of nowhere now!* she thought as she studied the endless ranges of barren hills dancing in the afternoon mirage.

1745hrs came around at last, the time Rose had decided on. But the sun was still high in the sky and it was fearfully hot. So she sighed and rested for another fifteen minutes, fidgeting and swatting at the flies and ants.

"Time to go again, Bubby Bee," she said.

"I not Bubby Bee. I Ball of Bounciness," Belinda answered.

But she stood up and accepted another drink. Happy that Belinda was at least partially rehydrated, Rose put the half empty bottle back in the backpack and swung it on.

And then it was slogging across the rough ground carrying Belinda, with fear seeping in as worry about being seen in the open became the dominant concern. Rose considered going down the gully, but it was too rough: big rocks and steep little drops which she would have to carry Belinda down.

*Too dangerous! If I trip or slip, we could be badly injured,* Rose reasoned. And in that environment there would be small chance of rescue or survival! *So the potentially deadly option of walking on the open hillside it is!*

Then her hopes got a lift. Rounding a bend in the track Rose got a long view ahead and saw that the track continued on down a long spur and then went on across the valley. It appeared to then follow beside the main creek that was flowing out of the valley. This looked to go through a distant gap in the next line of hills.

"And it is going northwest!" Rose croaked.

But, God, she was feeling weak and unsteady on her feet! Several times she stumbled and even small slips on loose gravel caused her concern. Struck by a bout of dizziness, she stopped and put Belinda down. Belinda took her hand and then tugged at it.

"Come on, Rosie! You can do it," she said.

Rose had to smile. "I hope so Belinda," she replied.

It was as though a current of hope and energy flowed into her and she started walking, Belinda walking with her. For at least a hundred metres this lasted and then Belinda stopped and put her arms up.

"Well done Little Girl," Rose praised.

"I not little girl! I big girl!" Belinda retorted.

"You are certainly heavy!" Rose replied.

But she managed a smile and Belinda patted her. A surge of affection swirled through Rose, and she hugged Belinda and then gritted her teeth and forced herself to keep walking. It was hard going as the track was rough and almost directly into the setting sun.

But after ten minutes she came down off the slope and was able to walk in the shade of the trees on the flat. There was very little undergrowth here and the spinifex grew in isolated clumps. Rose was able to get off the track and progress with less effort. A small tributary dry creek was easily crossed. The road curved more to the northwest and then the sun went behind the low hills to her left front. That was a huge relief, and Rose plodded on for another ten minutes before halting in a small dip away from the track.

Belinda accepted her drink bottle again and that eased Rose's worries too. She emptied another of her big beer bottles and refilled Belinda's from the fourth. Her own drink bottle, the sample bottles, and the 'Whisky' she was keeping as the emergency reserve.

The track then led across a wide flat ringed by rocky little hills. The sparse vegetation remained, and the soil became more and more sandy and devoid of ground cover. Even the spinifex thinned out. Big areas of exposed bedrock became common and then Rose found herself in a weird environment that was more stone than vegetation. The ground was now studded with boulders, many much higher than her. The hills ahead loomed up in the dusk as just masses of rocks. On their tops were huge boulders that brought to her mind the word 'Tors' from a trip the family had done to Dartmoor when she was ten.

But Dartmoor had been cold and rainy, even in the English Summer. And this was still sweltering hot, even though the sun had dropped from view. The hills became black silhouettes that made them look even more rugged.

With full darkness setting in Rose looked for a good place to camp. She wasn't keen on stopping among the rocks so pushed on for another few hundred metres until she came to what she wanted, a dry creek with a sandy bed. Turning right, she walked along it until she was sure they would not be lit up by the head lights of any vehicle that passed by. Not that she expected any.

*Not much traffic on this road,* she thought.

Having selected a bivouac site, she put Belinda down and then took off the backpack. They both had a drink and then Rose tried to entertain her little sister as it got darker and darker. Millions of stars began to twinkle, and Rose got Belinda to lie beside her. She began pointing out various constellations, being distracted by seeing several satellites tracking across the sky and then by a meteorite or piece of space junk burning up in the atmosphere.

Belinda wanted to know what that was so Rose dredged around in her mind for information and tried to explain satellites and space junk. As she did, Belinda pointed up.

"What that?"

Rose looked and nearly burst into tears. It was the lights of a jet airliner passing over. She realised then that she had been able to hear it for some time. Having flown over the area a few times herself she understood.

"It is an airplane Bub. The big ones all fly over Mount Isa," she explained.

Explanations of international air routes held Belinda's interest for a few minutes but obviously she did not understand. But she did know what aeroplanes were.

A long explanation of the Southern Cross and how it rotated across the sky took up another twenty minutes. But as the Cross was already low in the southern sky and starting to set among the treetops, this was not entirely satisfactory.

*I need a pencil and paper, or a whiteboard,* Rose thought, remembering how Captain Ross had explained it in the field one night.

A soft *thud, thud, thud* noise sounded near them. "What that?" Belinda quavered.

Immediately there was a skittering sound of grit on rock followed by louder and faster thud, thud, thuds. Belinda moved to grab hold of Rose.

Rose smiled, until she realised that Belinda was terrified. "Only a wallaby, or maybe a kangaroo," she explained.

And, of course, there were ants, little black ants that had a painful nip this time. And the air got quickly colder, and Belinda began to shiver and Rose cuddled her in and tried to get her interested in the stars again. Another aeroplane helped, going northwest this time.

"Going to Darwin or Singapore," Rose explained.

"What singapoo?" Belinda asked.

Trying to explain distant cities, especially one with an airport like Singapore's, kept Rose busy for another half hour. Then an aircraft came from the northeast. The tiny strobe light on it attracted Belinda's attention.

"That one going to Singapoo?" she queried.

"No mate. That one is probably going to Sydney or Brisbane."

"Me live in Sydney," Belinda replied.

"We do," Rose agreed.

"Want Mummy!"

It took a while to calm her down again and it was another aircraft. "Going fast!" Belinda said.

Rose agreed and watched the tiny lights move rapidly across the sky. She was very familiar with aircraft and had the surreal thought that the people in that aircraft would be home in bed soon, quite unaware of the two girls in desperate trouble far below them.

Belinda began asking more questions. Rose answered them all but really just wanted to relax.

"You are a ball of inquisitiveness, aren't you?" she commented.

"No I not! I Ball of Bounciness," Belinda replied.

Rose had to laugh. "Yes you are!" she agreed.

*I hope my kids aren't as wearing,* she thought.

Then she smiled. For a few minutes dreams of meeting 'Mr Right' and of Knights in Shining Armour kept her mind contented, until images of the spotty-faced and randy Year 10 boys at school who made what they thought were witty comments but were really only crude suggestions caused her another wry smile.

Luckily, Belinda dropped off to sleep in that time, so she was able to lie back and hold the little girl to try to keep her warm. Her mind then became her problem as all her fears and worries surfaced. What bothered her most was that, at one level, nothing had changed in three days.

*We are still on the run in the bush, still in danger of dying from heat or thirst, and getting weaker all the time from lack of food,* she worried.

But there was also a good dollop of satisfaction in there too. She had evaded the men for all that time, and she suspected that they must be very worried also.

*I have thrown all their plans in a heap,* she told herself.

Remembering that Captain Ross had said that when fighting the main target was the mind of the enemy commander, Rose started to speculate on what Cousin James was after and what he might be thinking.

*What is it that he wants?* she puzzled. That led her back over the conversation she had first overheard when Lucas had appeared on the scene. *If he really meant to kill us, why didn't he just shoot Dad and then Mum from a distance and then come hunting us?* she wondered.

The comment by Lucas about their goose being cooked if they did not find the two girls made her determined to keep on hiding.

*We will get to safety tomorrow,* she told herself. And she dropped off to sleep.

She woke just after midnight. Once again it was cold, and Belinda was curled up against her. Rose tried not to move lest she wake her while she checked her watch. With hours to wait till the moon came up all she could do was lie and think. This was mostly brooding but some of it was planning and a little bit of fantasizing about her 'White Knight' appearing to save her.

But that didn't sit well with how she felt. *I can save myself,* she thought. And as she thought back over the previous three days she experienced a fierce surge of satisfaction and of confidence. *I can do this! I know what to do and I think I have the strength to do it,* she thought. It was a good feeling.

So was the urge to make sure that the men were brought to justice. Rose was not a vindictive person, and was not one to bear a grudge, so the notion of revenge was not quite there, but she did want the men punished.

*They have hurt me and my family and they have no right to do that!* she thought as the moon began to lighten the eastern sky. *Zero three fifty,* she noted.

That was bad. It only gave about two hours of moonlight to walk in. Resolving to make the most of it she woke Belinda, gave her a dink, had a big one herself (Emptying the fourth big beer bottle, *Only mine and the tiny sample bottles and the Whisky bottle to last all day if I don't find water!* she fretted). By the time the first sliver of moon was visible above the skyline, she had the backpack on, Belinda on her hip, and was up and walking.

For safety and speed she walked along the vehicle track. The two wheel ruts were clearly visible in the moonlight and the moon gave her direction. Belinda was cold and shivering again but apart from getting her to walk for short distances Rose could not think what else to do.

Rose found the next couple of kilometres eerie and spooky. The landscape of big rocks cast weird shadows and had strange shapes. Swooping night birds did not help either. But it was the sudden bounding away of several wallabies that really gave Rose a fright. Belinda also jerked and pointed.

"What that, Rosie?" she asked, obviously scared.

"Only wallabies," Rose answered, her heart still hammering from the sudden fright.

"Wobbilies," Belinda replied.

"Wallabies," Rose corrected.

"Wobblies! Daddy calls them wobblies," Belinda insisted. "Where Daddy? Want Daddy?"

"So do I mate," Rose said, almost overwhelmed by a sudden bout of misery. Catching her emotions she took several deep breaths and added, "We are going to find Daddy now."

There were more wallabies and birds, but it was the curlews making their eerie long calls that scared them both next. The curlews were a long way away, but their mournful cries carried on the still night air, making the hairs on Rose's neck stand up.

By 0430hrs the pair were on a downhill stretch. The road was rough and caused frequent stumbles and trips, but it was not only downhill, it was in the right direction. As she plodded slowly along Rose calculated that the highway could not be more than twenty kilometres away.

*I will make it today, even if I only manage one kilometre an hour!*

There was another dry creek at the bottom of the slope, and they rested there until nearly 0500hrs. Then they continued on across flat country. The track was mostly smooth sand and Belinda was able to walk for nearly half a kilometre, which was a huge boost to Rose.

Another creek was crossed just on daylight and Rose paused to consider staying there. *It will be full daylight soon. Is it worth the risk?* she thought.

She decided it was, that she needed to cover as much ground as she could while it was still cool. So she walked up out of the creek and set off across another kilometre wide plain. This one was bare, sandy soil studded with some sort of prickly green bush and with almost no grass or spinifex. As there looked to be plenty of cover Rose pressed on.

She came to a low rise studded with rocks and paused there for a drink and short rest. 0600hrs on her watch got Rose up and walking again.

"Another half hour," she resolved.

It was nearly a kilometre to the next rise. This was also studded with large boulders, but the intervening ground was like the previous area, almost no trees, a few bushes and sparse ground cover. For safety sake Rose detoured away from the track on the northern side. She aimed for a large clump of rocks on the crest a hundred metres from the track.

*We should find some shade there and should get a good view,* she reasoned.

It took ten sweaty minutes to get there, the first rays of sunlight striking the rocks as she arrived. But as she plodded gasping up the last few metres, she heard a sound that chilled her blood: a vehicle behind her!

Glancing back she saw a white utility coming through the rocks on the ridge she had just left. It was making slow progress on the rough track, but her mind was now in a fluster of terror.

*If I can see it, they can see me!* she thought.

But what to do?

# Chapter 16

## CADET TRAINING

For less than a second Rose dithered. Then she dropped to her knees, putting Belinda down at the same time. She threw herself flat behind the next bush. As she did, she heard glass clink but this time only a trickle of water dripped onto her back. She didn't care. Her priority was to get Belinda safely under cover. One quick grab had the little girl in behind her and the bush.

*Must get those pink clothes out of sight,* she thought.

Belinda was so surprised that for several seconds she did not react. Rose hugged her to her front and placed her hand over her mouth.

"Sssh! It is the bad men. No noise," she hissed.

By then her heart was hammering as though she had run a hundred metres. Her vision went blurry and she found she was trembling violently.

*Did they see us?* she worried.

She knew it was all over if they had. There was no way she could outrun the men in such open country.

But was it the men? Or was it just an innocent grazier or stockman who might help? Rose had to know, and she had to keep track of what the vehicle was doing. So she took off her hat and very cautiously edged forward to peer through the side of the bush.

*Look through, not over, Captain Ross said.*

And it was as well that she did. The ute was driving steadily forward across the flat. But it wasn't speeding and the engine noise was fairly constant. She began to hope that whoever was in the vehicle had not seen them. Now she thanked her cadet training for getting her to detour away from the track.

To her relief, the ute drove along until it was almost level with her. Then it stopped on the crest and she was able to get a good look at it. Into focus leapt the head of the man Norris. He was driving. Next to him, on the far side, was Lucas. A surge of anxiety followed when Lucas opened his door and got out. But his actions did not indicate any hurry or urgency and he wasn't looking in her direction. Instead, he walked to the front of the vehicle and climbed up on the bull bar. Only then did he cast a quick glance up the slope in her direction.

Rose held her breath and then let it out in a long sigh of relief when she saw Lucas raise the binoculars slung around his neck to his eyes. He then stood and carefully scanned the country ahead of the ute. After saying something to the driver he then did another sweep of the country to the west.

*He hasn't seen us!* Rose thought. She was sure that if they had such men would just have driven the vehicle to where she was hiding or at least started running up the slope. *And he hasn't got a gun either,* she added.

But when Lucas jumped down and began scanning the ground Rose bit her lip. The suspicion that the men had discovered her boot prints somewhere along the track made her feel quite nauseous with anxiety.

*I should not have been lazy. I should have just walked cross-country,* she rebuked herself.

But it was done now and could not be undone. So the men suspected she and Belinda were in this area. That was bad.

*I will have to be much more careful,* Rose told herself.

To her intense relief, Lucas jumped down and got back into the vehicle. The engine revved and it drove on. A minute later it was out of sight over the crest. Rose at once got to her feet, lifted Belinda by one arm and then hurried forward to the rocks, hauling her sister to a more comfortable position as she did. Belinda objected strongly but Rose didn't care. She was too scared.

"Sssh, Belinda Bub," she cried. "That was the bad men. Be quiet!"

Thankfully Belinda did but she continued sobbing. Rose ignored her and crouched behind the nearest rocks. Carefully she peeked around the lower edge. Then she let out a long sigh. The ute was driving down into the next valley and showing no sign of stopping.

The next valley was wide and flat with the usual dry creeks seaming the bottom. But this one had a thick growth of grass and lots of dark trunked trees, iron barks Rose thought they were. The vehicle track went down and along the valley and then to the right of some rocky knolls and on out of sight to the northwest. The white ute was just visible through the tree canopies and Rose watched it anxiously until it vanished from sight around the far hill.

And her eye had noted something else. Down in the valley, on the left of the track among the trees, was a windmill. But did it have water? She knew they must get more water today or they would be in deadly peril again. But was this the time? Was it worth risking moving in daylight and possibly being seen? Could she afford to wait until nighttime?

"No, I can't! If those men suspect we are somewhere along this road then Cousin James will be along with his helicopter soon. That will be too hard to hide from out in this open country," Rose reasoned.

So how to get there unseen? She settled Belinda in some shade and gave her her drink bottle and then knelt under cover and studied the lay of the land. Lessons from Cadets were at the top of her mind. In particular she remembered walking for an hour or so through bush at Macrossan when Captain Ross was giving them very practical instruction on patrolling techniques.

*Lines of Advance, that's what it was called,* Rose remembered.

Captain Ross had pointed out that they might have to make big detours and walk much further to reach an objective unseen by using gullies and other dead ground.

Rose did not want to walk further, particularly in such heat, but she was feeling guilty about having been lazy and thereby leaving tracks, so she decided to do it. With that aim she carefully studied the country. And out of that came a plan.

Collecting Belinda's now empty water bottle and repacking it she remembered the clink of glass. A quick check did not reveal any broken glass in her backpack, so she felt happier. She pulled it back on, picked up Belinda and then backtracked, her ears now listening for the helicopter.

The route she followed took her back fifty metres and then north behind the row of rocky outcrops until she came to a dip. After a careful check (*Keep off the skyline)* she sidled through a low saddle and hurried down into the top of a re-entrant. She was still visible from some points along the road but by hurrying down she was soon hidden from most directions by the tree canopies. The re-entrant, now a gully, did what she expected and led down to the valley floor. At each bend and twist Rose stopped for a careful survey of the terrain ahead.

In this way she reached the low ground at a creek junction near the windmill in about half an hour. There was then a delay as Belinda indicated that she needed a pee. Rose found a small section of undercut creek bank and attended to that while crouching there.

"Good girl!" she praised as she buttoned Belinda's pants back up.

The vehicle track had to be crossed. Rose moved to crouch in the gully at the last bend before the track, hugging Belinda to her front. After listening intently for a minute or so she stood up and hurried forward, hoping that the other indents in the soft, dry sand would mask her boot prints. The track was easy to cross, she just stepped on the grass between the wheel ruts. Then it was on up the gully to a barbed wire fence. This was crawled under and they went on for another hundred paces until she was level with the windmill.

She sat Belinda in the shade and stood to study the area. To her considerable relief she saw there were both a water tank and a drinking trough attached. For a hundred paces around, right to the creek, there was no grass at all. It was a dusty wasteland. There were no cattle visible and obviously hadn't been for quite a while as all the cowpats were grey and small.

*But is there water in the tank?*

She knew there was only one way to find out, go to it. But that meant walking out into the middle of that big, open clearing.

*And what if that helicopter comes along when, Shit! The helicopter!*

Rose heard it just in time. *Belinda's bright pink hat!* she thought, as she whirled around, grabbed Belinda and dragged her down against the steep bank of the creek. Just in time she curled her legs up as the helicopter went buzzing low overhead. It had come from the north and went straight on. Within seconds it was gone.

*If it had circled it must have seen us,* Rose thought.

For a minute or so she just crouched there, quivering with fear and listening for the machine's return. When it didn't, she attended to a frightened and upset Belinda. Then she went back to considering if it was worth the risk going to a water tank that might be empty.

*And is one of the men watching?* she wondered. *If they are sure we are along this road then they must watch the water sources surely?*

She began methodically scanning the area, particularly the rock-studded hills just beyond the clearing for any sign of the men. In her mind was another cadet exercise. This had been a problem-solving Leadership Selection exercise along the bed of the Fanning River. The story was that they were a patrol in enemy territory trying to get to safety. But they had lost their section commander and 2ic and had no map. The group had arrived at the edge of a clearing and in the middle of it was a hutchie with some camp gear, and an open map.

It was, Captain Ross had explained later, a variation of the old 'Body and the Sniper' scenario, where some tempting bait was put out in the open and the sniper then lay in wait under cover.

*So where is the sniper?* Rose worried.

At that moment, a Kookaburra came flitting through the trees. It went to land on a branch just above her head but, seeing her, gave a squark and flew off to a tree on the hillside on the other side of the clearing. It then began its "Hooo Haaa Hooo Ha!" chortle.

*Well, I don't think there is anyone over there,* Rose reasoned, noting that it was the hillside closest to the road.

*So the solution to the Body and the Sniper was not to walk out into the open but to scout carefully right around the back of the clearing first,* Rose remembered.

That got her looking around. The creek she was in came from the west, from hills a few hundred metres away. It was made up of three tributaries which joined about fifty metres to her left. She decided that the sniper could be anywhere along the tributary coming down from the north.

"And if I check it out, I can get up onto the western slope of the hill without being seen," she told herself.

But there was the downside that if there really was a sniper in hiding she would walk right into him, and get caught, or shot! But it seemed like the right thing to do so she picked Belinda up, interrupting her game with pretty rocks, and started walking, scouting cautiously up the creek.

It was a sweaty and nerve-wracking half hour. After turning right up the tributary Rose found a nice shady spot due west of the windmill and told Belinda to stay there. Belinda did not want to but Rose insisted. "You look for diamonds Ball of Bushiness," she said. Belinda looked around and then sat down and picked up a stone. Rose immediately hurried on up the creek bed. The creek became smaller and smaller as it went up the slope and near the top of the saddle between it and the next hill to the west it was just a knee-deep rill. Rose did not have time to crawl, and thought it pointless anyway. Nor did she go right up. From where she reached she could see behind the bigger rocks on the hillside and it was obvious no-one was hiding behind them.

Satisfied it was safe she turned and walked quickly back to Belinda. Happy that the little girl could be left for a few minutes more Rose turned to face the clearing. Now that the time had come to walk out into the open, she found she was trembling and almost hyperventilating.

*If that helicopter comes over while I am there, or the vehicle comes back, I will be seen for sure.*

In her mind, Rose rehearsed what she intended and then, after taking several deep breaths, she strode up out of the gully and into the open. Walking across that fifty metres of bare, dusty ground she found a real test of courage. At any moment she expected to hear a shout, or a shot. She tensed in anticipation and her skin seemed to crawl.

But nothing happened and she reached the water tank. The first thing she did was what she had seen Captain Ross do at Macrossan Army Camp, she knocked on the water tank. To her relief, it did not give an 'empty' ring.

*It's got water in it!* she thought, relief coursing through her.

But how to get it out? The steel water trough was empty and burning to the touch, being out in the direct sun. Rose studied the arrangement of pipes and taps, almost in a fluster of anxiety. There was a big screw valve on the pipe that emptied into the trough, so she tried that. It was very stiff and hot to the touch, but she used all her strength and suddenly it came loose and a trickle of water dribbled into the trough.

"Yes!" she cried.

By turning it a bit more water began to flow. She quickly turned it off and then knelt on the side of the trough away from the road and pulled off the backpack. All the bottles were lined up, even her own and the full Whisky bottle. Then she prepared their coverings and lay them in a neat line. By then she was trembling and having trouble with her fingers being 'all thumbs'. She kept stopping to listen and to glance up.

Then she began filling. As each bottle was filled, she placed on the plastic wrap and hair tie and then nested it in the backpack. With each bottle she felt a little spurt of relief and achievement. When she got to her own, she first drank as much as she could, then filled it and put it in the pack. The Whisky bottle got the same treatment. Then she stood and cupped her hands to wash her face and to drink some more. She would have loved to wash Belinda and her clothes but knew she was taking a fearful risk. Trembling slightly from excitement and over-exertion she carefully screwed the tap tight again.

By the time she had picked up the backpack and pulled it on she was gasping and sweating. There was a small amount of water in the bottom of the trough, and she hesitated for a few seconds, wondering if she should somehow dry it up or drain it.

"No, it will dry up quickly," she said.

Turning, she hurried back across the yard, scuffing out her tracks as she went. Glancing back she saw that several bush birds had already come fluttering down from the surrounding trees and were starting to bathe and drink. That caused her a smile.

*Good!*

By then she was at the gully and Belinda was wailing and calling for her. Rose slid down into the gully and handed her a drink.

"Here, Bub-O, more water," she said.

"Smelly water?" Belinda asked suspiciously.

"No, from a different place, from that water tank over there," Rose replied. But she had some trepidation as the water had smelt a bit and tasted pretty awful to her.

To her relief, Belinda a took a big drink before pulling a face. "Not like!" she cried. "Want cordial!"

"Too bad! It's all we've got. Drink it!" Rose ordered.

To her considerable relief, Belinda did so and then Rose took the bottle and swung off the pack to put it away. But as she did, she heard the sound of a vehicle. Bobbing up to look she almost blanched with alarm. A white 4WD was stopped at the gate on the access track to the windmill!

*Is that the men?* she wondered.

A man got out of the passenger side and walked to the gate and then she knew: It was Marvin.

"Bloody hell! Let's get out of here!" Rose gasped.

She pulled on the backpack, grabbed Belinda up and went hurrying down the creek to the point where another tributary came in from the west. Luckily, it was deep enough for her to walk along without bending and she turned up it and moved as fast as she could. The bed of the creek was the usual mix of sand and pebbles and the occasional big rock or log, so she had to take it carefully in case she tripped. An accident would put an end to it all! But she could hear the vehicle moving and panic began to well up.

It was a spider web that brought her to a puffing standstill while she clawed at the sticky mess on her face and clothes, and on Belinda. Frantic with a bout of arachnophobia, she looked anxiously for the spider itself. There was no sign of it. But the incident calmed her and she slowed to walk more carefully, stopping from time to time to peek back over the top of the bank to check on the vehicle.

To her dismay, she saw Marvin again climb out of the front passenger seat. He reached back in and took out a bag of some sort and then a rifle. After speaking to the driver he turned and walked over towards the trough. As he approached the trough, the birds took flight. Rose's heart went into her mouth and she swore at having made another mistake.

*Oh bloody hell! He will see the water and know we have been there!*

But Marvin just glanced into the trough and then around the area before turning to wave at the 4WD. The driver waved back but from that distance Rose could not identify him. The 4WD swung away and headed back out to the gate. By then Rose was in a dither, wondering if she had splashed water or left boot prints. To her enormous relief Marvin did not walk around to her side of the trough. Instead, he walked back to the tree beside the access track and then sat down in the shade with his back to one.

At that, Rose gave a wry grin. *Not much of a sniper that one!* she thought, her contempt giving her a little boost. *I am better than these guys. They might be grown men but they are out of their normal environment.* Which was very comforting. But what to do now?

Belinda was getting fractious, and Rose feared she might call out so she decided to get further away. As she did, she saw the 4WD turn right on the road and head off to the southeast.

*Going to check that water trough where all the cattle are?* she wondered.

She had been planning to hide for the remainder of the day, both because of the heat and the danger of being seen but she now thought that she would move further away from the place in case Marvin did find her tracks and start searching. The obvious route was west along the gully she was in, so she took it.

Ten minutes later she was around behind the second hill and nearly

149

half a kilometre away. The gully was petering out but there were plenty of trees and a ridge of the hill to hide her, so she puffed her way up to a low saddle. Sweating and feeling decidedly weak she came to a standstill just below the crest. Now moving more cautiously she edged up to look over.

And got a surprise. The ground sloped down for about a kilometre to the bottom of yet another parallel valley and running north, south along it was a gravel road. There were lots of small knolls and clumps of rocks between her and the road, but it certainly gave her pause. Lifting her gaze, she again experienced that sense of endless space and loneliness the view of ridge after ridge gave her.

*Dad said poor old Burke and Wills passed through this area,* she thought. *Poor old Burke and Wills!*

But what to do? For a couple of minutes she stood there, biting her lip in indecision, while Belinda fidgeted and wanted to be put down. Then Rose shook her head.

"No, I need to get across to the other side of that road and find a good place to hide," she told herself. In her mind it was a sort of boundary of the area the men might search.

So she picked a route that offered the most cover and began walking down a re-entrant on the western slope. But she was now feeling so weak she had to stop every few minutes to rest. Each time she chose a clump of bushes or rocks or a dip in the ground. It was the helicopter more than anything she was worrying about.

Each time she picked her next hiding spot and then hurried across the open ground to it. It concerned her that the trees were becoming fewer, and also the ground cover was more open. Now she moved cautiously from one clump of rocks to another. As the country appeared to be more open to the north she reluctantly edged away more to the south. Twice she stopped to have a drink and to give one to Belinda.

At about 0845hrs they reached a jumble of rocks. Ahead appeared to be a large area of open country. There was only one more rock pile ahead of her about 25 metres away. It had a large, flat-topped boulder standing on a wide shelf of rock, with several smaller rocks scattered around among dark green, prickly bushes and big clumps of spinifex.

*I'll just go forward to that for a better look,* Rose thought.

She had in mind the depressing thought that they might have to do quite a detour to get around the open area. But it was very hot and they were both sweating.

*We'd better have a drink and a rest before we cross that open country,* she thought. But now Geography was against her. The sun was coming from behind her and that meant the shade was on the far side of the next rock pile. *We can't rest there,* she thought.

Looking around, she saw there was a nice patch of shade among some bushes just beside them. So she put Belinda down in the shade of one of the large rocks.

"You wait here, Bubby. I am just going to those rocks there to have a look," she said.

Belinda nodded and sat down, her attention now taken up by another small lizard that was peeking out of a crack between the boulders. Rose then moved forward and scanned the country ahead from under cover on the right of last rock pile.

She now saw, with some concern, that there was nothing but short grass and spinifex for about half a kilometre before a line of trees that marked another creek line. To the north it was even more open.

*Do I risk crossing this now? Or is now the time to hide somewhere?* she thought.

And then her eyes focused on a white object in the heat shimmer to the north. And her heart went into her mouth. It was a vehicle. As it got closer, she saw it was a white ute. Dismayed she crouched and peeked between some smaller rocks and bushes. To add to her anxiety, her vision went blurry and she had trouble blinking sweat from her eyes. Flies added to her discomfort. But her whole attention was the ute. It was driving steadily across the open towards the rise she was on.

*Did they see us?* Rose wondered. *And is it the men, or just some innocent grazier or stockman?*

With a sinking feeling in her gut she felt sure it would be Lucas!

But had he seen them? She wondered if the men had been observing from a long distance but frowned. She knew she had been very careful with her fieldcraft.

*Maybe they will just drive on by?* she thought hopefully, noting that the gravel road was only about 50 metres further down the gentle slope.

Quickly she slipped back behind the rock pile, thinking to get back to Belinda. But then she paused. She realised she could not cross that 25 metres of open ground without being seen until the view from the vehicle was blocked by the rock pile. But even that would be risky, she thought, as the vehicle was moving quite fast. Deciding that the risk wasn't worth it she remained behind the rocks, looking back anxiously to check that Belinda wasn't visible. There was no sign of her so Rose crouched behind the rocks, edging around the pile as the vehicle went out of sight on the other side. She was in the sun and it was unpleasant, but she hoped it would only be for a few minutes until the ute had driven by.

But to her consternation she heard it stop and then a door slam. Rose's heart leapt into her mouth. *Someone just got out! Did they see us?* she wondered.

She was now very anxious to get back to Belinda but could not tell if anyone in the ute could see the place where she had left Belinda. So all she could do was hide where she was and hope. There was a gap in among some smaller boulders on the south side of the rocks that was just big enough, so she slid into it, her heart now hammering with fear.

And then she heard the thud and crunch of boots on rock and saw Lucas come around to her side of the rock shelf, and he had a gun!

# Chapter 17

## LUCAS

Rose experienced a spasm of paralysing terror. She was sure he had seen her and that she had no chance. But Lucas stopped and looked around before turning to the big rock next to the one Rose was hiding behind. She saw that he had his binoculars slung around his neck and a radio hanging by a clip from his left shirt pocket. The rifle was a bolt action sporting rifle similar to one her father owned. It had no sling and Lucas was carrying it in his hand at the point of balance. By this time Rose was trembling and holding her breath, while silently praying.

Lucas tried to spring up onto the rock, but the rifle hampered him and he slid back down. It was obvious he needed two hands. Muttering swear words, he lowered the rifle and rested it against the rock on its butt.

*Not good practice that, leaving your rifle,* Rose thought.

But she also had an impression of why. The rifle looked brand new and had lovely yellow lacquered wood and stock.

*He wouldn't want to scratch that,* she thought.

As she thought this Lucas used both hands to lever himself as he sprang up. Now he was above Rose, and she could only stare up at him in horror.

*If he glances down, he must see me!* she told herself.

But his focus was upwards and he scrambled up onto the top of the large, flat-topped rock. Then he straightened up and looked out in all directions. All Rose could do was stay still, tensed and trembling. But the notion of trying to get the rifle did flit across her mind. Lucas lifted his binoculars to his eyes and began scanning the country to the east, looking over Rose's head.

*Oh, I hope Belinda stays under cover and quiet!* she thought.

And then Belinda spoke!

"Are you one of the bad men?" she said, in a loud and clear voice.

Rose looked over her shoulder, aghast. There was Belinda, standing out on the rock ledge to her left.

*Oh no!* she thought.

Lucas lowered his binoculars and a look of astonishment crossed his face, rapidly followed by a smile.

"Are you Belinda?" he said.

"Hmm, I Ball of Busyness," Belinda replied. "I got a butterfly," she added, holding up her right hand, where a small yellow butterfly was perched on her finger.

"That's nice. Where's your sister?" Lucas asked.

By then Rose had recovered from her shock. She knew she had to act, and there, just a few paces away, was the rifle. The plan of action she had half formed crystalised and she instantly acted on it, stepping sideways out from cover. As quietly as she could, she walked towards the rifle. Luckily, her rubber soled boots made no sound and she reached the rifle before Lucas looked down. As her right hand closed around the barrel, her eyes had already taken in the key details.

*This is like dad's,* she noted.

She had been taught to fire it on a trip the previous year. She had also twice fired army rifles on cadet camps. As she swung it up her brain said: safety catch, bolt, telescopic sight, trigger.

"Here I am," she cried, swinging the butt up to her right hip. Then she quickly stepped back in case Lucas jumped.

Another look of astonishment crossed Lucas's face, followed instantly by a frown, and then anger.

"Put that gun down girlie!" he snapped. He went into a crouch. "Don't be silly. You could hurt someone!"

Rose had by this time lifted the weapon up so that the muzzle was pointed at him. *But is it loaded?* she wondered.

She had to know. Now training told. Using her thumb she pushed the safety catch forward and then she gripped the knob of the bolt and swiftly jerked it up and back and then immediately slammed it forward. There was the noise of a round being ejected and she glimpsed shiny brass in the sunlight and heard a bullet bounce and tinkle on the rocks. She understood she had ejected the round that had been in the breech, but she didn't care. As she had pushed the bolt forward and down, there had been a very satisfying metallic sound and a click that told her that another round had been chambered and there was now a live bullet in the breech ready to fire. Her finger went onto the trigger and she took two more steps back.

"Don't try it!" she snarled, sure that Lucas was intending to leap down and grapple with her.

When he saw her finger go to the trigger, Lucas went white and looked scared. "Careful, girlie! Point that gun somewhere else," he gasped.

It was the 'girlie' that did it. Fury boiled in Rose and she pursed her lips and raised the butt to her shoulder to aim along the top of the barrel.

"That's what my father said when you pointed it at him," she snapped. "Now don't move. I know how to use this thing."

"Careful," Lucas said, his hands going up and his tongue appearing to lick nervously at his lips. "We don't want a nasty accident."

"It won't be an accident!" Rose shouted. "I'm an army cadet. If I want to shoot you, I won't miss! Now climb down slowly. Belinda, come here!"

Belinda, now looking very worried, trotted over to her. "Sorry, Rosie! I didn't think," she said.

"It's alright, Bub-O," Rose replied, annoyed at the situation but unable to blame her little sister.

*It was my fault. I shouldn't have left her alone,* she rebuked herself. But her focus was mostly on Lucas. There was also the concern that he might not be alone.

"Is there anyone else in the vehicle?" she asked.

As soon as she spoke, Rose knew she had made a mistake. *If there is we dare not step out from behind these rocks,* she thought.

But then Lucas glanced that way and then hesitated before say, "No."

*There isn't,* Rose decided. In her mind she reasoned that there were not enough men for them to drive around with two men in every vehicle. *Not if they are trying to watch all the water points.*

Lucas took a step towards her, so she shook her head. More advice from Captain Ross came to her. "Do not ever go close to a prisoner or he might grab your weapon or brush it aside and hit you. Keep him at a distance. And do not aim at his head or chest. That doesn't intimidate people. Aim at their lower stomach. That will worry them. And make them sit on their own legs."

So Rose acted on this, directing Lucas do that. He did but with obvious bad grace. She could see he was looking for any opportunity.

"Okay, take off the binoculars and radio and place them on the rocks," Rose ordered.

Now she braced in case he flung one of the items at her, in the belief she was just a little girl who would not shoot. But their eyes met several times and he sensed her mood and meekly obeyed.

*He's scared I will shoot him accidentally,* she thought.

Belinda was a problem, so Rose told her to go back to her shade. Reluctantly she did. Rose did not want to take her eyes off Lucas for a second. But she had to keep flicking them to both sides of the rock in case there was another person in the vehicle. Cautiously she edged sideways until she could just see the front of the vehicle and also had Lucas in the line of any fire. A searching look revealed an empty cab. That was a relief!

But what to do? *I can't take a prisoner with us,* she thought. "Are my Mum and Dad still alive?" she asked.

"Yes."

"Where are they? What have you done with them?"

"I don't know. The boss took them. I think your mother is a prisoner while your dad arranges our money," Lucas replied.

Rose was about to offer her opinion of Cousin James when it occurred to her not to let the enemy know what she knew.

"So why are you chasing us?" she asked.

"Just to keep you safe while… while negotiations go on," Lucas answered.

Rose nearly pulled the trigger at that. She realised it must have showed on her face as he looked very scared.

"Careful, girlie!" he croaked, lifting both hands.

"Don't call me girlie!" Rose snapped. "You may address me as Miss MacGregor!"

Lucas blanched and nodded. "Okay Miss," he meekly agreed. "What are you going to do with me?"

More advice from Captain Ross came to her. "Empty your pockets," she ordered. He was obviously reluctant to do so, so she put on what she hoped looked like a fierce face and said, "I will take them off your dead body if that's the way you want it!"

"No! No! It's alright," Lucas replied.

He hastily began emptying pockets. Rose watched notebook, wallet, coins, and mobile phone make a pile on the rock. Then she came up with a plan.

"Okay, turn around," she ordered. She did not want him springing at her like a panther as he went to get up.

Again he was reluctant to do so but complied. But when he had faced the other way, Rose experienced a savage surge of emotion and felt she wanted to hit the back of his head with the rifle. Then she shuddered.

*Oh! I didn't know I was like that,* she thought.

"Okay, get up and walk," she commanded.

Lucas got to his feet and glanced back. "Which way?"

Rose had been thinking about that. She reasoned that the vehicle track she had walked along during the night must join this gravel road somewhere to the north. So she pointed south.

"That way!"

Lucas made a face and shook his head but stepped down off the ledge and began walking. When he was about twenty metres away, he turned.

"Don't you go to the police," he called. "If you do your mother will die."

Rose nearly pulled the trigger at that. She lifted the muzzle to aim and snarled, "If you hurt my mother, I will spend the rest of my life making sure you suffer! Be sure of that!"

Lucas nodded and quickly turned and hurried away, angling across to the gravel road. Shaking with emotion, Rose lowered the rifle and then stood there gasping but relieved. Belinda came and joined her, obviously worried about getting into trouble.

"It is alright, Butterfly Girl, I love you," Rose said, patting her. For a few moments they just stood together. Then Rose shook her head. "No time to stand around weeping," she said.

Releasing Belinda, she walked over to the pile of personal belongings and placed the rifle carefully against a rock. Then she shrugged off her backpack and put it down.

But it was already full of the water bottles. *I need to keep all this stuff as evidence for the cops,* she thought.

But then that terrible threat made her pause. After a moment's thought she shook her head and knelt and opened her pack.

"I will take it all anyway," she muttered.

Somehow she crammed it all in, all the while watching Lucas who was now walking south along the gravel road and glancing frequently back towards her.

Rose stood and pulled the now heavy pack back on. "Come on, Bub-O," she said, lifting Belinda to her hip with one hand.

Picking up the rifle with the other she began walking towards the vehicle. She had in mind to get in and drive in it to safety. She had never driven a car in her life but had often watched it being done and thought she could manage.

*Be better than walking anyway,* she told herself.

To her surprise, she saw that Lucas had left the gravel road and was running off away from her towards the distant tree line.

*Running! Why is he running? And in this heat!* she thought.

But as soon as she got to the utility she knew why. She put Belinda down and then opened the driver's door and looked in.

"No key!" she cried. "Oh you idiot!"

Obviously Lucas had the key and he was a good two or three hundred metres away! For a moment a surge of anger caused her to bring the rifle up to shoot at him. But then sanity prevailed. She lowered the rifle and just stood there seething with anger and disappointment. A glance showed her it was an old-style vehicle. Part of her mind brought to the front the idea that car thieves could somehow join wires together to get such motors to go. But she had absolutely no idea how, so she just shrugged.

A glance showed Lucas still jogging away. "Oh well, bugger you too!" she cried, anger again welling up.

Pushing Belinda away she knelt and aimed sideways at the front tyre. *Two with one bullet I want,* she told herself

*Bang! Thwak! Pussht!*

Belinda screamed and began sobbing. Rose ignored her and stood up, angry that she had walked with Belinda all that way without putting the safety catch back on. Stepping to the front she saw that what she had intended had been achieved – both front tyres were deflating rapidly.

"Good!" she muttered. "Oh shut up Belinda! It's only a gun!"

Now she aimed at the front of the engine. She did not know much about engines, but she was aware that they must have coolant in the radiator or they quickly overheated and seized up. Her father had explained that.

*Bang! Wheeieee! Ting!*

Rose jumped in fright, afraid that the ricocheting bullet might hit her or Belinda. She was also appalled at the noise and the echoes that swashed around the hills.

*Ooh bloody hell! The other crooks might hear that!* she worried.

A glance south showed Lucas standing in the middle of the spinifex staring towards them. She was sorely tempted to fire a shot in his direction and did raise the rifle, making him hurry on away from them. Then she gave a wry grin and this time remembered to click the safety catch on. Another glance showed light green liquid dripping out onto the ground.

"Good! Now he will have to walk!" she muttered. She turned and leaned the rifle against the vehicle.

Belinda was standing nearby sobbing, her hands over her ears and tears streaming down her face.

"Oh shut up Bub-O! It is only me shooting. You've been with people shooting before," Rose snapped.

She was tired, dispirited, and hungry and in no mood for temper tantrums or sympathy. Something of this transmitted itself to Belinda. She stopped crying and Rose relented to the extent of kneeling and drawing her into her arms.

"There, there, Baby Sister," she soothed.

"I... sniff, not... sniff.. baby!" Belinda cried.

"Then don't cry like one. Come on, let's see what Mister Lucas has in his car," Rose said.

After another glance to check that Lucas was well away, she moved to look into the cab. The first thing she saw was a packet of shop bought sandwiches in a triangular clear plastic container.

"Oh goodo! Here's our lunch!" Rose cried.

Even though she knew she should be moving she spent a minute breaking the packet open. She held the packet down and Belinda stopped sniffling and at once snatched a sandwich and stuffed it into her mouth. Rose took the next one and had a big bite: scrambled eggs and lettuce.

Rose dug around in the glove box, all the while chewing and swallowing. But there was nothing else of use so she turned ready to walk. But that presented a problem: How to carry Belinda, the rifle without a sling, and the sandwiches? That got her looking inside again. Then she looked into the back of the ute.

"Aah! That's what I want!" she cried. 'That' was a snatch strap for securing loads on vehicles. This one was 3-centimetre-wide nylon and would do. "That is strong enough to hold an elephant," she said. "It certainly should carry Bundle of Blubber."

"I not blubber! I big girl!" Belinda corrected.

Rose chuckled and set to work. She did not want the actual steel buckles and ratchet mechanism, so she spent a minute working out how to unclip and slide them off. They were tossed into the back and then she quickly measured the strap up into three loops. After tying a reef knot to hold the ends, she placed it over her right shoulder like a sash. Belinda was then lifted up to sit in two of the loops and the third was placed behind her back and under her arms.

"You will have to hang on Bub-O. I won't be able to hold you all the time," Rose cautioned.

But it was a massive improvement in her mind. She suspected she would have some very sore shoulders and muscles after a few hours, but it was way better than always lugging her little sister along in her weak and aching arms!

"Okay, let's get away from here," she said.

Picking up the rifle she turned and strode off north-westwards into the spinifex. As she did, she looked back to check on Lucas but could see no sign of him. Shrugging she kept walking, setting her direction by the sun.

She had only gone about fifty metres when she felt a tugging at the packet in her left hand. It was Belinda. She was poking her fingers into the two remaining sandwiches.

"What that one?" she queried.

Rose looked. "Tomato and cheese. The other one looks like ham and pickles."

"Martoes please," Belinda said.

Not waiting to have it handed to her she dragged it out, dropping a slice of tomato in the process. The sandwich vanished into her mouth in big chomps. Rose glanced down at Belinda's now distended cheeks and smiled.

"Good on you, Chubby Cheeks," she commented.

"I noff Chubbby mfff, cheekies!" Belinda objected, chewing hard the whole time.

Rose laughed and felt her spirits rise. She began eating the ham and pickles while striding through the spinifex and long grass. It was hot but she was feeling suddenly elated. It suddenly dawned on her that Lucas had given her a subconscious compliment.

*He said don't go to the police. He thinks I am going to make it,* she thought. And now she had a rifle and live ammunition. That was a whole new situation for the crooks. *They will be a lot more careful now they know I am an army cadet and that I am armed,* she told herself.

But there was still a long way to go. And it was very hot. Out in the open country the air was shimmering and felt too hot to breathe. Rose found she was sweating badly but was not as concerned. Three times she had found water and now she was confident she could find more.

*And it can't be more than about ten kilometres to the highway! If I was a fit soldier, I could walk that in two hours,* she told herself.

But she was not a fit soldier and when she reached the trees along the creek line she had to stop in the shade for a drink and a rest. Belinda wanted more food and cried when told there wasn't any.

Rose also took the opportunity to unload the rifle and to strip the rounds from the magazine, laying them carefully on the backpack.

"Seven," she counted.

Now she regretted not having picked up the bullet she had ejected but there was no way she was walking a kilometre back and then another just for that. Belinda was attracted to the shiny brass and copper objects and reached out. Rose shook her head and pushed her grasping hand aside.

"No Bub-O. Not for you. Bad. Danger! No touch," she said.

She spent a few minutes familiarising herself with the rifle, cocking and dry firing it and practicing aiming as she had been taught at cadets. Then she carefully refilled the magazine and reloaded the weapon, placing a round in the chamber and the safety catch on.

"The army call that 'Action'," she explained to a curious Belinda who had watched carefully every movement.

At 1000hrs, despite the heat and the risk, Rose picked Belinda and the rifle up and resumed walking, following along beside a big, dry creek with a sandy bed lined with large paperbarks.

# Chapter 18

## PERILS AND PLEASURE

After walking for about ten minutes, Rose noted that the creek was trending away from the road. The creek was 'flowing' northwest. But following the road meant walking out in the open so she opted to stay in under the trees. After another ten minutes of walking she was glad of that as the creek swung northwards for half a kilometre. It was very hot but manageable in the shade. Out on the open ground the hot air was shimmering and forming mirages. The distant lines of hills and mountains seemed to dance in the hot air.

They came to a creek junction and headed northwest again, then another creek junction of two tributary creeks coming in from the hills out to the northeast. Rose opted for going northwest along the main stream. She kept to the top of the northern bank even though it meant trampling through lots of long grass. But that kept them in the shade.

Belinda began to droop. Rose tried to keep her interested by pointing out birds, mostly cockatoos, but a few budgerigars and grey and blue coloured parrots, plus always the ubiquitous crows with their mournful 'Cark!'.

1100hrs came and went and another drink and rest. Rose did not stint the water anymore and Belinda at least stopped complaining about the taste and smell. But it was becoming a real effort to keep plodding along. The rifle became heavier and heavier, and Rose wished she had looked harder in the ute for a rope or belt to make a sling. And the loops of the snatch strap supporting Belinda began to cut into her shoulder and, as she had feared, her back muscles started to ache and cramp.

At the next rest stop she swapped it all to the other side and then had to walk with one arm around Belinda as she had gone to sleep, slumped in a ball against Rose's side. The rifle she kept swapping from her left hand to the crook of her right arm. By the next creek crossing at 1125hrs she had nearly had enough.

She also got a real fright. As she slithered down a cattle pad to the bed of the side creek and looked for a way up the other side Rose heard rustling in the long grass nearby, and then loud snorting. Into view burst a huge black pig. The sight of it almost froze her with fear. It was as big as her and looked very mean and tough. She had heard stories of wild pigs killing people and that didn't help as she was so frightened that she was unable to move for a few seconds.

Then she remembered the rifle and tried to heft it into a firing position, but Belinda was in the way. The bumping woke Belinda and she sat up, grumbling and wailing. The noise attracted the big pig's attention. It had not seen them until then.

"Oh no! This is bad!" Rose gasped, clicking off the safety catch and trying to aim with her sister wriggling and pointing and in the way.

For a few seconds the huge pig stared at them with its little yellow eyes. Then it put its head down and grunted loudly and pawed at the sand of the creek bed. Its curved white tusks filled Rose's focus and sent surges of adrenaline into her already alarmed blood stream. Rose was sure it was going to charge, and she desperately tried to position the crossed hairs in the telescopic sight on its head and hold them there amid Belinda's wriggling.

*I will only have time for one shot!* she thought, gulping deep breaths.

She knew it was one of those real-life crises that could not be avoided. Summoning up her courage she tensed to face it, only to have the pig suddenly grunt and swing away. It went racing off along the bed of the main creek back past the way they had come. Rose was simultaneously relieved and appalled.

"Oh my God! Look at the speed of the bloody thing!" she cried.

"You swear naughty words, Rosie!" Belinda reproved.

"Miss MacGregor to you!" Rose retorted. Then she grinned and clicked the safety catch back on.

"What that thing, Rosie?" Belinda queried.

"A wild pig, Bub-O, a bloody great big wild pig!"

"You swear again!"

"I did, and I will again if I see another pig," Rose assured her. Then she remembered to click on the safety catch before moving.

She set herself at the steep other bank and arrived puffing at the top in a cloud of fine dust, only to be confronted by another big pig. And this one was a sow with four large piglets. Once again fear gripped her and she swung the rifle to her hip, the range was only ten metres!

*This could be bad,* she told herself, having heard that sows were more dangerous. *Mothers defending their offspring.*

There was another few moments of tense stand-off and again Rose tried to get the rifle ready. But the pigs were already alarmed and obviously feared humans as the piglets went running down into the main creek through hidden tracks in the long grass, all squeaking and oinking as they did. The sow glared at them for a moment and then followed.

"Oh my God! That gave me a fright!" Rose said, wiping her brow.

"They only little pigs," Belinda commented.

"Piglets," Rose corrected, now shaking with reaction.

"Piglet pink," Belinda objected.

"Yes Bub-O, the piglet in *Winnie the Pooh* is pink," Rose agreed.

Then she smacked her forehead. *The safety catch! I forgot to take it off. That pig would have just attacked before I could fire!*

With her thumb she checked. Yes, it was on! Ashamed of her poor reaction and appalled at the images her imagination conjured up of such a huge animal mauling them, she shuddered. It was a relief to keep talking to Belinda.

The discussion on pigs and piglets carried them for nearly a kilometre. By then Rose had calmed down but she was nervous and kept looking anxiously around for other bush creatures that might hurt them. She saw a few kangaroos, but they just went bounding off, and there were plenty of Galahs to cackle and screech at them from the trees overhead. But not much else.

From 1215hrs to 1245hrs Rose rested them at a point where the main creek was making a very obvious turn to the south. For most of the half hour she lay in the shade and kept them both hydrated, trying to appease Belinda when she demanded more sandwiches. All she could do was shake her head and try to distract her by showing her cicada shells stuck on the tree trunks. But Belinda did not believe that the things making the loud whining noise all the time had come out of them.

As the creek was heading south, Rose decided to leave it and strike off northwest along a cattle pad that was leading that way. It went out into fairly open country, but she decided there were just enough trees and bushes for cover. Most of the ground cover on the sandy soil was dry grass, weathered to light brown or grey. The path led up a long slope to the left of another of the seemingly endless stony knolls and hills.

While she trudged up the slope part of Rose's mind was on watching for signs of the men, part was brooding about what her parents (If they really were still alive) must be going through, and only a small part on the natural environment. A big chunk of her mind was taken up with her own sore feet, sore muscles, tiredness, and bodily aches.

She was just aware enough for some instinct to kick in and bring her to a stop. Shaking her head to clear it she focused her eyes downward, then stepped hastily back.

*A snake!* she noted. And not any snake but a Death Adder!

Rose had been lectured by her father on snakes, and she had been taught about them at Cadets in 'Bites and Stings' lessons so she knew that most snakes were very hard to identify. Most were some sort of browny-olive greeny colour and only by counting their belly scales from neck to anus, and by also counting their scales diagonally around the body, could they be accurately identified. But others had distinctive shapes or colours. And the Death Adder was one.

"Found in rocky areas," she muttered, glad that Belinda was asleep.

Taking another step back she stared at this specimen. With its distinctive shovel shaped head, fat body and tiny worm of a tail it was obvious as a type. But this one puzzled her. It looked misshapen and was having trouble curling into a striking 'S'. Then it came to her: the reptile had recently eaten a big meal and was too fat or too full to be able to bend easily.

Then she stared again. *Did that thing just change colour?* she asked herself.

When she first saw it, it had cross bands of light brown and grey, almost perfectly blending in with the grass it was lying in. But now it looked grey and yellow.

For a few more seconds she stared at it, amazed at the colour change, and then horrified by the way it moved its head slowly from side to side, while its little forked tongue kept flickering in and out.

*Smelling the air,* she told herself, remembering something she had read.

Then the colour change also came to her. "That is a warning, a threat gesture," she muttered.

It was a big snake for a Death Adder, as big as her forearms and as round. *I'm glad I didn't step on you before you had that meal,* she

165

thought with a shudder. Then she took another pace back, even though it was obvious the thing could not strike that far. *An ambush hunter,* she remembered, then shuddered again at the image of such a snake suddenly biting in a swift strike.

At the thought of dying out there in the wilderness from a snake bite, she shivered and then shook her head. A detour around the thing was made and Rose hurried on, picking her way with much more care around the tufts of grass and small clumps of rocks. In that way she came to the crest of the rise with yet another rocky hill to her right.

And stopped to gape!

A couple of kilometres away, but stretching right across her path for kilometres in either direction was water! The afternoon sun was reflecting on it and she stood there looking at it, amazed.

"A lake!" she gasped.

She smiled and the irony of it came to her. *Here I was fretting about finding water to drink and here is enough water for a whole city!*

It was so obviously a lake impounded by a dam to provide water for either some big mine or for Mount Isa that she could only stare. *Mount Isa probably?* she thought. That got her raising her gaze to stare at the lines of parallel ranges of stony hills that still seemed to stretch on forever. *Mount Isa is somewhere that way,* she thought. She found it dispiriting.

"No matter how many ridges I cross, there are always more," she grumbled.

But it was obvious that now she would have to just go north to get around the lake, or to the Highway. *It can't be far away now surely?* she asked herself, shielding her eyes from the glare and staring in that direction. But there was no sign of any civilisation, no road or building.

After scanning the surrounding country carefully, Rose set off northwards, aiming to reach the lake near its north end. She noted that the country was better timbered and that there was a lot more grass. There were also cattle, mostly greyish-white Brahmin types but some brown ones with horns. The cattle weren't in a big herd being scattered in small groups. Most of these ignored her if her route was at a fair distance from them, but a few tossed their heads and trotted off.

Belinda awoke and looked around. "Moo cows!" she cried, pointing.

Rose could only agree. Pointing to the cows and talking about birds (there were a lot more now) kept them both going until their next rest in a small dry creek which obviously emptied into the lake when it ran. With so much water close Rose had an even bigger drink and then helped Belinda to do a pee. That was just after 1400hrs.

It was fiercely hot by then, but Rose decided to keep going and to rest properly beside the lake. So she hoisted Belinda to her carry straps, picked up the rifle with a sweat slicked hand and resumed plodding. But now it became an ordeal. In the heat and with her sore eyes, chafed thighs and armpits, sore feet and aching muscles it took all of her willpower to keep putting one foot in front of another.

But it was worth it. The trees became a proper forest, mostly iron barks but a few other species like paperbarks. And there were clumps of a springy, scratchy weed with little bright red and yellow flowers that she thought was lantana. Belinda saw the flowers and wanted some and they helped amuse her for a few hundred metres more. The lantana clumps became larger and more numerous, and clumps of Madagascan rubber vine also began to appear. Rose was familiar with that because there was a lot of along the Burdekin River near Charters Towers.

Then she got a glimpse through the trees of sunlight reflecting off water and her spirits went up even more.

"Not far now," she told Belinda.

But that last few hundred metres felt like the hardest. A barbed wire fence had to be negotiated and then she had to weave her way through thickets of trees, bushes, and lantana.

They came out on the bank of the lake near the mouth of a small creek. The lake was low and there was a wide strip of dry sandy soil which marked the area between low and high water. Rose had been fearing to meet a lot of mud so was relieved. She put the rifle against a log and lowered Belinda to the grass in the shade and then took off the backpack and flopped down, exhausted but jubilant.

Belinda immediately wanted to have a swim, but the sunlight was reflecting straight into their eyes from that direction and Rose felt very exposed where they were. She had a clear view across and along the lake and realised she had been stupid.

*Not good fieldcraft! We need a better spot,* she reasoned.

So she picked everything up again, took Belinda's hand and walked slowly north along the top of the 'beach'.

This led them into the mouth of the small creek and there she found what she wanted, shallow water and a proper sandy beach at the point where the creek entered the lake. Better still there was lots of shade and cover from all directions, including above.

Once again, she put everything down and flopped down. Sighing with relief she stretched her legs out and lay back on the clean, white sand. But not for long. Belinda was insistent on having a swim. Muttering under her breath Rose groaned and sat up. She looked at the glassy water stretching out into the lake. There was no breeze so no waves. She realised she badly wanted a wash too. So she stood up, groaning and aching in every muscle, and walked to the edge of the water.

And then a horrible thought came to her: were there crocodiles? *This is northwest Queensland,* she told herself.

Downstream in these rivers, in the 'Gulf Country' around the Gulf of Carpentaria, she knew there were thousands of them, big estuarine or saltwater crocodiles. Her father had warned her.

"They are called saltwater crocs, Rose, but don't believe that. They live quite happily in fresh water. They infest all the rivers right upstream for hundreds of miles."

Rose stared at that inviting water with dread. *Oh my God! Should I take the risk?* she worried.

She had been on wildlife safaris in Arnhem Land with the family and seen giant saltwater crocs suddenly appear and leap up to grab food being held for them. They were scaly creatures bigger than her, and she knew they could move very fast.

*And they just appear from underwater with no warning and surge up and grab you and drag you back in!* she thought.

With the images of that and the 'Death Roll' she shuddered. "What a horrible way to die!"

And then she was given a clue. Over on the other side of the lake, a few hundred metres away, she saw several cattle with calves wandering around on a sandbank. Several put their heads down to drink and others waded in to drink.

*Surely if there are crocs the cattle would be a lot more wary?* she reasoned.

A glance at the nearby beaches and muddy stretches revealed hundreds of animal tracks leading down to the water.

"It must be safe," she decided.

But she resolved to keep it a safe as she could and restrict the bathing to just a tiny shallow bit of the creek beside the beach, 10 metres of very shallow water in behind a log and a tree trunk.

So she stripped Belinda, while repeatedly glancing to check the water for ripples or swirls of mud or anything that might indicate the presence of submarine monsters. But the only ripples were coming from the cows splashing around on the other side. And Belinda was hard to restrain.

Rather than risk a tantrum and possible screaming, having no idea how close any road or habitation might be, she took off her own boots and led Belinda by the hand into the shallows and washed her. The water was just cooler than the air but refreshing for all that. But the whole time Rose was scared and stayed tensed ready to pluck Belinda up if a croc appeared.

Belinda loved it and after a while Rose left her sitting in the shallows playing with the water and trying to catch tiny fish. She then carefully stripped herself, feeling very self-conscious being nude with her sister, and also worried lest a person come along.

As she waded gingerly in, Belinda looked up. "You 'Rudie Nudie', Rosie," she cried.

Rose blushed and covered her front with her arms. "I need a bath too," she commented.

Placing herself between Belinda and the lake she lowered herself to knee deep and carefully washed her whole body and face. It was bliss and she relished the feel of a gentle breeze evaporating the water off her skin.

Then she washed all of Belinda's clothes and waded self-consciously up to drape them over bushes in the sunlight. To her relief, Belinda did not seem to even notice, just kept calling for her to come and play or to look at some new wonder. Rose then rinsed her own shirt. The stale sweat had been giving it a very sharp odour and she was sick of that. Rather than hang the shirt up to dry she put it on wet. That was very pleasant and, as she suspected it would in that climate with such low humidity, it began to dry very quickly, cooling her as it did.

But after a while she became guilty at taking such a risk and waded ashore to stand in the shade while her skin dried. As she did, she kept watching over Belinda carefully, the rifle ready beside her. She also carefully inspected her body.

*Heavens, I'm just a mass of bruises and scratches!* she noted.

Large parts of her legs, her hips, waist, and arms were blotched with bruises, yellow, black and blue. And there were little sores and scratches everywhere.

Touching her sunburnt face she shook her head. *My face must look a sight,* she lamented. And her broken fingernail still hurt. But then it came to her that it was all surface trivia. *I am still fit and healthy, and I've had lunch!* she thought. *And I've got a rifle, and we are still free. I must go and rescue Mum and Dad.*

That idea got her dressing. Once she had her boots on, she moved to refill all the water bottles. Having tasted the lake water she decided it was better than the water from the windmills. First, she emptied them all and then carefully washed them. Next, she arranged caps. But some of the plastic wrap was lost or torn or no longer usable. So when she refilled them all she used short lengths of stick as 'corks'. It wasn't very satisfactory, but it was the best she could manage.

*I should reach the highway later today or tomorrow so it shouldn't matter,* she told herself.

The hardest bit was getting Belinda out of the water and dressed again. The little girl had sparked up remarkably and happily babbled and even danced a bit. As she picked her up, Rose said, "Come on, Beach Babe. Time to go!"

Belinda looked offended. "I not a beach!" she cried.

"No, it means you like to be at the beach," Rose replied.

She then had images of being on the beach at Manly in her swimsuit. She regretted that her figure did not look all that good in a bikini, too chubby she thought, so she always wore a one-piece. Thinking of relaxing on a Syndey beach made her sigh. Then she shook her head and returned to the task.

Dressing Belinda was a challenge. And then Belinda wanted stay there. But Rose was determined. A check of her watch said 1550hrs. "Time to go, Bub. We have to find Mummy and Daddy," she said.

"Want Mummy!" Belinda agreed.

Rose pulled on the backpack, placed Belinda in her carry loops and hefted the rifle at its point of balance. Then she set off northwards, weaving her way through the scrub that grew thickly along the lake banks.

And then got another shock. A long arm of the lake cut across her front. It was deep and muddy and the banks thick with lantana and weeds so there was no way of crossing it. The only option was to detour east for a kilometre.

By the time she had done this she was puffing and sweating and ready for another rest. She had this in the bed of the large creek that led into the backwater. Now anxious about the time she only allowed herself five minutes and then puffed her way up the far slope and out onto another wide, rock-studded ridge. This had few trees and most were only about 3 metres high so she had to weave around them. It was tiring going. 1730hrs came around.

Suddenly a man's voice spoke from directly behind her. Rose jumped in fright and spun around, lifting the rifle to both hands as she did. And then another man spoke, again directly behind her. Panic started to rise as she could not see anyone. It was the word 'Over' that gave her the clue.

"That bloody radio!" she cried.

Putting Belinda down she shrugged off the backpack and extracted the radio. She had forgotten it but now realised it could be a vital tool in avoiding the men. Then another man spoke. It was Cousin James.

"All stations, the girl has one of our radios. Switch to alternate frequency, over."

Four radios replied, each just giving a number, not a name. Never having really heard the other men speak, Rose could not identify any.

*But four? I thought there were only four of them altogether?*

It was a worry and she puzzled over that. She was also annoyed as she did not know what the enemy's alternate frequency was. But she had done enough cadet field exercises and radio training to have an idea. She studied the keyboard on the front of the hand-held radio and found what she wanted.

*Scan button!* she thought. With a real feeling of achievement she pressed it and listened and soon found that the men had switched to Channel 28. She did the same and then listened.

They all checked back in with radio checks, not very well done by one she thought was Marvin, and army style by Lucas.

*He's been in the army alright,* Rose concluded. But she also knew that people who worked at mine sites did a lot of radio work and were good at it.

"Oh well, Bub-O, we can't stay here listening," Rose told an interested Belinda, who wanted to play with this new toy.

Rose hooked the radio to her pocket, pulled on the pack and picked up her little sister. After picking up the rifle she set off walking north again, moving out across a wide, open ridge. Then the radio began again. It was Cousin James and he warned them all that Rose now also had a rifle and was to be approached with caution. That drew a few sarcastic and pointed replies from men who obviously did not like Lucas.

"So what do we do boss? Over," called one, Norris Rose thought.

"Just watch and call us and we will deal with her," Cousin James snapped.

*Deal with me? What does that mean?* Rose wondered. She had a sick feeling in her stomach that it meant shoot her on sight.

The next call was to tell all the men to move to where Norris had his camp for more instructions and to be there within the hour.

*That is good news!* Rose told herself. *They will be all in one place and not scattered around watching every road junction or waterhole!*

Heartened by that, she hurried across another open space of about a hundred metres. She was very conscious that the sun was starting to sink, and she wanted to cover as much distance as she could to get to safety.

And then she heard it, much too late!

The helicopter came from behind and went clattering overhead a few hundred feet up before she had time to do anything. It then turned sharply and began to circle.

"Seen! Oh no!" Rose cried, her nervous system again going into overdrive.

# Chapter 19

## HELICOPTER

Rose stared up at the circling helicopter appalled. Her emotions went into overdrive, intense fear mixed with anger at being seen and a sharp sense of being defeated. "Damn!" she swore.

Belinda jerked up and pointed. "Cheppycopta!" she cried happily.

Rose stood there dithering for a few seconds while the helicopter went into a sharp right turn. She could see pilot looking at her and another man in the front. But should she run or prepare to fight, defend herself?

One of the images that was chilling her was from TV *Landline* programs of feral animals being shot from helicopters. It had been deadly, the shooters rarely missing. A quick glance around showed her that there was no chance of running. The nearest trees that might provide cover were a hundred paces away and the helicopter was coming back around, weaving to the side so that the port side was towards her.

And there was a rifle poking out of the open cabin window!

Rose heaved Belinda up out of her straps and just dropped her to the ground, then stepped aside and lifted the rifle. But she wasn't quick enough, that damned safety catch again! As she clicked it off and went to aim the helicopter swept past very low, only a few metres off the ground and 25 metres away. Very clearly she saw Cousin James's face. And he was aiming a rifle at her!

Several things happened simultaneously. Rose leapt sideways, Cousin James fired, and the pilot grabbed at his right arm, an appalled look on his face.

*Crack!*

Rose saw the brief puff of smoke of the rifle's discharge and knew the sound was the bullet snapping past her.

"Crack! Thump!" Captain Ross had explained. "The bullet is going faster than sound so you hear it first. Then you hear the sound of the gun going off. It's the one you don't hear that hits you!"

*Missed!*

Rose thought, bringing the butt of her rifle into her shoulder. Now she was savagely determined to protect Belinda and herself. She lifted the barrel and tried to follow the rapidly zooming machine. As she did, she experienced a wave of chill as shock and fear swept through her.

But she stood her ground and steadied her aim. The helicopter swung around and Rose got a glimpse of the pilot gesturing furiously and then his face turning in her direction. But how hard it was to hold the target in the circle of the telescopic sight, and to get the proper 'eye relief' (Where the telescopic sight goes black if the focus distance is wrong)!

Giving that up, Rose just aimed along the barrel. The helicopter flew into her line of sight and she pulled the trigger.

*Bang!*

Quickly she reefed the bolt back and slammed it forward again. *Do it quickly, Dad said, or the expanding cartridge can jam in the breech!*

Then she gasped with dismay. The helicopter did a sort of convulsive jerk and then spun sharply away. For a terrible few seconds, she feared she had actually shot the pilot. An awful feeling of guilt welled up. But then the helicopter came under control and turned away. She watched it circle, now about two hundred metres away. She could not see much but what was obvious was that the pilot was arguing or fighting with Cousin James.

That gave her hope. This grew as the helicopter did a sharp turn and then flew straight off to the west. *What is it doing now?* Rose wondered.

Gasping and trembling with reaction she lowered the rifle across her front and watched, dimly aware that Belinda was crying and grabbing at her left leg.

The helicopter kept flying straight and vanished into the distance. *Heading for Mount Isa Airport?* Rose wondered.

She was amazed that the incident, so potentially deadly, had ended so quickly. All she could think was that the pilot had been hired but was not part of the gang.

*If so then Cousin James will have some explaining to do!*

Rose sat down, resting the rifle across her knees. Then she remembered to apply the safety catch again as Belinda hugged her and also burst into tears. For a few moments all Rose could do was sit there sobbing and shaking. It took her nearly ten minutes to calm down.

What got her moving was the notion that Cousin James could use the radio to call his gang to home in on this area. She hadn't heard him call but that was even more worrying as she suspected he may have changed channels on the radio again. But she was very emotionally battered, realising she had deliberately shot at other human beings with serious intent.

*I am a horrible person!* she thought. But then she shook her head. *No I'm not! I was fighting for our lives,* she told herself. *And we had better move. Here we are still out in the middle of this big open area ten minutes later,* she rebuked herself.

Picking up Belinda and the rifle, she hurried on across the bare ground to the trees on the northern side. Here she found a hide among a clump of trees and weeds and stopped to have a drink, finding her mouth dry with emotion.

The sun was now striking in low through the trees and that got her moving again. "We need to cover as much ground as possible before dark," she told a complaining Belinda. It was nearly 1800hrs by then.

*Only another hour or so to dark,* Rose noted anxiously.

So she hurried on through the bush, going northwest up over another low, stony rise, the sun now striking the left side of her badly sunburnt face. As she walked, she scouted as well as she could. But all they saw were more cattle and then a couple of horses. These excited Belinda and she wanted to chase them so she could have a ride.

"Sorry Bub-O, no gee gees today," Rose replied.

"Want!"

"No, now be quiet. There might be more bad men around."

That seemed to work, and they covered another few hundred metres quickly. After crawling under another fence, Rose found the vegetation closing in again, lots of trees and lots of undergrowth: lantana, spikey bushes, rubber vine, even Scotch thistles.

"Ouch!" Rose cried as the bristles on a thistle brushed her thigh. "Bloody Scotsmen, bringing things like that to Australia!" she grumbled.

And then she smiled. It was an old argument between her mum and her dad. Her dad had suggested it was more likely to have been by a Scots woman who wanted something familiar in her garden.

Suddenly she came to a well-used dirt road. It wasn't graded but there had been a lot of traffic along it. That gave her pause for a minute and then she turned left and tried to follow it while walking through the scrub. But the tangle of weeds and lantana grew so dense she had to detour out onto the road frequently, anxiously aware that she was leaving a trail of clear boot prints in the grey dust.

*Can't be helped. They know we are in this area by now,* she rationalised.

And then she smelt cooking! Steak and frying onions! The tantalising aroma was wafting on the slight breeze. *People! And food!* Rose thought, her mouth salivating at the smells. She turned left towards it. *They might just be ordinary people and I can get them to take me to the police,* she thought.

But that also gave her pause. *Do I dare go to the police? Lucas said mum would die if I did. Oh, what can I do?* Rose agonised.

But she did think that they would be safe from immediate murder if there were a lot of witnesses, so she kept moving. The shrill sound of children's voices added to her hopes.

The children were calling, "Come on, Dad! We want a swim!"

*That sounds good*, Rose thought. To be safe and to get food! She hurried along the vehicle track towards the sounds, only to stop in her tracks, aghast.

On a low rise on a loop of the track stood a caravan and a grey 4WD dual-cab ute. On her side of the caravan were a collection of folding chairs, some camp tables, and a man with his back to her cooking on a large gas barbeque. And the man was Norris!

*Norris's camp! Oh no!* Rose thought.

Just to her right along the road she was on was a low bank covered with lantana and weeds. She quickly scuttled over to it, placing her hand over Belinda's mouth as she did. The lantana scratched but she barely noticed that as she pushed quietly in among it and crouched.

"Ssssh! Bub, bad men," she whispered.

To her relief, Belinda looked scared and nodded, holding her lips together to keep in the noise. Rose shuddered with delayed reaction and then moved to where she could see.

Norris was busy turning sausages and pieces of steak with tongs. Next to him was a table loaded with trays, bread rolls in plastic bags, saltshakers, plastic plates and so on. Several 'Eskis' were positioned on the ground nearby. It all looked very ordinary but was chilling to Rose.

*Is this the gang's hideout? Are they keeping mum a prisoner in that caravan?* she wondered.

That question was answered almost immediately. Out of the side door stepped a tired looking woman in dirty shorts and a floral blouse. Three primary school age children in bathers followed her: girl, boy, girl.

*Five or six, seven or eight and nine or ten,* Rose estimated.

"Come on, Dad!" the children shrilled, dancing and running around, the boy kicking a soccer ball.

Norris nodded and turned to the woman. "Take over cooking, Merle. These blokes will be here soon," he said.

The woman looked tired and down, but she nodded. Stepping forward to take the tongs she said, "How many of them are there? How much of this do I cook?"

"Cook the lot, there could be six or seven blokes and they will be hungry," Norris answered.

*They will be!* Rose thought with a chortle of malicious glee, *especially Lucas!*

"Yeah well, I got to feed the baby too!" Merle answered angrily. "So don't be long."

Norris called the children to him and hurried off down to the left. Rose heard splashing and shrieks of fun and realised there must be an arm of the lake there. Noting a clothesline hung with washing, which indicated the family had been there for a few days, she gave a wry smile.

*Obviously no crocs in the lake,* she thought. But she still thought she had done the right thing on the 'better to be sure than sorry' principle.

Then she got a real shock. The radio, which she had forgotten about, suddenly came to life. "Norris, you there, man? Over," called a man.

Rose gasped in fright and quickly reached up to click it off, her panicky fingers having to fumble with the switch. *Oh you drongo!* Rose berated herself. She prepared to sneak back out of sight.

But that food! Seeing it and smelling it was close to torture! Several ideas swirled in her mind: use the rifle to just take some food; or try to sneak up somehow? And then the problem resolved itself but gave her the option of taking a terrible risk. A baby cried from in the caravan and the woman put down the tongs and wiped her hands before walking to the door and going in.

"Now! Now is my chance!" Rose muttered. She found her heart suddenly hammering hard and she gritted her teeth. "Do it! Even if they see you, they know you are somewhere close," she told herself. So she put Belinda down. "Stay here and be very quiet Belinda," she said.

Gripping the rifle ready to fire, safety catch off, Rose pushed through a gap in the lantana, scrambled up the low bank and hurried across to the table. As she did, her eyes kept flicking to the door of the caravan and also to her left towards the lake. Luckily, the swimmers were just out of sight over the rise although she could see part of the lake in the distance.

*She's feeding the baby. I should have a couple of minutes,* Rose mused.

And then she blushed with embarrassment as she imagined what the woman was doing. Rose was just at that age where she was very self-conscious about her breasts, and even though at a certain level she understood that breast feeding was perfectly natural and that she would almost certainly do that herself if she had babies, she was still embarrassed. It was only a few months since she had often seen her own mother feeding Belinda and she blushed at that memory.

But now she was at the barbeque. The woman had moved all the meat she was cooking off the barbeque. On the hotplate a dozen eggs were frying. There were several trays loaded with already cooked sausages, steak and rissoles. For a few seconds Rose dithered, trying to decide what to take and worrying whether it would be noticed. Then she shook her head.

*Act girl! Get on with it!*

There was a loose plastic garbage bag lying with several others. Leaning the rifle against the table Rose picked it up, flicked it open, instantly regretting the noise, and then scooped a pack of six bread rolls into it. Grabbing the tongs she picked up six cooked sausages from a tray holding several dozen and dropped them in. Two rissoles from a batch of a dozen cooked ones followed, then two fried eggs. Two tomatoes from a nearby tray followed. On the table was a dish with tiny packets of salt and pepper. A handful were stuffed into her trouser pocket.

*Salt! We need that. Salt gets sweated out and it makes the nerves and muscles work properly,* she thought. She was so anxious her vision was going blurry.

Shrieks and laughter from her left alarmed her and made her think that the swimmers were returning so she put down the tongs. *That's enough. Hopefully they won't notice what is missing,* she thought.

Clutching the garbage bag on one hand she picked up the rifle and walked quickly back to where she could just see Belinda peeking through the bushes.

Pushing back into her hide Rose held out the bag. "Got us some food, Bub-O," she whispered. She found she was hyperventilating and so boosted by the thrill of what she had just done that she was trembling.

"Hungry! Want!" Belinda cried in a loud voice.

"Sssh! Quiet! Not here," Rose replied. Then she remembered the safety catch. Clicking it on she went to stand up. But the sound of an approaching vehicle sent her back to a crouch in the weeds. Fear and adrenaline surged again.

To her horror a white 4WD with Marvin and another man in it roared in, and it came along the track she was next to! All Rose could do was cover Belinda's pink hat and clothes and crouch low, heart palpitating with fear.

But the vehicle went past so fast that it stopped with a skid at the loop that led back up to the caravan. It revved its engine and reversed and for a horrible moment Rose thought they had been seen. But then it (and her and Belinda) were enveloped by the cloud of dust it had stirred up. Rose covered her mouth and nose, but Belinda started to cry out and cough. Luckily, this was masked by the man with Marvin also coughing, and swearing horribly, and by the roar of the vehicle's engine. It swung right and roared up to stop near the barbeque. Marvin and the other man climbed out, stretching and calling out.

The woman came to the door of the caravan, baby still to her breast. "Help yer selves, you blokes," she called, gesturing at the barbeque.

Rose managed to calm Belinda and stop her coughing. *Time to get out of here!* she told herself.

She hoisted Belinda to her hip and clutched the rifle and garbage bag in her left hand and started moving at a crouch behind the thin screen of scrub and weeds.

She had only moved five paces along the edge of the bottom track and could see a track junction ahead, where the bushes finished, when she heard another vehicle approaching from the north.

*Oh where will I hide?* She thought, thinking that the line of lantana and weeds on her left was too thin. *Can I cross the track and push into that in time?* Rose thought, glancing at the wall of lantana on the other side of the track.

# Chapter 20

## DIFFICULT CHOICES

Rose knew she had to make a difficult choice, one that might lead to disaster, and make it in a split second as the vehicle was approaching very fast and sounded just around the bend ahead of her. She glanced again at the wall of weeds and lantana across the track and then shook her head.

*We would never make it in time!*

So she went for the other bad option. Kneeling she pushed Belinda down and lay over her to try to cover all that pink.

"Sorry Bub. Sssssh! Bad men!" she hissed.

Belinda looked hurt and started to cry out, but Rose let go of the bag and rifle and put her hand over her mouth and then remembered to hide her own face. Quivering with fear, she hunched over Belinda, very aware that her backpack might be sticking up above the weeds.

And there was the vehicle, heading straight towards her. Out of the corner of her eye she watched it approaching. And suddenly its brakes came on and it slid to stop only ten metres away, wheels grating dirt and grit. Rose experienced such a spasm of fear that her heart seemed to choke her throat. And then the following dust enveloped the vehicle and her.

As before, she heard men swearing and cursing (They had also been driving with their windows down) and then the clash of gears. The engine note changed and the vehicle began moving. Rose risked a glance, blinking in the fine, grey dust. To her enormous relief, she saw that it was turning to her left to drive up the other track towards the caravan.

And sitting in the passenger's seat was Lucas! *Oh no! That is bad news!* Rose thought. But she had to smile at the sight of Lucas coughing and waving his hands to clear the dust!

The vehicle pulled up just to her left rear, close to the caravan. Its engine was turned off and the driver and Lucas climbed out. Rose still did not know if she had been seen or not, so she did not bolt as her first instinct told her to. Trembling with anxiety, she remained crouched over

Belinda, trying to soothe her little sister's protests at being treated so roughly.

But Rose quickly realised she had not been seen as she heard the other men begin calling out ribald comments, teasing Lucas for losing his rifle and his ute. Lucas was not amused.

"Shut up you blokes! Where's this food? I haven't had any bloody lunch," he snarled.

At which Rose grinned. *No, you haven't! We ate it!* she thought with malicious pleasure.

Now she was torn, stay and listen and risk being discovered, or try to get further away? Two things decided her: Belinda whimpering and hearing one of the men say, "What are we doing now?"

To which Lucas replied, "Waiting for the boss. He is going to brief us."

*That will be a while,* Rose thought. *He went back towards Mount Isa in the helicopter about half an hour ago. He will have to drive back here, unless he comes back in the helicopter.*

But she did not think that likely as it was already getting dark, the last of the sunlight even then on the treetops.

For a minute or so, Rose watched the men standing around the tables. They were all busy getting food or drinks. *Nobody will notice I took some,* she thought.

Then she realised that Belinda was tugging at her shirt front. "Wosie!" Belinda whimpered.

"Yes, Bubie?" Rose whispered back, acutely aware that her stomach was making noises.

"Are they bad men?"

"Yes, Bubie. Be very quiet and we will go away from them," Rose agreed.

"Hungry!"

"Ssssh!" Rose looked around to choose which way to go.

Her decision-making was then complicated by the sound of children getting closer. *Norris and his kids coming back from the lake.* She saw she could not go back the way she had come.

"And if I go on along this track, they will probably see me," she muttered.

She noted that the two tracks not only joined but the road went on for 50 metres or so before there was a bend. That only left the option of going across the track and through the lantana. The problems with that were that there wasn't much cover in the screen of bushes between the two tracks and the lantana looked very thick.

But the voices were getting closer, and she could not risk staying in case one of the children discovered them while playing. *With my luck that little boy will kick his ball into here,* she thought.

After taking a few deep breaths, Rose struggled to her knees. First, she picked up Belinda and then she gripped the rifle by its barrel with the garbage bag held between it and her fingers. Then she slowly stood up and edged back across the track, continually glancing to her left to check that Norris and his kids could not see her. As she moved, she remembered her boot prints and did a bit of scuffing.

There looked to be a bit of a gap in the lantana a few metres to the north side, so she risked being seen and made her way there. Then she began backing into the tangle. It was worse than she had thought, and she was quickly held, half in and half out of the tangled scrub. Desperate to get out of sight, she pushed back, hearing lantana crackle and bend. Dead leaves showered down inside the back of her shirt and her hat was swept off. This was snatched up and stuffed between her and Belinda.

"Ow!" cried Belinda, luckily drowned out by the cries of the children.

Rose glanced and saw that a prickly stem of lantana was scraping across Belinda's ankle, pulling the sock and drawing blood. Quickly she reached down and pulled Belinda's leg free. Then she kept moving, slowly making her way backwards out of sight.

And then another problem emerged: the prickles were tearing the plastic garbage bag. "Bugger!" Rose muttered.

She did not want to have the bag rip open and spill all the food. Trying to retrieve it among the lantana in the dark would be a real problem. Very carefully she unhooked the bag and lifted bag and rifle so they were in front of her and clear of the vines.

Moving backwards slowly, she was able to get right in among the lantana. To her enormous relief, the vegetation opened out a bit and she found a small gap between the clumps. Turning around carefully, she readjusted her load and set off facing forwards, Belinda, hat, the bag, and the rifle all gripped tightly to her front. Even so, the bag caught several more times and she nearly lost it all.

A small clear space allowed her to go left, north, and she went that way, now confident that she was out of sight. Noise was now the problem as she had to push through some bits of scrub. To her the crackling sounded very loud but there was no change to the chatter of the men around the food so she thought she would be alright.

It took her ten minutes to make her way through the tangle to the road going north. This was just around the first bend. By then it was twilight and visibility was fast going. To her dismay, she saw that the road was lined with what looked like an impenetrable tangle of weeds and lantana for the 75 metres or so to the next bend.

*If I walk on the road, I will leave foot prints,* she fretted.

But speed seemed more important, so she stepped out onto the road and moved along it backwards, trying to scuff out her tracks. It was slow but she felt happier with every step. By now the men could barely be heard but she saw the glow of a light spring up among the trees back at the caravan.

"Even better!" she thought, knowing from cadet exercises that the light would impair the bad men's night vision.

Once around the bend, which went left, Rose found she could get off the road among more scattered bushes and clumps of lantana and rubber vine. She stepped off on the left side and walked as quickly as she dared away from the road and then northwards. The red glow of the sunset on her left gave her the direction. As she did, she had to almost consciously suppress her fear of snakes. Each step was a little test of courage.

*Like soldiers walking into a minefield,* she thought.

The road wound its way through the trees and she found herself next to it a hundred metres further along. She was just about to stop and rest when she heard a distant motor. It was in front of her and heading her way fast.

*Cousin James arriving?* she wondered.

Which was bad news as he would soon give orders and the men would start searching. The glow of headlights appeared among the trees a few hundred metres ahead so she turned and quickly walked away from the road, seeking good shelter. Once she was at least fifty metres from the road she crouched down behind a big clump of lantana and watched the vehicle go racing past.

Driven by the urgent need to get away, Rose stood and rearranged her load, settling a tired little sister in her straps on the left and putting her hat back on her head. Then she hurried on, still marching north. But not for long. Five minutes later, she came to a vehicle track that went northwest across her front. It was only two wheel ruts in the grass and did not look very well used.

*Should I go along this?* she wondered.

"Yes," she told herself. "Get away from that other road. Those men will be driving along that."

So she turned left and began striding along one of the wheel ruts, until she remembered boot prints. Then she walked in the grass and weeds in the middle, until memories of the Death Adder slowed her down and drained her of courage. But having made the decision she persevered.

A couple of hundred paces further on, she came to where the track split at a big, dusty clearing with big trees. She stopped and looked anxiously around, puzzling over what she was looking at in the last glow of sunset. Then it came to her: that red mirror effect was the sunset reflected on water; and the long grey thing was a concrete dam.

That made sense. She knew the lake must be impounded by a dam, so she walked across to the end of it. It was only a metre or so wide at the top and a few metres high and looked to be between 75 metres and 100 metres long. She was about to step out onto it when she shook her head.

*That will not be a good place to be seen,* she thought.

Quickly casting around she saw that a dirt track went back south on her side of the lake and that the right hand one went down into what was obviously a riverbed on the downstream side of the dam. She opted for that. But it was a rough track with lots of washouts going down into the riverbed and then lots of stones and potholes, so she had to go slow and pick her way.

*I'll look stupid if I sprain my ankle now,* she told herself.

Where she was crossing the riverbed it was dry, but she could see patches of long grass and reeds indicating pools or swamps. The whole riverbed had been cleared of trees, but they began again in a thick belt a hundred metres downstream to her right. She found it a relief to get across, fearing to be caught by a vehicle in such an open and difficult place.

By this time the sun had fully set so she was having to go very slow, picking her way in the starlight. She struggled up the riverbank on the far side and came to a gasping halt. In the starlight she could just make out the wheel ruts curving back to the left. She deduced that the track was going southwards along the west side of the lake.

"No good to me," she said.

"What no good, Rosie?" Belinda asked.

"You awake, Bubby? You are good girl! You did very well back there being quiet," Rose said, hugging her.

"Hungwy," Belinda replied.

"Me too! Let's find somewhere safe to eat," Rose agreed.

And that meant away from a vehicle track. She set off into long grass and soon found herself almost wading in it as she angled northwards. That was such hard going that when she came to a cattle pad which looked to be going northwest, she decided to follow it. That was much easier going, even though she knew a tracker would soon find her boot prints. But she could not imagine the men walking around such places in the dark, even with a torch.

*So it will be daylight tomorrow before any such discovery might be made.*

The cattle pad led up out into more open country with scattered trees, short grass and spinifex and many clumps of rocks. She found one with a small dip on its western side and decided that would be a safe and suitable place. Carefully feeling her way she went down into the dip and then lowered bag, rifle, and Belinda to a shelf of smooth granite. With a sigh she sat down and took off her hat and then shrugged off the backpack.

"Oh thank God for that!" she muttered, mentally adding, *and to Captain Ross and my cadet training.*

Despite Belinda's impatience, Rose carefully arranged things. Rifle and hat put safely aside, she reached into the plastic bag and began taking out food. The inside of the plastic garbage bag was all sticky with cooking oil and fat, but she ignored that as trivia. When her fingers closed on a sausage, she at once pulled it out and passed it to Belinda.

"Here, Hungry Girl! Eat that," she said.

Belinda let out a little squeal of delight and at once stuffed the end of the sausage into her mouth and bit it off. As her sister chewed, Rose felt her own mouth salivate but she resisted the temptation to join in.

*Salt, Bubbie needs some salt,* she thought.

So she dug out the little paper packets and then had to stare in the starlight to see what they were. Each had a tiny sachet of salt and another of pepper. Knowing that pepper would result in a tantrum she stared hard but could barely discern the printing. So she felt the outside and then tore one sachet open and tasted it on a fingertip. It was salt.

She went to add it to the sausage Belinda was eating, only to discover it was all gone! "Oh you little greedy guts!" Rose said with a chuckle.

"Nover! More!" Belinda said, reaching out a chubby hand and fingers.

Rose found one in the bag and carefully dusted salt onto it. "It's got salt on it, Bubbie," she warned.

The chubby fingers closed on the sausage, and it was instantly stuffed into Belinda's mouth. Even in the starlight Rose could see her cheeks and jaw working.

*Good!* she thought. *Now one for me.*

She found another sausage amid the greasy mess and was sprinkling salt onto it when a flicker of light attracted her attention. She paused and looked anxiously towards where she had seen it. Then it came again, and she saw treetops being lit up. At first she thought it was a torch beam, but then she saw it was stronger than that.

*A spotlight!* she thought with dismay. She tensed ready to grab everything and either run or hide.

But then she saw that the beam was actually a long way away, back on the east side of the river. And it was moving fast, flashing around among the trees. It dawned on her that the light was not being carried by a person walking but was on a vehicle, moving along a road. At that, she sighed with relief. The men obviously had no real idea where she was. Equally, she was now glad she had opted to get away from the road and to cross the river.

"I don't think they will look for us over here," she told herself.

But she also reasoned that it would make it very difficult for her to walk north near the road to get to the highway. "Drat!" she muttered. It seemed that every time she tried to go in a particular direction, she was forced to go in another.

Satisfied they were safe, Rose bit off a mouthful of sausage and began chewing. It was bliss! After days of hunger she relaxed and enjoyed eating. Belinda wanted another sausage, but Rose found her a piece of steak. After adding salt she handed it over.

"Chew on that, Bub-O. That will slow you down," she said.

She reached back into the bag and her fingers closed on one of the tomatoes. She dug this out, grimacing at the slimy feel and regretting that it was almost certainly going on the sleeve of her shirt. The tomato was placed aside on the rock. The packet of bread rolls followed and then the other tomato.

Now Rose did a bit of thinking about food. She remembered sliding two fried eggs into the bag, so they were found and put on the rock. Next, she dug out the steaks and then felt around, discovering the badly broken up remains of two rissoles. The biggest piece of a rissole was extracted and salt added. She chewed on that with real pleasure.

*Lucky I'm not a gourmet eater!* Rose thought.

It was one of her mother's little tragedies, they often went to flash restaurants or upper-class dinners or parties, but she preferred plain food and they had trouble providing that. And the high-class chefs were horrified that she wanted hard fried eggs (Turned over please) and liked her steak charred.

As she sat there happily munching food she liked, she noted another vehicle moving north with a spotlight. *They must be going to search along all the roads and tracks,* she deduced. But would they keep it up all night?

She got the answer to that almost immediately, and straight from the enemy. Not having heard the radio for hours she had forgotten it but now she turned it on. Immediately it squawked out loud and clear. It was Marvin.

"Hey Boss!" he called, "I'm at that road junction. How long do I have to stay here?"

Cousin James answered, "All night, and stay awake! And you others, keep driving back and forth along that highway. If you need to go and get fuel let me know so we can make sure there are at least two vehicles covering that ten kilometres all the time. That kid must not reach the highway or contact anyone, got it!"

There were few 'Roger, overs' but their radio procedure was poor. Cousin James ended by rebuking them for it and then snapped, "So stay off the radio unless you have something to report! Out!"

"Well, that was interesting, Baby Boo," Rose said, clicking the radio off as she did.

"I not Baby Boo!" Belinda cried through a mouthful of half chewed food. "I Ball of Bounciness."

"You will be if you eat all this," Rose agreed with a grin. But she was also dismayed.

*If those men are watching road junctions and driving up and down the highway with spotlights it is going to be very hard to get there and then flag down a vehicle,* she thought.

"With my luck the car I wave down will be one of them!" she muttered.

That got her thinking while she ate. The deduction was that she needed to walk more than ten kilometres to the side so that she was outside the stretch of highway the men were patrolling.

*They can't watch all one hundred kilometres between Mount Isa and Cloncurry,* she reasoned.

Belinda had finished her steak, so Rose handed her a tomato. There was a murmur of delight, followed by squelching, munching sounds. Rose shuddered, picturing the mess that must be accumulating on Belinda's cheeks and around her mouth.

*And on her shirt and pants!*

After that Rose fed her small pieces of fried egg, which she ate but without enthusiasm. At the same time she ate the other egg, really enjoying that even though it was cold. She could almost feel her energy level returning as the food went down. When Belinda demanded more Rose undid the packet of bread rolls and handed her one. She began to happily munch on that.

Rose enjoyed a steak with lots of salt in a bread roll. *That's enough for now,* she thought.

So she had a big drink, the lake water tasting a bit muddy but still better than the cattle trough water. Belinda was happy to drink it as well.

The girls sat there for more than an hour and Rose felt both satisfied and determined. *Cousin James and his henchmen are really worried,* she thought. *So now I need to get help, adult help.*

But who? And how? That terrible threat to kill her mother was now haunting Rose and causing her lots of mental anguish and indecision. She did decide that she needed to move further away from the dam area. But then she debated whether she should risk moving in the starlight or wait until the moon came up.

*We often walk in starlight on cadet exercises,* she remembered.

So she decided to go, for at least another kilometre or two. She packed everything ready and pulled on her pack. She then made Belinda comfortable in her straps before picking up hat, plastic bag, and rifle. For a minute she stood staring down, checking that she had not left anything behind. A patch of white caught her eye and she bent and picked up a used salt and pepper sachet. Then she set off following the cattle pad. It went on northwest, heading across a wide rise with yet another stony hill on her right.

It was easy walking, but the effort soon began to tell. All her chafed bits began to rub and her muscles began their usual complaints. Her feet still felt heavy and had sore soles. And it was cold! A breeze had sprung up from the west and was enough to quickly chill Belinda and to make the evaporating perspiration on Rose's arms and face feel quite unpleasant. But she persevered and plodded on, thankful that Belinda had fallen asleep.

At a few minutes to ten she finally stopped, eyes gritty and exhaustion making her stagger. She had crossed three dry creeks and was on the rise to yet another rocky knoll. Her estimation was that she had walked five kilometres in three hours. And in all that time she had not seen a single light or heard a single vehicle. It was through she and Belinda were the only humans on the planet.

*Australia certainly is big, and empty!* she thought.

Having decided to stop she plodded on until she found a nice clump of rocks. Hoping there wasn't a resident Death Adder she put everything down and settled them both in a hollow out of the breeze. After walking a few paces to have a pee she returned and snuggled a slightly shivering Belinda close against her and then sat staring out into the night. She did not think the men would find them while they slept.

*And they will bloody well regret it if they do!* she told herself, gripping the rifle tightly.

# Chapter 21

## DETERMINATION

Rose set the alarm in her watch for 0400hrs. Now she was determined to reach safety that day. When the alarm went off, she started in fright and then quickly stopped the soft beeping noise and stood up.

*I wish I had a map,* she thought as she crouched for a morning pee in the cold. *Sick of this blistering hot during the day and freezing at night. I need to end this.*

She wasn't sure how she would save the situation, being deeply bothered by the threat to her mother's life, but she knew the drama could not go on. Misery welled up when she thought about how upset her parents must be, not knowing whether she and Belinda were free or dead in the desert.

"Poor Mum!"

As she stood there worrying, Rose heard a noise that made her stiffen. It was a vehicle! But was it the men? She turned in the direction of the noise and saw the unmistakable beam of vehicle headlights a few kilometres to the north. But the light was heading east and the sound was of a big vehicle's engine.

"That might be a truck on the Barkly Highway," she told herself. It sounded too big to be one of the men's vehicles. Then she saw another glow of lights going the other way. "That is the highway!" she told herself.

It looked tantalisingly close, but there was no way she was going to head directly towards it. *Not until I've got further away from where the men are searching.*

To check if she could glean any more information from the enemy, she turned on the radio. But it was silent. Belinda was woken and persuaded to have a pee as well. The little girl was shivering and began crying.

"Mummy! Want Mummy!" she sobbed.

Rose cheered her up as much as she could by pointing to stars and the moon, which was just coming up. She was cheered up herself by noticing what looked like the loom of lights off to the west.

*Is that glow from Mount Isa?* she wondered.

Remembering Captain Ross pointing out the loom of Townsville and Charters Towers on weekend bivouacs at Macrossan. Townsville, she knew it was a hundred kilometres from Macrossan and Charters Towers 20.

*Have I walked that far?* she wondered, trying to add up the distances over the last four days. She knew Mount Isa was a town of about 20,000 people, twice the size of Charters Towers. *So maybe it is?* That was hopeful! Although what she would do when she got there, she did not know.

After picking everything up and getting Belinda comfortable, she started walking northwest again. Her logic was that she had to get past the ten kilometres of the Barkly Highway that she believed the crooks were patrolling to catch her. But that meant extra distance. She gritted her teeth and made her legs function.

As usual all the aches and pains quickly returned and then slowly subsided to a dull consciousness of hurting, seemingly all over. It was easy going, almost no ground cover. Even the spinifex grew in scattered little clumps. It was downhill for half a kilometre to the inevitable dry creek, the bed of rocks and pebbles. Then it was up a similar long, gentle slope to a low, rolling north-South ridge which she crossed at about 0450hrs.

The pattern then repeated itself except that ahead of her, several kilometres away, the silhouette of another line of jagged rocky hills showed up against the loom of Mount Isa's lights (She was sure that was what it was now). In yet another dry creek bed she rested for ten minutes and then forced herself to get up and plod up a very long, gentle slope for nearly two kilometres. The ground changed to being almost bare and composed of a layer of pebbles which crunched under her boots.

By 0600hrs with the first glimmer of dawn behind her she crossed another watershed, passing between two stony ridges. Finding another spot out of the wind, which had swung around to the south and become even colder, she sat to rest. The usual dawn wonder of grey to pink to red brought her some relief. But daylight meant danger, so she made herself get up and move on.

A few minutes later the radio crackled and she started in alarm. Then she put her ear to it. It was a man whose voice she did not recognise.

"Hey Boss, how much longer we gunna keep this up? Over."

"As long as we need to," snarled an angry Cousin James. "Just keep driving back and forth. Over."

"What about breakfast? And I need fuel," the man said in a voice that clearly carried disgruntlement.

"You go now. When you get back, tell me and Carson can go. Over"

"Okay Boss, out."

Rose almost cheered on hearing that. The men had been driving back and forth all night and were obviously not happy! She switched the radio off again to conserve its battery.

And then she got a real glimpse of hope from the highest point on the gap. Off to the west she noted a sort of pale smudge above a black vertical line. It was silhouetted against the sky. Then she saw another thin vertical line with peculiar banding. When she realised what she was looking at Rose let out a little cry. "See those little things sticking up Belinda? They are the chimneys at the Mount Isa Mine."

For a few seconds she savoured that sight of possible salvation. The first bar of sunlight reached out to touch the rocks on the high points to right and left and ahead and then lit up those two massive chimneys, the red and white banded one in particular. But daylight also revealed some big hills almost in their direct path and in the distance, between her and Mount Isa, a range of rugged mountains.

That helped her choose the best route. As she went down to the next creek she angled more to the north to go around that end of the hills. Belinda began to whimper and grizzle.

"Bwekfast!" she cried.

Rose reluctantly stopped and dug out a bread roll and gave it to her. Then she picked her up again and resumed walking. *I just want to get this over!* she thought, gritting her teeth to ignore the pain as she struggled across another steep little gully.

There were more creeks and gullies down there and lots of rock outcrops. But almost no ground cover, just the sandy soil with a few tufts of grass of spinifex, a scattering of small trees or big open patches of the 'gibber' plain.

She remembered her Geography teacher talking about them: areas where the small pebbles, gibbers, were cemented together by mineral salts and which were then polished smooth by windblown sand so that they shone in the sunlight. And to her amazement, they did.

As she came up out of the next dry creek through a thicket of twisted and spindly mulga trees, Rose saw that her route was blocked by a single big hill. The choices were to turn right and go directly north or turn left and go around the southern end of it.

*Have I come ten kilometres yet?* she fretted.

She decided that she hadn't so she set a course to the south of the big hill. Knowing that the men were out on the highway made her determined to avoid them.

By 0700hrs they were on the crest of yet another parallel ridge directly south of the hill. She had to stop as her fingers were cramping and Belinda was still shivering. Rose found a spot among some rocks and organised a better breakfast. By turning the plastic bag inside out she was able to collect all the crumbled pieces of the rissoles, and these were placed in bread rolls with some salt. There wasn't much mince in each, but it added to the taste and made them palatable. Belinda ate hers while chattering away about the dragonfly she could see nearby. Rose allowed her to have a big drink, confident now they would be safe by sundown. A crow came and perched on a nearby branch, cocking its head and eyeing them with its beady little eyes.

After 20 minutes Rose made herself get up. It took over five minutes to pack up, load up and get stiff and sore muscles into action. The empty plastic bag was left, shoved into a crack between two rocks.

The downslope was a problem. The area to the right was cut up by a cluster of gullies and she took the easiest path, which was to the left of them. But then she discovered that she had a larger creek between her and the highway. She could now hear traffic noises all the time, a steady rise and fall of distant motors. She knew from experience that it was a very busy highway. Fairly frequently she heard louder engine noises and guessed they were from 'Road Trains': huge trucks with three or four trailers. They were very common on the Flinders and Barkly Highways.

Her path was now down another long slope with what looked like five or more kilometres of relatively flat ground ahead. The creek she was walking beside was trending northwest, so she stayed roughly parallel to it, keeping a hundred metres or so away to avoid the small gullies that fed into it. There were three larger tributaries she had to cross, resting at each. The slope was, to her amazement, mostly covered with her old friend the sticky bushes. Luckily, they were widely spaced on that barren ground so she could weave a course through them without getting seed pods all over her. But they did restrict visibility to about fifty metres.

*Except from above,* Rose noted, looking up at the clear blue sky.

But she was no longer worried about the helicopter. She believed Cousin James was in a vehicle somewhere behind her and that the helicopter pilot had not been part of the gang.

*He certainly acted appalled when Cousin James tried to shoot me,* Rose reasoned.

But it was slow going and she had to keep stopping to rest. It became a real teeth-gritting slog: walk, rest, walk, rest. 0800hrs came and went and she was still among the bushes. A fence had to be negotiated. It wasn't until 0825hrs that she reached another big creek that cut across her path. This one flowed north and she decided that was far enough.

"I will cross over and follow it to the highway," she told Belinda.

The creek was 25 metres wide with steep banks and it took her a few minutes to find a safe way down. The bed was the usual rocks and sand and full of paperbarks. She thankfully rested in the shade of one for five minutes before yet again struggling to her feet and pushing up onto the other bank.

She came out on a wide area of flat country almost bare of ground cover. There were plenty of the gnarled and twisted mulga trees but there was almost no spinifex or grass. The whole area was gibbers. It was pleasant enough in the shade but by now the air was hot and Rose made the unpleasant discovery that the gibber plain was not a nice environment. She found that in the direct sunlight they not only produced a horrible glare but that they were hot, reflecting the sun's rays and radiating absorbed heat. She could feel the heat through the soles of her boots. Because there was very little spinifex Rose tried getting Belinda to walk but after less than a hundred metres the little girl put her arms up to be picked up and began to complain of being hot.

Reluctantly, Rose hoisted her up again and then went to settle her in the straps. "Sit still Belinda!" she snapped, being tired and grumpy and hot.

"Chooken!" Belinda cried, wriggling and pointing.

*Chooken?* Rose wondered.

Her eyes followed Belinda's pointing finger. To her surprise, she saw a large emu only about 50 metres away. The giant bird was picking at something among a patch of grass. But Belinda's cry had alerted it to their presence, and it stopped eating and lifted its head to study them.

Rose had to laugh. "That is not a chicken, Baby Bee. That is an emu," she explained.

"Eemoo!" Belinda cried, jerking excitedly and staring.

Rose was fascinated as well. She had seen them in the distance on various drives but had never seen one this close. Forgetting the heat, flies, and discomfort she held her little sister while she studied the bird. The tiny head and big eyes she found curious, as was the long neck, but it was the spindly legs and huge three-toed feet with their nasty looking talons that really interested her. She had never heard of anyone being attacked by an emu, not like the jungle cassowaries, so she was not afraid.

Belinda wanted to go to the emu but Rose shook her head. "No. Too big for you," she said.

As she did, her eyes noted sunlight reflecting on silver in the distance beyond the emu. *Buildings!* she thought.

For a few moments her hopes shot up as she thought it might be a farm. That would mean someone to help, an adult. *And it will all be over.* But then she shook her head. *What story will I tell the people?* she wondered. The threat to her mother's life made it difficult to come up with a simple and plausible tale.

She began walking towards the buildings. That alarmed the emu which trotted further away and warily watched them from a distance. Belinda was upset but Rose did not care. She hurried through the 'forest' of mulga and across the gibber plain, heedless of the heat and glare and the crunch of her boots breaking the pebble crust. But as she got closer, she became cautious and slowed to stand behind a tree to study the place. What she saw was disappointing. She found she was looking at a long, open-sided shed with only a back wall of corrugated steel sheeting. Nearby were two small, corrugated iron buildings which she thought might be toilets, and some sort of store shed. Beyond them was an open structure with stalls and a roof and no walls. For a few moments she thought it might be some sort of equine facility with horse stalls but then she noted a long earth mound in the distance.

*No. It is a shooting range, a rifle range,* she told herself.

And there was obviously no-one there. That cast her down and she quietly swore. Belinda was uncomfortable so Rose placed the butt of the rifle on the ground and leaned the muzzle against the tree trunk, and immediately reproved herself for such bad practice.

*Captain Ross said never put a rifle barrel against a tree trunk. Pieces of bark could fall into the muzzle and when you shoot that could burst the barrel or blow out the breech.*

So she moved to lean it across a small branch. She lowered Belinda in the shade and took off her backpack to have a drink. It was nearly 0900hrs and it was hot already. And the flies were becoming more annoying.

Belinda jerked in the middle of drinking and pointed. "Eeemoo!"

Rose looked and saw the emu stalking off in the distance, heading for the creek they had recently crossed. But it was the traffic noise that was her focus. She was anxious now, even scared. She knew that going near that highway was a real risk. But it had to be done! Reluctantly she put away the drink bottle and pulled on the backpack, picked Belinda and the rifle up and walked out into the blazing sunlight.

The glare was so intense she had to squint as the sunlight reflected up off the polished gibber plain. She shook her head and gritted her teeth.

*Get it over with girl!* she told herself.

She estimated that the highway could not be more than a kilometre or two away now and there were straggly belts of trees between her and it. She went directly north and soon came to a gravel road that obviously led from the rifle range to the highway.

Rose settled down to a steady slog. Sweat dripped from her nose, and trickled into her eyes, the salt stinging and annoying. Her shirt became damp from perspiration. Belinda grizzled and wanted food and then demanded they follow the emu. But that bird had now vanished. As she glanced around Rose noted that the heat shimmer had begun.

"God it's hot!" she muttered.

She reached a sparse belt of trees. A small water course ran across the range and the road went into a tiny dip to cross it. Beyond, on her left, was another huge open space and she realised that was another rifle range, a long clearing extending away from her for a kilometre or so to the foothills of more rugged, stony hills. The gravel road wound on into a small area of trees and grass and as she plodded towards it she glimpsed a huge truck go roaring past.

*The highway is just there!*

The knowledge that she must now take a huge risk got her heart beating faster and she took several deep breaths. The distance to the trees and a gate reduced with every step, 100 metres, 75 metres, 50 metres, 25. Rose was scared and knew it. Her mind was racing with plans and options.

*What story do I tell that gets us to safety but doesn't set alarm bells going or warn the crooks?* Through the screen of bushes and trees she could see cars and trucks whizzing by every minute or so and in both directions. *I shouldn't have any difficulty waving down a vehicle,* she thought. But would it be the men!

The need to have a story immediately ready was reinforced when she saw that there was a caravan attached behind a white 4WD parked on the gravel area just outside the gate. There were two people there. Which brought Rose to a standstill.

*How do I explain the rifle?* she puzzled.

She knew it was against the law for children under 18 to have firearms unsupervised. But she liked that rifle and had grown attached to it!

With a vague notion she might need it again she decided to hide it. Off to her right was a stand of mulga trees growing among several clumps of bushes. Deciding there would do she turned off the road and walked over to the bushes. The rifle was then safely placed out of sight. But leaving the weapon took more courage.

*Now I am defenceless,* she thought. It was a very uneasy sensation.

That done she shifted Belinda to her other hip and started walking towards the gate. "Don't talk about bad men, Belinda," she said. "You tell people about the emu or the birds."

On arriving at the gate, Rose stopped and examined the gate. It was locked by a chain and padlock. She looked along the fence both ways to find the easiest place to crawl under the fence. As she did, she studied the two people. To her disappointment they looked quite elderly, in their seventies or even eighties. 'Grey Nomads' was the expression she had heard her parents use. There was a thin man with a grey moustache and grey hair and a more solidly built woman in slacks and cotton top. Both wore leather shoes and hats. They had been doing something to the wheel of the caravan. Both stopped and stared as Rose proceeded to take off the pack and place it under the fence.

Now that the moment had arrived Rose was torn. *What story do I tell, and do I go to the police and possibly put Mum at risk?*

# Chapter 22

## MOUNT ISA

Rose crawled under the barbed wire fence and stood up, heart hammering with anxiety and indecision. As she dusted her hands and clothing, she was aware that both of the old people were staring at her in astonishment. Feeling both anxious and unreasonably embarrassed, she tried hard to give a smile. She turned and carefully lifted Belinda over the fence and put her on her hip before facing the old couple again.

The old lady half-frowned and half-smiled. "Are you alright?" she asked.

Rose managed the smile. "Yes, thanks. Can you give us a lift to Mount Isa please?" she asked. She was very conscious of the cars whizzing by and the threat they represented.

Both old people looked surprised. The old man replied, "Are you in trouble? You look like you've been in the wars."

*We have!* Rose thought. But she converted the smile to a wry grin. "We have had a bit of trouble."

The old man gestured behind her. "Should you have been in there?"

Rose looked and got a nasty little shock. On the gate were big signs saying: DANGER, KEEP OUT and 'Department of Defence Firing Range, Entry Prohibited' along with a lot of fine print she did not have time to read but sounded all legal and threatening. All she could do was shrug.

"We are alright. We just need a lift. We haven't done anything wrong."

The old man looked doubtful, but Belinda broke the ice when she suddenly jerked around and pointed out at the highway.

"Big twuck!" she cried.

A road train consisting of prime mover and three big tipper ore wagons went roaring past. The driver did not even glance at them. But the driver of the next vehicle coming from the direction of Mount Isa did. It was a white 4WD and the man driving stared hard at them. Rose did not recognise him but that stare really bothered her.

*We need to get off this highway quickly, before the men come along,* she thought. "Please, we just need a lift. We've had a bit of trouble, but we haven't broken the law."

The old man gestured to the sign and shook his head. "Apart from that, trespassing on Defence land," he said.

"We didn't know! We came from the other direction," Rose said.

The old woman frowned. "Do your parents know where you are?" she asked.

Rose shook her head. "No, and please, we need to get back quickly so they don't get more worried," she said, pleading now.

The old man frowned. "We don't have a child seat," he said, gesturing to the 4WD vehicle in front of the caravan.

Rose began to get anxious and could feel tears starting. "Please! We must get there so Mum and Dad don't get into trouble! It is only for a few minutes."

That wasn't quite how she'd wanted to word it, but it seemed to work. Another 4WD raced past on the highway, heading for Mount Isa this time and she became even more anxious.

The old woman looked at the old man and said, "We can do that, Cyril. We can move a bit of stuff in the back."

"Oh alright," Cyril, replied.

He obviously wasn't happy but moved to put the tools away and to open the back passenger door. Rose heaved a sigh of relief and then got another little problem.

The old woman asked, "And what's your name, dearie?"

Rose was tempted to lie, to use a made-up name or her middle name but then she glanced at Belinda and shook her head. *Baby-Boo is sure to call me Rose and then they will think I am a liar,* she thought.

"Rose, and she is Belinda, the Ball of Busyness," she said, deliberately omitting their family name.

At that, the old woman smiled. "She looks like she could be. You can put her down now dearie. You look quite worn out. Have you walked far?"

"A fair way," Rose answered, not wanting to get drawn into any explanations.

From the old couple's demeanour and speech she had a suspicion that they knew nothing, that there was no public search going on for two little girls missing in the bush. That was good. But she kept holding Belinda.

Old Cyril frowned and said, "Have you run away from home or something?"

Rose shook her head. "No, but we have been walking in the bush. Mum and Dad don't know where we are and we want to get back before they... before they realise and get worried and... and make a fuss."

Both of the old people frowned at that, and Rose did not think that Old Cyril was convinced.

"Would you like a cold drink?" the old woman queried.

"Yes please!" Rose agreed and Belinda squealed with delight.

The old woman, Violet, the old man called her, went around to the other side of the car, opened the door and reached in to get a cup and then filled it from a small fridge in the back. Belinda was given the drink first and as she went to put it to her mouth Rose said, "What do you say?"

Belinda looked guilty and stopped, the cup just short of her mouth. "Thankoo!" she said. Then she gulped it down so fast that a good deal went down the sides of her mouth and onto her shirt.

Violet looked concerned. "My, you are thirsty!" she said.

She refilled the cup and handed it to Rose. It was cold fruit cordial and to her it tasted just wonderful. She managed to restrain the urge to quaff it down but did take a few big gulps.

By then Old Cyril had cleared a seat. "You will both have to squeeze in here," he said.

The middle of the back seat was still stacked with suitcases, plastic boxes and pillows. Rose nodded and handed the cup back. Carefully she lowered Belinda and then took off her backpack. This was placed on the floor of the car and then she seated herself. Old Cyril held out the seat belt.

"Put this on first and then you will have to hold the little girl."

Rose did so and Belinda allowed herself to be picked up by the old lady and was seated on Rose's lap. Rose sighed with relief and now tears did start.

*Safe, at least for the moment!* she thought. They were in a car with other people and on the way to safety! It was cramped and uncomfortable, but heaven compared to lying in the spinifex!

Old Violet went back to the Eski and then came back and held out two small chocolates. "Would you children like a chocolate?"

Rose sniffled and wiped away her tears and nodded. "Yes, thank you."

Belinda snatched the one offered to her. Rose grabbed it. "You say 'Thank You', Bubby-Boo!" she reproved.

"Sorwy!" Belinda said. "Tank ooo!" Then she looked baffled. Holding out the chocolate she said, "Open please."

Rose did. Belinda almost snatched the chocolate from her and it began to rapidly vanish, smears of it appearing around Belinda's mouth. As Rose began to open her own, she noted the two old people talking quietly at the front of the car. The old man cast her an anxious glance and she blushed.

*They don't know what to make of us,* she thought. *They think we are up to some mischief.*

But she did not want to make any explanation and was mightily relieved when both adults got into the seats in front and the car was started. Rose was even more relieved when they pulled out onto the highway and started driving towards Mount Isa. After a few minutes travel, they ended up stuck behind another large Road Train, more ore tippers. Rose did not care about that. The car was ten times faster than walking.

*We will be in Mount Isa in a few minutes,* she thought.

But then what? When she had first thought about it she had the plan of getting to Mount Isa and then of finding a phone and trying to locate her parents or some relative she could trust. But she now realised she knew only her parent's mobile numbers and she had no money and nor did she know any place where she and Belinda could hide or wait.

*I don't know a soul in Mount Isa,* she thought.

Then she realised she did. She knew a few cadets who had been on annual camps or leaders courses with her. But none of them were friends and she wasn't sure where to find them or what story to tell.

It was all very worrying and the 'what to do next' rapidly become very urgent as she saw they were driving through the outskirts already. Ahead through the windshield she saw those huge chimneys standing up tall against the sky. The chimneys were still kilometres ahead but were so high they dominated the place.

They drove in along the main road, passing a motel Rose thought the family had stayed at once, and she recognised a caravan park on the right. Then she saw a telephone box on the footpath outside a shop.

*A phone! But who can I call?* she wondered. *Apart from Mum and Dad's number I don't know any numbers at all!*

All she could think of was somehow getting connected to the office at the Mt Egbert Mine.

She found she was shivering with anxiety and reaction. Belinda was no help, looking out and babbling away in baby language and pointing at things. Then Rose thought she heard the old couple say the word 'police'. Bitterly, she realised she probably had no choice.

*Lucas might have just been saying that to deter me from going to the police because that's what they don't want,* she thought. But it was a horrible dilemma. What if he wasn't bluffing?

Rose sobbed and then wracked her brain while watching the buildings they were passing: a museum she had been to when she was much younger, businesses and ahead on the left, a large shopping centre she remembered shopping at.

As they approached it, the old man called over his shoulder, "Where do you want to get out?"

With a sob, Rose replied, "Take us to the police station, please."

The two old people exchanged significant glances and the old man replied, "Do you know where it is?"

Rose shook her head. "No. I don't live here," she said, then realised she was giving away information she had not meant to.

Old Cyril muttered and said something to the old woman and they drove on past the big shopping centre. Rose expected them to use a GPS navigator or at least a mobile phone to find the police station, but they used the more old-fashioned method of following street signs.

As car and caravan swung into the street indicated by the sign at the corner, Rose looked out ahead and saw the police station on the left. Her heart sank into her boots with dread. Then she glanced over the top of the pile of pillows and luggage. And gasped!

Sitting in a white 4WD parked on the other side of the street was one of the men she had seen at the barbeque! *One of the men! And he is watching the police station!* she thought, aghast.

At that moment, the old man was driving slowly, obviously looking for somewhere he could park the car and caravan.

"Oh don't stop!" Rose cried. "Drive on! There's one of those men."

Both old people glanced back and gave her a sharp look. This increased to actual surprise when Belinda also called out, "Bad men!"

"What do you mean by one of those men?" Old Cyril queried.

He kept driving straight ahead, much to Rose's relief. "There are men looking for us," she admitted. "I... I can't really explain but please, just drive somewhere else."

Old Violet called from in front of her, "This is very serious, isn't it?"

"Yes Miss, er... Missus," Rose admitted. She was trembling now as fear and disappointment swamped her nervous system. "Very serious. Please, the men must not see me going to the police station."

Rose was actually afraid the men might just shoot her on the footpath but did not dare suggest anything so outrageous. Nor did she have any real proof that this might be so. But she was sure she had seen one of the men.

*And if they have someone sitting all the time watching the police station the men must be really worried.*

With that thought the dreadful threat of her mother then being killed swamped Rose's mind. She sobbed and battled tears, trying to come up with plan.

Old Cyril had driven to the next intersection and turned left. Rose noticed that they were right in the business district of the town, people and cars everywhere and was appalled that she did not feel at all safe.

*We were safer in the bush!* she thought.

Old Cyril drove around several streets and ended up on a street outside the big shopping centre. There were long parking spaces there beside the footpath, designed for car and caravan combinations and luckily one was empty, and he was able to drive straight into it. After parking he pulled on the handbrake and switched off the engine then turned to look hard at her.

"I think you had better explain."

"I can't, not really," Rose replied.

She was still shivering with reaction. Her whole plan of reaching safety and handing it all over to the adults had just crumbled and she felt more at risk than before.

"Try," Old Cyril coaxed.

At that moment, two children and a lady walked past, having just come from the shop and they were eating ice creams. Belinda saw this and pointed.

"Want!" she cried.

"Belinda, not now!" Rose croaked, tears starting again.

"Want!" Belinda shrieked, "Hungwy!"

She started kicking and Rose was sure a full-scale tantrum was about to burst forth. Luckily, Old Violet thought so too.

"What a good idea," she said. "I am sure you children would like an ice cream." She got out of the car.

Rose knew it was a good idea but she did not want to be seen walking around a shopping centre. But she could not see any alternative. *If I am going to persuade these people to help I have to co-operate and tell them something.*

So she told Belinda to calm down. "We will get you an ice cream, Hungry Bub."

Belinda nodded. "I hungwy!" she said, but luckily the storm was averted and she smiled.

When Old Violet opened the door and held her arms out for her, she put her own arms up. Rose did not expect Belinda to go to Old Violet and was also scared lest it was some sort of trap, but it was too late. Belinda happily allowed herself to be lifted out. Rose then climbed out and stood on the footpath, leg muscles stiff but trembling and every nerve alert. An open place like that was the last place Rose wanted to be in broad daylight. She was aware that the next street up was the main road and she kept glancing nervously around.

Old Violet lifted Belinda slightly in her arms and sniffed. "Unless I am mistaken, I think this young lady has done something," she said.

Rose blushed. From the smell it was all too obvious! "Can we go to a change room?" she asked (Only later did she realise she could have suggested the caravan).

Old Cyril locked the car and the four of them walked down across the busy car park to the shopping centre entrance. As they did, Rose felt very much like the proverbial beetle crossing the white ceiling.

*If any of those men drive past now our goose is cooked,* she thought, then realised she had used the same expression as Lucas. *Oh what story can I tell these people?*

Part of her problem was that she now thought they were a nice old couple, and she had a vague notion that telling them the truth would implicate them and possibly put them at risk. Belinda obviously liked them as she kept chattering to Old Violet and pointing around at things. It was very obvious that Old Violet was a mother.

*Even a grandmother,* Rose surmised.

Thankfully, they went through the sliding doors into the air-conditioning but then a different fear took over, that one of the men might be doing some shopping! Rose found she was so upset that her vision was blurring and she found she was gasping as though she had run a race.

She was further confused when Old Violet said, "Little Belinda isn't wearing a nappy is she?"

Belinda made a face. "I not little! I big girl!" she cried, but they all ignored her.

"No Missus, only panties," Rose replied. She understood that presented a problem. *We will have to wash them somehow.*

"Do you have any clothes in your backpack?" Old Violet queried.

Rose shook her head. "No Missus. We were just spending the day fossicking."

Old Violet nodded and glanced at a nearby shop. "Have you got any money?"

"No Miss," Rose replied, shaking her head.

"Would your parents mind if we buy her a few clothes. They can pay us back later if they want." Then she looked embarrassed. "If they can that is."

Rose gave a wry smile. *Dad can buy the whole shop if he feels like it, no, the whole chain of shops!*

She nodded and said, "That will be alright. I am sure they will make it up to you. They will appreciate it."

"Okay, you take little sister… she is your little sister isn't she? Take her into the change room and we will be with you in a few minutes," Old Violet said.

Rose looked at the nearby Parent Room sign and nodded. She took Belinda and walked over to the door and watched as Old Cyril and Old Violet both turned and walked towards the shop. But Rose was reluctant to go in.

*Is this just a cunning ploy to get us in a room while they get security or the police?* she worried.

Belinda began to wail and cried, "Ice cream! Want!" so loudly that people turned to look.

Embarrassed and anxious Rose tried to pacify her. "Got to change you first, Bub-O. Then we get you an ice cream."

"Hungwy!"

"Yes Bubby Tubby," Rose said. "You will be fed. Just be patient please."

Still anxious about being somehow tricked or trapped she stayed standing just outside the Parent's Room, aware that she was also taking a risk of one of the men walking by. It was a horrible dilemma. But she need not have worried. A few minutes later she saw Old Violet and Old Cyril coming back out of the shop carrying a bag. They gave a happy smile and Old Violet then led the way into the Parent's Room.

As soon as they were all in and the door was closed Old Violet held up a lolly. "Can she have this?" she asked Rose. Rose nodded and Old Violet unwrapped the lolly and handed it to an already grasping Belinda. "Suck on this sweetie," she said. Then she turned to Rose. "Okay, lay her on the change table and we will get Miss Pooey Pooey cleaned up."

"Oh Miss, you don't have to," Rose protested. "I can do it."

"Stop fussing, girl. You look exhausted and I have done this a thousand times. Now just lie her down."

Rose went to do so and then saw herself in the mirror on the wall. For a second she stared, in surprise more than horror. Then she lay Belinda down and stepped back to study her image. What surprised her was that she had thought she must look a real wreck. But in fact, apart from dark rings under her eyes in a tired face and a few straggly wisps of hair she looked quite normal, if sunburnt and tanned.

By now Belinda was happily sucking on the sweet and made no protest at being laid flat. Old Mr Cyril made a face and Rose guessed he was one of the old-fashioned parents who thought this was all 'Women's Work'. She watched anxiously as, with deft and obviously practised hands, Old Violet undid Belinda's clothing and peeled it off.

It was a poo alright, big and smelly and all squashed over the inside of the panties and trousers. Old Violet picked the trousers and panties up and began rolling them up.

"Will you get into trouble if I put these in the bin?" she said. "I don't think we can clean them really. I mean, will it be a problem for your parents?"

Rose shook her head. "No problem. We will be alright," she replied, thinking of her mother's usual shopping expeditions. She sensed that Old Violet was a bit embarrassed in case Rose's parents were poor. Old Violet continued rolling and walked to the nearby rubbish bin.

And then Rose remembered the amethyst. "Wait!" she cried. "Let me look for Bubbie's gem."

"Gem?"

"We were looking for gems in a dry creek bed and Belinda found what I thought might be an amethyst. The only place I could find to put it was in her empty water bottle. Later on I refilled the water bottle and she drank it all. I... er... I promised we would look for it when it passed through."

Old Violet laughed and clapped her hands. "Good on you! Here, wash them in the sink and try not to let it go down the plug hole."

Old Cyril now came to the rescue. "There are some rubber gloves in that dispenser there."

Rose took the gloves and pulled them on and then gingerly placed the trousers and panties under the running tap. She then began to slowly and carefully feel if there was a stone in the faecal matter. While she did, this Old Violet deftly wiped Belinda's bottom and buttocks clean with wet wipes and then a wet washer and then dried her with paper towel. Powder was added. Belinda gurgled and was happy and kept sucking on the lolly. As Old Violet began dressing Belinda in new pale pink panties and a pair of bright green trousers, Rose closed her fingers on something hard.

Very carefully she rubbed it and then gripped it. Using the now washed-out panties as a sieve to stop accidentally washing the stone down the drain she rubbed and washed it clean and then held it up against the light between finger and thumb. It was about the size of a small pea and glowed clear pink.

Old Cyril nodded. "Looks like a gemstone alright. Look at this Violet, it looks like the one you found at Rubyvale a couple of years ago."

There was discussion of the gem, which was dried on paper towel and passed from hand to hand. Belinda was sat up and she demanded to see it but had difficulty holding it in her pudgy little hand.

"Diamond for Mummy," she explained to Old Violet. Then her face crumpled and tears began. "Want Mummy!"

Rose retrieved the gem and slipped it into her shirt pocket. She calmed Belinda while Old Violet started putting on her socks and little sandshoes. As she did, Rose again checked her appearance in the mirror. She noted that her khaki shirt looked a bit crumpled and grubby and had dried salt stains on it , and she was hotly aware that it smelt with the sharp tang of stale sweat. It made her want to get away as quickly as she could.

"Thank you," she said. "You can leave us here now if you wish." She rolled up the soiled pink trousers and dropped them in the bin.

"You sure you will be alright?" Old Violet queried, obviously curious but concerned.

"Yes thanks," Rose replied. "I don't want to get my... er... cause my Mum and Dad any trouble."

"Mummy! Want Mummy!" Belinda wailed.

"Let's get her that ice cream," Old Violet suggested.

So they made their way back out into the crowded shopping mall and along to a shop that sold ice creams. Rose was offered one too but she actually wanted more substantial food and asked if they could get her a salad roll. She was soon seated at a small table chomping hungrily into a bread roll full of chicken and salad.

"So, can you tell us what the story is?" Old Cyril asked.

Rose was glad she had a mouthful at that moment as she could shake her head and say nothing. "It is along story, and I don't want to involve you. It could cause you... er... cause you trouble." (She had been about to say harm.)

"You are sure you do not want to go to the police?" Old Cyril asked.

Rose shook her head emphatically. "No! If those men see me or Belinda then... then... oh, then my Mum and Dad might be hurt!" she replied. Overcome with emotion she burst into tears.

Old Cyril looked really worried. "It's alright, Rose. We can phone them and they can come here," he suggested.

Both of the old people looked really mystified and anxious. Old Violet went and purchased milkshakes and Rose gratefully drank this.

"Thank you. My dad will... will thank you for this," she said.

"Who is your dad?" Old Cyril asked.

"Better you don't know at the moment," Rose replied. She then politely refused to explain what was going on, fearing that the old couple could then come to harm by knowing too much. "You'd better go. You don't want to be seen with us. We will manage," she added.

That clearly alarmed the old couple. Reluctantly they agreed and they stood up. The Rose remembered her backpack with its incriminating evidence.

"I will just get my backpack out of your car," she explained. She picked up a happy and replete Belinda and they all walked back out of the shop.

Actually, Rose was far from sure what was the best thing to do but she was hopeful she could cope. *I will find a phone and call the office at the mine,* she thought. *They should be able to tell me where dad is, or get a message to him.*

But even as she thought this the chilling notion that her father and mother might both be dead struck her with almost paralysing emotional force.

They were walking back across the car park by then and she was feeling so torn she felt desperation welling up.

*Oh what should I do?* she thought.

# Chapter 23

## CAPTAIN ROSS

As she walked across the car park, Rose was in near despair. *What will I do?* she thought.

Belinda didn't help by leaning away and calling, "Down! Walk! Want to walk!"

"Not in the car park, Miss Bossy Boots!" Rose replied.

"I not Bossy Boots! I Ball of Bossiness!" Belinda retorted, but she gave up the walk request.

Both the old couple walked with them and were now looking very concerned. "You can't just go off on your own," Old Cyril said.

Rose shrugged. "We've been on our own for four... no, five days."

"And where are your parents? Do they know where you are?" Old Cyril asked.

Rose could only shake her head and press her lips together, not wanting to answer any questions. Her vision went blurry from a wave of emotion, and then cleared. By then they were at the line of ornamental trees at the far side of the car park and were stepping across to the footpath near the old couple's car. As they did, Rose glanced to her right at a man getting out of a white 4WD that had just pulled up behind the old couple's caravan.

Then she stopped and gasped. "Captain Ross!" she cried.

*Oh thank God! Saved!* she thought, running towards him.

A tubby, middle-aged man wearing baggy khaki trousers and a checked long-sleeved shirt had just climbed out of the passenger seat of a Toyota Prado towing a grey camper trailer. On hearing his name, the man turned and then put out his arms and braced himself.

Rose, still clutching Belinda, was so relieved to see him that she dashed over and threw herself into his arms. That was something that had never happened before, and in the normal course of events, never would.

"Captain Ross!" Rose cried again, clinging to him with relief washing out of her.

Of all the people on earth, other than her own parents, Captain Ross and his wife, Anne, who was also an Officer of Cadets, were the two most important people in her life.

Captain Ross showed his surprise on his face, "Why... why it's Rose... I mean Corporal MacGregor. What on earth?"

He looked down at the top of her head, she had now buried her face in his shoulder, squashing a protesting Belinda as she did. His eyes met those of the old couple who looked equally astonished.

Anne Ross, Lieutenant (AAC) and a very strong-willed and capable woman, got out of the driver's seat and walked around to join them. Gently she patted Rose's shoulder.

"What's wrong, Corporal MacGregor?" she asked. Even though neither was in uniform the cadet style of address came as a habit.

Rose shuddered and clung to them. Now everything would be alright! *Ma'am and Captain Ross will know what to do,* she told herself.

She became aware of Belinda's protests and eased herself away. "Sorry, Bub-O," she said. "Oh sir, thank God! Please help us!"

A frown of concern appeared on Captain Ross's face. "Help you? What's the trouble?" he asked.

His wife moved to stand beside him, also looking worried. She glanced at the old couple who were also obviously concerned.

Rose did not know what to say or where to begin. She shook her head and tried to marshal her thoughts.

*How much do I tell them?* she worried.

Captain Ross looked at the old couple and raised his eyebrows, then put out his hand. "Christopher Ross," he said. "This is my wife, Anne."

Old Cyril shook hands. "Cyril Goodhew, and wife, Violet. We picked these two up beside the road a few kilometres out of town, at some rifle range."

Captain Ross looked surprised. "Rifle range! What is going on?"

Rose realised she really had to tell Captain Ross and Lt Ross the whole story. She looked anxiously around. "Sir, can we please go somewhere private? I... we... must get out of sight, off the street, in case we are seen," she said.

"In case you are seen! By who... I mean whom?" Captain Ross asked. "Who might see you? The police?"

Rose shook her head. "No sir. We haven't done anything wrong. Please!"

Old Violet now said, "In the caravan, quick!"

She turned and hurried to the door of the van and unlocked it. Rose did not really want the old couple involved but it was obvious that Old Violet was curious to know the story. And the caravan was just there a few paces away. So she shrugged and hurried to the door.

Lt Ross locked their car and she and Captain Ross followed Old Cyril. As he did, Captain Ross said, "Are you family?"

Old Cyril shook his head. "No. We don't know any more than you. We just picked them up beside the road and brought them here. We aren't related; never seen them before in our lives."

They all stepped inside and Rose sighed with relief, both at being out of sight and out of the blazing sunlight.

Old Cyril closed the door and that cut off the glare and made it much more pleasant. Lights were turned on and Rose and the Rosses were ushered to seats around a small table. Rose sat down on the edge of the seat and tried to order her thoughts again. She hugged Belinda on her lap.

"Well?" Captain Ross queried. "You were at the rifle range. What were you doing there? That's a defence range. I know, we've done camps there," he said, indicating Lt Ross as he did.

"Eemoo!" Belinda said.

"Eh?"

Rose smiled. "She means emu. We saw an emu there. This is Belinda, Miss Busy Bee. She had never seen one before."

"So what were you doing there and how did you get there?" Captain Ross asked.

Rose knew she had to answer. "We were hiding from some men so they could not use us as hostages," she replied.

"Hostages! For what?" Captain Ross queried. The old couple looked shocked.

"Some men. They had guns and said they were going to shoot Mummy and Daddy, but Daddy said he would pay them not to. They agreed but said they would keep us as hostages until they got their money," Rose explained.

Captain Ross's eyebrows shot up and Lt Ross gasped. She said, "So how did you get away?"

"Bubby and I were in a creek bed nearby looking for gems," Rose began.

"Diamonds for Mummy," Belinda cried. "We found one. Show her, Rosie."

Rose felt in her pocket and extracted the small stone. "I don't know if it is a gem of not. I thought it might be an amethyst," she said, handing it over.

It was briefly examined by Lt Ross and longer by Captain Ross who held it up to the light. "Might be," he said with a shrug. "But go on, how did you get away?"

"The men hadn't seen us, so we hid and when they went looking further away we walked off along the creek in the opposite direction," Rose answered.

Old Violet looked puzzled. "Do you mean hostages for ransom?"

Rose nodded. She had not wanted to reveal her identity and did not know if Captain and Lt Ross knew who she was. She looked at them.

"Sir, do you really know who I am?"

Captain Ross nodded. "Yes, we do. Your father spoke to us when you joined cadets and asked us to treat you like any normal person."

Rose was amazed. "Oh sir, you have! You have never given me any special help or favoured treatment. I thought you didn't know. Thank you!"

"I didn't need to give you any special stuff. You are capable enough to have earned your promotions and awards by your own efforts," Captain Ross replied, and Lt Ross nodded.

Old Cyril now spoke to Rose. "Er... excuse me, it may be none of our business, but we seem to now be involved. Who are you please?"

"Rose MacGregor. My dad is Roderick MacGregor. He owns MacGregor Mines and Enterprises," Rose replied.

Amazement showed on both the old couple's faces. Old Cyril looked thoughtful and nodded. "So your father is Rod MacGregor, the mining magnate?"

Rose nodded. "Yes. Sorry, I just didn't want to involve you in something dangerous," she explained.

Old Cyril nodded again. "Okay, now things start to make sense," he replied, looking at her with a whole new interest.

Rose felt a surge of regret and then said, "If you like, you can tell us to go and we will look after ourselves. These men are dangerous and have guns. You could be putting yourselves at risk. You too sir and ma'am."

Captain Ross reached out and squeezed her hand. "That is the most wonderfully brave and selfless thing I have ever heard," he said. "Of course we won't abandon you."

"Thank you, sir," Rose said and then bit her lip and tried to hold back tears. Belinda turned and said loudly. "Bad men! Rose make bad man give us lunch."

Captain Ross frowned. "So why don't we just call the police?" he suggested.

Now Rose did burst into tears. "B... be... because... sniff... I ... heard that Lucas... blub!... say... say that if the police found out they would k... kill my mum!" she cried.

"Mummy! Want Mummy!" Belinda said, also crying.

All the adults looked appalled. Captain Ross shook his head and said, "I see. That is bloody serious. It will take some thinking about."

"It... It's. It's all...sniff... I have b... b... been thinking about for days," Rose said.

"Days! How long has this been going on for?" Captain Ross cried.

Rose frowned and tried to add it up. "Four? Five. I'm not sure. I've lost track of the days. It was Monday I think."

"Today is Friday. That's five days! What have you been doing all that time?" Captain Ross queried.

"Walking, hiding," Rose answered.

Then she burst into exhausted tears again. Old Violet got her a cup of water and she gulped it greedily. Then Belinda wanted one and that was quickly poured.

Captain Ross shook his head in disbelief. "Do you mean in the bush out there at the rifle range?"

Rose shook her head. "No. We were at an old mine near a place called Kalkobi. It's an old, abandoned smelter."

Lt Ross gasped in astonishment and that was also the look on Captain Ross's face. "But... but that... that's over near Cloncurry! That's at least... Oh... at least fifty or sixty kilometres away! You can't have walked all that way."

"I did sir, and carrying little Miss Bundle of Busyness all the way," Rose replied, annoyed that they should doubt her. She met his gaze. "And it was thanks to you and ma'am that I could, sir. It was cadet training and experience that gave me the knowledge and skills to do it."

Belinda now interrupted. "I not little miss. I big girl. I Ball of Mischief!"

That eased the tension. "I'll bet you are," Captain Ross agreed. "My God! Wait while I go and get a map,"

He stood up and hurried out and Old Violet took the opportunity to organise drinks and a toilet break. For Rose going to a proper toilet, even one as cramped as the caravan facility, was a pleasure. Belinda was also persuaded to go and she happily explored the interior of the small toilet. She and Rose were given more water, and the adults were all provided with tea or coffee and biscuits.

Belinda reached out to take a biscuit. Rose pushed her hand away. "You ask first, Miss Greedy Guts!" she reproved.

"Bicket please!" Belinda asked in a really sweet little voice. Then she turned to Rose. "And I Miss Busy Bee to you!"

Both Belinda and Rose were handed biscuits. Rose munched on hers while Captain Ross sorted maps and spread a couple out on the table.

As he did, Old Cyril said, "Excuse me…er… Chris, was it? May we ask how you know these girls? She keeps calling you two captain and ma'am."

Captain Ross smiled. "I am a teacher at Gold City State High School, History and Geography, and Anne is a teacher aide and is working in admin in the office. We are Officers of Army Cadets, part-time volunteers, and run the Charters Towers Army Cadet Unit. Our home base is currently at NGC, I mean at Northern Goldfield College. Rose is a cadet, a second year with the rank of corporal. She is a student at NGC."

Old Cyril's eyes lit up. "Well fancy that! I went to boarding school in the Towers sixty, no, seventy years ago!"

Old Violet raised her eyebrows inquisitively and looked at Rose. "So Rose, if your dad is one of the richest men in the country, how come you are going to a small regional boarding school?"

Rose smiled. "Because he didn't want me spoiled. He wanted me to have normal teenage years. I think he was right. I really like NGC and have made some really good friends there, nice girls. Mostly off cattle properties out here in the west. They don't know who I am. They just think I am from out this way and that dad works in the mines," she explained.

The adults all nodded and obviously thought that a good idea. Old Violet nodded and said, "We had a look at your school office when we were in the Towers a few days ago. It is a lovely old building."

"It is," Rose agreed. "It is a very pleasant place NGC."

Captain Ross agreed then said, "It is, now let's get back to business."

"I Ball of Business," Belinda added.

There were smiles all round and nods. Captain Ross said, "So, start at the beginning Rose and tell us the story."

So Rose started. But she had only just recounted what she could remember of the men arriving when she realised that Belinda had put her head down on her shoulder, and had a half-eaten biscuit in her hand. "Can I lie Bubby down?" she asked, seeing a bed further along the corridor.

"Of course!" Old Violet replied.

She led Rose past the small lounge and kitchen. Rose eased the biscuit from Belinda's pudgy fingers and Old Violet took Belinda from her and eased her onto a bed. Belinda opened her eyes and looked around then smiled and lay back. "This dood!" she said. She stretched and wriggled and then closed her eyes, stuck her thumb in her mouth and rolled on her side. Within minutes she was asleep.

They returned to the table and Rose resumed her tale, as well as she could remember. At each stage she emphasised how her cadet training or experiences had helped.

"Water and heat were our main problems," she explained. "We really only had my water bottle."

"So how did you know where to go?" Captain Ross queried.

"We had been to Fountain Springs, that's a pool in the mountains, the day before," Rose explained.

Lt Ross nodded. "We know, we went there last year. It is a lovely place."

Captain Ross frowned. "But Kalkobi is on the eastern side of range of hills and nowhere near Fountain Springs."

"When we got out of the car at Kalkobi dad pointed west and said that Fountain Springs was on the other side of the hills we could see," Rose agreed. "So I walked over them. It was hard going because of the heat, and we did a lot of it at night. That's why I am so tired. We did a lot of the walking at night."

"Why?" Old Cyril asked.

"Cooler, and the moon was good for navigation," Rose answered. "And it made it less likely the men would see us."

"Do you really think that these men are dangerous?" Old Cyril queried.

Rose nodded. "Oh yes. Cousin James tried to shoot us from the helicopter."

"Shoot you!" Old Violet gasped.

"Yes," Rose agreed.

"From a helicopter! What did you do?" Old Violet asked.

"Shot back," Rose replied. Then she realised she possibly should not have said that.

Captain Ross looked suddenly very serious. "Shot back! What with?"

"The rifle I took off a man named Lucas," Rose replied. She was resigned now to having to tell the whole story.

"A rifle! Where is that?" Captain Ross asked.

"Back in the bush," Rose answered, even then not wanting to give too much detail, subconsciously thinking that she might need that rifle again. She shrugged. "I didn't think people would pull up to give us a lift if we had a gun."

Old Cyril nodded at that. "You are right there! We would not have been happy if you had walked out of the bush with a rifle."

Captain Ross gave a big sigh. "Okay, this is serious legal stuff. It needs to go to the police now."

"Sir! Oh no! Sir please don't! The men might kill my mum! Please!" Rose begged. She began to breathe so rapidly she went dizzy with apprehension.

"We must!" Captain Ross insisted.

"We will run away if you do," Rose gasped.

Captain Ross frowned and looked hard at her. "But we are now involved. This could get us into trouble as well."

"Sorry sir, but please no. At least wait until we have tried to find my dad to speak to him," Rose pleaded.

But Captain Ross was shaking his head as he and his wife looked at each other. Both looked very worried. Rose felt her heart begin to beat faster and the anxiety built.

Captain Ross frowned and said, "No, I think this must go immediately to the police."

# Chapter 24

## ROSE PLEADS

Rose felt her hopes crash. Anxiety shot up and desperation and dread became her dominant emotions. What was particularly bothering her was the concern that she might have misunderstood the conversation between her father and Lucas and that it might all be a terrible mistake.

"Sir, please no! Please hear me out!" she cried.

"Okay, but it had better be a good argument," Captain Ross agreed.

"Sir, is there any public search going on for two missing girls at the moment?" Rose queried.

All the adults shook their heads. "Not that I've heard," he answered.

Old Cyril agreed. "We listen to the news on the radio nearly every hour. There's been nothing."

"And if my father went missing that would be news?" Rose suggested.

Old Cyril answered. "It would be. There's been no mention of him for a couple of weeks that I can remember," he said. The other adults all nodded.

"So these men have kept it all quiet," Rose said. "My dad said he could not organise the ransom money from out there in the bush, so he must have gone to one of our offices to do that. That's why they said they were taking my mum and us as hostages."

"Yes, that sounds likely," Captain Ross conceded.

"So my dad must be at least pretending to live a normal life while he arranges to get the money," Rose said. "So we should be able to find out where he is and contact him."

"How much were the men demanding?" Old Cyril asked.

"Twenty million dollars, half in used banknotes and half in gold. Dad said it would take a few days, possibly a week to organise," Rose replied.

All the adults shook their heads in amazement, but Rose had overheard his parents discussing business deals in the billions. She thought she might be starting to talk Captain Ross around, so she kept trying.

"So my dad must be out there somewhere doing that. I think we can contact him without the men knowing."

"Where might he be?" Lt Ross asked.

"Well, our nearest big mine with all the office and communication facilities, airfield and so on, is at Mt Egbert," Rose replied, picturing the huge mining complex she had visited half a dozen times.

"Where is that?" Old Cyril asked.

"Near a place called Kajabbi, somewhere north of here," Rose answered. "Oh please sir, please try to contact my dad before you go to the police. Please! That Lucas sounded like he meant it when he said it."

"I suppose we could call the mine and ask for your father saying it was something to do with cadets?" Captain Ross suggested, and Rose nearly cheered, feeling a surge of hope.

Lt Ross gave a wry grin. "Say she hasn't paid her term fees to pay for bus hire and camps and so on," she suggested. She looked at Old Cyril and Old Violet. "The army only provides uniforms and one camp a year. Everything else the cadets have to pay for, and half the parents don't like paying."

"How much?" Old Cyril asked.

"Only $100 a term," Lt Ross said.

Captain Ross pursed his lips and then nodded. "Okay, let's hear the rest of this story and then I will decide. So go on Rose. You and Little Miss Ball of Bossiness, have crossed the hills, looking for water. How did you navigate?"

"By the sun and the moon like you taught us sir. I tried the Southern Cross, but it was setting by the time the moon came up and Orion was only just coming up."

"Very good. So how did you know which way to go?"

"I just went west as I reckoned we would see the mountains of the Fountain Range, and we did," Rose answered.

"Yes, they are very distinctive," Captain Ross agreed.

Rose next described how they had made their way to Fountain Springs and how she had bathed Belinda and then used the discarded beer bottles to increase her water capacity. That earned her looks of admiration and approval.

Old Violet said, "That is why your backpack was so heavy then?"

"Yes Missus. Can I have it please?" Rose asked.

Old Violet went out to get it and the backpack was brought in and unpacked like Exhibit A. Rose was amazed at how much was stuffed in there. She pushed all Lucas's belongings to the side and mentioned how she had broken a couple of the small beer bottles when diving for cover and then later found the bigger ones at another old mine site.

Then she went on to describe how the men had arrived at Fountain Springs just as they were leaving, how she had walked to Ballara and then hidden under the overhang of the old goods platform.

"The sticky plants saved us," she explained. "And I was able to overhear the men."

"Oh yes, we've met those sticky plants," Lt Ross commented.

Rose went on to describe the walk up the old railway to Hightville and on to the Wee MacGregor Tunnel. "I thought they had us, but their vehicle got stuck on a rock and we made it around the bend," she said, "and then my cousin James arrived in a helicopter."

"Who is Cousin James?" Lt Ross asked.

Rose had to think hard, wrinkling her brow to reconstruct the family tree. "My grandfather's brother's son I think," she said. "There was old Hamilton Arbuckle MacGregor who came out from Scotland in 1910 to drive the trains on the railway there; and his son was... er... was Robert Arbuckle MacGregor and he had two sons, about the 1940s, I think. The oldest was my grandfather Alexander Arbuckle MacGregor and he only had one son, my dad. The other son of Robert was Magnus. Magnus was killed in a car crash a few years ago but he had a son, who is Cousin James. I think that's right."

Lt Ross wrinkled her brow. "Is this Cousin James somehow involved in an inheritance deal? Is he in your father's will or something?"

"I don't know," Rose answered. "I've never really heard my parents discussing anything like that. I just assume it was all being split between Busy Bee and me, unless Mum and Dad have more kids."

"Do you think they will?" asked Old Violet.

Rose nodded. "I hope so! I'd like a little brother."

"It all might go to him," Old Cyril suggested. Rose shrugged and smiled and found she didn't care. "Won't bother me. I might just marry some guy who owns a cattle station. I like the people from out here, more than I like most of the people I meet in Sydney."

"Sensible girl," Lt Ross said.

"So will you please try to contact my dad first sir?" Rose asked.

Captain Ross nodded. "Alright, but you do realise that possibly places us all in some serious legal trouble later. Do you others agree? Now is the time to pull out if you don't."

He looked at each adult in turn and Rose was relieved to see them all nod. Old Violet gave a smile and said, "What can they do? Put me in jail? That's one of the few things I haven't experienced yet."

Rose mentally heaved a gigantic sigh of relief. She had been tensing to just run out of the caravan to try to contact her father. Now she felt confident they would achieve it as she trusted the Rosses to do their very best.

Captain Ross indicated the map. "So you were here at the Wee MacGregor Tunnel. What happened next?"

Rose described the helicopter landing, hiding in the culvert, sleeping all afternoon and then walking down into the valley and finding the big beer bottles, "And the Dewar's Whisky bottle," she added, holding it up. Then she made a face. Seen in the light it was full of floating things.

*Oh well, it hasn't made me sick yet!* she told herself.

The night walk to the cattle trough and then up into another range of hills was described and how they had slept through the heat of the day in the shade in a rocky gully. Captain Ross nodded.

"You have managed the heat very sensibly," he complimented.

"It was the cadet lessons on heat sir," Rose replied. "You and ma'am saved us."

Both Rosses looked pleased. Lt Ross smiled. "Thank you, Rose. That is a lovely compliment."

The business of taking the rifle off Lucas and the subsequent shooting of his tyres and radiator took a lot of anxious question and answer and once again every word of the conversation that Rose could remember was analysed.

*Oh I hope my mum is alright and not dead,* she thought, apprehension once more almost overwhelming her.

Both the Rosses were amused by her descriptions of how she had outwitted and avoided the men at road junctions and windmills and at her scathing comments on the men's abilities and poor self-discipline.

"They are only crooks," she added. "They have obviously never been soldiers, not even cadets, except Lucas. He's the really dangerous one."

Rose now discovered that she had been to Lake Mary Kathleen on the east Leichhardt River. She enjoyed relating how they had swum in the dam, and her fears about crocodiles and how she had washed Belinda's clothes and her own shirt. Old Violet nodded and tactfully asked if that was the only wash she had had.

When told it was, she said, "You can have a shower in here if you like and we will find you another shirt."

"Sorry Missus. I know I must smell," Rose apologised, blushing with shame at the idea of such poor hygiene.

There was then the helicopter incident and the adults all looked deadly serious. Captain Ross asked where the helicopter had come from.

"I think Cousin James just hired it here in Mount Isa. I am sure the pilot did not know what was going on. He looked pretty annoyed when Cousin James aimed a rifle at us, and he grabbed at him. They had an argument and then they flew away, straight back here, I think. We never saw the helicopter again."

"Hmm! That might already be the subject of a police enquiry," Captain Ross suggested. "These crooks must be getting very worried."

The adults also applauded her use of the captured radio and Rose positively glowed at their praise. Then they laughed and really congratulated her on her raid on the barbeque.

"Apart from two sandwiches each from Lucas's lunch that is the only food we had in all that time," Rose explained. "That is why Belinda, little Busy Bee, was so keen to grab food."

"That's alright. You have done fantastically well!" Old Violet said. "We will have some more tea and coffee and cake, I suggest."

This was done and Rose found a small plate loaded with fruit cake and cream biscuits along with a large glass of orange cordial on the table in front of her. She went on to describe the night walk to avoid the vehicles with spotlights and how she had crossed more lines of hills.

"I was getting a bit worn down by then," she added.

"I'd say you would be," agreed Lt Ross. "You have done a mighty job, and carrying your little sister all that way!"

"Not so little!" Rose said with a groan. But she glowed at the praise. "She is a mighty little bundle of mischief," she said.

Old Violet chuckled. "She is a great kid, lots of spirit," she agreed.

"Certainly," agreed Rose. "And that sounds like her now."

It was. Belinda was awake and busy exploring the bed area. She greeted the idea of cordial and cake enthusiastically and while she consumed this

Rose described the morning walk to the rifle range. Captain Ross had pencilled on the map the route that Rose had most likely followed and now he got busy calculating the distance. When he had he whistled and looked amazed.

"You have walked nearly sixty kilometres, and much of it cross-country and in the dark. That is a tremendous effort. Well done!"

Rose blushed at the praise but shrugged. "I was able to do it because of Cadets sir, all those lessons on navigation, how to be safe in the bush and night fieldcraft exercises. It is you and ma'am who should get the credit," she said.

"Well thank you. It is good to know that cadet training comes in useful sometimes," Lt Ross said.

Rose again shrugged. "And here we are. So, can we please go and find my dad?" she asked, her apprehension returning.

To her relief, Captain Ross nodded. "Okay. Where do you suggest?"

"The Mt Egbert Mine," Rose answered.

The map was consulted. "Northwest of Kajabbi," Captain Ross indicated. "Hmm! We were going east to Julia Creek, but I guess we are now going to Kajabbi to start with."

Old Cyril frowned. "What's at Kajabbi?"

Captain Ross answered. "Not much, a little country pub and half a dozen houses scattered around among a lot of overgrown allotments and scrub. It used to be a railway town fifty years ago."

"We stayed at the hotel at the start of our holiday," Rose added.

"Did you? That might be a suitable place for us to hole up while we do some inquiries," Captain Ross suggested.

Lt Ross nodded. "We could camp out the back again and the girls can act like they are part of our family, and it has food, showers, toilets and a laundry."

"Sounds good to me," Captain Ross agreed.

"What about us?" Old Cyril asked.

"You can just go on your way if you like," Captain Ross said.

"Oh, we feel a bit involved now," Old Cyril said, looking a bit hurt.

"What were your plans?" Captain Ross asked.

"We were going to spend a few days looking around Mount Isa."

"You could do that and keep your ear to the ground while you do," Captain Ross suggested. "We could phone each other each day to pass on any information. And, if need be, you could be the ones to go to the police here when we decided it is the right time."

Rose felt anxious at that but had to accept that it would probably become necessary. She was old enough to understand that to try to deal with a gang of armed men on their own would really be asking for legal trouble.

*Or worse if the gang twigs we are onto them. They might murder us as well!*

The old couple reluctantly accepted this and then lunch was called for. Captain Ross looked at his watch and agreed so Rose checked her watch and was surprised to see it was 1250hrs! The women then suggested some delays while they purchased more food and did a bit of necessary shopping.

Old Violet said to Rose, "You take those smelly old clothes off and have a shower. We will get you something better."

Rose blushed and nodded. She checked that Belinda was alright and then went into the tiny shower space and took off her clothes. A towel was produced and she proceeded to luxuriate in a hot shower. During it she rubbed and scratched at all her stings and cuts and lamented all her bruises and her broken fingernails. But it felt wonderful, and she was surprised she did not feel worse.

By the time she had finished the women had been to the shops, telling the men to stay there to look after the girls as men could not be trusted to remember to buy all the things a girl might need. Rose was handed new undies and a new bra, to her great embarrassment but relief. New long pants, khaki, and a dark green long-sleeved shirt were passed in.

*At least they know Mum and Dad can pay for it all now!* she thought.

When she came out, she found two large bags filled with new clothes, toiletries and even little items like hair ties for Belinda, towels and new toothbrushes for them both.

"Oh thank you! You didn't have to," she exclaimed.

"We enjoyed it," Lt Ross replied, beaming. "Now get little Ball of Bounciness and bring her to lunch."

"She's tubby enough to have for lunch!" Rose commented.

She went and found Belinda playing with a little fluffy bunny that she had just been given. But she was 'hungwy' and happy to leave it and come to eat. Lunch was more salad rolls, a couple of pies and sausage rolls, Cheerios and tomato sauce for Belinda and some cheese and then a lemon tart for Rose and a small cup cake with pink icing for Belinda. It was a very happy meal.

Rose now discovered that while she had been in the shower Captain Ross had cleared space in the back seat of their Prado, placing the excess luggage into the camper trailer, a Jayco 'Swift' that they had owned for several years. The two new bags were packed in and Rose remembered her own now worn and grubby backpack. It was placed in the Prado, still with its load of bottles and other items.

All of the preparations took nearly two hours. During this Rose lay down beside Belinda and quickly drifted off into a deep sleep. She was woken from this at 1500hrs and told to quickly go from one vehicle to the other. Her hat was handed to her and she held it over her face while she did. Once she was seated in the Prado with her seat belt done up a pillow was placed on her lap and Belinda, now wearing a new, pale pink hat with a bunny picture on it, and clutching the new fluffy toy, was carried from the caravan to her by Old Violet.

Satisfied all was ready the adults checked phones and phone numbers and Rose noted Lt Ross writing down the registration numbers of the old couple's car and caravan.

*I must make sure they are rewarded,* Rose thought.

There was some handshaking and quick farewells and the Rosses walked back to the Prado and got in. Lt Ross was still the driver.

"We swap every two hours of driving," Captain Ross explained, "and we only came from Dajarra this morning."

Another check was done that everyone was ready. "Okay, let's go. Keep your head down and face covered Rose," Captain Ross instructed.

The motor was started and the vehicle pulled out onto the street. Rose felt her spirits really lift.

*Good! Now we can contact Daddy and find out where Mummy is.*

# Chapter 25

## THE GREATEST OUTBACK PUB IN AUSTRALIA

As the vehicle turned right onto the Barkly Highway Rose felt so elated she wanted to cry out or sing. A feeling of great confidence filled her, and she happily hugged Belinda and chatted to her. Belinda, however, was more interested in looking out the window.

"Big twuck! Brrrm!" she cried as a road train went past the other way.

Rose looked at it and smiled then noticed that the vehicle following the road train was a white 4WD. She experienced a momentary stab of alarm until she saw that the diver was a middle-aged woman with purple hair and ridiculous, purple-rimmed glasses.

But it did make her more wary. *Those men are still out there,* she thought.

So she pulled her hat to one side to shield her face and sat lower in the seat. Belinda's new hat was removed and she was allowed to look out and play.

As the vehicle drove out eastward along the main road, Rose mentally ticked off the landmarks she recognised. She also carefully scrutinised all the vehicles they passed. There seemed to be a large number of white ones, and a dismaying large proportion were white 4WDs!

Then they were out of the main part of town and passing through the more scattered buildings on the outskirts, single houses in wide lawns; a caravan park; horses in paddocks, and sheds. Ahead the Barkly Highway went up over a rise and a mountain filled the windscreen. The road curved to the left to go around it. There were black cattle in the field on the right; another ore carrier rumbled past coming into town. The highway was a very good, two-lane, bitumen road and they could drive at over 100kphs.

Then they were out in the open country, spinifex and bushes and a few trees. The mountain was soon beside them and then behind them. The traffic thinned out and Rose knew something was nagging at her. A white ute came into view as they went over another rise. She focused on that and noted that they were past the big hills and were driving over a lower rise and the road was curving left onto much flatter country.

Captain Ross half turned and called, "This is your rifle range coming up on the right," he said.

Then Rose remembered. "Oh sir, please stop so we can pick up that rifle."

But there was a road train, a fuel truck with three tanker trailers coming towards them. It was slow and had a tail of five vehicles and there was nowhere on the left to pull over.

Lt Ross shook her head and said, "I will have to find a safe place to pull off to turn around."

Rose could only nod in frustration. Between the vehicles flashing past in the opposite direction she glimpsed the gate into the rifle range. Unable to safely stop they drove on, rounding a long curve to the left. They crossed a concrete bridge that Rose thought must be across the creek where they had seen the emu. And then they had to drive on for half a kilometre with an impatient grey car close behind before they found a wide area of bare earth on the left that allowed them a chance to pull off the highway. Rose realised it was a turn-off to a side road but was not interested.

After waiting for several vehicles from both directions, Lt Ross swung the Prado and trailer across the highway and headed back towards Mount Isa. Luckily, there was a gap in the traffic and they had no difficulty in pulling over safely on the patch of bare earth outside the rifle range gate.

As the vehicle came to a stop, Captain Ross unclipped his seatbelt and got out. Rose also undid hers and then opened the door. A wave of heat and glare hit her and she winced. She had to lower Belinda to the dusty area.

As she pushed the pillow aside, Captain Ross said, "I can get it if you tell me where. It will be better if you stay in the car out of sight."

Rose shook her head. "I can find it easily, sir. It will take longer to tell you than it will be for me to get it. You hold Belinda please."

Captain Ross reluctantly conceded this, and Rose waited until a vehicle came from the east. It was a delivery van of some sort. She waited until it roared past before stepping out. Rose ran across to the place where she had rolled under the fence. For a second she hesitated, reluctant to get her clean new clothes dusty.

*Don't be ridiculous!* she told herself. *Your mum's life is depending on you!*

With that motivation she almost threw herself down and was under the bottom strand in a few seconds. She rolled to her knees and stood up and was dusting herself when she heard another vehicle coming. That sent her scampering into the bushes, even brushing through a couple of the ubiquitous sticky bushes!

Ten seconds later she had the rifle in her hand. As she held it up, she noted that it was already covered with a fine layer of dust. Brushing at it she started walking back. Conscious of Captain Ross's attitude to weapon safety, she remembered to check the safety catch and to carry it safely. Carefully she placed it through the fence, making sure it was not pointing at her. Quickly she dropped down and rolled back under the fence.

As she stood up, Rose heard more vehicles coming from the east so she hastily placed the rifle vertically against her body to hide it and then began walking slowly back towards the Prado.

*Act naturally,* that's what Captain Ross tells us. *Act as though you own the place and nobody notices. Never scuttle or run. That just looks suspicious and attracts attention.*

Even so she dipped the front of her hat to hide her face as the vehicles went roaring past: a big semi-trailer followed by two cars. Captain Ross was standing there smiling and was busy amusing Belinda by pointing out the antics of a crow further along the road. But as soon as the vehicles were out of sight he reached out for the rifle.

Rose really wanted to hold onto the rifle but understood that he was the adult. So she surrendered it, saying, "Weapon is loaded, sir, at 'Action'. Safety catch on."

"Good!" Captain Ross replied, holding Belinda towards her.

Rose took Belinda who looked at the rifle and cried, "Bang! Bang! Rosie shoot gun!"

"I did too," Rose agreed.

She watched Captain Ross carefully place it in on top of the luggage beside where she was sitting, muzzle pointing away from her. A rug and a pillow were placed over it.

"Okay Rose give me little sister and get in," Captain Ross said.

Rose did and a minute later she was in and had her seat belt done up and Belinda sitting on her lap. Her door was slammed and Captain Ross got in the front. Another minute later, Lt Ross had the car half turned to do a U-turn while she waited for a safe gap in the traffic. Another minute after that they were speeding east along the Barkly Highway. Rose realised she had been very tense and now let out a big breath.

As they recrossed the concrete bridge, Captain Ross pointed ahead to the left. "That road junction there is the start of a gravel road that goes to Kajabbi. But it is fairly rough and we are going to do two sides of a triangle by going to Cloncurry and then north along the Burke Development Road, all good bitumen highway, to past a place called Quamby. There we will turn west along a good, graded road to Kajabbi. But not only is it better roads for our trailer. It will give us a chance to see if there are vehicles with men in them parked at road junctions going south off the highway. Now, I appreciate that is a risk to you and Belinda so if you don't want to take it then say so and we will go along the Lake Julius Road."

But it seemed a very good idea to Rose. *I want to know if those men are still watching the highway too,* she thought.

"Highway please!" she said, adding, "Always good to know what the enemy are doing."

"You are right there," Captain Ross agreed. "Now you keep low and let us do the looking."

Rose said yes but as there was no traffic at that moment she stayed up watching. To her right she noted a large stony hill. *That's that thing I went to the south of this morning,* she thought. Then she shook her head: was it only this morning?

Off to the south she could see all the lines of rugged hills in the seemingly endless rows of parallel ridges. *God, how did I manage to cross all of them, and in the dark!* she marvelled. Then there were vehicles coming so she slid low and hid under her hat till they had passed.

In the front, Captain Ross had a 1:100 000 scale military topographic map open and was tracking their progress with his fingertip. "There is a road junction on the right coming up," he commented.

There was, but it had a locked gate and was just two wheel tracks in the spinifex. No vehicle was parked there. Nor was one parked at the next gate. Rose started to relax. The sun was now behind them and the scenery was, as always along this highway, magnificent and beautiful.

*I love the way the white trunks of the gum trees stand out against the light green of the spinifex in the sunlight,* she thought. But then she pulled a sour face. She definitely did not like spinifex!

And then her anxiety level was sent shooting up. The next road going off to the right was a good, graded gravel road with a cattle grid at the turn-off, and parked just beyond in the shade of a tree was a white 4WD. Rose stared hard from under her hat but while she could see there was a person sitting in it she could not identify them.

"Might have been," she commented.

"That is the main road that goes to the East Leichhardt Dam," Captain Ross replied. "And here is the East Leichhardt River."

Rose was just in time to glimpse the sign before they were out on a long concrete bridge. *That dam saved my bacon,* she thought, looking hard upstream at the thick belt of trees growing in the riverbed.

Thinking about it made her feel thirsty, so she lifted up her drink bottle and had a drink. Belinda wanted a drink as well and managed to spill some down her front. Rose didn't care.

*It's only water. It will dry,* she told herself.

A range of big mountains now blocked the way ahead and the highway curved to the right to go around through a narrow, rugged pass. As they did, several white 4WD s went past in the other direction but they were going too fast to see if they were being driven by any of the men.

As they came out of the pass there was another gate on the right, but there was no vehicle there. The road went up and down over more ridges. They came up behind a large triple-trailer ore carrier but not for long. The Barkly Highway had passing lanes every few kilometres, so they were able to get past. And faster vehicles, ones doing the 110kph speed limit or more, were able to pass them. A couple were white utes or 4WDs, but Rose did not recognise them.

After a few more kilometres of travel a big range of rugged hills loomed up on the right. There was another gate on the other side of the hills but no vehicle. They roared past a sign pointing down a road to the left that said: MARY KATHLEEN.

Captain Ross said to Lt Ross, "That was a very pretty place."

"What is, sir?" Rose asked.

"It was the site of a fairly large town back about half a century ago. They mined uranium and when the mine closed the entire town was removed, except the bitumen roads and concrete slabs among lots of lovely big gum trees. You should visit it one day. There is a huge open cut mine which is pretty spectacular too," he explained.

Then Lt Ross called, "Here is the Fountain Springs Rest Area on the left. Does anyone need a toilet?"

Rose did not want to get out of the vehicle but she did need the toilet so said so. Lt Ross pulled in to the gravel side track and parked as close to the toilet as she could. The only other vehicle there was a small camper van with two young people who looked like European backpackers, hardly any clothes, tousled fair hair, sleepy looks.

Rose hurried into the toilet with Belinda and managed to persuade her to go as well. Then she put Belinda out with Lt Ross and went herself. Feeling very relieved but scared of being seen she scuttled back into the Prado and climbed in. Belinda wanted to look at the kookaburras that were chortling in a nearby gum tree but was picked up by Lt Ross and plonked in her lap.

"Chuckleburras Rosie!" Belinda cried, pointing and wriggling and making it hard for Rose to do her seat belt up.

Lt Ross got back in, and they pulled out onto the highway again. Captain Ross pointed ahead. "The turn-off coming up on the right is the one to Ballara and Fountain Springs," he explained.

"I love Fountain Springs," Rose said. "It saved our lives!"

Belinda obviously recognised the name. "Swim!" she cried.

But then the fear returned. There was a white 4WD parked at the turn-off and Rose thought she recognised Marvin sitting in it. She crouched low and peered from under her hat, hoping he would not recognise Belinda. But she wasn't really worried as she was sure a man like that would think all babies looked the same.

Rose nodded and looked out at several roads going off to the left and at a really big range of rugged mountains with a radio mast on top.

*Glad I didn't have to climb that,* she thought.

Feeling hot despite the car's air conditioning she had another drink of water. She closed her already drooping eyelids and dropped off to sleep, barely disturbed by Belinda's squirming and comments.

\* \* \*

Rose woke to find the vehicle pulled up outside a single-story, country pub. Next to the vehicle was a veranda and steps leading up to a door into what was obviously the bar. Rose looked and blinked.

*Oh, we came here with Mum and Dad a week ago,* she remembered. With that memory came a wash of near misery and apprehension. *Oh, I hope they are alright!*

She realised she had slept through many kilometres of driving, including the junction of the Barkly Highway and the Burke Development Road near Cloncurry.

The door was opened by Captain Ross and Belinda lifted out and put down. She at once went crawling up the stairs.

"This is the Quamby Pub. Another toilet break and you can have a drink if you want," he said.

"Whisky?" Rose asked mischievously as she undid her seatbelt. When she saw the surprised look on Captain Ross's face, she shook her head. "I'm just joking. I actually meant a fruit juice or flavoured milk if they have them."

Before she got out Rose looked cautiously around but there were no other vehicles there and no other people. She got out and stretched before following Belinda up the stairs. The veranda was lovely, polished wood and the cool shade inside the bar was most inviting. She knew that in Queensland it is against the law for children to go into a public bar. But she had been there only a week before with her parents and knew the place. She also vaguely understood that the law was not strictly enforced in remote rural hotels.

A nice lady appeared behind the bar to serve them. Rose hoped she would not recognise her or Belinda, but she did not do more than give her a brief smile. Yes, they had fruit juice. Rose was handed two and then set off after Belinda, who was heading out of the very nice bar area onto a really pleasant outside 'deck' dotted with flowering plants in pots and small sculptures made of bits and pieces of scrap steel welded together.

Belinda only noticed these when Rose was kneeling trying to get her to put the straw in her mouth. Belinda started to suck and then pulled her head away and pointed. "Eemoo!" she cried.

It was, not a real one, but a very good steel sculpture of an emu made out of bits and pieces of old machinery. It had to be examined, and Belinda stopped from touching it while she sucked on her drink. Then she spotted another animal sculpture.

"Wobbolie!" she said, pointing.

Rose had to laugh. "Or a kangaroo," she suggested.

"Wallyobolie," Belinda insisted.

This went on for ten minutes while the Rosses went to the toilet around the back and then sat to drink soft drinks. Rose got a chance to go but Belinda resolutely declined while she squatted and talked to a sculpture of an echidna. Then Belinda was off along the veranda to make friend s with a ginger puppy that had appeared.

Lt Ross watched her and then shook her head. "Certainly a real Ball of Busyness!" she said.

Rose had to smile. "She can be," she agreed.

She saw Captain Ross glancing at his watch so looked at her own and was astonished to find that it was 1650hrs. Five minutes later they were all back in the car and driving out onto the road, the Burke Development Road Rose was informed.

"Poor old Burke and Wills! I felt like them a few times," she said.

"You must have, out in that wilderness all on your own," Captain Ross agreed.

Belinda shook her head. "You not on your own, Rosie. I with you," she said.

Which made them all smile. "Yes, Busy Bee, except that next time we say hide and be quiet you are not to walk out and ask the bad man if he is a bad man," Rose said.

"Sowwy," Belinda said, looking abashed. "I just want to show him my butterfly."

"It was a very nice butterfly," Rose agreed.

After ten minutes of driving north they turned left onto a gravel road. Rose tired of Belinda's endless comments and began to doze. But there just enough corrugations and bumps to keep her awake. And they were driving almost straight into the setting sun, which was unpleasant.

They did not pass a single vehicle on the 30 kilometres drive before dipping down to grind across the stones in the dry bed of a big river. Rose remembered it from other trips but only now learned from Captain Ross that it was actually the Leichhardt River.

From there it was only a drive of a few minutes through fairly thick bush to the tiny town of Kajabbi. Lt Ross pulled off the road to the right opposite the hotel where there was a turn-around at a monument. Rose had been to the hotel with her family and was familiar with it but now studied it more intently.

KALKADOON HOTEL read a sign. She knew that the Kalkadoons were the local Aboriginal tribe and that they had been fierce warriors who had stoutly resisted white settlement back in the 19th Century. The hotel was a typical one-story bush hotel with a veranda and corrugated iron roof.

'The Greatest Outback Pub in Australia' proclaimed another sign. At that, Rose started to smile at the memory of her father laughingly debating the claim with the licensee, and then she sobbed, anxiety becoming dominant.

*Oh, I hope we can find my dad!* she thought.

# Chapter 26

## BAR FLY

Lt Ross walked across the small strip of bitumen and up into the hotel. Captain Ross turned and said, "We are just booking in. There is a place for caravans and camper trailers in the back yard," he explained.

Rose nodded. "I know, sir. I've been here. We stayed here last week for two nights. There are rooms at this end," she answered.

"Oh, have you? I didn't know that," he said, obviously surprised.

Rose pointed northwest along the road. "One of my dad's mines is along this road," she explained.

"Oh yes, which one?" Captain Ross asked.

"Mt Egbert. It's a huge open cut thing with rock crushers and lots of trucks and buildings, a workers camp and offices and workshops and stuff," Rose explained.

"I knew Mt Egbert was along there but have never been to the mine," Captain Ross said. "But I did not know you dad owned it until today."

Rose nodded. She knew that the road to the mine had lots of gates and DANGER, KEEP OUT signs and security but had never really paid much attention. When she had been with her dad they had just driven in and out past the gate guards without any trouble.

Captain Ross frowned. "Maybe staying here isn't a good idea. Do you think the people will recognise you or Belinda?"

Rose thought hard and then shook her head. "Maybe Belinda, but not me. Adults don't pay much attention to kids." What she thought but didn't say was that she did not think she was pretty enough for people to look at and remember.

By then Lt Ross was on her way back. The adults briefly discussed other options but then decided it was only for one night so they should be alright. Captain Ross walked across the road and around to the backyard to open the back gate while Lt Ross swung the Prado and trailer around and went back to the corner of the block.

"We stayed here last year for a couple of nights," she explained. "So we know where to go."

Turning right and going past a really old, ramshackle house, and then right again, she turned the vehicle into the large back yard of the hotel. There was already one caravan backed up against the fence on the left, just inside the gate and another parked lengthways over on the right so Lt Ross drove past the first caravan and then swung the vehicle to reverse the camper trailer over against the fence on the left, the western one. This was only twenty metres from three small, corrugated iron sheds spaced across the back lawn: showers and male and female toilets. There were a man and a woman in their thirties cooking outside the caravan opposite them but no-one else was visible.

Captain Ross arrived after closing the back gate. "Maybe you and Belinda had better stay in the car until we have the camper trailer set up" he suggested.

But Rose had had enough of being cramped and so had Belinda. "We can help sir," she said.

"No, you just keep this little tornado out of the way," Captain Ross replied.

Belinda gave a whoop of joy when she was put down on the grass. "Puppies!" she cried, obviously recognising the place.

She trotted over to where two little Kelpie pups were rolling on the grass. Rose remembered her playing with them on their previous visit, so she wasn't worried. She moved to keep an eye on her. While she did, she watched the camper trailer being set up. It was quickly obvious that the Rosses were a practised team.

The dolly wheel was put on and the Prado unhooked and driven forward a few metres, then reversed to half beside the trailer. Four 'legs' were put down and then adjusted for height to level the trailer. A set of steps was folded out. Then the top was unclipped and wound up with a handle at the back. A bed was pulled out at the front and legs clipped in under it and then another bed at the back. A door was fitted and then adjustments made to Velcro strips to seal around the door and windows, and so on. Rose was impressed.

The back of the Prado was then emptied, suitcases, bags and food boxes being passed in. It was nearly 1800hrs by then but that far west there was still plenty of light. Captain Ross signalled Rose to come, and she scooped a wriggling and protesting Belinda up and walked to the steps at the side of the camper trailer.

She had never been inside such a thing but as soon as she stepped up she liked it. It felt spacious and airy. On her left was a cupboard and bench seat and then the end bed. Directly in front was a small fold-up table and another bench seat and then a bench with cupboards and small refrigerator under it. At the far end was a double bed and on the same side as the door a washboard, sink and gas stove. Captain Ross was busy putting a kettle on the gas stove.

"Have a seat," he said, indicating the bench seat on the left. Rose slid in and Belinda stood on the seat and looked around. "Will she drink Hot Chocolate?"

"Oh yes, and may I have one too?" Rose replied.

Hot chocolate and coffee were quickly made and then Captain Ross seated himself next to Lt Ross facing her. "Okay, this is our plan. We are going to have showers and then have a meal from the hotel. We adults will then engage any adults in casual conversation to try to pick up local gossip and to sound out if they know anything about the Mt Egbert Mine. We just want you two girls to stay in the background and, as much as you can, out of sight."

Rose nodded. Lt Ross now spoke. "We are thinking we might call you by your middle names in public. What is your middle name Rose?"

"Corinda," Rose replied blushing. "It's my mother's first name." She didn't like the name herself.

"And Little Miss Bundle of Busyness here?"

"Her middle name is Joy."

At that, Belinda stopped playing with a strap and looked around. "I Bundle of Joy, Mummy said. And I not little!"

"You are a bundle of joy!" Lt Ross agreed, smiling. "Now, let's get organised for quick showers. There are two so they won't take long."

This was done as soon as the hot drinks were finished. Captain Ross went off to organise dinner in the hotel and Lt Ross got Rose to go and have her shower. "I will look after Bundle here," she said.

Rose was appalled: ma'am washing a little girl! "Oh ma'am you can't!" she cried.

"Why not? I've had children of my own. I'm a grandmother for heaven's sake! You just hurry and have a shower. Same clothes will do."

Rose accepted this and so, luckily, did Belinda. While Rose was soaping herself in the first shower, she could hear Belinda giggling and talking and splashing in the other. It only took fifteen minutes and by the time she was back in the camper trailer Belinda was there all happy and damp, with her hair being dried. Captain Ross went off to hurry through a shower and then came back dressed in a short-sleeved, casual shirt and trousers. Lt Ross then hurried off.

While Captain Ross was lacing up his boots, old black army boots, Rose noted, she said, "Sir, what about the rifle?"

Captain Ross nodded and gestured to the bed behind him. "There. I brought it in with a roll of bedding and stuff," he replied.

Rose had not noticed and was impressed. But she was also starting to worry. The walls of the camper trailer were just thin aluminium and underneath the beds was only thin plywood. The windows and upper parts were just cloth and plastic or mosquito mesh.

*None of this will stop a bullet,* she thought.

By 1900hrs they were all dressed and ready and strolled over past the toilets to the back stairs. A wide veranda took up half the rear and all of the west side of the hotel. Six round tables, each with four chairs were placed around the area. Captain Ross led them to the table nearest the servery and they sat, one to a chair. That was a problem for Belinda but quickly solved. A girl a year of two younger than Rose came out of the kitchen and brought a highchair. Through the servery window Rose saw a young woman in her twenties, slim with black hair and obviously the cook.

Belinda liked the highchair and happily chattered away. She kept looking around, exclaiming at seeing pups, moths and various birds. A man came out of the back doorway of the public bar and walked past them to the next table. He was a thin, elderly gent with white hair and a prickle of beard stubble. He wore only shorts, T-shirt, and thongs. His eyes looked very pale blue and watery and even to Rose he did not look the picture of success. However he gave them a pleasant good evening and sat with his back to them. There were no other patrons.

The young girl returned with menus and then stood to write down their orders. Rose was familiar enough with all this and was able to order for Belinda. "Joy here will have chicken nuggets and chips," she said.

"I Bundle of Joy!" Belinda agreed. "What you having, Rosie?"

Rose met Lt Ross's eyes and grimaced. "I will have Chicken Kiev," she replied, while thinking, *This idea with the names isn't going to work.*

Gravy and salt appeared and Rose began to salivate. The lights came on and she felt very exposed, but as there was only the one man and the hotel staff she did not feel too threatened. A light came on at the next house in the street to the west, but she saw no-one there.

The meal was a great success. Rose enjoyed the chips and gravy more than the Chicken Kiev, but she also made herself eat the vegetables. The main course was followed by dessert, ice cream for Belinda and cake with custard for Rose. She savoured every mouthful and felt more relaxed than she had for a week. It was a really nice meal.

Captain Ross excused himself. "I need to spend some time in the bar," he said. "As I don't drink much this could be a challenge."

With that he turned and walked through the back doorway. As he did, the man at the next table turned to look at him and then turned away. That sent a little niggle of concern through Rose.

*Is that man one of the bad men?* she wondered.

That concern returned when they stood up to go. The man again turned and studied them, then looked away.

There was a short halt along the way to let Belinda play with the puppies. These were now tied up at a shed to the east side so could not pursue when Lt Ross urged them to move on.

After that it was back to the camper trailer. Lt Ross set up a small TV that could take DVDs and she had a couple that were just right: *Tinker Bell and the Pirates* keeping Belinda happy until she lay down on the single bed with her head on the pillow and her thumb in her mouth. She was soon fast asleep. Rose was also very tired, so she nerved herself to go to the washbasin outside the 'ladies' to clean her teeth on her own in the dark, with a small torch loaned by Lt Ross.

As she started back, she suddenly felt cold and vulnerable. She looked anxiously around and then shone the torch. The thin beam was shone on the grass ahead of her, thinking that snakes must live in all the overgrown gardens and allotments that made up much of the 'town'.

*Stop being silly and scaring yourself,* she told herself. *Nobody knows you are here.*

It was organised so that Rose and Belinda shared the single bed, Rose closest to the edge to stop Belinda rolling out of bed. The Rosses would share the double bed. Rose now learned that usually Captain Ross had the single bed because they had to lie side by side in the double bed in such a way that when the outside person wanted to get out of bed they had to climb over the other one.

She had only just climbed up and lain down when Captain Ross came back. He set about preparing for bed, while quietly telling Lt Ross that he had really learned very little except that sometimes miners from Mt Egbert dropped in for a drink.

"They are discouraged from doing so because it leads to accidents, drink-driving, that sort of thing," he explained.

That was discouraging and Rose found she was close to tears. She had been pinning high hopes on learning where her dad was here at Kajabbi and it had come to nothing.

*Well, not nothing. I have had a really good feed, and I am safe and comfortable in a proper bed out of the weather,* she told herself.

And promptly fell asleep.

She slept soundly for eight hours, being roused by Belinda's chuckles as she talked with Lt Ross. They were obviously playing a game and that pleased Rose but then made her feel guilty.

*I should be doing that! We are ruining sir and ma'am's holiday,* she thought.

She opened her eyes and saw that it was daylight. Belinda was sitting at the table doing a cat's cradle game with string. That made Rose smile. And then she heard steps outside and Captain Ross came up the steps. He had obviously just had shower and shave and was in his casual clothes again.

"Oh, hello Rose, I mean Corinda. How did you sleep?"

"Marvelous!" Rose cried.

She felt very rested and all her sore muscles and aches seemed to have gone away, until she went to get up. Then they returned and she groaned. But sore muscles were just a minor inconvenience and she was soon up and on her way to the toilet. As she stepped out, she saw the man with the white hair come out of the male toilet. He headed for the caravan on the other side of their camper trailer. He gave her a nod but did not look happy or well.

Rose looked anxiously in all directions but the world looked reassuringly normal, so she hurried to the female toilet and then to the washbasin outside to wash her face. As quickly as she could she hurried back to the camper trailer.

Breakfast was a most enjoyable and tasty meal. Both the Rosses cooked, producing cereal first (Coco Pops with milk) then bacon and scrambled eggs on toast with fried tomatoes and then small cardboard containers with fruit juice in them. During the meal they all chattered happily away but were mostly careful to avoid discussing their real problem or the adventure the girls had just endured.

The moment the conversation started to stray onto those topics Captain Ross would point to the next caravan.

"Sssh! We don't want that fellow to hear anything," he said softly.

"Is he a problem?" Lt Ross asked.

Captain Ross looked thoughtful. "He might be. He asked me a lot of questions about myself last night. I told him I was a teacher but at Townsville Central State High School."

That all worried Rose. She knew that Captain Ross had once taught in Townsville. She said, "Sir, are you going to phone the mine to ask about my dad?"

Captain Ross nodded. "Yes, after they are all at work after nine," he said.

Washing up was done. Rose helped. Hot water was boiled and collected from the shower. Lt Ross washed and Rose dried. Captain Ross put away and then proceeded to clean the rifle. When he took it out and laid it on the bedspread

Belinda saw it and called loudly, "Bang! Bang! Rosie shoot helicopter."

"Ssssh! Don't say anything about that, Baby Bee, please," Rose gasped.

Captain Ross proceeded to empty the magazine, laying the bullets on a cloth after wiping them. He had a proper cleaning kit and flannelette so was able to pull the barrel through. As he peered through it to check it was clean Rose watched fascinated. As a cadet she had never stripped a rifle or cleaned it. It impressed her to see that Captain Ross appeared to know exactly what he was doing.

When he had finished, he placed the bullets back in the magazine, carefully pointed it to one side and then worked the bolt of put a round in the chamber. Then he clicked the safety catch on.

"At action. That means loaded and with the safety catch on," he instructed.

Rose knew that and nodded. She then puzzled over how to keep

Belinda happy and occupied all day. While all this was going on she glimpsed half a dozen vehicles, all work utes or white 4WDs, go racing past without stopping. Most were heading towards the mine and two had mining logos and orange lights. Only one went towards Cloncurry and it was also a mine vehicle.

Captain Ross checked his watch and then went out to use the public telephone that incongruously stood outside an overgrown and vacant allotment in the next street. That left Rose almost weeping with anxiety for her parents. And continuing to entertain Belinda she was finding a real trial. One of the things that was bothering her was whether the mine could trace a phone call to a public phone box. From TV programs she believed that the police could, but she did not know.

*The police can certainly track where mobile phone calls are coming from.*

 Ten minutes later Captain Ross was back and by his demeanour Rose could tell he had not succeeded. Lt Ross spoke first.

"What happened? Did you get him?"

Captain Ross shook his head. "No. I got the mine office alright and then got passed on to some secretary who wanted to know who I was and why I wanted to speak to him. I had to give her my real name and the cadet story. She said he was not available at the moment and insisted I give my mobile number and said he would call me back when he was free."

Hearing that appalled Rose. *When he is free! Does that mean he is a prisoner?*

But that did not make sense. Surely if the mine management knew there was a problem, they would call in the police? The mobile phone was a problem too. She knew that there was very good mobile phone reception in the area because of all the mines. But could the crooks get access to that information? It was very worrying.

The next part of the plan was put into action at 1000hrs. Rose was left to mind Belinda. Lt Ross went to sit on the side veranda of the hotel where she could see both the main road and the camper trailer; and Captain Ross took himself to the public bar to chat to anyone there. Rose stayed on the lawn close to the back veranda where she could see in the back door of the bar. Belinda played with the puppies.

Two more vehicles went past in the direction of the mine. Then one pulled in and two council workers appeared and went into the bar. A few minutes later a man Rose had not seen, tall, short curly grey hair, walked past with the young primary school girl who had been serving the night before. They both went into the bar. Soon after that the girl came back out and went off to the laundry.

A few minutes later, Captain Ross came out back looking worried. "Bit of a problem," he said softly to Lt Ross.

"What?"

"The man with the curly grey hair is the owner's brother. That isn't the problem. The problem is that he lives in Townsville, and all his kids have gone to Ross River State School and at the moment he has a son and daughter at Townsville Central State High School."

"What did you do?" Lt Ross queried.

"Just told them that it is a big school and I did not know them," Captain Ross replied. "But he isn't the only problem. That old guy with white hair, a bar fly if ever I've seen one, is asking more questions."

Rose felt her anxiety shoot up and she wished they could just get it over with. *Oh, where are Mum and Dad? Are they still alive?* she fretted.

Then she shook her head and decided that her father might still be alive if the people in the office at the mine thought so. Then Belinda fell over and began to cry and she had to go to her. She wasn't really in the mood for entertaining any babies at that moment, not even her little sister!

But she was also curious. Adults said all sorts of things that she did not always understand. "Sir, what's a bar fly?" she asked, keeping her voice low as she understood they would not want the man so described to hear her.

Both adults made a face. Lt Ross answered. "A bar fly is a person who is habitually found in the bar of a hotel during the daylight hours when honest people are either at work or at home," she said.

"Oh!"

Captain Ross then added, "This one says he is staying here because it is free to park caravans in the back yard. But he appears to have enough money to keep drinking and to shout people. I've had to refuse a couple of times and I don't think he likes me. Anyway, I'd better get back. I'm not learning much but I am now ready if someone comes."

With that hopeful comment he went back into the bar and Rose went to pick Belinda up after she had tripped over the puppies again. She got her laughing by tickling her and then by getting her to try to bite her own big toe, well the pink sandshoe toe anyway.

The council workers left and there was relative silence for a few minutes. A TV was going in the bar, sports and ads mostly. As always in NW Queensland a crow 'caarked' from time to time. Rose found herself tiring.

*After morning tea I will try to have a lie down,* she thought.

The heat built and there was very little breeze. Flies arrived to annoy. Rose became drowsy. She heard another vehicle arrive from the direction of Cloncurry, but it parked at the front out of sight.

Suddenly Captain Ross was there above her. "Your dad is here! Quick, get Belinda and get into the camper trailer out of sight. I will try to get a message to him, and he might be able to come and see you. Quick!"

*Dad is alive! Dad's alive and he's here!* Rose thought.

# Chapter 27

## SELF CONTROL

Rose's first impulse was to rush into the bar to hug her father. For a few seconds she literally danced on the spot with boiling emotions. But then she remembered the plan detailed by Captain Ross.

"We won't know if he has one or more of the men with him and whether he is a free agent or not," he had said. "Nor do we know if Cousin James has others watching to report to him. If we let him know you are alive and free, and they find out that will put you back in deadly peril again."

*There is that man, the Bar Fly,* Rose thought.

At that moment, she saw Captain Ross move to sit next to her father at the bar. He did not greet him, except casually, and it looked like her father did not recognise him. The Bar Fly was a bit further along the bar talking to the man from Townsville.

*How can Captain Ross tell my dad without everyone noticing* she wondered.

But she also realised she had to move, and fast. Without a word she stood up and lifted Belinda up and started walking across the lawn towards the showers and camper trailer. Belinda objected, reaching back over Rose's shoulder. "Puppies!" she wailed.

"Shhh! Bad men, Bub-O. We must be quiet and play hide and seek," Rose hissed.

At that, Belinda jerked upright and looked around. "Where bad men?" she said, but much softer.

"In the hotel bar," Rose replied.

By then they were passing between the showers and the female toilet. Rose suspected that she and Belinda were visible through the back door of the bar but could only shrug and hurry on. She detoured around the back of the Prado, which was parked in a way that hid the steps of the camper trailer door from the back of the hotel. Feeling such a turmoil of emotions she could not describe them she opened the door and stepped up inside.

As she did, she came up with a strategy to keep Belinda quiet. So the first thing she did was flop Belinda onto her back on the bed and then snatch up the new fluffy toy.

"Oooh look! Your new bunny!" she cried, proceeding to snuffle the toy into Belinda's face and neck. It worked. Belinda began to giggle and play.

Rose moved the bunny to tickle Belinda's tummy. "Has your new bunny got a name?" she asked.

When Belinda shook her head and said no, Rose again attacked her with it, eliciting more gurgles and giggles and 'please stops'. Rose did and held the toy bunny up.

"Should we call your bunny 'Hippity Hop'," she suggested.

But Belinda shook her heads emphatically. "No. He name Bunny," she said.

Lt Ross had strolled down off the veranda and across the lawn and she now came up the steps and pulled the door shut. She then undid a couple of the sliding curtains on the side facing the hotel and slid them across. That caught Belinda's interest, so she was allowed to play with them as well.

Rose met Lt Ross's eyes. "Oh Miss... I mean Ma'am, I am so happy! My dad is alive!" she whispered.

Lt Ross smiled and nodded. "Yes, but we aren't out of the woods yet. Let's keep Little Miss Ball of Mischief amused while we wait."

Rose didn't want to wait. She wanted to shout for joy, to rush over and hug her dad. But she had to use all her self-control to act naturally and to keep Belinda engaged and happy. She held up the bunny.

"I wanted to call him 'Hippity Hop," she said, only to be interrupted by Belinda almost shouting, "No! He Bunny!"

The game went on. As the minutes dragged by impatience began to build. *Oh, what's going on in there?* Rose wondered.

She wished she was inside the bar to follow what was being done and said. But she understood the basic problem very well: Captain Ross had to pass information to her father without attracting the attention or suspicion of anyone who might be working for the gang.

Ten minutes went slowly by, and it became progressively harder to keep Belinda amused. With the curtains drawn and cutting out the breeze the temperature in the trailer quickly built and perspiration was added to the little annoyances. To help cool them Lt Ross turned on two small ceiling fans. Rose found that the tension was literally nail-biting, and she had to consciously put her hands away from her mouth. But a glance at her left hand made her shake her head.

*Oh my poor nails! They are so wrecked!*

And then she saw her father. He had walked out of the back door of the bar and down the back steps. She noted that he looked normal: hair cut short and trimmed, clean shaven, casual short-sleeved shirt, long grey trousers and shiny polished black shoes.

*Dad always shaves in the morning, no matter what,* she thought.

That got her remembering the advice he had given her. "Always do the morning routine as a drill," he had said. "Make as much as much as possible a drill and save your mental energy for the things that matter." He had gone on to say, "Then, when things really go wrong in your life stick to the drill. That way you at least start the day with some feeling of normality and that makes it easier to face the real challenges."

*That's good advice,* she thought, watching her father with deep affection and thinking he was a handsome man.

For a moment he went out of sight behind the female toilet and then re-appeared heading for the male toilet. To her disappointment he went inside.

*Does he just need to go to the toilet; or doesn't he know yet?* she wondered.

Several long minutes dragged by. *What is going on?* Rose fretted.

And there he was, strolling directly towards the camper trailer! He looked calm and relaxed and she marvelled at how he could have such self-control as she was rapidly losing hers. Her heart was hammering and emotions swirling. Tears began misting her vision. Through a gap in the curtains she watched him walk to the bottom of the steps. There was a knock on the door and Lt Ross reached down and swung it open.

"Come in," she said.

Rose's dad nodded and stepped up, Lt Ross moving back to let him up. And then he saw Rose and she lost it.

"Daddy!" she sobbed, flinging her arms around his neck. He grabbed her to him, and she buried her tear-stained face into his shoulder. She was now trembling so much it took her a while to realise that he was also shaking with emotion.

"Oh Rose! Oh God, you are safe!" he said.

For the first time in her life Rose saw that her father was crying and she loved him all the more. She hugged him tighter and kissed his cheek. "Oh Daddy! You are alive!" she managed to say.

By then Belinda had sat up and realised what was going on. "Daddy! Daddy!" she shrieked, reaching out and launching herself at him. She would have fallen to the floor if both Rose and her father had not put out an arm each to catch her. She was squeezed into the hug.

"Sssssh! Sssh! Bub-O!" Rose croaked. "Bad men might hear."

"Shhh! Sorwy!" Belinda cried. "Daddy!"

There were more tears and kisses. During all of this Lt Ross had pulled the door shut and was standing back beside the sink. Rose shuddered with relief and eased back to look at her dad. Then an awful question rose to the forefront of her mind.

"Dad, is Mum... is Mum alright?" she croaked.

To her intense relief, he nodded. "I believe so," he answered.

He released her and reached into his pocket, Belinda still gripped firmly in his other arm. With difficulty he opened his mobile phone, tapped on the screen and showed her an image. It was her mother with a newspaper held up in front of her.

"This was sent at zero eight hundred this morning. I believe it is what they call a 'Proof of Life' image," he said.

Rose was appalled at the language. "Proof of Life?" she queried.

"It is what the crooks send during ransom negotiations," her father explained. "To prove that the hostage is still alive and well."

At that moment, Belinda caught sight of her mother's image. "Mummy! Mummy!" she cried, jerking and pointing at it. "Want Mummy!"

"Yes, Bubbie Bee, we will get her," their father said.

He then hugged and kissed Belinda to distract and calm her. While he did, Rose studied the image and now realised that the newspaper had todays date on it. She nodded with understanding.

"So what happens now?" she asked.

Her father eased Belinda to sit on the table while he put his mobile phone away and fished out a brown envelope. "This will probably tell me," he said.

"What is it?" Rose asked.

"A letter the hotel licensee just handed me," he said. At that moment, her father glanced to his right and then shook his head. "Oh, my apologies, Mrs Ross. I have been so rude."

"It is alright, Mr MacGregor. Your children are the priority," Lt Ross replied.

"Rod, please," Mr MacGregor said, putting out a hand to shake hers. As he did, his gaze travelled past her and a look of alarm crossed his face. "You've got a rifle? Good!" he said.

Lt Ross nodded. "Rose took it off a man named Lucas while she was walking to safety," she explained.

At that, her father looked at Rose and smiled. "Well done, Wubble Bubble. How did you do that?"

Rose blushed with a mixture of embarrassment at him using her baby nickname and pleasure at his praise. "It's a long story. Tell you later. Please tell us how we can rescue mum."

Mr MacGregor nodded and looked serious. "Yes. I had better get back into the bar before any of those characters wonder what I am doing for so long." With that he tore open the envelope and smoothed two sheets of paper on the table, fending off Belinda's grasping reach as he did. "Not now Bubbie. Important. Business stuff. Please!" he said.

Bellinda nodded. "I Ball of Business," she said.

"Yes, you can be," her father agreed.

Rose helped by picking Belinda up and kissing her cheek, distracting her. Mr MacGregor quickly read the two pages, one of which had a sketch map drawn on it. For a moment he looked grim.

"These are instructions on where to drop the ransom," he said. "I have to do it this afternoon at a place called Dobbyn. It's an old abandoned mine site near Mt Egbert."

Lt Ross nodded. "We know. My husband and I have been there. It is the end of an old railway. We like to go to the ends of all the old railways in Queensland," she explained.

"That's right. Well, I will have to get going. I'll try to get back in touch. The crooks don't have anyone with me, but they have the girl's mother as hostage. I don't know who they are or who to trust," he said.

"Cousin James is the ringleader," Rose said.

"Is he now! I might have guessed. What else do you know?"

Rose quickly listed the crooks she had seen or suspected: Lucas, Marvin, Norris and his family, two other men driving white vehicles.

"I don't know if there are any here, but Captain Ross doesn't trust the old guy with the white hair in the bar," she ended.

"My, you have been busy!" Mr MacGregor said with a low whistle. "How do you know all that?"

"We kept bumping into them all week," Rose answered. "But it's a very long story, Dad."

Mr MacGregor now looked at Lt Ross. "How did she make contact with you, Anne?" he asked.

"By sheer chance. We met them at a shopping centre in Mount Isa," she explained.

"Mount Isa! How did you get there Rose, did you walk out to the highway and get a lift?"

Rose shook her head and got all bashful, not wanting to boast. Lt Ross did it for her. "I gather she walked cross-country all the way from Kalkobi to the Mount Isa Rifle Range, sixty kilometres, dodging those men and finding water along the way."

Rose's dad looked amazed and then his admiration showed on his face. "Oh well done! I was afraid you had both died of thirst out in the desert."

Rose shook her head. "No, Dad. I knew what to do. Cadets taught me that. Thank you, Ma'am."

"And with Bub Belinda?"

Rose made a face. "Yes, I lugged Miss Ball of Mischief most of the way," she agreed.

At which Belinda objected. "I Ball of Bossiness!"

There was a brief moment of laughter before the tension returned. Mr MacGregor looked at his watch and looked grim. "Anyway, I have to follow these instructions, so I had better get going."

Rose was appalled. "Daddy, they might just take the money and shoot you," she gasped. That horrible notion had been in her mind for a while.

Mr MacGregor shook his head. "Not this time, I don't think. I told them it is only half the ransom, to show good faith, that it was all I could collect in that time, so probably not now."

"Can we help?" Rose asked, almost frantic not to lose her father again. "Can we copy the instructions and be nearby in case you need help?'

Her father shook his head. "Take too long to copy. And if these crooks are any good, they will already have someone at the drop site watching from under cover," he said.

"Mobile phone," Lt Ross said. "Quick, smooth that paper and hold it flat." She took out her mobile phone and opened it to 'camera'. Quickly two photos were taken.

"Good work! Well, I had better go. I will find a way to keep in touch. Love you, Rose. Love you, Belinda!"

There were hugs and kisses and tears all round and Belinda did not want to let go. Rose found she could hardly see for tears and was sobbing with emotion. The door opened briefly and her father was gone. The door closed and he was visible walking firmly towards the hotel.

"Oh poor Daddy!" Rose croaked. "He is so brave."

"And such self-control," Lt Ross added. "And so have you, Rose. You really kept yourself together then. You are a very capable girl."

"Thank you, Miss... er... Ma'am."

Belinda began to get hysterical, calling loudly for Daddy and the Mummy. She would not listen to Rose and it was only when she was offered a small chocolate that her attention was diverted and she began to calm down. Rose slumped onto the seat and went back over everything her father had said.

*Somehow, we have to rescue Mummy and also keep dad from being in more danger,* she thought.

But how to do it? Then she remembered the two photos. "Ma'am, may I read those notes please?" she asked.

Lt Ross called put the message on her phone and sat beside Rose while they read. It was simple enough. It read:

DRIVE TO THE DOBBYN HEADFRAME AT 1500HRS
GO ALONE.
LEAVE THE PACKAGE BEHIND A BUSH 75 PACES NORTHWEST
OF THE HEADFRAME
GO BACK TO YOUR OFFICE.
FURTHER INSTRUCTIONS SAME WAY
DO NOT TELL THE POLICE OR CORINDA DIES

When Rose read that last line she burst into tears. "Oh poor Mummy! What can we do?" she sobbed.

At that moment, everything looked black. *We are back where we were on Day 1,* she thought. But then she smiled and told herself they had some advantages. *No we aren't! We are free and the crooks don't know where we are. And we have Ma'am and Sir to help.*

The sound of a vehicle accelerating towards the northwest along the main road came to her and she bent to look through a gap in the curtains. But she was too late. All she got a glimpse of was a flash of white beyond the next house and a swirl of dust. Once again apprehension rose up to choke her and tighten her chest.

A few minutes later, Captain Ross came sauntering back to discover them all eating ice cream. "Oh, I can see I am missing out!" he cried. "Well, how did it go?"

He was provided with a bowl of ice cream and a spoon and sat to listen while Lt Ross described the reunion. During this Rose was bursting with curiosity about what had happened in the hotel.

"Sir, how did you let my dad know we were here without the other men there knowing?" she asked.

"It wasn't easy," Captain Ross replied. "I had already written messages on beer 'coasters' and had them in my pockets. But what I was really worried about was him saying hello and letting people know he already knew me. But when he walked in he paused at the door and looked around and then strolled over as calm as you please and plonked himself on a bar stool so he had me between him and the other men," he explained.

"I saw that," Rose agreed.

"Well, he ordered a beer from the barmen, who I gather is the owner, and then the barman said hello, he obviously knew who he was, and then reached under the bar and picked up a brown envelope which he handed to him. 'This was dropped of by a fellow about an hour ago Mr MacGregor,' the barman said. Well, your dad, as cool as a cucumber just put it in his pocket and turned to me and held out his hand. 'I'm Rod,' he said."

Belinda was listening and piped up, "I like cucumber."

"Do you, Bubbie? That's good. Well, I shook hands and told him I was Chis and he asked what I did, and I said, I was a teacher from

Townsville and he said he was at the mines. All this was loud enough for the others to hear. He nodded to them and had a drink and at the right moment I nudged him and slipped him a beer coaster that said, 'Your girls are safe. In the camper trailer'."

There was a pause while Captain Ross swallowed another spoonful of ice cream. Then he went on. "He got up to chat to the other fellows and that is when I came out to tell you. You did very well to just slink away."

"It is hard to slink with Miss Trouble Bubble here," Rose said.

"I Miss Busy Bee thank you," that young lady retorted before returning to her ice cream.

# Chapter 28

## WHAT DO WE DO NOW?

Rose was following the description carefully, picturing the scene in the bar. She was puzzled. "So did Dad know who you were?"

"Oh yes," Captain Ross assured her. "As soon as he got a chance to whisper to me without being noticed he said, 'The moment the office sent me a message saying that a captain from the army cadets wanted to talk about your cadet fees from last term I knew that Rose had somehow contacted you.' He knew that because he had paid the whole year's fees at the start of the year," he explained.

Rose nodded. "Dad has always been very good at faces and names," she commented.

Captain Ross also nodded. "Your dad must have excellent self-control. When he read that message on the 'coaster' hardly a muscle moved in his face, and he kept on chatting about tourist sights in this area."

"I am very proud of him!" Rose said, then burst into tears, to Belinda's puzzlement.

"What wrong, Rosie?" she queried.

"Nothing Bub-O, just saying I am proud of Dad," Rose replied between sniffles.

"Daddy here! Want Daddy!" Belinda cried.

They managed to placate her and Captain Ross went on to describe how Rose's father had said he needed to go to the toilet and then finished his beer and strolled out.

"I had to make a special effort to keep the other men's attention while he was away. He was here quite a while, and I was getting worried. What happened?"

They took turns to describe the meeting in the camper van. Captain Ross then asked to see the message on the phone. He read it and his face took on a very grim cast. "What was the second page?" he asked.

It was a sketch map showing how to get from Kajabbi to the Dobbyn Headframe. Both the Rosses nodded.

"We know exactly where," Lt Ross said. "We went there last year."

"So what are we going to do?" Rose asked, anxiety gripping her.

Captain Ross frowned. "I'm not sure what we can do. I think your dad is right and the crooks will already be watching the place."

"Could we sneak in from outside the area?" Rose suggested.

Captain Ross pursed his lips. "That is what I was thinking of doing," he said. "But that will be terribly dangerous."

"Oh are you!" Lt Ross snapped angrily. "And what about us?"

Captain Ross looked worried. "I thought you could just wait here and be ready to call the cops."

"Why wait here? How does that make us safe?" Lt Ross queried. "We would be more split up. You, I presume, intend to take the rifle, so we would also be defenceless. If those men turn up, they get three more hostages easily."

"But... but we can't just leave Rose's dad to go out there on his own," Captain Ross said. "It doesn't seem right."

"It doesn't seem right that you would have to go with a rifle and possibly shoot someone, or get shot yourself," Lt Ross said. "I know it doesn't seem right but think of the risk, and the probable legal consequences."

"You can visit me in prison," Captain Ross retorted. He was obviously upset but determined.

"I might not want to!" Lt Ross snapped. "And I don't want to organise your funeral."

"But we can't just do nothing!" Captain Ross cried.

Belinda now joined in. "Want Daddy! Take me to Daddy!"

Rose hushed her. "We can't, Bubby. He has gone to work."

That silenced her, work being a concept that had somehow lodged in her mind as being important. "Want Mummy then," she persisted.

"We are looking for her mate," Rose said. Then she looked at both the Rosses in turn. "I'd like to go and help my dad," she said.

"You can't. You are just a chi... a minor in law. We couldn't let you."

"I will just go then. If you won't take me, I will hitchhike. I'd like my rifle please," she said.

"Rose! Be sensible! You can't and we can't let you!" Lt Ross insisted.

"Then you will have to tie me up or lock me up," Rose cried, now so anxious to do something to help her father that she knew she wasn't thinking straight.

Captain Ross now shook his head and looked at Lt Ross. "What about a compromise. We all go to a place nearby but safely back away from any action. That way we can be on the scene in minutes instead of hours if we are needed. And we may be able to help."

Rose liked that idea. "Safer than just sitting here," she said. "The longer we sit here the more likely it is that the crooks will learn we are here and in this camper trailer stuck in the back yard we are sitting ducks."

That made both the Rosses look uncomfortable. But it was Lt Ross who answered. "I agree with that. So we will do that. I think I know a place we can be safely out of sight."

"Oh Miss, thank you... er... I mean Ma'am," Rose cried.

"We aren't at cadets Rose. You don't have to keep calling me ma'am."

"Yes, I do Ma'am. I'm not going to call you by your first name and Mrs Ross is too long," she replied.

Captain Ross now looked at his watch. "Okay, it is twenty past eleven. It is about thirty kilometres from memory and will take about half an hour. And the place I have in mind to hide the vehicle is a couple of kilometres back and might take an hour to walk forward from. So let's have a quick lunch and get organised, water bottles, rations, First Aid gear and so on."

That mention of First Aid gear chilled Rose, and she sent up a silent prayer hoping her father would be safe. But she was also pleased and excited. She at once thought about how to carry food and water.

"I will want my backpack and a long cloth or straps to carry Belinda," she said.

"Do you think you are up to that?" Captain Ross queried.

"I've just walked fifty kilometres with her. A couple more won't be much," she said.

Lt Ross was obviously very concerned and even hinted that it was time to call the police. But that horrified Rose and Captain Ross backed her up.

"We can't risk any harm coming to Mrs MacGregor," he insisted.

A military topographic map of the Dobbyn area was produced, and they began eating, drinking and packing.

"Drink plenty. We will dehydrate quickly in this heat," Captain Ross said.

Rose made a face at that. *I know that sir, better than you,* she thought.

But she was glad they were doing something. She was not sure what Captain Ross had in mind, but just to be trying was enormously satisfying.

Clothing was a bit of a problem. Both the Rosses had their army camouflage uniforms, which they intended to put on before starting to walk, and Rose's dark green shirt and khaki longs were adequate. But Belinda's bright pinks and greens were not. A dark blue pair of romper pants was found in her bag, along with a dark blue hat with a unicorn badge on the front.

After drinking and eating hastily prepared sandwiches (honey and peanut butter for Belinda, and honey for Rose), they all made toilet visits and Rose carefully filled her collection of water bottles and placed them in her backpack, which went into the now half empty Prado. Pillows and rugs, including an army camouflage summer sleeping bag that Lt Ross was using as a seat cover, were added. The rifle was smuggled into the back of the Prado, wrapped in a rug.

It was all a bit of a rush and twice Rose noticed the white-haired old man looking in their direction.

*I hope he's not one of the enemy,* she thought.

But the old man finally just walked past looking a bit unsteady on his feet, and went into his caravan.

They were all in the Prado and outside the back gate by 1235hrs. By then Rose was in a ferment of impatience.

*Oh hurry up! We will be too late otherwise,* she fretted.

Captain Ross navigated. They drove back around past the front of the hotel and then northwest along the main street. By then it was very hot and the road seemed to disappear into the heat shimmer. After passing a couple of very old and poorly maintained houses, they were out of town. To Rose's surprise, they then drove along a very wide section of bitumen.

"This looks like an airfield," she commented, noticing broad white markings painted across the road.

Lt Ross answered. "It is. It is an emergency landing strip for the Royal Flying Doctor Service. Look, there is the windsock."

Rose was impressed with that idea and she made a point of showing Belinda. But Belinda was looking tired and soon snuggled into her and put her head on her shoulder. But she did not drop off to sleep because immediately past the end of the runway the road became graded gravel. This was just sufficiently corrugated and potholed to make it bumpy.

Captain Ross kept moving his fingertip on the map and every few minutes lifted the map so Rose could see it. She had been along the road only a week before and the first section, until they passed the good road going off to the Mt Egbert Mine, she had been on many times. It was all impressive scenery but she had no eye for it.

A white 4WD came into view from the other direction. Rose went tense and she mentally rehearsed trying to get the rifle ready while having to cope with Belinda on her lap and the problem of taking cover. But it was just a mine vehicle with the logo of another company on it. It went past with the driver giving a friendly wave. Rose relaxed and tried to tell herself it was unlikely the men knew where they were.

The car wound northwest and then north, passing through a variety of vegetation types. There was a lot of spinifex and rugged hills, all of which gave Rose some bad memories and anxiety. But there were also a few very pleasant, forested areas with a fair grass cover. There were plenty of beef cattle in those areas, which got Belinda mooing and singing.

Captain Ross pointed out a few remnants of the old railway: embankments and even some wooden sleepers, grey with age. But mostly the country was dry and none of the creeks had water in them. They passed only one water tank with cattle clustered around it, the road spattered with their droppings. They also crossed a haul road for another mine, clearly marked with warning signs.

After about half an hour they came out of the stony hills into more rolling country. This was covered with plenty of trees, grass, spinifex, and various bushes.

*Including my old friend the sticky bush!* Rose noted.

They passed a vehicle track going off on the right. "The next track to the right is the one we want," Captain Ross said, sending a frisson of anxiety into everyone, except Belinda, who had at last gone to sleep.

It wasn't much of a track. It went down a gentle slope past some rusty old car bodies. Captain Ross got out and scuffed out their vehicle's tracks at the junction and then led the way on foot, pushing bushes aside (And discovering the sticky bush in the process, to his annoyance). They managed to get the car a good hundred metres from the main gravel road and out of sight over the crest of the long slope.

They all got out, Belinda waking during that. Captain Ross showed them the map. "We are about two kilometres from the Dobbyn Headframe, which is here, and we are on the other side of the main road. I suggest we go back to the main road on foot and cross over, then move parallel to it through the bush. Make sure you take your food and water. Ma'am and I will change into our camouflage uniforms now and Rose, you carry that camo bedspread thing. And all go to the toilet now, so you don't have to go later."

They scattered to do this and then all had big drinks of water. Rose wondered what the temperature was, and Lt Ross consulted her mobile phone.

"Still works. Good reception too. Must be because of the mines," she said, and read the air temperature: 38 degrees Celsius. "Bit hot. We will take it slow."

Both Captain Ross and Lt Ross now dragged sets of basic webbing out of the back of the Prado. "We always carry our webbing in case of emergencies," he explained. Swinging his on, he said, "I will go fifty metres ahead as scout."

Rose was jealous of that webbing. *I wish I'd had my webbing last week!* she thought.

"Okay, let's move!" Captain Ross said, hefting the rifle to check it.

Dressed as he now was in his army camouflage uniform, he looked the part. The sight was simultaneously reassuring and worrying to Rose. She understood that if it came to a gun battle both he and Lt Ross could be killed, and even if they weren't they could be in terrible legal trouble.

*This isn't an approved cadet activity,* she thought, remembering the jargon he and ma'am often used. *They could be chucked out of cadets for doing the wrong thing.* She was also aware that what they were doing was terribly dangerous. *There could be shooting. And if those men do shoot Dad, what can we do anyway?*

Exactly what they planned to do when they got closer to the area was not clear and Rose assumed the adults knew what they had in mind. She was just glad to be with them and with Belinda. But she was scared. There was so much apprehension she found she was breathing rapidly again. By thinking about it she controlled her breathing and calmed herself.

The group pushed their way through the scrub back to the main road. Captain Ross had crossed by then but held up his hand to halt and then put it behind his ear. They listened but Rose could not hear any sound of traffic, just cicadas.

"Be very quiet, Bubby," she whispered. "Bad men here."

Belinda nodded and put her finger to her lips. Rose smiled and kissed her cheek, then moved with Lt Ross to cross, scuffing out their boot prints as they did. Once across they followed Captain Ross away from the main road for a hundred paces. Then they turned right and began walking slowly forward.

After a few minutes they stopped while Captain Ross scouted ahead. Rose moved over beside Lt Ross. "Ma'am, where are we going?"

"Captain Ross plans to go to a big creek a few hundred metres this side of the Headframe area," she replied. "There is plenty of cover there."

Rose had not been there so could only nod. But she could picture the area around the headframe. The headframe itself was a huge steel structure that had once stood over a mine shaft. It was now preserved as a historical heritage structure, and it stood in a large area of bare gravel surrounded by dry but fairly open bush and a few trees. She remembered having her photo taken there.

They moved at a very slow walk, Captain Ross just visible flitting through the cover ahead of them. It was hot, there were flies and there were sticky bushes! Rose began to doubt the wisdom of the plan.

*If the crooks are watching the place they will be hiding somewhere in the bush around the clearing. And there may be more than one of them,* she reasoned.

She pictured stumbling on the enemy at close range with a resulting deadly exchange of fire. That caused her to shudder and consider trying to persuade the Rosses to change their plan. Also, she could not see what they could do to protect her father.

*We can only react afterwards and then go and get the police,* she thought.

It was a horrible prospect, but she was determined and kept plodding on, despite sleeping Belinda getting heavier and heavier by the minute. They had a rest after twenty minutes and Lt Ross offered to carry Belinda for a while. Rose was glad to accept, and she found the next twenty minutes much easier. At the end of it Captain Ross came back to where they were crouched in the shade. He pointed to his right.

"There is a clearing just over there with some rusty machinery and old gravel scrapes and so on. We are right next to the old railway now, see."

Rose had to look and then wondered how she had not noticed. Only about 25 metres to her right was a very obvious earth embankment with a level top, the earthworks of the old permanent way. Captain Ross grinned.

"I have been here before. The big creek is just ahead there. We can go a bit further safely."

So they did. And the big creek was just that, big. It had high banks of dusty black earth that were so high and steep that they had to scout to the left for fifty paces to find a path down. This was a dusty cattle pad and Captain Ross insisted that Lt Ross come last and scuff out their boot prints. The creek bed was also a problem. It was 50 metres wide and just open sand.

"A tactical obstacle rather than a physical one," Captain Ross explained.

He moved to scan the other bank carefully while they crouched in the end of small gully. Then he strode quickly across, his boots sinking into the sand and gravel. Once on the other side he went up a gully and scouted both ways along the top of the bank, rifle at the ready.

Rose looked to her right and was surprised to see four big concrete structures standing in line across the creek bed. Then she shook her head. *They are the bridge supports for the railway bridge,* she thought.

She was surprised at how big they were but supposed that they needed to be if a huge steam engine was going to safely cross the bridge.

Then Captain Ross signalled them to cross. Rose walked as quickly as she could, lugging Belinda again. She found the sand hard to walk on and arrived panting and sweating at the far side. Captain Ross met them.

"I was hoping for more cover here in the creek bed. I think it is safe to push on a bit further," he said.

They made their way up another cattle pad to the top of the bank and Rose found they were in among lots of trees and bushes, the dense growth along the creek banks. To her right she could just detect the earthworks of the old railway. There seemed to be plenty of cover and shade. But then she gave a wry face.

*That means there is plenty of cover for enemy snipers too!* she thought.

They crept forward, slowly. Tension was now palpable, and Rose was braced to cover Belinda's mouth or to dive for cover. The vegetation was close: visibility only ten to fifty paces. It was 1445hrs and she knew Captain Ross wanted to be in position by then.

They came to a small creek or gully, possibly a flood overflow channel. The bottom was covered with dry leaves and deadfall and suddenly Captain Ross froze and held up his hand to stop. Rose was only a couple of paces behind him now with Lt Ross on her heels.

"Stop!" he hissed, warning clear in his tone. He moved the rifle barrel to point down beside her.

Rose's gaze followed the line of the barrel, and she gasped in shock. There, only a metre or so away, was an enormous brown snake!

# Chapter 29

## REAL COURAGE

*S*nake!

Rose froze in fear. At a glance she took in the length, well over a metre, thickness, and the brown colouring. She saw with horror that it was drawing back its head. Her gaze focused on those tiny, evil eyes and the flickering forked tongue.

Captain Ross brought the butt of the rifle to his shoulder and he tried aiming. "Stand still, Rose," he muttered.

But Rose had now noticed something else, the snake was having difficulty drawing itself into the striking 'S' shape. *It is moulting,* she thought.

She croaked back, "Don't shoot, sir, it is shedding its skin."

*And if he shoots then the enemy will know we are here!*

Keeping her eyes on the snake and tensing ready to try to spring back Rose slowly moved her right leg back half a step. The snake moved but did not strike. But Belinda moved and sighed.

*Oh, don't wake up, Bub-O!* Rose thought. By now her heart was hammering with fear and her breathing rate had shot up.

Taking courage with an effort she moved her left leg back a pace. Leaves crackled and the snake did a twitch but still did not move. Instead it hunched back and went lower. Exhaling in long deep breaths Rose again moved her right foot back a whole pace. By then she was well over a metre from the snake.

*I will take another step back,* she told herself, very aware that she was terrified.

Slowly she did so, more dead leaves crackling under her boot. The snake reacted by lowering its head to the leaves and looking around. Thinking she was now safe, Rose took two more steps back.

*I am definitely out of range now,* she reasoned.

Captain Ross obviously thought so too as he lowered the rifle and also stepped away, up the slope out of the dip.

At that, the snake turned and began sliding away. As it did, the pieces of old skin and areas of shiny new skin became very obvious in a patch of sunlight. Rose had seen snakes vanish in a flash but obviously the shedding process restricted it as it only slowly dragged itself out of sight into a big clump of spinifex up on the top of the other bank.

Captain Ross breathed out and shook his head. "Oh, that was no fun!" he muttered. "I'm glad I didn't have to shoot. Trying to hit a moving snake with a rifle is a very chancy business." He slipped the safety catch back on and theatrically wiped his brow. "Sorry about that. I should have seen the bugger, but I was trying to peek over the top to see if I could see the headframe."

Rose now realised she was still holding her breath and getting dizzy. She let her breath out and took a deep one, then turned around and went back along the dip, her eyes now scanning the leaf litter anxiously. Lt Ross moved with her and Captain Ross followed, coming back down into the dip while casting anxious glances back over his right shoulder.

"I can't really see the clearing from here," he muttered.

That was a worry. They walked 25 metres east along the dip, passing between a line of low concrete pillars that had once supported the old railway. Twenty paces further on they came to a dense stand of trees and stopped in a nice open hollow with plenty of shade.

It was decided they were close enough and Lt Ross took the camouflage sleeping bag and unrolled it. It was spread in the shade and Rose lowered Belinda onto it. As she was put down Belinda twitched her arms and legs and snuffled but she stayed asleep. To Rose's relief, she rolled on her side and put her thumb in her mouth.

Captain Ross nodded with satisfaction. "You two stay here with bub while I try to find a spot where I can observe."

"You take care," Lt Ross replied, obviously concerned.

Captain Ross gave a thumbs up and then moved up behind a bush on top of the bank and peered through. He then lay down and aimed the rifle. "This might do," he whispered. "I can see the headframe. Come and look, one at a time."

Lt Ross went first and then nodded. As she turned to come back down Rose got up and made her way carefully up to lie beside Captain Ross. At first all she could see was long grass and spinifex clumps close to her but by lifting her head slightly she could see over them and noted an area of dry, open bush with a covering of short grass and spinifex and with scattered, spindly black-trunked trees. There were some dark coloured objects which she could not identify but no sign of the headframe. The only real clue was a brighter area of sunlight beyond which indicated a clearing.

"Use this," Captain Ross said, passing her the rifle.

Rose took it, fumbling with sweaty fingers to grip the smooth wood and then to find the eye relief and focus. Through the telescopic sight the scene sprang into clear images. The dark-coloured objects resolved themselves into rusty old pieces of machinery and few rusty 44-gallon drums.

Then she focused on the strip of reddish gravel she could see and saw that it was the clearing, which she knew was about a hundred paces across. And there was the headframe. She was surprised she had not seen it earlier, but it was also black with rust or paint and its thin legs were mixed with the spindly black trees.

"Yes, this will do," she whispered.

"No point in trying to get closer. That will just be an unjustified risk," Captain Ross replied. He indicated another shallow gully or dip ten metres ahead. "I could get into that and go closer but only by crawling."

Rose's gaze followed his pointing finger and saw that there were more low concrete bridge supports to her left where the railway had once crossed the second gully. From where they lay, she saw that the gullies led east into thicker stands of trees and bushes which were closer to the clearing and the road.

"If there is a sniper he could be in those trees," she suggested, her anxiety making her croak.

Captain Ross nodded but then pointed to her left front. "Or up on that low rocky rise there in among those bushes. There is a huge open cut mine pit over beyond that."

"I know sir. Dad showed me," Rose said, remembering looking down, astonished at the size of the huge hole excavated in the side of the hill she could see in the distance.

At that moment, she heard a vehicle. It was coming from behind their right shoulder, from the direction of Kajabbi.

*Is that Dad coming from Mt Egbert?* Rose wondered, her anxiety level shooting right up again.

Lt Ross heard it too and crawled up beside them. Into view came a white 4WD. It slowed and turned off the main road into the clearing and came to a stop near the headframe.

"Five to," Captain Ross muttered, checking his watch. He then opened his left basic pouch and extracted a pair of binoculars. "Have a look, Anne," he offered.

Lt Ross took the binoculars but Rose barely noticed. Her vision was focused on the man who had stepped out of the vehicle. It was her father. Her heart gave a little jolt, and she swallowed as apprehension tightened her throat and chest. Her father reached into the back seat and took out a brown hat of the type bush people wear (Not the American 'Cowboy Hat' style. Rose knew he did not approve of that). Her father then reached in again and lifted out a rucksack, a heavy rucksack judging by the effort it took,

*Must have gold in it,* Rose thought, knowing that gold was very heavy.

With anxiety making her breathing and heart rate fast she kept the cross-hairs on her father as he walked to the headframe. Now almost holding her breath with anxiety she watched him start pacing off to her left front.

*Towards where that sniper might be,* she told herself.

Lt Ross focused the binoculars. "Now there is one very brave man," she muttered.

"It certainly takes a lot of courage to walk right out there in the open knowing you could be shot dead at any second," Captain Ross agreed. Then he shook his head. "Sorry Rose."

Which caused Rose a mixture of extreme anxiety and great pride. *Real courage!* she thought, wondering if she could do a thing like that. To her credit, she thought she could. *If it was to save my family.*

Through blurry, anxious eyes she watched her father stride into the edge of the spinifex and bushes at the base of the low rise. He halted, swung the rucksack off and lowered it out of sight. Without even glancing around he turned and started walking back towards the vehicle.

*If he is going to be murdered, it will be now,* she thought, tensing and getting ready to use the rifle.

An anxious minute later, her father was back at his vehicle and no shot had been fired. He opened the driver's door and slid into the seat. Rose exhaled and sighed with relief. She did not think the crooks would shoot now. She heard the vehicle's engine start and then watched with relief as it started moving. Her father swung it around and drove it back out to the main road. There he turned it right and it vanished in the direction of Mt Egbert.

Rose gasped and lay down, trembling with reaction. "Safe!" she muttered. She was about to get up when Captain Ross put his hand on her shoulder.

"Stay still. We will wait awhile."

Rose understood why, to see if the crooks were there. *They can't be far away if they want to collect the ransom money,* she reasoned.

A glance behind showed her Belinda still sleeping in the shade. Another glance around behind her showed no sign of any reptiles.

So they stayed there, lying behind the bushes in the long grass. Time soon started to drag. It was very hot. There were flies. And there were ants. These began to trouble Belinda and she muttered and began to move around. Rose knew she should go back and be ready to keep her quiet if she woke up. But she really wanted to see if there were any men hiding nearby. When Lt Ross moved back down to Belinda and began brushing ants off her Rose felt a mixture of relief and guilt.

In the heat she became drowsy and found her eyelids starting to droop. A small black ant nipped her on the sweaty left wrist and she gave a stifled yelp before crushing the tiny creature and flicking it away. Flies kept crawling at the sides of her eyes and at her nostrils, obviously seeking moisture. Then she realised she was thirsty. She lay the rifle down and quickly slid back down into the hollow. After a quick drink she crawled back up into position and then rested her arms on the rifle stock.

*Movement!* Rose blinked, focused her eyes and stared. *Yes, there is someone there!* she thought as a person stood up among the bushes at the crest of the rise about 50 metres from where her father had placed the ransom.

The person was wearing some sort of shaggy costume. Rose had seen them at cadets and recognised it as a 'Yowie' suit, a costume made of pieces of hessian cut in long strips (Scrim) and sewn on to old camouflage clothes or onto camouflage netting.

Captain Ross saw him as well and touched Rose's arm. "A sniper," he whispered. As he said it, the sniper pushed the scrim back from around his head to reveal his face.

"Lucas," Rose said. "And he's got a new rifle." She could clearly see an object that could only be a rifle, even though it was wrapped in hessian and scrim.

At that moment, a second person stood up nearby but he was in dark blue work clothes. Rose lifted the rifle to squint through the telescopic sight. Into focus leapt the face of Cousin James.

*You bastard!* she thought, a spurt of intense anger surging through her as images of all the fear and pain she had endured because of him flitted across her mind.

She brought the butt of the rifle into her shoulder and reached up with her right thumb to click off the safety catch.

Captain Ross reached across and firmly clicked it back on. "No Rose. Even if you hit him, it is wrong. You do not want to take a life and spend the remainder of yours feeling guilty, never mind the religious concept of damning your soul. He isn't worth it. Let the justice system deal with him."

Rose experienced and massive surge of relief and shame. *I nearly lost control then,* she thought.

"Thank you, sir," she whispered.

"Take these," he said, handing her the binoculars while at the same time lifting the rifle away from her with his other hand.

Now shivering with reaction, Rose focused the binoculars and looked across to where Cousin James and Lucas were walking through the scrub down to where the ransom had been placed. To Rose's annoyance the distance was just sufficient for the afternoon heat shimmer to distort what she was seeing. But it was clear enough for all that. Cousin James bent down and picked the rucksack up. He was obviously surprised by its weight and made a comment to Lucas and then laughed. The rucksack was unbuckled, and both men looked inside and even from that far away Rose saw them grin. The sight of her enemies being triumphant made her grind her teeth.

*Mongrels!* she thought.

Then Cousin James reached down to his belt and lifted a small radio or mobile phone to his head. On seeing it was actually one of the hand-held radios Rose muttered a swear word.

*Oh you idiot!* She told herself. *You should have brought that radio with you.*

"What was that, Rose?" Lt Ross whispered.

"Oh Miss… Ma'am, I took one of those radios off Lucas. It is in my backpack. We could be listening in to learn their plans."

Rose quickly handed her the binoculars and slid back down to where her backpack lay on the sleeping bag. Quickly she unbuckled the top flap and felt around inside. It took her a minute to find the radio and then another half minute to turn it on and lift it to her ear. As she did, she crawled back up to join the Rosses.

But all they heard was a crackle of static and "ger, Over." After that there was nothing. Rose saw Cousin James put the radio on his belt and the two men walked out to stand beside the headframe. They kept looking out towards the main road and were obviously waiting. While they did Lucas leaned his rifle against one of the uprights and then took off his 'Yowie' suit.

A couple of minutes went by and then Rose heard a vehicle approaching. To her surprise, it came from the north. It was another white 4WD and was travelling fast. As it got closer it slowed and then turned in to the clearing. It was driven over next to the waiting men and they placed the rucksack in the back and then got in. Rose could not see the driver clearly enough to identify him but thought it might be Marvin.

The vehicle moved off with a roar and a spray of dust and gravel. It went back out to the main road but then, to Rose's surprise, it turned right and went off in the direction of Kajabbi. For a minute or so she could hear it as it went down across the big creek and then off into the distance.

"I didn't expect it to go that way," she said, relaxing and standing up.

Captain Ross also stood up and slid his binoculars back into his basic pouch. "No. That is a worry. I think we had better wait a while before we go." He looked at his watch and Rose noted it was 1520hrs.

The three of them moved back down into the dip and all had big drinks. Belinda was stirring on by then and she had to be coaxed to drink and then to go to the toilet in the bush. Rose took the opportunity to go herself, eyeing every clump spinifex with a very wary eye as she did.

*Bad enough having the spinifex prickle my bum,* she thought. *But I don't want to be bitten on it!* The silly joke about the army snipers came to her and she managed a smile. *But what do we do now?*

That was what the Rosses were discussing when she carried Belinda back. Belinda was put down on the sleeping bag and at once began crawling around on it, reaching off to pick up sticks and gum nuts. Rose had another drink and sat down, suddenly feeling quite drained.

"Do we just go back to the hotel?" she asked.

Captain Ross shrugged. "I don't see what else we can do. I think we will just have to wait now until your father can get us a message to tell us what to do," he said.

"I hope he didn't go back there hoping to see us," Rose said.

That was an awful thought. But what was really bothering her was worry about her mother, where she might be and how to get her to safety.

Captain Ross held up his mobile phone. "He has my number. I wrote it on the 'coaster' I gave him so he can easily get a message to us."

Lt Ross also looked at the phone and said, "If there is service."

Captain Ross checked and nodded. "There seems to be good service in all this country. I suppose it is because of all the big mines. It is amazing really because nobody else seems to live out here."

Rose could only agree with that. She had not seen a single building between Kajabbi and where they were. *It is just more empty wilderness.* She was about to tell herself she had had enough of this sort of country when she shook her head. *No, I like it!* she thought. She realised that it did not frighten her anymore.

"Oh well, let's get back to the car," Captain Ross said, bending to pick up the rifle.

Rose stood up and plucked Belinda away from her play and set about distracting her by getting her to look for the crow she could hear in a nearby tree. Lt Ross scooped up the sleeping bag and quickly rolled it and shoved it through her web straps. After a quick check that nothing was left lying around, they started walking.

As before, they went in single file, Captain Ross leading with the rifle. He followed the route they had used to get there, but walked much faster. Worry about snakes kept Rose looking continually at the ground ahead of her but he just seemed to stroll along. He was obviously very 'at home' in the bush. It took only a couple of minutes to reach the big creek and a couple more to cross it. This time they did not brush out their tracks.

Walking back through the bush quickly raised a sweat in the afternoon heat and Rose found she was puffing and perspiring. And Belinda felt like she was getting heavier.

"You are eating too much Bubby," she said. "You weigh a ton!"

Belinda looked indignant. "I not! I Ball of Blubber Daddy said."

"You are," Rose agreed.

*And he got into trouble from Mummy for saying that. Oh, I hope mum is alright!*

Then she tried to distract her by looking for the kookaburra that was cackling at them from a big gum tree. However they saw no sign of it, until it suddenly swooped low overhead and landed in another tree ahead of them where it set up more of its maniacal sounding laughter.

They got another good nature distraction for Belinda when they were back near the Prado. They had just crossed the road when Captain Ross stopped and pointed to his right. Rose looked but could not see anything unusual. It was only when Lt Ross gave a clearer indication that she saw the ears of a big kangaroo poking up above the spinifex. It was a big roo resting in the shade of a tree. He was about 50 metres away and visible along what might have been the overgrown clearing of an old road.

It took a while to get Belinda to look and when she saw it she let out a little cry that was so loud it disturbed the animal. The big roo had been watching them, its ears twitching, but now it stood up, obviously alarmed. And that alarmed Rose.

"Holy Mackerel!" she gasped. "Look at the size of it!"

It was full-grown male red kangaroo and stood taller than her. She had heard stories of kangaroos attacking people, of boxing with them and of standing on their tail to use the claws on their powerful hind legs to rip people open so she experienced a real spurt of anxiety. But when Belinda squeaked again the kangaroo turned and began bounding away.

"Kangawoo! Kangawoo!" Belinda cried, clapping her hands.

They resumed walking and five minutes later were back at the vehicle. Rose had been worrying that the crooks might have seen it but Captain Ross did a careful circuit of it first and then checked it before opening the doors. Before getting in they all had another drink. The rifle was wrapped in the cam sleeping bag and placed in the back, along with their webbing and Rose's backpack.

The Prado was turned in the scrub and driven back out, Captain Ross driving this time. "We take turn and turn about," he explained.

Rose nodded, aware that her mother left all the driving and vehicle stuff to her father.

There was obvious tension on the half hour drive back to Kajabbi, worry in case they encountered the crooks along the road, even an irrational fear of ambush. In the whole distance they only met one other vehicle, a dark blue Prado going towards Dobbyn.

"I wonder where they are going?" Captain Ross queried.

"Probably to some station homestead," Lt Ross suggested.

They passed the cattle at the water tank and the turn-off to Mt Egbert without incident and then they were back at the section of bitumen forming the emergency landing strip. Captain Ross slowed to study the sky and the road before driving on along it.

As they approached Kajabbi he drove slower, and Rose joined in peering ahead to see what vehicles might be parked outside the hotel.

"We will look silly if we just drive in and the crooks are there celebrating," Captain Ross suggested.

But there were no vehicles in front of the hotel so they relaxed a bit and the Prado was driven slowly past. It all looked normal so they turned right into the next street and then right again into the street at the back. The caravans were still there and the camper trailer. Lt Ross got out to open the gate and they drove in. She closed the gate and followed on foot. Captain Ross reversed the Prado in where it had been and switched off the motor and got out. Rose opened the door to put Belinda down.

As she did, the owner of the hotel hurried across the back lawn. "G'day," he called. "I hate to say it, but I think youse have been burgled!"

# Chapter 30

## DISCOVERED?

*B*urgled! Rose clutched her throat in alarm. *Have the crooks discovered we are here?*

She turned to look at the camper trailer and saw that the door was open and swinging gently in the breeze. She picked Belinda up and got ready to run.

Lt Ross also glanced at the open door and said, "Do you know who by and when?"

The hotel owner shook his head, glancing at Rose and Belinda as he did. "Aw! Not really. Three blokes in their late twenties or early thirties, all dressed in yellow 'Hi vis' work shirts. They came into the bar about an hour ago. They asked if Mr MacGregor from the mine was here, and I said no and then they walked over here and one of them got up and undid the Velcro around your door there and stuck his arm in and unlocked it. I don't think they broke anything. Sorry, but it looked like one of them had an automatic pistol in the back of his pants, so I stayed in the bar," he explained.

Captain Ross made a face. "Probably just as well you did. Tell me, did Mr MacGregor come here this afternoon?"

The hotel owner nodded. "He did, about half an hour before the three men. He asked if the people in the camper trailer were here and then came over and knocked. When he got no answer, he came back and thanked me and then drove off."

Lt Ross pursed her lips. "Do you know Mr MacGregor?"

The hotel owner nodded again. "Sure. He's stayed here a couple of times." He then paused and looked hard at Rose. "He and his family stayed here for a night a week or so ago."

"Don't they have accommodation at the mine?" Captain Ross asked.

"I guess. Never been there, but he said he likes to get out and meet ordinary people."

At that, Rose nodded and said, "That's Dad. He likes to keep in touch with real people, he says."

And as soon as she said it she stopped and thought, *Oh, you bloody idiot! Now you have told him you are his daughter!*

Both Captain Ross and Lt Ross frowned and gave her hard looks but all she could do was feel ashamed and shrug. The hotel owner also looked hard at her.

"Sorry, I thought so but didn't like to ask. When I saw you yesterday, I was sure I had seen you and the little girl before."

Belinda had been listening and now looked indignant. "I not little girl! I big girl now!" she cried.

"You are! You are certainly a heavy girl," Rose replied, now feeling very foolish and quite scared.

*We have been discovered. That is a real problem.* Then another horrifying thought crossed her mind.

"Did you call the police?" she asked.

To her relief, the hotel owner shook his head. "No. I thought it all so odd I decided to wait until you came back. Do you want me to?"

Rose shook her head emphatically. "No, please no."

At that, the hotel owner frowned and looked worried but then nodded. "Okay. I will leave it to you."

Captain Ross asked, "Did these three men say anything or give any clue as to what they wanted?"

The hotel owner nodded and gestured to the next caravan. "Yeah, they went and talked to old Brody there."

Rose glanced that way and was just in time to see the face of the old white-haired man withdraw from watching them through a side window.

"The Bar Fly," she muttered. "I wondered."

At that, all three adults nodded. The hotel owner pursed his lips. "Bar Fly! Yes, that's a good description."

"Well, now we can guess where he gets his money from," Captain Ross added. "Did he tell you anything?"

"I haven't questioned him," the hotel owner answered. "I wasn't sure if it was my business. I don't think the men took anything. They just looked inside and came away muttering."

"I might question him now," Captain Ross snarled.

Lt Ross put her arm on his sleeve. "No! Just leave it."

The hotel owner looked worried. "Is there something I can do? Are you sure you don't want to call the police?"

At that, Rose got really alarmed. "Oh no!" she cried at the same time as Captain Ross saying, "I don't think that is necessary."

And Lt Ross said, "I will just have a quick look inside to see if anything has been taken."

At that, the hotel owner looked decidedly worried. "It is something serious, isn't it?" he queried.

Captain Ross nodded. "Yes, but it is family business. Mr MacGregor wouldn't like it becoming public knowledge yet."

The hotel owner looked far from happy at this but nodded. "Okay, well, if I can help."

"Did you tell the men where we had gone?" Captain Ross answered.

"I said I thought you had gone to Mount Isa along the Lake Julius Road," the hotel owner answered, pointing off towards the south. He shrugged. "I didn't actually see which way you went but I remembered you talking about that road in the bar last night."

"And which way did the men go?" Captain Ross asked.

The hotel owner pointed south. "That way, along the Lake Julius Road. That was about half an hour ago."

Captain Ross glanced that way and nodded. "Have you seen these men before?"

"Yeah, they have been past a few times, usually only one or two of them. I overheard them telling Old Brody that they were camping at the Rodeo Ground over at Quamby," he said, pointing east.

"We've been to Quamby," Captain Ross replied, looking very thoughtful.

Lt Ross rejoined them after being in the camper trailer for a few minutes. "It doesn't look like anything has been taken. They obviously searched the cupboards and our suitcases and under the bench seats, but everything seems to be there."

Rose was now becoming very anxious. "They must suspect we are staying here," she said. "What do we do now?"

"Go somewhere else till your father settles this little problem," Captain Ross replied.

"Yes, but where?" Lt Ross said, then glanced at the hotel owner.

He took the hint. "Look, I'll tell them you just drove off and I wasn't looking. If you want, I will contact the cops. You call me if you need any... er... need any help. You've got the hotel number?"

"Yes," Captain Ross agreed. "Thanks. Well, we might move to another caravan park. There's one at Quamby isn't there?"

"Behind the hotel," the hotel owner said.

Lt Ross shook her head. "Let's go back to Mount Isa."

"Alright. Thanks mate," Captain Ross said. "We will pack up and go." He glanced at his watch. "Nearly five thirty. We should make it before dark if we move fast. But we will go along the bitumen. I don't want to we meet these fellows on the other road."

"Okay, I'll leave you to it," the hotel owner said, looking very hard at all of them again. He then walked away towards the back of the hotel.

As soon as he was out of earshot, Rose cried, "We aren't going to Mount Isa are we?" She obviously did not think that was a good idea.

Captain Ross shook his head slightly. "No, that was just for the enemy's consumption. I have a plan. Okay, Rose, you go and play with Belinda, over there with the puppies, while we pack the camper trailer and hook it on. Keep a good lookout and be ready to run over here if there is a problem," he instructed.

For the next twenty minutes Rose did that. Belinda was happy, except when she ran and tripped over a puppy, with resulting tears. These were quickly solved by Rose picking her up and kissing her and then blowing 'raspberries' on each of her fat cheeks until she giggled. Then it was back to playing. Rose snatched the opportunity to quickly go to the toilet and, with some difficulty, persuading Belinda to do the same.

During this time, the Rosses packed things as quickly as they could. Many things which should have gone into the back of the Prado were put on the floor of the camper trailer. Lt Ross was not happy about this as it affected the weight and balance for towing, but Captain Ross assured her it would only be for a short time. The beds were slid in and the door hinged up and then the top wound down and locked tight.

Rose was then called to help fill water bottles, leaving Belinda for a few minutes. During this whole time Rose kept listening for the approach of any vehicles and looking anxiously around. Two vehicles came from the west, but both were mine vehicles and did not stop. Twice she noticed a face peeking out of the old man's caravan. The couple in the second caravan just said hello and went to have showers and started cooking. Rose would have loved to have had a shower but there was no way she was going to place herself at that much risk.

*I don't want to be caught in the nuddy by those men!* she thought.

The Prado was backed up and hooked onto the camper trailer at 1750hrs. By then the sun was well down to the west and Rose was getting very anxious. Worry about the men returning, added to anxiety over her mother and father put a real strain in her nerves. And this was on top of hours out in the sun and walking through the bush in the heat, which all left her feeling exhausted.

"Okay Rose, bring bubby," Lt Ross called.

She began walking towards the back gate, so Rose just ignored Belinda's protests and wails to stay with the puppies and hurried her to the Prado. To shut Belinda up she gave her Bunny. As quickly as she could she slid into her seat and did up her seat belt. Captain Ross lifted Belinda in and the door was closed. Captain Ross hurried to his seat and got the vehicle and tow moving. By then Rose was in a fever of impatience to be gone before the men returned.

As the vehicle began moving, Rose glanced towards the old man's caravan to see if he was watching. He was and she curled her lip and poked her tongue at him. His face quickly vanished.

*Horrible man!* she thought,

As soon as they were through the gate and Lt Ross was in her seat, Captain Ross began driving. They went left in the back street and then left along the next. As that street was also the start of the Lake Julius Road to Mount Isa if they had turned right Rose sighed with relief.

*At least we are out of the hotel yard and moving away from our enemies!*

As they came to the intersection, Lt Ross asked, "Which way are we going?"

Captain Ross pointed. "North, along this road," he replied.

Rose had suspected that. She did not think he had intended to go left and back towards Dobbyn. That was a dead-end road into the wilderness.

Within a hundred metres they came to another decision point, an intersection with the signpost pointing right indicating to Quamby and Cloncurry. Instead Captain Ross drove straight on northwards.

"I'd like to stop and brush out our tracks but think that would be a waste of time," he said. "The next vehicle along, if it isn't the crook's, will do that."

Rose was curious. "Where does this road go, sir?" she asked.

"North to a couple of cattle stations. The first one is called 'Coolullah' but just before then there is a turn-off to the east which goes out to the main highway, the Burke Development Road that is," he replied.

The road was a good, graded gravel one and he soon had the tow up to nearly the speed limit. Dust trailed up behind them. On both sides there was just bush, more trees and grass than spinifex. And there were lots of cattle which caused them to have to slow to a crawl on three occasions. This put Rose in a fever of impatience at the thought of the crooks catching them up, but at least the cattle amused Belinda.

After a while, with the sun now slanting in from low to the west, Captain Ross slowed and then stopped at the second dirt track Rose had noted going off on the left. It led through a wire gate into an overgrazed paddock with dozens of cattle in it camping around a windmill, water tank and water trough.

"This might do," he said. "Has that wire gate got a padlock?"

It did not, so Lt Ross quickly got out and opened it, holding it taught so the wires would not tangle. Captain Ross drove through and stopped. Leaving the motor running he opened his door and got out. Then he leaned back in and said, "We are going to brush out our wheel tracks before we close the gate."

Rose liked that idea. It took the Rosses a couple of minutes to do that. They used small branches broken off the sides of bushes away from the road. The gate was then closed and Captain Ross drove slowly forward towards the cattle, which were by then all starting to get to their feet and shuffle around. Lt Ross followed on foot, brushing out the wheel tracks until they were close to the water trough. By then the cattle had all moved aside. They were obviously used to vehicles and people as some came closer, obviously excepting food.

Lt Ross kept her bush and kept walking as Captain Ross drove on into the trees beyond the dusty clearing. Rose glanced back and saw that the cattle were already moving back to the area they had driven through.

*They should hide our tracks really well,* she thought, remembering how she had hoped the cattle would cover her own boot prints the previous week.

Captain Ross drove carefully into the bush for about a hundred metres, aiming away from the road, which was unfortunately almost directly into the sun. The route he chose wound between trees and around bushes and logs. He kept going until the windmill and cattle were just visible through the scrub. As the bush was getting more and more dense, he stopped and got out. Lt Ross dusted the bare patches he had driven over and stood up a few clumps of grass until she joined them,

"I don't think they will find us in the dark easily," Captain Ross said.

Rose shook her head, a dismaying memory coming to her. "They used spotlights when they were looking for Bub-O and me," she said.

"Did they indeed!" Captain Ross cried. "Okay, we had better cover the taillights and reflectors. Hop out Rose and hold Belinda while we do a bit of camouflaging."

The back of the Prado was opened. Out came basic webbing and her backpack and then two army packs. "We usually take these in case we need to camp," Captain Ross said apologetically.

The back of the Prado was then closed and two camouflage plastic Shelter Individuals which were clipped together were taken out of a pack.

"Oh, a hutchie!" Rose cried.

She was very familiar with them as that was how the cadets camped when on bivouacs. She learned that this double one was ma'am's as it was draped over the rear end of the white Prado to hide it from anyone on the road.

Next the camouflage sleeping bag was tied across the rear end of the camper trailer to cover its taillights and reflectors. Captain Ross used a small folding step and a length or rope that came out of the pocket in back of the driver's seat. That done Captain Ross walked back fifty paces to check if that was sufficient camouflage.

By then it was 1825hrs and the sun was down among the trees. Captain Ross picked up his pack and webbing and the rifle and said, "Grab your backpack Rose and bring Belinda. We are going to hutchie up in those trees further into the bush."

Rose had expected them to put up the camper trailer to sleep in, or at least clear the car seats, but now understood they were going into a 'hide', well away from the vehicles. That this was good tactics was obvious.

*The crooks won't expect that,* she told herself.

Lt Ross pulled her pack and webbing on and picked up a food box and followed. About 50 paces from the vehicle Captain Ross found a small area of bare sand in among a fairly dense clump of trees and bushes.

"This will do," he said, putting down his pack and webbing and leaning the rifle on it. "Now just sit here on this sleeping bag Rose and entertain little Miss Ball of Energy while we put the hutchie up."

The two Officers of Cadets went into an obviously long practiced routine. Another double hutchie was pulled out of the top of the captain's pack and flicked open. Rose noted that the hutchie already had cords attached all around it. Two corners were quickly tied up at waist height to two trees which were the right distance apart. The centre of the double hutchie, where the Shelters Individual were clipped together, were then tied slightly higher between two more trees, making a slightly sloping flat roof. It was high enough for them to sit under. The second hutchie was then pegged down at an angle to form a windbreak. Two plastic groundsheets were spread under it.

Belinda had watched all this with interest and now struggled to get down and free. "Cubby!" she cried. "Want cubby!"

She was allowed to crawl in under the flat roof and immediately she lay down with her head on one of the packs. They all smiled and Rose felt a real easing of anxiety. She had been concerned about sleeping in the bush with Belinda but now saw that it would be no problem. After just sleeping in the open on the ground for five nights Belinda obviously thought this was a very good little 'cubby'.

When Bunny was produced by Lt Ross this situation became positively happy. Captain Ross watched Belinda for a minute or so then said, "Will she be alright if we sleep here in the bush and have no lights? We need to hide ourselves from those men until we have more information to act on," he said.

Rose smiled. "She will be fine, sir. She was no problem when we had to sleep out in the open when we were being hunted."

"We are probably still being hunted," Captain Ross replied.

This sent chills of anxiety through Rose. She had known that but hearing it somehow made it worse. "What will we do, sir? Will we have a piquet?"

Captain Ross nodded. "Yes. We will organise a sentry roster in a while and that means one person on alone, which is never a good idea. But we will have an advantage."

He bent and opened his right basic pouch. Rose thought he was going to get out his binoculars but instead he produced an impressive looking monocular sight.

"This is a fancy night shooting sight," he said, holding it up for her to see. "You have used the unit's infra-red night vision gear. This is like that but much more powerful."

"Where did you get it sir?" Rose asked.

Lt Ross answered that. "Remember that the cadet unit gets grants from the RSL when we put in submissions? We asked for the purchase of another night sight, but this was sent to us in error. The manufacturer did not have the model we asked for so they sent this. You cadets have never been allowed to use it because the laser in it is not eye-safe."

Rose dimly understood that and nodded. Lt Ross went on, pointing to the gadget. "It can be switched on here and it just amplifies the available natural light, same as the ones you cadets use, or you can push this button and that switches on an infra-red beam. Remember that infra-red is invisible to the human eye. It is very powerful and can damage people's eyes if the beam is directed into them. It also marks the target with the famous red spot you see in the movies. It is a very good piece of kit."

"How far away can you see people in the dark ma'am?" she asked.

"At least a hundred metres or more. It is good, and a very clear image," Lt Ross answered. "But remember, if the enemy have infra-red equipment they can see your beam, same as a white light torch. Also remember that it is only battery powered so we can only use it for short periods of time."

Rose felt enormously comforted by them having that sight. "So it should only be used when we hear a vehicle," she stated.

"That's right."

Rose nodded then looked towards the direction of the road. "But what happens if the crooks do discover us?" she asked both OOCs.

Captain Conkey answered that. "We will get ready to move, and if they get close I will fire a warning shot to dissuade them. If they keep advancing, they will bloody well regret it!"

Rose nodded at that, and she had a searing flashback to her own thoughts of having to shoot in the dark if the men had found her and Belinda.

"Good," she said, noting yet again that she was not quite as nice a girl as she had previously believed. She was now sure she would fight to protect those she loved.

Captain Ross gave a grim smile. "I reckon that one shot will be enough. These men are only criminals, not soldiers doing their duty. But, if they persist, then we will just withdraw on a compass course further into the bush and hide in a dip or gully and repeat the process if need be. But I don't think they are up to that level of skill. And I don't think they will be very keen. It is a terrifying business to advance in the dark towards an enemy who has a loaded gun and will shoot. It takes a lot of courage."

Rose nodded and felt enormously comforted. She knew that Captain Ross had been a regular soldier when he was younger and that he had been in real battles. Memories of seeing his medals on ceremonial parades like Anzac Day reinforced this trust. She was sure he would keep them safe.

*And only if those crooks discover where we have gone to!*

---

# Chapter 31

## NIGHT IN THE BUSH

Captain Ross looked around and listened. The evening stillness was starting, broken only by a soft sighing of the wind in the trees and the murmur of the cattle. The sun was now casting very long shadows. He carried his pack and webbing to a nearby patch of bare ground and then carefully positioned the rifle across it. He put his webbing beside it then sat down, facing towards the cattle and the road.

"Let's have some food before it gets to dark," he said.

"Are we staying here all night sir?" Rose asked.

"Unless the crooks find us, or unless your dad contacts us by mobile phone with instructions," Captain Ross replied. He took out his mobile phone and checked it. "We have service but I'd better charge this up. Anne, start cooking please while I do that."

Rose knew that the Prado had a second battery. This was in the passenger foot well and her right leg had been rubbing against it. She knew it ran the small fridge in the back and, she now learned, it could be used to charge mobile phones, cameras, and laptops.

*How handy is that! I must get dad to have one installed,* she thought.

Lt Ross opened her webbing and took out a hexamine stove and dixies (Pan Set Messing in army jargon). She also took out her Cup Canteen Steel and opened the folding handle and locked it in place. Water was added to a mess tin and the cup. The stove was opened out and stood in a clear area of sand and the packet of hexamine inside taken out. Then she opened the packet of hexamine (A hard, white chemical solid fuel). Using her knife she carefully scored across the centre line of one of the small square blocks of hexamine. Deftly she pressed on both side and snapped it neatly in two. Rose knew this was standard practice in their cadet unit. Hexamine was only issued with cadet ration packs during the Annual Field Exercise and was hard to get at other times as they had no entitlement. Yet they did four or five weekend bivouacs a year and needed it to heat meals. So they only used half squares unless it was very windy.

Next Lt Ross took out a box of matches and struck one. This instantly attracted the attention of Belinda. She hurried over and knelt to stare with fascinated interest as Lt Ross picked up the block of hexamine and held the flame under the bottom corner until it had caught fire. The hexamine was placed in the bottom of the stove and the dixie of water lifted on. Belinda went to touch the stove, but Rose was ready and blocked her hand.

"Hot! Burnie! Don't touch, Bub-O," she warned.

Belinda had been at campfires and barbeques often enough to understand so she now sat back and watched intently as the flames grew and licked up around the sides of the mess tin. Rose stared at them also and began to relax. Field cooking was one of those activities she enjoyed most on bivouacs, and she had been a cadet long enough to associate the smell of burning hexamine with food. She began to salivate.

She wished she had her own stove and dixies. For a moment she pictured the cadet Q Store back at NGC. All the cadets in the unit were issued with pack and webbing, hutchie, and mosquito net, plus the stove, Cup Canteen Steel, Knife, Fork and Spoon set (KFS) and dixies. The main items all had the same number on them in felt pen. The cadets were never allowed to take this camping gear home, but when they came for a weekend bivouac or annual camp they got issued with it, the same items each time. It was all handed back at the end of the activity, so the unit never lost any. Only the mess tins and KFS were taken home, to be properly washed and cleaned, ready for use.

Lt Ross now looked up at Rose. "What would you and Bubby like to have?" she asked.

That was a bit of a problem. Rose felt quite dehydrated and worn out after a long day in the sun and she did not really feel like food. But she knew she needed to eat for energy. "Have you got any soup ma'am?" she queried.

A can of chicken and corn soup was found in the food box, and this was opened and poured into another mess tin. Belinda watched this with obvious interest. Then she cried, "Hungwy!"

Lt Ross quickly passed her a biscuit and she began munching on it immediately.

"Say 'Thank You', you greedy little monster!" Rose said.

"I not monster! I Ball of Mischief!" Belinda replied.

Which made them all smile. Hot drinks were quickly prepared, Hot Chocolate for the girls and coffee for the adults. Rose held the cup for Belinda, who still had part of her second biscuit In one hand. Belinda took big gulps with deep breaths between each one.

It was just dark enough by then for the flames to make a bright glow and that was worrying to both adults.

"Be ready to blow that out if a car comes along," Captain Ross commented as he rejoined them.

He sat and took out his own stove and cooking gear and set to work preparing himself a hot drink and a meal, a can of Beef Stroganoff in his case.

Belinda wanted some of this, so she was offered a taste on a spoon. She at once licked her lips and nodded so his meal mostly went down her throat, to everyone's satisfaction. Another biscuit and a big drink of water seemed to fill the little girl up. Rose relaxed even more and enjoyed her own meal of soup and bread. And then Belinda reached forward and touched a hot mess tin.

"Waah! Wah! Oh sob, sob!" she cried, bursting into tears.

Rose at once lifted her clear and looked at the fingertips and then stuck them in her mouth to suck them (No ice!). She was annoyed with herself for letting it happen.

Lt Ross looked concerned. "Is it bad?" she asked.

Rose pulled the fingers out and held the chubby little hand up for her to see. "I don't think so, Ma'am. I think she just got a fright. Maybe a small blister?"

There wasn't and after a few minutes of cuddling, kissing, and wiping her tear-streaked face Belinda calmed down. A big drink of cool fruit juice helped.

The evening meal took about half an hour. By then it was dusk and the remaining flames were blown out (So the piece of remaining hexamine could be used again). They then sat and finished the meal in the growing darkness. At Lt Ross's suggestion Belinda was taken out to do a pee. Rose went at the same time and so did Lt Ross, each walking off in different directions into the bush. Rose found it a bit of a challenge as there was not enough open ground to get away from the long grass properly and she kept thinking about that snake!

Mosquito nets were next. Two dark green army nets were hung up from the flat hutchie, side by side. It took the two OOCs only a few minutes, even in the dark. Rose could only shake her head. She and her friends and the newer cadets often took half an hour or more to tie those four slip knots!

By then it was fully dark, and Rose was worried Belinda might get upset but she seemed quite happy and when a rug and pillow was placed under the left mosquito net she sat there humming and talking baby talk to Bunny. The layout was all heads towards the sloping 'back wall' hutchie, with the packs and webbing stored up under it. Under the flat hutchie was to be Rose on the left and then Belinda, both under one mozzie net; then Lt Ross and Captain Ross on the right. He placed the rifle on the outside on the groundsheet.

"You won't need the rifle during sentry duty," he said. "We have the night sight. If anyone hears anything they are to wake everyone anyway and I can use the rifle if need be."

Rose half suspected that he was remembering when she had put the cross hairs on Cousin James that afternoon and did not want any tragedy on the spur of the moment. She could only nod, and then slap at a mosquito that had buzzed on to her arm. It was very dark, and mostly very quiet.

Captain Ross said, "It is coming up to nineteen hundred now. Time to go to bed and to start our sentry roster. I thought I would do the first for two hours, till 2100hrs. That is the time when the men are most likely to be out searching for us."

Nobody objected so he went on. "Anne, you do from 2100hrs to 2300hrs and Rose can take over and do from then until 0100hrs. I will then do the 0100hrs to 0300hrs watch and Anne, you do the last two hours and wake us all at 0500hrs. It will be getting light by then and we need to pack up and stand-to."

This time Rose did object. "Oh sir, you and ma'am are doing two lots and I am only doing one. That's not fair."

"Yes, it is. You had a very tiring week before this and haven't fully recovered. You can do two tomorrow night, if we need to," Captain Ross replied.

*Tomorrow night!* Rose thought with dismay. Somehow she had hoped it would all be over by tomorrow. Now she realised that it might not be.

"Yes sir," she responded.

Captain Ross went on, "And Rose, when you are on sentry duty and want to check the time make sure you hide the light in your watch. It can be seen from a long way away."

"Oh sir! I'm a corporal!" Rose retorted, quite unable to keep the asperity out of her tone. She was annoyed that he had felt the need to remind her.

"Sorry, I know you are a section commander, and a good one, but we are in great danger and it pays to be sure rather than sorry," Captain Ross replied.

"Yes sir, sorry sir," Rose muttered, her feelings partly mollified.

Captain Ross said, "We are to sleep fully dressed and with our boots on. That way we can get up and run if need be. When we are on sentry duty, we are to stand here next to this tree at the end of the hutchie. No sitting. People can go to sleep sitting down. And if you need to go for a pee no torches either."

*Now that might be a challenge!* Rose thought.

Lt Ross also wasn't happy as she grumbled, "It's alright for you men! Oh, sorry, Rose."

"It's okay ma'am. I do know a bit about boys," Rose replied, blushing yet amused at the societal fiction that made adults assume that young people, teenagers, knew very little about such things, when in fact they were secretly fascinated by them.

"And whoever is awake has to entertain young Bundle here," Lt Ross added.

*That might be a challenge too!* Rose thought as she knelt and helped Belinda find the pillow in the dark. Captain Ross took up the night sight and stood while she and Lt Ross lay down. And of course Belinda wasn't ready for sleep so there followed nearly an hour of quiet, but wearing, playtime and soft singing of nursery rhymes and other songs until she finally drifted off and snuggled against Rose.

Rose stretched out, her mind still wide awake with worry about her parents and how they might evade the men the next day. She was comforted by the fact that her father was still alive and well.

*And I think Sir has some plan too,* she thought.

She could just see Captain Ross's lower body silhouetted against the night sky as he stood there on guard. Knowing that gave Rose a great feeling of being cared for and safe and she drifted off to sleep.

It was a restless sleep, broken by dreams and by Belinda snuffling and moving but sleep it was. She was in the middle of a nice dream where she was at school and showing off to one of the handsome Year 11 boys when Lt Ross shook her boots.

"Wake up Rose. Time for piquet," she said softly.

"Oh yes ma'am!" Rose muttered.

But she immediately gently disengaged Belinda's little hand and crawled out, despite wanting to go back to sleep. She used a water bottle to have a drink and wet her face and then she was ready. Lt Ross placed the night sight in her right hand, reminding her which buttons did what as she did. Then Rose was alone on sentry duty.

She had done this half a dozen times before on cadet field exercises, but this time it was real! She found herself breathing fast and feeling quite anxious. Every sound made her start, and it took her a while to settle to the job.

*If it scuttles or hops it is not a human,* she told herself, remembering Captain Ross's advice during cadet lessons. *But what is that rustling sound?*

Images of the brown snake leapt into her mind, and she found herself staring into the blackness, her heart in her mouth and terror starting to freeze her muscles. Then she remembered the night sight. With fumbling fingers she brought it up to her right eye and experimented with it, turning it on and twirling the focus adjustment to scan the ground close around the hutchie. There was nothing. She made herself relax. After a quick scan towards the cattle she switched the night sight off.

*I don't want the battery to go flat just when we really need it.*

Then her ears seemed to magnify every sound. Mostly it was just the breeze in the leaves but there were little crackling noises and various birds making odd noises. A big one nearby kept going 'Hoot! Hoot!' and she could hear curlews giving their eerie wail off in the distance. Silence again. The sudden *flap! flap!* as some night bird flew low overhead made her jump in fright.

*Hop! Hop! Hop!*

Rose tensed and then moved. The animal hopped rapidly away. *Kangaroo or wallaby,* she told herself.

Another long period of relative silence. Rose stared up at the stars and then around in the starlight. It certainly was dark. That actually comforted her. No enemy could find them in this unless they also had a night vision device. They might have one, but she didn't think so.

*I don't think Cousin James's plans included anything like this.*

Two bulls began snorting and bellowing. There was the sound of shuffling and stomping from where the cattle were camped, then a bit of dust drifted by before silence settled again.

Then Captain Ross began to snore, loudly. For a few minutes Rose was too scared to go and do anything about it, he was the OC after all! But then she knew she had to. Cautiously she moved around to the side of the hutchie and bent down to feel for his boots.

"Sir! Sir! You are snoring," she hissed.

A grumpy Lt Ross's voice came from the dark. "Roll on your side, Chris!" she ordered.

To Rose's relief, he did. The snoring stopped but he did do a bit of snuffling and grunting. Then he did a very loud fart. Rose blushed and tried not to giggle. She moved back to her sentry post.

From time to time Rose worried about what might be happening to her mother and father and she wished she knew what her father was planning. He had obviously gone off to do something, but where and what she had no idea. She hoped it was to get more money for the ransom, or even to get her mother.

*Poor Mum! She must be beside herself with worry. She won't know if Bubby and I are alive or dead,* she thought. She was sure the crooks would not tell her anything. *Even if the crooks now know we are alive and somewhere in the area.*

That both heartened and bothered her. *If the crooks know we are with the Rosses, then they must be very worried and their plans must be coming adrift,* she decided. Hiding her watch from the direction of the road she turned on the light. 0037hrs. Still another 23 minutes!

They were a very slow 23 minutes. Finally it was time and she again went around to shake Captain Ross's boots. He gave a low groan and then said softly, "Thanks. I'm awake." He stood up and stretched and Rose handed him the night sight.

"Nothing, sir, no vehicles," Rose reported.

"Hmm. Good! So there was only that one going north very fast at about 2030hrs and then another coming back slowly at 2115hrs," he said.

Rose had slept through that and was surprised, but then not surprised.

*There doesn't seem to be much traffic on the back roads out in this part of the world.*

She carefully crawled back under the mosquito net and felt for where Belinda was before lying down beside her and making herself comfortable. It was not cold, but she could feel a bit of a chill starting so she pulled the rug over Belinda and lay next to her on the plastic groundsheet.

*At least I've got a proper pillow,* she thought. She did not think she would go to sleep easily but she did. This time it was a deep sleep with no dreams she could remember.

Lt Ross shook her boots gently at 0500hrs. Rose groaned and opened gummed up eyes. It was still dark.

"Yes, ma'am. I'm awake," she croaked. Her throat was dry so she sat up and had a drink. Then she moved carefully to avoid waking Belinda. "Do you want me to wake the tornado?' she whispered.

"No. Let her sleep. We will pack the hutchie and the mosquito nets though," Lt Ross answered.

She had just woken Captain Ross. He at once rolled onto his knees and stood up. Stretching and groaning he looked around. "All quiet?"

"Yes. Not a thing. No vehicles, only one animal, a dog or dingo with some unfortunate little marsupial creature in its mouth," Lt Ross replied.

"I'll just get my mobile phone," Captain Ross said. "It should be charged by now."

"Here, take the night sight and recharge it," Lt Ross replied.

She handed him the night sight. Rose was standing looking around by then. The first glimmerings of dawn were just starting and that gave her flashbacks to her other dawn risings. It was quite light and looking around she saw that the moon had only just begun to show in the east.

*It will come up after daylight tonight,* she thought. That meant no moon all night and she hoped they would not be hiding out in the bush by then.

The mosquito nets were untied and rolled up, an easy task for Rose. Then the double hutchie was untied and folded up. During this Rose kept looking around and listening. Captain Ross had said they would 'Stand-to' but she wasn't sure if he really meant that. At cadets they did it on field exercises with an opposing force. Packing up in the dark and then being ready to 'march or fight'. Webbing on and lying behind her pack was no novelty to Rose and she thought it would be a good idea now.

*Those men aren't up to this sort of thing. Well, maybe that Lucas is, but not dopey Marvin or his crony Norris,* she thought.

Captain Ross had opened the Prado with the manual key and collected his mobile phone. He crouched inside the vehicle to turn it on and check it. Then he came hurrying towards them in the half light. Rose could tell he was excited.

"Message from Mr MacGregor," he said to them both.

Rose's heart leapt in a mixture of hope and alarm. "What does it say sir?" she queried.

"Meet me Cloncurry Caravan Park tonight, is all it says," Captain Ross read. He then smiled and slid the phone into his pocket. "Good! Your dad is okay, and I think things are moving, and I have a plan!"

# Chapter 32

## TIME SPENT ON RECONNAISSANCE

That statement sent Rose's hopes even higher. She was elated that her father had been able to contact them, and she just wished it was right away instead of hours later.

"What is you plan, sir?" she asked.

"I will discuss it during breakfast," he replied.

"Are we staying here, sir? I thought we might get driving as soon as possible," Rose said.

Captain Ross shook his head. "No. I don't like the idea of driving along bush roads in the dark when I have no idea what we might meet,"

That concept caused Rose a shudder of apprehension as she pictured trees dragged across the road to block it and men with guns hiding in the undergrowth. *We would be trapped and it would be deadly.*

She was about to say this when a wail from Belinda got her hurrying to where the little girl was sitting up and looking anxiously around.

"Hello, Bubby-Boo!" Rose cried, scooping her up and kissing her. "Did you sleep well?" She knew she had but felt she had to say something.

Belinda calmed down a bit and then pointed. "Cow!" she cried.

Rose looked and was puzzled. There was no cow there. "Cow?"

"Jump over da moon!" Belinda said, sweeping her arms up.

"Yes, it did!" Rose agreed. She carried Belinda over to say hello to the Rosses. And as she did, she sniffed and then grimaced. "Oh! I think we have a poo bear here," she added.

"I not Poo Bear!" Belinda retorted, standing on her dignity. "I Miss Busy Bee MacGregor to you, thank you!"

Rose had to laugh. She had not thought Belinda had even heard, much less understood, her very frosty rebuke to Lucas that day.

"Yes Ma'am," she agreed.

"I not Ma'am. She ma'am," Belinda replied, pointing to Lt Ross.

Lt Ross sniffed and then nodded. "Yes, I think we have a little problem. Never mind. We can easily fix that. You take her clothes off, Rose, while I get a wash basin and water."

The wash basin was in the back of the Prado and there was a jerry can of water in a bracket on the tow bar of the camper trailer. Captain Ross carried it over and in a few minutes, just as the sun was starting to turn the sky pink, a happy little girl was standing in the wash basin. The water was obviously a bit cold, but she soon forgot that and then sat down and began happily splashing. Soap and a towel were produced and then a hairbrush and new hair ties.

Ten minutes later, scrubbed clean and in clean new clothes Belinda sat in the first rays of sunshine while her hair was redone and tied in neat pigtails. Captain Ross took the soiled panties between finger and thumb and walked off into the bush with them and an entrenching tool.

"No point in trying to wash these," he said. "We will buy new ones at a shop in Cloncurry."

Rose could only agree. When Captain Ross returned, she took the entrenching tool and went off into the bush to do the serious part of her 'morning routine'. Later the adults did likewise. During this the camp was all packed away and the packs and webbing re-arranged for breakfast. The cover was taken off the back of the Prado to give access to the fridge and food brought out.

Belinda at once became interested. A slice of bread with honey kept her happy while stoves were set up. Breakfast followed, Rose and the Rosses all staying alert and continually glancing towards the road. Rose was able to enjoy a cup of hot Milo and then had a can of Spaghetti and Meatballs heated for her by Lt Ross. Belinda wanted some but turned her nose up at the first mouthful so was given little frankfurters from a can. Fruit Juice and a packet of cereal with milk rounded out a full meal.

As they were cleaning up, Captain Ross explained his plan. "There is an old army saying," he said, "That time spent on reconnaissance is seldom wasted. I intend to do a reconnaissance of the Quamby Rodeo Ground and Racecourse."

"Oh! Why?" Lt Ross asked, obviously not happy with the idea.

"Because the man who owns the Kajabbi Hotel said that the crooks had told the old man with the white hair that they were living or camping at the Quamby Rodeo Ground. That is worth a look."

"Is it worth the risk?" Lt Ross queried, plainly concerned.

Captain Ross nodded. "We have no other clue on where to look. If we can locate Belinda's mum, we can just call the police," he said.

"No! These men are armed! You could get shot!" Lt Ross snapped.

Captain Ross looked stubborn. "We must! I don't think it is all that risky. These guys are only crooks. And I think there are only four or five of them. If three or four are out looking for us then only one or two can be there on guard. And they will be watching the room or building where they might have Mrs MacGregor prisoner. They can't be looking out to watch the country around the place at the same time."

"No! I don't like it! I don't want you to do that. How will you do it anyway?" Lt Ross snapped, plainly upset.

"By wearing my cams, taking my webbing and the rifle and by you dropping me off in the bush a couple of kilometres from the place. I will do a recce and then we can RV somewhere," Captain Ross answered.

Rose now found herself torn. She did not want Captain Ross put at risk or Lt Ross upset, but she did want to know where her mum was! And Quamby was the only clue they had. But she kept silent, understanding this was for the Rosses to resolve. But she could see that Lt Ross was wavering.

He did win. Very reluctantly Lt Ross agreed and went back to cleaning her mess gear and packing up. Captain Ross organised his uniform and refilled his water bottles from the jerry can. This was now returned to the trailer and locked in. Rose had no other task than minding Belinda, who was full of energy and wanted to run around. Rose had to hold her and distract her by looking at birds. Luckily, a flock of happy jacks flew in and then a pair of kookaburras started laughing from a nearby tree.

The only alarm during all this time was a single vehicle which came from the north and went past at high-speed leaving a trail of dust at 0710hrs.

"Probably a mine worker who has to be at work by eight," Captain Ross surmised.

By 0730hrs everything had been loaded in the vehicle and the camp area had been cleared of everything other than a few boot prints. Even the used matches were picked up. Captain Ross changed into his camouflage uniform and then spent a few minutes manoeuvring the camper trailer to get it turned around among the trees. Rose and Belinda then got in and Lt Ross took over as driver and started driving back out.

The cattle were no problem, moving aside to let them pass. Captain Ross walked ahead and opened the gate. As they approached the road

Rose found her anxiety shooting up again. Once they were out on that road they were at risk of discovery, or worse. But the gate was easy and once it was closed Captain Ross scuffed out their wheel tracks and then got in.

As he did, up his seat belt he gave an audible sigh of relief. "I was trying to work out what to say to the landowner if he had suddenly arrived to feed his cattle and asked what we were doing in his paddock," he explained.

Rose now realised they had turned left and were driving north. "Sir, aren't we going to Quamby?" she asked.

Captain Ross nodded. "We are, but we are not going back to go along the gravel road from Kajabbi. This is longer but I think our chances of meeting the men are much less. We are going north for thirty or forty kilometres to the 'Coolullah' turn-off and then east out to the Burke Development Road. That is a very good two-lane bitumen highway with a lot more traffic and they can't easily stop us on that so I reckon we will be safer," he explained, showing her the map.

That made sense to Rose, and she approved. *The crooks won't have any idea where we have gone,* she reasoned. *They must be very worried men.*

There was then a drive of about half an hour along a graded gravel road. Rose noted that mostly it was through more 'normal' savannah woodland country. But what kept her busy was entertaining Belinda. She had to resort to as many of the old travel games her parents had used that she could remember. 'I Spy' was no good because Belinda was too young to know the Alphabet or spelling. So it was mostly who could see the first black cow or the biggest white tree or a crow, and so on. Belinda really wanted to see a kangaroo, but none was visible.

"Want Kangywoo!" Belinda cried.

"They are probably sleeping in the shade of a tree because it is so hot," Rose suggested. The demand for a kangaroo became a desire to see another 'Eeemoo'. Rose found it all a bit wearing.

Soon after that they came to the bitumen Burke Development Road and turned right. Rose quickly saw that Captain Ross was right, there was a lot more traffic, vehicles passing the other way every few minutes, mostly 'grey nomads' towing caravans on their way to the 'Gulf Country'. Several vehicles overtook them from behind.

And Belinda still had to be kept happy! Rose noted that there were plenty of dead kangaroos on the road, but she thought that Belinda did not understand what roadkill was. And she had no intention of telling her. So she got her looking at the hawks, eagles, and crows.

They passed the eastern end of the Kajabbi Road and Rose became even more anxious. Somewhere ahead was Quamby and she was starting to feel really guilty about Captain Ross risking himself by going to see if that was the gang's hideout.

"Sir, you don't have to do this," she said.

"Yes, I do. I want to sleep at night and just doing nothing when I can do something doesn't sit well with me," he replied.

It was only about twenty kilometres to go at that stage and Captain Ross was carefully tracking their progress on his map. After a time he said, "Anne, see those hills just ahead? Find a place to pull over when you get to them. Then go on and park the vehicle and trailer in the back yard of the Quamby Pub. You and the girls then go and stay on the deck outside the bar and I will meet you there. Keep an eye out for the crooks and their vehicles."

"How long do you think you will be?" Lt Ross asked, still not happy.

Captain Ross shrugged. "It is about three kilometres from the hills to the Rodeo Ground, that could take an hour. Allow another hour for me to do a close recon of the place. That is two hours. And another hour to get to the pub. Make it four. It is 0845hrs now so if I am not there by 1300hrs and don't answer my mobile then drive to Cloncurry and tell the police the whole story," he said.

Rose wasn't happy at him saying to tell the police, but she said nothing. *If something happens to him it is my fault and the police must be called in, even if it puts mum at risk,* she thought.

Soon after that they drove up among the small range of stony hills. There was a gravel area on the left that allowed Lt Ross to get off the road safely. As soon as the vehicle stopped Captain Ross got out, now very conspicuous in his camouflage uniform. At that moment, there was no traffic but as he was leaning in the back to get his webbing a big fuel tanker came from behind. He stayed there until it had gone around the next bend and then swung his webbing on, mostly hidden between the vehicle with its back door open and the camper trailer. He paused to listen and then pulled the rifle out from its wrapping.

A white 4WD came roaring past from behind but it just kept going and Rose didn't think the driver had seen anything. Captain Ross closed the back and swung the spare wheels in and locked them. He checked his binoculars and then the rifle.

"Okay, I am off," he said.

"Good luck sir," Rose called back.

"I will also depend on skill Corporal MacGregor," he replied.

With a grin and a wave he turned and vanished into the bushes and spinifex in a small gully.

Lt Ross let out a small sob and then shook her head. "Oh silly man!" she cried. But Rose could tell she was proud of him.

Lt Ross put the car into motion and drove on. A few minutes later they came out of the hills and onto the turn-off to the Rodeo Ground. In the distance across a wide grassy clearing was a row of buildings. These were hard to see clearly because the hot air was already distorting images. Rose stared at the buildings, wondering if her mother was there.

*Oh, I hope Captain Ross is safe,* she thought.

And there was the Quamby hotel on the left. The caravan park area was just beyond. It was a large, mostly gravel area on a long slope up to another stony knoll. There were only two caravans parked there and both were close to the main road, so Lt Ross drove right up and did a U-turn and parked partly behind them but ready to just drive out. When she turned the motor off and got out Rose noted that she was shaking so much she was unsteady on her feet.

Despite that Lt Ross took Belinda while Rose got out. The car was locked and they strolled down past some sheds to the hotel. The same very nice lady was in the bar.

"Do you want to stay in the van park?" she asked.

Lt Ross bit her lip. "We w... we aren't sure. We are waiting for someone. If they arrive, we may but if they don't we will just drive on."

Rose wasn't happy with that and stepped forward. "We will pay anyway, for any inconvenience."

The lady and Lt Ross both looked at her in surprise. Lt Ross then nodded. "Yes, yes we will."

They were all then distracted by Belinda starting to jerk and point. She wriggled so much Rose could hardly hold her.

"Porkykidna! Porkykidna!" she cried.

Rose's gaze followed Belinda's pointing finger and then laughed. It was one of the steel sculptures, of an echidna. "Oh, you mean an echidna," she said.

"Porkykid?" Belinda queried as she was lowered to the floor.

"Is it alright if she plays with them?" Rose asked. "She thinks it's a porcupine."

"Porkypin!" Belinda agreed and ran out the door to the sculpture. Rose followed, leaving Lt Ross to talk to the lady.

A few minutes later, Lt Ross carried out two cups of hot chocolate and a coffee and scones with jam and cream. They helped. Lt Ross and Rose sat at a table where they could see any vehicles pulling in but were not obvious because of pot plants. Here they relaxed to enjoy their morning tea. Belinda, however, was a real ball of energy, hurrying from one sculpture to the next. Rose began to weary and was just glad to sit and sip the drink.

Time then began to drag. For a while they carefully observed all passing vehicles and particularly the ones that pulled in. But none of them had any of the men in them. After a time Rose became hot and felt sticky and grimy. She arranged to have a shower and was given the car keys to get her bag and a towel.

Lt Ross smiled. "I will mind the Ball of Atomic Energy here. You just watch out when you are out of sight up there," Lt Ross cautioned.

Rose had forgotten about the men but with that warning she stopped at each corner to look and only then went on. She got her bag and the towel from the Prado without any trouble and quickly made her way back to the hotel, only 50 paces but feeling like hundreds. She glanced nervously at a white 4WD which went roaring past along the highway. No, not the men.

An elderly couple had arrived and came to sit on the side deck. Rose gave the keys back to Lt Ross and went to the showers, which were luckily just a few paces away with the entrance visible from where Lt Ross was seated. The hot shower was bliss and Rose took her time, twenty minutes instead of five. After she had dressed, she lingered to study herself in the mirror. But it wasn't her looks that held her attention. They were as ordinary as she remembered, except for the dark rings under her eyes and the straggly hair. It was her character she was assessing. She found that the whole week had been a revelation.

*I didn't know I was like that,* she thought. But now she knew she had a very strong personality and a savage streak she had not suspected. *And I am very determined and capable,* she told herself. She knew now she had many skills and that gave her even more confidence. *Captain Ross is right. He's always telling us that character is more important than intelligence.* But she also accepted that she was bright. Which gave her a whole new perspective on the future.

It was Belinda wailing and wanting 'Wosie!' that ended her reverie. Reluctantly she came out and the moment Belinda saw her she ran to her with arms outstretched. "Wosie!"

Rose knelt and hugged her and burst into tears. "Sorry," she said to Lt Ross who came to help. "I've had nearly all I can take at the moment."

"We will have another morning tea, or lunch and see if she will have a sleep." The drinks and biscuits helped but even more help was the 'blue' cattle dog that came along from the sheds at the back with a man Rose thought was the publican. He allowed Belinda to pat the dog. The publican then asked if he could take her to see the chooks.

"Oh yes please!" Rose agreed.

Lt Ross stood. "You rest and watch the cars. I will go with them."

So the publican took Belinda by the hand and led her up the slope, Lt Ross following, while Rose just slumped in her chair and tried to relax. But it was vey hard. Anxiety over Captain Ross on top of worry about her parents was draining her nervous reserves and she knew it.

Suddenly, in a period of relative silence between the men now noisily drinking in the bar and the passing traffic she heard Lt Ross's phone ring. Rose had been idly watching her and the publican with Belinda. Now she saw Lt Ross answer the phone and then look towards her. Lt Ross pointed towards her vehicle and then to where Belinda was just vanishing around behind a shed, being led by the hand by the man. Rose nodded and stood up. As she did, Lt Ross set off at a fast walk and vanished from view behind the hotel, obviously heading for the van park.

*I hope that is Captain Ross who just called,* Rose thought. Only then did it hit Rose. *Belinda has gone out of sight with that man,* she thought. That caused a niggle of concern but the next thought caused a real stab of alarm. *And I have no idea who that man is. He might be one of the gang!*

Her heart leapt into her throat. Angry at herself for dropping her guard she set off at the run.

# Chapter 33

## WHERE TO NEXT?

Panic started to grip Rose by the throat as she bounded down the back steps and went running up the slope towards the sheds.

*Oh no! What have I done!* she thought.

As she ran past the back of the hotel she glanced to her right, hoping to get Lt Ross to come back but she caught just a glimpse of her as she went left around the next shed.

Rose ran on, now almost in a state of panic. She raced up past the next shed and then stopped, gasping. A wash of relief swept through her. There was Belinda crouching at the wire netting of a chicken coop with her finger through the wire to try to attract the chickens. The man stood there beaming. A dozen fluffy and very new chickens clustered near a warm box or coop.

Feeling foolish but relieved, Rose tried to pretend she had not been anxious or in a hurry. She strolled over to join them. Belinda looked around.

"Rosie! Rosie! Look, chookens!" she cried.

Rose smiled and crouched beside her. "Chickens, Bub-O," she corrected. "Chickens. Chick, chick, chick!"

Belinda laughed delightedly and clapped her hands. "Chick, Chick, Chick!" she called. The chickens looked at her but only came a little way.

The man said, "I'll get them some feed."

He turned and walked off into the next shed. Rose glanced around and saw the camper trailer out beyond that line of sheds. Just visible on the other side were the heads of Captain Ross and Ma'am. Captain Ross was peeling off his camouflage shirt.

*Oh thank God! He is safe,* Rose thought. *He doesn't seem very excited, so I suppose he didn't find anything.*

The man returned with an old can full of chicken feed. He held it down so Belinda could reach in. "Just throw a small handful in," he instructed.

Rose was about to suggest that was not a clear enough instruction but was too late. Belinda plunged her hand in, scooped up a big handful and sent the mix of grain and oats in a big spray that started outside the cage and then swept in a curve for several metres. But it worked. The chickens came at the run and began pecking with great energy.

Belinda shrieked with pleasure and then reached in to scoop out another big handful. The man was just in time to pull the can away before she spilt it all on the ground. The chickens were showered with more feed. Rose held Belinda's hand back next time.

"Slow down, Miss Ball of Busyness! Just little bits at a time," she said.

The game went on for a few more minutes. Belinda wanted to get in with the chicks to hold them, but the man wisely said no. The 'bluey' cattle dog again claimed Belinda's attention and she was given a ball to throw for it. While this was going on Captain Ross and Lt Ross walked over. Captain Ross was now back in casual civilian shirt and long trousers but wore thongs and had a towel over his shoulder. As he got closer, he gave a shake of his head.

Rose felt her hopes plummet and tears prickled her eyes. She gave a nod but with the man there could not ask.

Captain Ross said, "I will just have a shower and a shave. Then we will have lunch."

Belinda now saw him. "Captain Woss, Captain Woss, look, chookens. Chick, chick, chick!" She jumped up and down laughing and clapping her hands.

Rose was worried about that 'captain' but the man did not seem to notice and did not ask. Instead he went off to show Captain Ross where the showers were. Lt Ross joined them and also shook her head.

"No luck," she whispered. Then she was drawn into admiring the chickens.

Worry about the crooks now got Rose anxious. "Aren't we a bit obvious out in the open here at the hotel?" she suggested.

Lt Ross nodded. "We are, but it is as good as anywhere. The crooks can hold us up anytime really. It is just as public as a shop or caravan park in Cloncurry."

Rose had to agree with that. "I suppose so," she replied, not quite convinced. In her mind she could picture the gang arriving with guns and simply taking them prisoner, or shooting them.

*These people here couldn't do much to stop them,* she thought.

They managed to get Belinda away from ball throwing. As they strolled down towards the hotel, Lt Ross went on, "Besides, if that racecourse or rodeo ground or whatever it is was the crook's base, then they won't suspect that we will be so close. They would expect us to run as far away as we can."

Rose nodded and did a quick calculation in her head. "I suppose if we had just driven all night we could be anywhere in half of Queensland by now."

"Yes. We could have reached Townsville, or Longreach. We could be anywhere," Lt Ross agreed.

Rose didn't exactly feel sorry for the crooks, but she did give a malicious smile while picturing their possible confusion. The only real worry was that if the crook's plans went too much astray, or they got too worried, they might decide to cover their tracks by murdering her mum before trying to vanish.

1230hrs came around and Captain Ross re-appeared, now shaved and showered and in clean clothes and with his boots on.

"Lunch!" he declared.

He went into the bar and got menus and soft-drinks for himself, Rose and Belinda and a whisky for Lt Ross. Then he moved to a table on the deck and sat down. Rose saw a highchair over to the side and got that. Then she had to capture Belinda to put her in it.

"Come here, Little Miss Whirlwind! Sit and calm down!"

Belinda managed to look down her nose and said, in a very good imitation of Rose's tone, "Miss MacGregor to you!"

"Oooh! You cheeky little monkey!" Rose cried, glancing anxiously towards a young couple in a nearby table to see if they had heard. They hadn't and Rose had to grin when Belinda giggled and covered her mouth.

As soon as the nice lady had taken their order and gone away, Captain Ross leaned forward. "Sorry, no sign of your mum. There are a dozen huts and sheds. Most of them are locked and, judging by the long grass around them, haven't been visited for months. A couple were unlocked but again the grass had not been trampled down at all. Only one has been used recently and all the grass is flattened around it. There is a lot of rubbish inside and around: empty beer bottles, fast food packets, that sort of thing. They are a real pack of pigs this gang. But there is a back room with a barred window and a bolt on the outside of the door. That might have been used as a prison. But they would have had to have a person there all the time to stop the prisoner breaking out." he explained.

"Do you think the gang have been there, sir?" Rose asked.

"I do. But they have now gone. That might be because they think we know it is their base, or because they have another place."

"Do you think my mother was there?" Rose asked.

Captain Ross shrugged. "She might have been. But there is no evidence I could see. Those police forensic people might be able to find some but there are no obvious clues.

That was very discouraging for Rose, but she managed to keep smiling and kept Belinda entertained until the food arrived by the usual little games and songs. But 'Incy Wincy Spider' and 'This little piggy' were staring to wear thin by the time it did.

Despite the reconnaissance not locating her mum, it was a merry meal. Sir had two meat pies with peas, Ma'am had a salad, Rose had chicken nuggets and a sausage roll, and Belinda enjoyed chicken nuggets and chips. Ice cream followed. Fruit juice and soft-drink kept them hydrated.

When they had finished, Rose looked at the two OOCs in turn. "Sir, Ma'am, what are we going to do now? Where to next?"

Captain Ross smiled and answered immediately. "To Cloncurry. We will find your dad and maybe do a bit of planning."

"Is that safe?" Rose queried.

Captain Ross shrugged. "No, not really, but we have to take some risks and it is a town with a police station so it is less likely that something will happen there. And your dad has said to meet him there at the caravan park. So that will do. We will stay out of sight and rest as much as we can."

That became the plan. As soon as lunch and the showers were paid for, they all walked back to the Prado and got in. Captain Ross took over as driver and by 1330hrs they were out on the highway heading south at 100kph.

During that next stretch of road, Belinda luckily put her head on Rose's shoulder and quickly went to sleep. Rose followed a few minutes later, crumpling in her seat. She slept the whole distance to Cloncurry, waking only as they slowed to turn left onto the Barkly Highway just out of town.

Through sleepy eyes she looked out at the Cloncurry River and then the houses and buildings along the main street. Rose had been to Cloncurry several times so was familiar with its layout. As they drove slowly along the main street, she looked out at all the people and vehicles and felt a sense of unreality. She also felt a rising sense of excitement.

*I will see dad soon!* she thought.

There were several caravan parks, but Lt Ross had been on line on her phone and booked them into the one Rose's father had said, the 'Oasis' van park on the main street. Rose had stayed at a motel over the road so knew roughly where they were. As Captain Ross turned the Prado into the front entrance, she sighed with relief.

But only for a few seconds. Belinda woke up and looked out. Spotting play equipment on the front lawn she pointed and cried, "Swing! Swing!"

"Later, Bubby, later."

"Swing! Swing now!" Belinda cried.

"No! We are seeing Daddy first," Rose answered.

She was feeling too drained for playing and also worried that the play area was too open to view from vehicles passing along the main street.

"Daddy! Want Daddy!"

And there he was! Mr MacGregor was standing on the front porch of the very first cabin past the front office. The Prado was stopped in front of the office and as Rose opened the door her father was down the short set of steps and hurrying towards them. Belinda was put down and she at once ran towards her father.

"Daddy, Daddy!" she cried. Mr MacGregor swept her up in his arms and there were kisses and tears.

Rose followed, flinging off her seat belt and running to her father's embrace. There were more kisses and tears amid fierce hugs.

"Oh Daddy, I love you!" she gasped.

For fully a minute the three of them stood there until they were joined by the Rosses on their way to the office. They stopped and beamed at the reunion. Mr MacGregor lifted his head and looked at both.

"Oh thank you! Thank you for looking after my precious ones!"

Both Rosses grinned. "It is an honour to look after two such wonderful young people, sir. You should be very proud of them," Captain Ross said.

"Rod please, not sir. After this I hope you will count yourselves as my friends for life," Mr MacGregor said.

Belinda lifted her head. "Daddy, we saw chookens."

"Did you my precious?" Mr MacGregor replied smiling at her and kissing her tear-streaked cheek.

Rose gave a wry grin. "More like precocious!" she suggested.

They all laughed at that and that eased the emotions. Mr MacGregor pointed across the road from his cabin. "I have booked that drive-through site for you. If that is acceptable. Now, you are free of any responsibility for my girls if you wish and I will take it from here."

Captain Ross frowned. "Have you informed the police?"

Mr MacGregor shook his head. Captain Ross then asked, "Have you called in your own security people then?"

Again Mr MacGregor shook his head. "No, not yet. But I do not wish to place you two at further risk."

Lt Ross now spoke. "Then you still need us, and we are willing to help. Until this thing is settled, we consider ourselves involved."

"But... But!"

"No buts!" Lt Ross replied. "Now you take the girls into your cabin out of the sun and out of the public view and we will book in and then park our camper trailer. Then we can discuss our next move. Go on! I am sure these girls both need the toilet again and you need to talk to them. We will be with you in a few minutes."

Mr MacGregor nodded and turned to lead them. He carried Belinda and Rose walked beside him, her arm around his waist and her heart bursting with affection. She was just so happy and so relieved! It was also a relief to get into the cabin and its air-conditioning and out of the heat and glare. It was a fully-equipped cabin with two beds, kitchenette and refrigerator, cupboards and a separate toilet and shower.

As soon as Belinda was lowered to the floor, Rose led her to the toilet and persuaded her to go. She waited to help her with her clothes and then washed her face, using a damp face washer, ignoring the spluttered protests and squirming. Then she pushed her back out.

"Out you go, little monster. Go and talk to Daddy," she ordered.

Belinda did and Rose was able to use the facilities and freshen up. Feeling much better, she came out and again hugged her father, who was having difficulty understanding about the 'Porkykids' at Kombi.

"She means the steel sculptures at the Quamby Hotel. We were there this morning. There is one of an Echidna," Rose explained. She then looked through the blinds and saw the Rosses busy unhooking their camper trailer from the Prado in the van space just across the entrance road. "Are we safe here, Dad?" she asked.

Mr MacGregor looked at her and nodded. "We probably aren't safe anywhere much. We can't hide away and be on guard twenty-four hours a day."

"We did last night. I felt really safe, the safest I have felt in a week," Rose answered.

"Oh yes, how was that?" her father asked.

Rose proceeded to tell him how they had driven into the bush past all the cattle and then how the Rosses had organised the camp for secrecy and security and how they had done sentry duty all night. Mr MacGregor was amazed and impressed. He shook his head in admiration, particularly at all the little details that added to their safety, like the infra-red night sight.

As Rose was finishing, there was a knock on the door. It was the Rosses. Rose moved to unlock the door and they were let in. Mr MacGregor stood up and shook their hands as he ushered them to the two chairs.

"Rose has just been telling me how you kept them safe last night. That was a mighty job. Thank you!"

"She did her fair share," Lt Ross replied.

Mr MacGregor smiled at Rose. "She is a good kid," he said.

"Dad! I'm not a little kid!"

"Still a kid to me mate. You and Bubby will be my little girls until the day I die," Mr MacGregor replied.

At which Belinda looked unhappy. "I big girl now," she insisted.

This took the sharp edge of the horrible thought that had crossed Rose's mind as her father spoke. *There might not be much more to his life. He could be dead tonight or tomorrow!*

There was then an hour of describing what had happened since they had last seen Mr MacGregor at the Kajabbi Hotel. When he learned they had driven to Dobbyn and watched the ransom being handed over, he was amazed and appalled.

"You took a terrible risk," he said.

Rose objected. "Not such a risk dad. Captain Ross and Lt Ross, they know what they are doing. And besides, if we had stayed sitting there at

Kajabbi those men would have just taken us hostage and we would be worse off."

Mr MacGregor had to concede that. He was appalled to learn of the sniper hiding on the low rise near the headframe. "I thought they must be watching," he said. "I suppose they could have just shot me and taken the money."

"It was only half of the ransom wasn't it?" Lt Ross asked.

"Yes."

"So they are greedy. They want it all. I wouldn't trust them an inch!" she added.

"I agree. It will be the final ransom payment and prisoner swap that will be the really dangerous time," Mr MacGregor agreed.

"You still don't want to involve the police?" Captain Ross asked.

"I'd like to but I don't dare. I can't see how these men would know I had unless they have a contact in exactly the right position in the police. But they might have and I am afraid to take that risk with Corinda's life at stake."

Hearing her mother's name Belinda looked around. "Mummy? Where Mummy? Want Mummy!"

They calmed her and described how they had walked back through the bush to their vehicle after the crooks had driven away. At that, Belinda, who had been listening cried, "Kagawoo!"

Lt Ross explained. "We saw a kangaroo, the biggest I have ever seen. He was a big red and he stood taller than me."

Rose squeezed Belinda to her. "She's seen nearly all of Australia's wildlife this last week," she commented.

"What wildlife, Rosie?" Belinda asked.

"Animals and birds and snakes and things," Rose replied, shuddering at the memories of those snakes.

Lt Ross described how they had driven back to the Kajabbi Hotel and learned that three men had searched their camper trailer and how the old white-haired man had been passing information to the crooks. Mr MacGregor pursed his lips. "Yes, I did wonder," he said.

Rose quickly went over again how they had spent the night safely in the bush and then Lt Ross commented on what a good girl Belinda had been in the bush in the dark.

Belinda then piped up, "I very good girl! I Ball of Mischief!"

They all had a laugh at that, to Belinda's puzzlement. Mr MacGregor then looked at Captain Ross. "You've been a soldier, Captain?"

"Yes, when I was young," Captain Ross replied.

At which Rose said, "Oh Dad, Captain Ross has been a real soldier. He has fought in real battles. You should see all his medals!"

Captain Ross blushed. "Thank you, Rose. I hope your father will one day."

Rose nodded. "You must come to the Cadet Passing-Out Parade in November, Dad," she added, a plea in her tone.

Her father had not come to the end-of-year parade or dinner the previous year when Rose had been presented with 'Best Attendance' and 'Best Cadet' awards and it had been a disappointment to her. She really wanted to impress her father.

Mr MacGregor smiled and nodded. "I will. I will even award an annual scholarship for the cadet with the most initiative and determination. But if I do come to the parade and your friends learn who you are, they may not be your friends anymore."

"If who my father is matters to them like that, I don't want them as friends," Rose replied.

"So what have you been doing all morning then?" her dad asked.

Between them they described driving out to the highway and then Captain Ross's reconnaissance. On hearing about that Mr MacGregor looked very serious and shook his head. "You took a terrible risk for a stranger Captain. I thank you for that, and I owe you."

"Not such a risk when you know what you are doing, sir... er... Rod. But we didn't find anything. And I think the gang must be very worried. I don't think they have any idea where we are. Do they know where you are and what you have been doing?"

Mr MacGregor nodded. "I suspect so. I have had to go to Brisbane to collect the other half of the ransom and I used the company jet for that. But so that the people at the Mt Egbert Mine didn't suspect that something was wrong I told them that Mrs MacGregor and the girls had gone to visit their aunty and that I had a business meeting. It was better to use the Cloncurry Airport than the one at the mine for that."

Lt Ross asked, "You have the ransom?"

"I have. It is in that cupboard," Mr MacGregor replied. "Now I am just waiting for instructions on where to take it and when."

That notion sent tremors of apprehension through Rose. Having watched one ransom hand-over she now dreaded the second.

"We can come and support you again," she suggested.

"I'd rather you didn't," her father replied. "I want you safe. You got away with it last time because the crooks did not know you were there. But I suspect they now know about Captain and Ma'am here so will make it much harder."

"How so?" Lt Ross asked.

Captain Ross answered that. "Last time they sent a text message and gave you about six hours to make the drop. That is probably because they did not know your exact movements. But you said they told you to be in Cloncurry. So, even if they aren't watching you, us, right now, they can calculate driving times and will probably make it a much shorter time. We took nearly two hours to get into position last time. If we don't have enough time, it will all get messy."

Mr MacGregor nodded. "I agree. I think they will give me a very short time, an hour or so, to get to the place."

Lt Ross frowned. "So now we just wait until the crooks tell you where to go next?"

Mr MacGregor nodded. "That's right. Then we can make a plan."

# Chapter 34

## WAITING

Rose was not happy with that. "So we just wait?"

"Yes."

"We will still come with you dad," Rose said in a most determined voice.

"No you won't! And particularly not the Little Gem," Mr MacGregor said, looking at Belinda and rumpling her hair and ears.

"I not a gem!" Belinda objected. "I got diamond for Mummy. Rose, you show diamond please."

Rose had luckily transferred the amethyst to the pocket of the shirt she had on, so she dug it out and passed it around.

"Ball of Business had just dug this up at Kalkobi when Lucas and his mate Marvin arrived," she explained.

"Me have it pass through," Belinda added, which puzzled them all until Rose explained how it had gone into her 'Finds' bottle and that had been filled with water when she needed every little bit of storage.

"She drank it by mistake and had to wait until it had passed through her system."

Belinda beamed at this and insisted on taking the amethyst to look at it. Before any of them realised what she was doing she put it in her mouth.

"Belinda!" Rose cried. "Spit it out!"

But it had gone, swallowed again. "Oh well, we will just have to examine all your poos again, Bub-O," Rose said. "And this time you can search through them for it!"

"Wowsie!" wailed Belinda.

Lt Ross interrupted. "Let's change the subject. What about afternoon tea?"

This was organised, coffee for the adults and Milo for the two girls. Biscuits and cake were found from the cupboard and the camper trailer. While they sat and enjoyed the refreshments Captain Ross said, "We need to go to the shop for a few things and we need to refuel the Prado.

Do you think you and the girls will be alright if we leave for a couple of hours?"

Mr MacGregor nodded. "Yes. I don't think this gang will try anything in town where there are lots of witnesses. I think they are trying to avoid any publicity and any police attention."

"We still have that rifle. Do you want it?" Captain Ross asked.

Mr MacGregor shook his head. "No. I am not going to start a gun battle with the girls here. You keep it."

"Okay. It is in the Prado if you want it," Captain Ross said.

Lt Ross now spoke up. "Are there any things you might want at the shop while we are there?"

There were and a combined shopping list was compiled. Mr MacGregor reached into his pocket. "Do you need any money?"

Lt Ross looked a bit offended. "We can worry about that later. Just look after these wonderful girls."

"I will," Mr MacGregor assured them. "And I would like you to be my guests for dinner tonight at the restaurant over the road so don't worry about buying anything for that."

Captain Ross looked doubtful. "Oh, I don't think that is a good idea. I think we need to keep out of sight as much as possible and give the enemy as little information as we can. We can have a celebratory dinner after it is all over. What about a take-away here after dark?"

Mr MacGregor nodded. "Okay, do you want to get that while you are out?"

This was agreed to, and the girls asked what they wanted. Lt Ross wrote this on her shopping list. "Thank you. Well, we'll be off. Goodbye girls. See you in a while," she said. They both moved to the door and went out. Rose's father locked it behind them.

As the Rosses said goodbye and went out, Rose experienced a spurt of anxiety. It suddenly dawned on her just how important they were in her life and what a great comfort it had been to have them around for the last two days. She experienced a stab of worry that in fact they might just leave and not come back. Then she felt ashamed of having such doubts.

Once the Rosses had driven off Mr MacGregor offered more biscuits and then, seeing Belinda's eyelids drooping, picked her up and hugged her to his shoulder. He began to walk up and down ten steps each way while humming a nursery rhyme.

"You have a lie down too Rose, please," he said. "You never know what might happen next, or when."

Rose accepted this advice and took off her boots and lay down on the single bed. Her father kept walking up and down until Belinda was sound asleep and then gently lay her on the double bed before sitting in the sole armchair and closing his eyes. For a while Rose lay there with her own eyes closed, trying to relax and pretending she was asleep, and then she was.

It was dark when Rose woke. She looked around in the dim light from a streetlight outside and for a moment wondered where she was. Then she remembered. Looking around she saw that her father was asleep in the armchair and Belinda was still snuffling in the other bed. Rose did a quick trip to the toilet and that woke her father. She checked her watch: 1830hrs.

Her father sat up and yawned. "Any news?" he queried.

Rose shook her head. "No Dad."

That sent her anxiety level shooting up again. *Surely the crooks won't want to make the hand-over in the dark?* she thought. That would be a whole new level of danger!

Belinda woke and had to be tended to and then entertained. Bunny helped. Rose was in the middle of telling the story of the 'Little Engine That Could' when the Rosses knocked on the door. They had carry bags full of take-away food so the lights were turned on and they arranged themselves on chairs and beds to eat. Rose had trouble making the food go down her throat as she was feeling so miserable about what might be happening to her mother that she was physically ill. Knowing that she might need all her energy to help save her mother Rose forced herself to eat.

The TV was turned on to help amuse Belinda. She happily sat on the bed and watched 'The Teletubbies', 'In the night garden', 'Peppa Pig' and 'Thomas the Tank Engine'. During that Thomas puffed his way through a tunnel and Belinda turned and looked at Rose. "We go through tunnel," she said.

Rose was amazed that she remembered. "We did," she agreed. "And you were very brave in the dark."

Turning to her father Belinda continued, "Rosie carried me, and she tripped and hurt her fingernail."

*I did too! And it still hurts,* Rose thought, curling her fingers to look at them and then opening both hands out to look at them. *Oh, my nails and my hands are a mess!*

After that, they sat and talked about life, school, past events, and travel. The Rosses were more widely travelled than Rose had expected, and they had a better knowledge in detail of many places overseas and in Australia than even her father. Rose's dad gave a wry grin.

"I travel a lot and sometimes very fast but all I see are plastic hotels that all seem the same and the inside of business offices. I don't get much of a chance to meet the locals. That's why we were doing this sort of holiday, to keep our mental feet on the ground."

At which Belinda piped up and said, "Rosie called me a Ball of Business."

"Busyness," Rose corrected as they all laughed.

The adults then discussed various plans about what to do when the crooks finally sent the information for the hand-over. Rose tried to listen but was fairly fully occupied keeping Belinda happy. But Captain Ross had a very good idea.

"One of the advantages of being a history teacher," he commented. "You have a lot of useless facts in your brain but in among them are some gems."

At the word 'gem' Belinda looked at him and then put her hands to her mouth and giggled. Rose was not amused. "Don't you laugh, you little Miss Mischief! You can squish through your own poo if you want your amethyst back!"

Which upset Belinda. "Aw Rosie! Sowwy Rosie. Will you please help me. I only little."

"I thought you said you were a big girl?" Rose retorted, half angry and half amused.

"Only sometimes," Belinda replied meekly.

"Yes, only when it suits you! Alright Bub-O, I will, but only if you go to the toilet now," Rose insisted.

That worked but a cursory check of the results convinced Rose a detailed inspection was not necessary.

"Too soon yet!" she explained.

Games, stories and talking filled in an otherwise long evening. At 2130hrs Captain Ross said, "Bed for us. We all need to be up and ready by 0530 I reckon. If you want, we will do sentry from over in the camper trailer."

"Do you think that is necessary?" Mr MacGregor asked, obviously alarmed and surprised.

"Maybe not. But I think we will do it anyway. We will look silly if the gang turn up in the middle of the night and take the girls as hostages too," Captain Ross replied.

Rose put her hand up. "Sir, do you want me to do a couple of hours?"

Captain Ross shook his head. "No Rose. We don't want any movement outside your cabin. We can manage thank you. But I recommend you sleep fully clothed and with your boots handy."

Rose nodded and her father agreed. The Rosses said good night and left. Rose took Belinda to the toilet again and then went herself before lying down. Her father turned the lights off. But neither could sleep so, in between amusing Belinda, they talked, the best father-daughter talk Rose could ever remember.

As they talked, it was borne in upon her that her father not only loved her but that he was now mightily impressed with her behaviour and performance during the last week. Rose glowed inside over that and reinforced it by being very proud of what she had done herself.

It was an anxious but satisfied girl who finally dropped off to sleep again just before 2300hrs. After a big drink and a check through the curtains at the silent world of the caravan park outside (Silent that is except for the roaring and rumbling of big trucks passing along the main road outside every few minutes!), she lay down. For a while she lay on the double bed with Belinda beside her, having insisted her father use the single bed.

Several times during the night Rose woke with a start and found she was perspiring despite the air-conditioning. Her heart was hammering and she lay there listening and wondering if it had been a bad dream that had woken her, or some suspicious noise. But all was quiet, except for another big truck, so she closed her eyes each time and drifted off back to sleep.

Dawn found them still waiting. The usual caravan park sounds of early risers packing up and driving out and people walking yapping dogs or talking loudly penetrated her consciousness. Her father woke and went to the toilet and then had a shower and shave. Belinda woke and had to be attended to and dressed in new clean clothes, although she hadn't soiled her panties, thank God!

Then it was Rose's turn to use the bathroom and toilet. As she brushed her hair afterwards, she heard voices and peeked through the tiny window and saw Captain Ross in a T-shirt and shorts walking back from the shower block. There had obviously been no alarm in the night.

*But we are still waiting!* Rose thought anxiously.

After dressing and hanging up the towel, she again looked out and this time saw Captain Ross standing outside the camper van making toast at a small table. The toaster was plugged into the side of the van. It was all refreshingly normal. But also very wearing.

*Oh, how long before these crooks send us a message?* she fretted.

To be ready, she sat and put on her boots and made sure her water bottle was full. Then breakfast followed, cereal, fruit juice, toast, and a banana. Belinda enjoyed the banana but did not eat much. She ended up squishing more of it through her fingers than went into her mouth.

"Stop playing with your food and making a mess Little Miss Messy!" Rose snapped.

"I Little Miss Mischief!" Belinda retorted.

"You will be Little Miss Sore Bum if I smack your bottom!" Rose threatened, although she had never actually seen her mother do that. But she had heard her threaten it and the threat seemed to work.

"Sowwy Rosie!" Belinda replied meekly, holding out two hands covered with raspberry jam and mashed banana.

Rose took a wet washer to them and then to Belinda's grubby cheeks and mouth. She was in the middle of that when there was a knock on the door. Her father checked. It was the caravan park manager.

"Sorry to disturb you, sir ,but you are Mr MacGregor aren't you?"

"Yes."

"A lad came in and handed me this as soon as the office opened. Said it was important and it was for you," the manager said, handing over a brown envelope.

Rose's heart rate shot up. *At last!*

She heard her father ask the manager if he knew who the boy was, but the man just shook his head.

"Never seen him before in my life. He just gave me this and then jumped on his bike and off."

"Thank you. It is important," Mr MacGregor said. He closed the door and turned to Rose, holding the envelope up. "Let's see what this says."

Rose could hardly wait. Belinda was told to amuse herself with Bunny for a minute and Rose sat beside her dad while he tore the envelope open. As before it had two sheets of paper: a message and a sketch map. The message read:

MARY KATHLEEN MINE
1000 HRS
FOLLOW MAP
COME ALONE

The sketch map was off the area from the Barkly Highway to the mine site, apparently an old open cut. At the turn-off from the highway was a gate symbol and the notation: 'Ignore Keep Out Signs'.

Rose's heart rate was now very high. Excitement and fear mingled. Her father read the note again and then said, "Go and get the Rosses please Rose, while I put my boots on."

Rose immediately clicked the TV on to give Belinda something to keep her amused. 'The Little Princess' was on.

"Good! Just your program. You are a little princess," Rose said.

She hurried out of the cabin and across to the camper trailer. The Rosses were washing up after breakfast. Rose didn't even knock as the door was open.

"Quick! We have a note!" she cried.

A minute later the Rosses followed Rose through the cabin door. Belinda did not look around from the TV and Mr MacGregor merely thrust the note at them.

"Sorry, but we need to move if we are going ahead with your plan," he said.

Rose felt her chest tighten with anxiety. The plan was a variation of the one they had used at Dobbyn, but it still carried a lot of risk.

Captain Ross nodded and said, "We are not just going to sit here minding the girls. You need some back-up and may need help. And the girls are probably safer hiding out in the bush than sitting here essentially prisoners in a cabin. So I'd like to go ahead. And this time I am contacting my police contact as soon as it is safe for your wife."

That idea really got Rose choked up, but she still thought they did not have many options. "Let's do it please," she cried.

The notion of her father needing help and of what her mother's situation might be were starting to haunt her.

Her father looked grim. "I don't like it, but I agree. Thank you for your support. I won't forget. Now let's get going!"

# Chapter 35

## RUNNING OUT OF TIME

Captain Ross looked at his watch.

"It is 0815 already. We need to move fast. We will see you at the rendezvous. Come on love." He turned and he and Lt Ross hurried out.

Hearing Captain Ross call Lt Ross 'love' really hit an emotional spot in Rose. *Love!* she thought. *Yes, love is the most important thing in the world. Not money but love.* Even as she grabbed her backpack and then picked up a protesting Belinda she smiled and gave her dad a quick hug and kiss.

"Love you, Dad!"

Belinda did not want to leave the TV. "Pwincess!" she cried, reaching back towards the TV over Rose's shoulder as she was hurried to the door.

"We are going to find Mummy, Bub-O," Rose replied.

"Mummy! Want Mummy!" Belinda almost shouted, twisting to look around for her as they went through the doorway.

The first part of the plan was simple. Rose and Belinda got into the back seat of the 4WD their dad was driving. He buckled them in with pillows and a rug and then got in the driver's seat and drove out onto the main road. There he turned right and drove west. Rose was so impatient that she kept wanting to urge her father to drive faster but he stayed right on the speed limit in the town, 50kph, when she wanted to do 150kph!

Her father said, "We don't want to be stopped by the police for speeding, not at this moment." Rose could only agree and try to be patient.

Once out of town across the Cloncurry River her father accelerated the vehicle and quickly had it up to 110kph. By then it was already 0825hrs! The driving was easy and good. The Barkly Highway is a very good two-lane, bitumen road with passing lanes every ten kilometres or so. Thus they were not really delayed by being stuck behind slow moving road trains carrying ore to the smelters in Mount Isa. By now Rose was starting to think she had had enough of the Barkly Highway!

By 0850hrs they were at the turn-off to Ballara. Here they turned left onto the gravel road. That gave Rose a few flashbacks to consider. She wasn't sure now whether she hated or liked that area.

*But I do like Fountain Springs. That place will always be good to me,* she told herself.

Her father only drove south along the gravel Ballara road for about half a kilometre, until the vehicle was out of sight from the highway. Then he swung it round and got out and opened up the back. As he did, the Rosses drove in. Their Prado was parked among the bushes and they both immediately got out and quickly changed into their army camouflage uniforms. Rose had never seen people lace boots up so quickly but even so was in a fever of impatience. The minutes seemed to fly by.

*Oh hurry! We do not want to be late,* she thought.

The knowledge that her mother's life might be hanging in the balance gnawed at her and made her feel ill in the stomach. But she also had a part to play in this plan and she now took out the radio she had taken off Lucas and clicked it on.

Within five minutes both Rosses had changed and were crawling into the back of the 4WD with their webbing and the rifle. The sight of that rifle filled Rose with a mixture of satisfaction and dread. But she knew she certainly felt safer out in the bush with the Rosses than she had back in the cabin.

The Rosses lay down in the back and Mr MacGregor pulled a camouflage sleeping bag over them, then closed the back door. Hurrying to the front, he said, "Lie down on the floor, girls, and I will cover you. You must stay down and not be seen. Do not get up until I say you can."

This was Captain Ross's History idea, the Trojan Horse. Rose thought it was a very good idea but was very aware it could go disastrously wrong. She got Belinda down with difficulty.

"We have to hide, Bub-O. There are bad men ahead," she explained.

That worked. Belinda looked scared and whispered, "I pwomise I won't show them any butterflies."

"Good girl. Now, stay very quiet," Rose answered, patting her and wishing she had an adult to comfort her.

Her father drove the car quickly back to the junction with the highway. Rose felt them turn left and accelerate and could only try to imagine where she was going. It was very claustrophobic and frightening under the rug. And it was already 0910hrs!

A few minutes later the vehicle slowed and then turned right. Her father then spoke. "There are signs here that say 'Danger, Keep Out' and 'Explosives in use' and one saying 'Road Closed, By Order'. It doesn't say by whose orders. I presume the crooks put them there to keep tourists away while they do this."

Rose was scared, she could not see and was afraid that the crooks might just stop the vehicle and find them all. And she still feared that the crooks might intend to kill her father after the hand-over. But all she could do at that time was go ahead with the plan. She felt the vehicle start bumping over potholes and washouts as it began travelling along a poorly maintained side road.

And then the radio crackled! It was Norris, she was sure. "Hey boss, a white Four-Wheel drive just passed me and MacGregor's drivin',over."

The reply crackled back at once. "Is he alone, over."

*That was Cousin James,* Rose told herself.

"Yeah, I didn't see anyone else in the car, over," Norris replied.

"Good! You stay here and keep watch. If any dumb tourist tries to come in, you turn 'em back. And if the cops arrive, you let us know and stay hidden, over," Cousin James instructed.

The vehicle went bumping down a slope. Rose's father said, "So they were watching the entrance. You were right Captain Ross. Let's hope they don't see you people get out."

The road seemed to be very rough to Rose, the vehicle bumping and swerving continually. "Sorry," her father called, "But it is a very rough road. Bitumen but lots of potholes. I am driving as fast as I dare but I don't want to blow a tyre or damage the suspension."

"Nine twenty, Dad," Rose said.

"I know Rose. I am driving as fast as I can."

The vehicle bounced and rattled across some gravel and then started going up a slope. Her father called back, "This is a very old road, but it hasn't been looked after for a long time."

More minutes of bone-juddering travel had them up over another rise and down across another creek. They did a sharp left turn and accelerated, and Rose badly wanted to peek out but knew she must not. Keeping Belinda quiet and calm was more of a challenge!

0925hrs slid by and then 0930hrs, and now Rose was getting really anxious and sweating. The car's air-conditioning was not working down under the rug. Belinda began to cry. To add to Rose's emotional stress, her dad now called out, "We still have a fair way to go. I think we are running out of time to carry out our original plan."

Captain Ross called from the back, his voice muffled by the sleeping bag, "Can't be helped. Go on as long as you can. I'll tell you when to stop. I'm going to look out to see where we are."

Rose badly wanted to look as well but she steeled herself to stay hidden. *One of the crooks might be looking. I mustn't give our plan away!* she told herself.

So she stayed under the rug and tried to quieten Belinda, who was now on the verge of being hysterical. Finally, after a series of particularly awful jolts, she decided she had to take the rug off. She pulled it aside and at once Belinda became less noisy, looking up with tear-filled eyes.

"Want Mummy!"

"We are going to Mummy now. Sit up Bub and calm down please,"

Rose sat Belinda up on the floor and looked around. She noticed a plastic drink bottle in a pocket in the door beside her. Quickly she unscrewed the cap and tested the contents. It was water.

"Here, have a drink," she said.

But when she held the bottle to Belinda's mouth the vehicle hit a big bump and water sloshed out, all down Belinda's face and front. She burst into tears again and sat there, chest heaving.

Finally, five harrowing minutes later, Belinda calmed sufficiently to take a few mouthfuls. Her father then called back.

"Hang on, the next bit is rough. We are leaving this road to cross a gully."

They did so, grinding up onto a stretch of very good bitumen road. From the back Captain Ross called, "This used to be the treatment works and offices. Just around the corner is an old boom gate and security set-up, and the concrete slabs where the buildings were. Keep driving. We still have fifteen minutes."

Rose glanced out and noted that the road curved to the right onto a large area of flat land. She got a glimpse of the concrete slabs in among huge clumps of weeds and bushes. But only a few metres on the road deteriorated to bumpy gravel and curved right and then began to wind its way around the clumps of prickly looking bushes. Ahead through the windscreen she glimpsed a mountain that seemed to fill the whole scene.

"We go up there," Captain Ross called.

Rose could not see exactly where but got an impression of very steep, rocky, scrub-covered slopes that appeared to climb up to the sky. It was a daunting sight and she hoped they would not have to climb it.

A couple of bumpy minutes later they came to a sharp little climb and then a T-junction. "Go right," Captain Ross instructed.

Rose noted that the road they turned onto was a bench cut into the side of the steep mountain and that it was also very rough, washouts, exposed rocks, potholes. The steep slope up was on their left.

Another bumpy minute of driving and Rose was hugging a frightened and almost distraught Belinda to her. She was feeling very fragile herself and it was obvious even to her that their plans had gone awry and that they had run out of time. Her watch told her it was 0950hrs.

*Only ten minutes. We won't have any time to try to creep into cover on foot,* she thought.

But Captain Ross had other ideas. "Stop just off the road in this slightly wider section please Mr MacGregor. I know it is nearly time, but the crooks know you are coming so I reckon they will wait a few more minutes. The next bit of road goes up through a cutting and then downhill to a sort of overgrown parking area. You are to park there and then walk to the right of the gully. There is an obvious footpath that takes you out to the bench cut shown on their sketch map. Just give us five minutes to get ahead and into some sort of cover."

"Okay, ten minutes if you need it. I agree they will wait a bit. I would for ten million dollars," Mr MacGregor agreed.

The 4WD came to a stop. Mr MacGregor got out and hurried to the back. The back door was flung open and the Rosses slid out, dragging their webbing and the rifle with them. Rose opened her door and climbed out, still clutching Belinda to her like a koala. Belinda luckily quietened down.

"Hush now, Bubby!" Rose said. "There are bad men. We must hide and be very quiet."

Standing there, scared and trembling, Rose looked for her father. He was having a hurried conversation with Captain Ross. But then he hurried around the car and hugged her.

"You take care of Little Miss I Love You please. And I love you, Rose."

Through her tears Rose saw her father had wet eyes as well. She gripped him fiercely. "I love you, Dad! Take care please."

"I will, as well as I can. Now get walking and stay safe. I will try to get Mummy back as quickly as I can. Now go! We are almost over time."

Rose sobbed but nodded. Still with Belinda clinging to her she let go and turned to start walking up the rough track. Captain Ross, now with his webbing on, went hurrying ahead, rifle at the ready and eyes questing all likely enemy positions on the slopes ahead and above. Lt Ross followed. Rose glanced back and saw her father standing there looking very grim and upset. She managed a wave, and he forced a grin and waved back.

*He is very brave. He could be dead in a few minutes,* Rose thought, and then she sobbed and could barely see.

The walk up to the crest was only a few hundred metres but took five minutes and left Rose gasping and sweating. The only good things were that the cutting was so deep that it cast a shadow they could walk in, and it funnelled a breeze. When she came to a gasping standstill near the top, that breeze instantly began to chill her perspiration.

*Nearly at the top,* she told herself. But then she shivered with apprehension at what the next few metres might reveal.

But there was no time to stop to get breath back. Captain Ross had paused under cover to scan the area ahead and he now gestured to the left.

"No time to rest. We are out of time. Come on, stay over to the left and under cover as much as you can. Then get into the gully leading up on the left of the clearing," he instructed.

Rose forced herself to keep plodding up, her chest heaving and heart hammering. And then she was at the top. And the view brought her to an involuntary stop. She actually gaped. In front of her the road went down to a scrubby clearing of bare earth with steep slopes on both sides. Just beyond there was the start of a gully, which quickly became a deep, steep-sided chasm, which led into a gigantic hole in the earth, the old open-cut mine pit. And as a massive backdrop was a series of bench-cut haul roads and grey cliffs that reared up beyond the pit and seemed to fill the whole sky.

Lt Ross came up, puffing and panting. "Keep going Rose. You can look at the view later," she said.

Rose nodded and resumed moving, having trouble keeping her footing on the loose rocks and stony outcrops. She saw that Captain

Ross was already fifty paces ahead and near the clearing which was the 'parking area'. She followed. It took a whole minute to get down and she was scared the whole way. It was obvious to even her that a sniper could be hiding anywhere on the steep, scrub-covered slopes that reared up to her right, right-front and her left.

Captain Ross vanished into a fold in the ground to the left and Rose made that place her objective. She was now so stressed that her gaze kept darting from place to place but not properly focusing. She found she was getting dizzy from breathing so deeply and she had to pause to shift Belinda to a more comfortable position. Lt Ross guided her left into the small re-entrant.

It wasn't much cover but by moving close in to the hollow behind the small spur and the bushes growing on it she found she was out of view of all but the steep hill to her right. She came to a stumbling standstill and had to let Belinda slip to the ground. Gasping and trembling she flopped down among the bushes, to immediately yelp and scramble up. They were a mixture of spinifex and some spiky shrub.

The sounds of rustling and scuffing above her told her that Captain Ross was climbing the slope, presumably to look for a good 'overwatch' position. And then she heard the vehicle coming.

*Dad! He is on his way! Oh no! We have run out of time. We aren't ready!*

# Chapter 36

## COURAGE

Rose looked back towards the road. Now she noted that directly across the clearing from her another gravel road went up a very steep slope between two even steeper hills. That road looked rough and washed out and she could not see any sign of recent use. She decided that the crook's vehicle was not up there. For a few seconds she scanned the bushes on either slope for any sign of a sniper.

Into view came her father's 4WD. Rose's heart leapt into her throat with anxiety, and she watched with absolute dread as he stopped it in the clearing near her, switched off, got out and then took another black rucksack from the back. She wanted to cry out, to call to him to take care, to not even go. But she knew he had to, if he was to have any hope of rescuing her mother!

*Oh, he is so brave!* she thought as he started walking across the clearing to the right.

Rose now turned her attention to where he was going. Putting the radio down she edged forward and peered through some bushes. That gave her a clearer picture of the layout of the mine. She now saw that where her father was headed for was what had once been a gravel road that went off to their front on a bench cut around the side of the very steep hill to her right-front. The section of road closest to her had been eroded but as it went out of sight, curving up and around to the right, it became wider and a proper gravel road. Her father began moving slowly onto the eroded section, along an obvious walking path.

Rose now saw that what she had taken to be a gully between her and the walking path was in fact the remains of a badly eroded haul road that went down steeply through a vertical sided cutting. This had been blocked off with boulders. Bushes grew among them. Closer to her was another foot path and she saw that it had also been a haul road but had been blocked by rocks and landslips.

She stood up to get a better view. She was able to see down the steep cutting and was amazed to see water, brilliant blue water. It filled most of the bottom of the gigantic mine pit forming a small lake. With its backdrop of dramatic cliffs cut by numerous bench cuts for haul roads it made a spectacular scene.

*Very pretty!* she thought.

Then she remembered seeing that scene on tourist posters and pamphlets. Her gaze lifted to the series of grey cliffs. With her family background and her father's profession Rose had a good understanding of how open-cut mining was done so she understood what she was looking at. Then a comment by Captain Ross during a lesson on Day Observation, came to her: "Check key details and make accurate counts if you can."

So she quickly counted the number of bench cut haul roads upwards, all the way to the top of the rugged, black boulders on the crest of the mountain. Ten.

Her father was past the walking path by then and moving up the gently sloping haul road. He was going slow and looking in all directions. But he was right out on his own and again Rose admired his courage.

*He is a sitting duck standing out there,* she thought, thinking of snipers positioned across to her left on the series of bench cuts that went out of sight behind the spur she was on. But surely they wouldn't just shoot him and take the loot? *What about Mum? What will they do to her.*

Belinda was fidgeting beside her so Rose gripped her arm and held her back in cover. "Ssssh Bubby! Bad men here," she hissed. Belinda stopped moving except her head, which swivelled to look around.

Her father kept moving slowly forward, keeping to the right against the cliff face and away from the steep drop on his left. Rose stared with anxious eyes and scanned the hill above him, then dismissed it.

*Too steep. A person up there can't see Dad,* she reasoned. The concept of the 'convex slope' came to her from a map reading lesson in cadets.

She shifted her focus to the other side of the huge pit. On most of the haul roads there was no cover, just grey rock. But back almost in line with the low crest her father was approaching, at the point where several haul roads went off the right-hand side of the mountain onto a flat grass-covered area were several clumps of bush.

*That might be a good spot for a sniper to be,* she told herself, remembering Captain Ross's advice that good soldiers always tried to have a withdrawal route.

At that moment, her father yelled, his voice echoing around the massive hole. "Well, here I am! Show yourselves! Bring out my wife and you can get your money."

There were a few seconds of terrible tension and then Captain Ross called softly from up the slope behind them. "I can just see over the crest. A man has come out from behind some bushes and he is holding Mrs MacGregor. Now they are walking towards us."

*Mum! She's safe!* Rose thought, then she sobbed.

Trembling with nervous tension she kept standing staring at the crest which was still about 50 paces past her father. Belinda was squirming and whimpering but Rose ignored her. She saw her father hold up the black rucksack. He was just standing there, obviously watching the two people approaching.

After an agonising period of about three minutes, Rose saw two heads come into view on the bench cut about a hundred paces past her father. To her surprise, it was Cousin James with her mother. He was walking on her left, holding her with his right hand. To Rose's relief, her mother appeared unharmed but tired. She was still wearing the same clothes that she had been kidnapped in. The pair walked forward until they were right on the crest about 25 metres in front of her father.

Her father now called. "Stop there! Now turn around and pull your shirt out and show me you are unarmed."

Cousin James let go of her mother and did as he was told. "You do the same!" Cousin James called back.

Rose's father put down the rucksack and pulled his shirt up, then slowly rotated. At that moment, a tiny flicker of sunlight caught Rose's eye. It came from the far side of the pit, from that left hand bush she had noted earlier. That cadet fieldcraft lesson on 'Why Things are Seen' instantly gave her the answer: sunlight reflecting on something. But what? Glass? Binoculars? No, a telescopic sight!

For a second terror froze her muscles. But not her brain. *The sniper! Lucas is there. They just mean to shoot Dad.* She looked and saw that her father was almost at the crest, at least his top half visible over the rise to the person in the bush. *I must do something!*

Rose turned to Lt Ross. "I just saw sunlight reflect off something in those bushes right across the other side of the big pit, at the right-hand end. I think that is where Lucas is with his rifle. I must warn Dad."

Lt Ross bit her lip but shook her head. "No. You must stay under cover safe," she said.

Belinda looked from one to the other and cried, "Daddy?"

But Rose was not to be stopped. She was certain. She turned and called up the slope, "Captain Ross, Captain Ross!"

"Yes, Rose?"

"Sir, far side of the pit, the haul road level with the flat area. Bushes. Left hand bush. I just saw sunlight glint off something."

"Roger!"

"I'm going to warn my Dad, Ma'am," Rose said.

She let go of Belinda and stepped out in the open. As she did, she saw her father bend and pick up the rucksack and start walking forward up towards the crest. Rose started to run, ignoring Lt Ross's calls to come back.

"Dad! Dad! Lookout!" Rose screamed, certain in her own mind that he was about to be shot.

Her father heard her and stopped walking and turned his head.

*Crack! Boo..ooo...oom!*

Rose heard the shot and heard it strike with a terrible smack. To her absolute horror she saw her father stagger back, drop the rucksack and fall hard against the cliff face.

"Dad!" she screamed, and ran.

*Whack! Eeeeeiee..ow! Boo..ooo...oom!*

A second shot smacked into the cliff face just beside her father's head, just as he crumpled to lie flat. The bullet ricocheted off with a blood-chilling shriek. The sound of the shot went echoing around and around the giant pit.

By then Rose was across the clearing and she started up the narrow footpath between weeds, rocks, and a nasty drop without any hesitation. Her father had been shot and she was going to him! For a few seconds her mother and Cousin James were out of sight, but as she came racing up and around the bend she was dimly conscious of more shots. She realised that Captain Ross had begun shooting. There were shouts from Lt Ross to come back and screams from Belinda but they barely registered.

As Rose rounded the curve, her father came into view, crumpled against the steep cliff face, blood showing on his face. The black rucksack lay nearby. A hundred paces... seventy-five... fifty! Rose ran as she had never run before, yelling but unaware of it. Her whole focus was her father.

But then it shifted. There, right on the cliff edge, were her mother and Cousin James, and they were fighting! Rose realised, with a stab of horror, that Cousin James was trying to push her mother over the cliff!

"Mum! Mum! Keep going!" Rose shouted.

That shout made Cousin James pause just for a second. He glanced in her direction and then turned and hit at her mother. She was trying to grapple with him but obviously wasn't strong enough. And Rose could see over the edge as she ran. To her horror, it wasn't just a short drop to another haul road but a ghastly sheer cliff down to rocks near the edge of the lake!

Rose kept running, passing her father and heading to help her mother. She was aware that shots were being fired but not how many or who at. To her dismay, she saw Cousin James punch her mother hard in the face, knocking her down. He then pushed at her, trying to tumble her over the cliff. She was only a metre or so from it!

"No!" Rose screamed as Cousin James bent to shove harder.

Then Rose tripped. She fell hard on her knees. Pain shot up her legs and her eyes misted, and she gasped in defeat. But desperation drove her. There, under her hand, was a cricket ball sized stone and there was Cousin James pushing her mother right to the edge!

Without conscious thought Rose got to her feet, stone in her right hand and, sensing she did not have time for a hard overarm throw, she threw it underarm. Now all those softball training sessions paid off. The stone flew straight and fast and struck Cousin James in the side of the head, just as he was about to heave her mother over the edge.

Cousin James went down with a cry, clutching his face. For a moment Rose feared he was going to pitch over the edge of the cliff, but he fell hard on his back and rolled away from the edge, obviously hurt.

*Good!* she thought.

Now up and running again she dashed over to her mother and grabbed her shirt. "Mum! Mum! This way!" she screamed, dragging her away from the cliff edge.

*My God! It's a long way down!* she noted, fear giving her strength. The shirt tore but Rose just grabbed more cloth with her other hand and kept dragging.

She got her mother clear and then hauled her to her feet. Her mother was dazed from the punches but was able to stand and start staggering along with Rose's support. They began hobbling back towards her father, Rose barely able to walk with her sore knees. Rose cast a frightened glance back to check that Cousin James wasn't about to attack. To her enormous relief, he was still lying flat. But then she saw movement in the distance at the bushes on the far side of the pit and her blood ran cold with almost paralysing terror.

*Lucas!* She had forgotten about Lucas and his rifle!

But then the movement resolved itself into a tiny running figure. It was Lucas and he was leaving his cover at the run, rifle in hand. The sound of a shot cracked by and the *Thump!* came from in front of Rose, Captain Ross shooting. Rose glanced back again and then let out a cry of triumph. Lucas was down! She saw the man go rolling on the rough ground, his rifle flying from his grasp and then skittering off over the edge of the cliff. But Lucas wasn't dead. He sprang up, looked frantically around for his rifle and then went limping quickly out of her view behind the curve of the hill.

Rose hobbled along, her arm around her mother, gripping her tight and babbling, "Mum! Mum!"

Her mother was also crying and sighing and gripping her with her left arm over her shoulder. By then they were approaching where Rose's father lay and her mother saw him and let out a terrible cry of anguish.

"Oh Rod!" she cried.

Letting go of Rose she staggered over to her husband and dropped to her knees beside him. Rose hobbled slowly over to join her, her knees and that damned left fingernail, all hurting like blazes!

Into view in front of her, coming up the path from the parking area, were Belinda and Lt Ross. Belinda had obviously given her the slip and was running over the rough ground at a most surprising speed. Lt Ross was puffing along behind calling on her to stop. But Belinda had seen her mother.

"Mummy! Mummy!" she screamed.

Rose was torn between worrying about Belinda going too close to the edge of the cliff and seeing what had happened to her father. She was filled with dread as she looked at him. Reaching him she dropped to her knees, and instantly regretted that, and began to examine him.

The first thing Rose noted was the blood on the side of his head but a quick check of it showed it just to be from a small contusion on the side of the skull. Rose had never seen a bullet wound but had heard about them and read about them and this certainly did not look like that. Almost frantic with anxiety she ran her hands over his shirt, looking for a wound. There wasn't one she could find. And then she realised he was breathing.

*He's alive! Oh thank God!*

"Rose! Rose lookout!"

It took a moment for the warning from Lt Ross to sink in. But when it did Rose glanced back over her shoulder and did freeze in fright. Cousin James, a very angry Cousin James with a blood-spattered face, and he was hurrying towards her!

Rose jumped up, looking frantically around for a weapon. She was not going to run. There was her unconscious dad and just a few paces away her injured mother clasping the Ball of Busyness to her, and quite oblivious to the danger.

Lt Ross was coming but she was also unarmed. Rose turned to face Cousin James, her lips compressed with determination but knowing she not only did not know how to fight with her bare hands but that he would be very much stronger. She steeled herself for pain.

But Cousin James was not interested in her. Only when he was a few paces away Rose realised he was after the black rucksack.

*The ransom!* she thought.

Even as he bent to grab at one of the pack straps Rose felt a surge of hate and anger such as she had never before experienced. Without articulating a plan she sprang forward and grabbed the other pack strap and pulled.

Cousin James looked at her in surprise, which quickly turned to blazing rage. "You, you little bitch! You've been bugging me for a week. Let go! Let go!"

He jerked at the rucksack, pulling Rose off balance. She scrabbled with her boots on the loose gravel to try to keep her grip, determined not to let him have it. Then her eyes took in a rip in the nylon of the rucksack.

*Is that a bullet hole?* she wondered. *Is that why dad is alive?*

For a moment she bent to peer more closely. Which she suddenly realised was a mistake.

*Thud!*

Her head seemed to explode from a punch. She gasped, flopped to her knees and let go. She was about struggle up when she felt an arm go around her neck and she was jerked to her feet. To her horror, she realised that Cousin James had her in his grip. He moved back, hoisting the rucksack to one shoulder with his left arm while hoisting Rose upwards again. That lifted her feet off the ground. Shooting pains seared up her neck and into her brain.

*He will break my neck! I'm going to die!* she thought.

A whole host of regrets began to flash across her mind: never having really lived, never having been to Paris, never having made love to a boy (man) (Better not let Mum and Dad know I have those sort of thoughts!).

Through eyes that were alternating between focus and blurred images Rose saw a sort of tableau in front of her: her father still on the ground, her mother clutching Belinda and looking horrified, Lt Ross looking angry and clenching and unclenching her fist, Captain Ross just coming into view around the curve. Captain Ross looked very 'army' and had the rifle in his left hand and a mobile phone in his right.

Cousin James shouted, "Stay where you are! Stay there or I will break her neck and throw her over the cliff!"

Terror swamped Rose's being. *Oh my God!* she thought.

She began to pray, but the sequence of the words was continually interrupted as each step back Cousin James took sent another wave of shooting agony up her spine. She tried to say he was strangling her, but she could not even open her mouth. She struggled to break free, but he just cuffed her hard with his other hand and kept walking backwards.

Rose began to black out from lack of oxygen.

# Chapter 37

## FLIGHT

Rose gasped and gurgled and was scared she was dying from being choked. She reached up with both hands and tried to pull Cousin James' arm away from her throat. When that didn't work she kicked at his shins, earning another hard slap on the left side of her face.

Rose could see her mother's distressed face and the look of dismay on Lt Ross's. Through blurry eyes she saw Captain Ross join them and slip his mobile phone into his pocket before lifting the rifle to his shoulder. Cousin James snarled and held Rose up in front of him while still shuffling backwards.

"Don't try anything you people!" he shouted, "Or I will break her neck and toss her over the cliff."

To demonstrate his ability to do so, he gave Rose's legs a swing and she experienced such a spurt of fear she was ashamed she might have wet herself. Being unable to actually scream she had mentally done so, and she was aware that her heart was hammering very fast.

To Rose's dismay, the group with her father stayed standing there and she was dragged back around the curve out of sight. Captain Ross appeared, keeping close to the cliff and holding the rifle ready. He was obviously trying to stay in cover from the sniper. Rose mentally wished she could tell him that Lucas had dropped his rifle.

*Captain Ross obviously didn't see that,* she thought.

Cousin James began speaking, and for a moment Rose thought he was talking to her. Then she realised he was speaking into his radio.

"Get that car down here, Marvin," he almost yelled.

Marvin's reply came through loud and clear. "It ain't a car, it's a ute."

"I don't care what it is! Don't be a smart-arse! Just get here!" Cousin James shouted back angrily.

"What about the 'over' stuff you are always carrying on about?" Marvin retorted. That caused Cousin James to unleash a flood of expletives. But he did at least ease his grip and stop carrying Rose. Setting her on her feet, he gripped her arm.

"Walk, bitch! And don't try to run or I will push you over the cliff."

As the bench cut went on all the way to the area of flat land ahead of them where the haul roads seemed to converge, Rose was very conscious of that drop beside her. She was also struck by just how blue that water down there was!

Now she could see around the bend and saw there was a large flat area. An overgrown road went up the rise directly ahead and over a saddle between a high hill on the right and the black topped mountain on her left. From among some bushes halfway up the road a white 4WD Dual Cab utility appeared. It drove quickly down, making two wheel tracks in the long grass as it did. At the bottom it did a U-turn and faced back up the slope.

Lucas appeared, limping out of some bushes nearby. He went to the front of the ute and climbed into the passenger seat. Rose had no choice but to walk with Cousin James to the vehicle. When he got there, Cousin James opened the left-hand back door and tossed the rucksack in.

"Is that the loot?" Marvin queried.

"From the weight of it, it is," Cousin James agreed.

"Didn't you check it before handing Lady Muck over?"

Rose bristled to at the insult to her mother but held her tongue. Cousin James was obviously nettled by being questioned.

"I didn't have time before this little bitch appeared and started shouting," he snarled.

Lucas looked at Rose through the car window. "You call her Miss MacGregor, Boss," he said, in a fair imitation of Rose's own tone to him.

"Eh! What are you talking about?" Cousin James asked as he shoved Rose up into the back seat in the middle beside the rucksack.

"When I first met her in the bush that's how Miss Hoighty Toighty spoke to me when I called her by first name," Lucas explained.

"Spoilt little rich bitch, I'd call her," Marvin growled, which also hurt Rose's feelings. She had always thought she was a normal, nice girl.

Cousin James shoved her across and climbed in, slamming the door. "Bloody little slut! She's spoiled everything," he growled.

Rose was really offended at that and pursed her lips but held her silence in case she got another smack. To her surprise, Lucas spoke back.

"There's no need for language like that, Boss," he said.

"I'll speak how I like!" Cousin James snarled.

"She's only a kid," Lucas replied.

That also obviously annoyed Cousin James. "Get this thing moving," he snapped at Marvin. Turning to Lucas, who sat diagonally opposite, he said, "Look in that glove box and see if there is a pistol in there."

Marvin started the vehicle moving and Rose felt her hopes plummet. *Oh, where are we going? What will these men do to me?* she thought, terrifying images of several disgusting or deadly possibilities torturing her imagination.

Lucas handed Cousin James a shiny new automatic pistol. Cousin James grunted with approval and clicked the magazine out to check it was loaded, then snapped it back in. Rose could do nothing but hang on. And hang on she needed to as the overgrown road was full of washouts, rocks and potholes and she was continually thrown about. It was so violent at times that the men cried out and told Marvin to slow down.

"There isn't that much hurry," Cousin James snarled.

Marvin shook his head. "Yes, there is! They got army people there and the cops will be on their way," he said.

Lucas answered that. "They aren't army. They are little Miss MacGregor's army cadet officers, teachers from her school in Charters Towers."

"That guy doing the shooting, he looked like he knows what he is doing," Marvin grumbled.

"He probably does" Lucas agreed. "He was probably in the army when he was younger."

*He was,* Rose thought, *And I wish he was able to shoot now!*

Cousin James agreed. "And Norris will give us warning if any cops turn up. But I reckon they won't even have started from Mount Isa yet."

That was a depressing thought to Rose. That meant it would be at least half an hour before a police car arrived at the turn-off on the Barkly Highway.

*Then they have to drive in here and find out what is going on.*

One of the things that was bothering her was that the overgrown road they were driving up wasn't on the sketch map the crooks had sent. She dimly remembered seeing a few roads marked on the army map Captain Ross had but she had not memorised them or studied where they went.

*There was no need. We didn't know it would be at Mary Kathleen then.*

The future was looking very black and potentially dreadful and she began bracing herself for death, and worse. The disgusting notions of defilement and rape she conjured up made her shudder and she remembered discussions with her friends at school about what to do if they found themselves in this situation. But that just made Rose begin to despair. That was then and this was now, and now was real!

The vehicle topped a rise and ahead of her Rose saw endless rocky ridges and stony knolls. That sent her heart into her boots.

*I hope we aren't going into all that country again,* she thought, while noting that she was facing south.

The old road went downhill for a few hundred metres and came to a junction with other old gravel roads. Here they did a sharp right turn and headed west. The road was better so speed was increased.

"Where are we going?" Rose plucked up the courage to ask.

"Shut up! You'll find out soon enough," Cousin James replied.

To Rose he was looking very agitated and unhappy. He kept nervously fingering the pistol and that worried her too. Then she thought, *It will be best if he just shoots me. I don't have to endure being ... being.*

She could not frame her darkest fears and began sobbing. That earned her a whack on the side of the head from Cousin James.

"Shut up, you little troublemaker!" he ordered.

A few minutes later they came out on a potholed bitumen road lined with bushes that half overhung it. They turned right. Speed was increased, except when they hit a really big pothole hard. Then the two men cursed Marvin, so he slowed down and instead swerved slowly around the worst of the potholes.

A gravel road went off to the left. They swung onto it and went down a long slope, across an old cattle grid, and came out in a long clearing. Rose gaped. There was a bitumen airfield at least a kilometre long, the sides all long grass and the painted markings hardly visible, but a proper airstrip all the same. The grass around the verge was waist high and the windsock was just a few rotted strips hanging from the hoop. But an aircraft stood there waiting, a twin-engine, low-wing type.

Marvin pulled the ute to a stop and switched off the motor. Cousin James looked out and grunted with satisfaction.

"Good! The plane's here. At least that part of the plan is working. Okay, out you get Miss I'm Special MacGregor!"

They all climbed out and Cousin James reached back in and hauled out the rucksack. This went over his left shoulder. He then pointed with the pistol to the aircraft and growled, "Get in!"

A man in his thirties, obviously the pilot by his white shirt with epaulets of black with two yellow bars on each, climbed out and walked towards them.

"Was that shooting I heard?" he asked, looking a bit worried.

"Nothing that concerns you," Cousin James replied. "You ready to go?"

"Yeah. Who's she?" the pilot queried, indicating Rose.

Rose opened her mouth to speak, to plead with this man to help her, to save her, but Cousin James brought the pistol up to her cheek and pressed it in hard.

"She's our insurance," he snarled.

The pilot shook his head. "I don't mind a bit of smuggling, but I won't be part of any abduction or whatever," he said.

At that, Cousin James let go of Rose's arm and used that hand to cock the automatic pistol. "You'll do whatever we tell you to, or you are a dead man right now!" he snarled.

The pilot blanched and eyed the pistol, which was now pointing at him. He put his hands half up. "Okay, okay, take it easy, Boss. I just prefer to know what I'm involved in."

Rose decided to add to the confusion. "I'm a hostage," she said. "My name is Rose MacGregor. My dad owns MacGregor Mining."

Cousin James snarled and whacked her hard, half stunning her. The pilot gaped as realisation sank in. Cousin James drew his hand back to hit her again. Lucas reached out and grabbed it.

"That'll do, Boss. Keep your cool! You make bad decisions when you get in a temper."

"Stay out of it!" Cousin James shouted. "Just get in the plane, all of you."

Marvin shook his head. "What about divvying up the loot now. Then we can go our own way."

Cousin James looked at him and scowled, then nodded. "Okay, in the plane as soon as we take off. Now get in. Marvin, get that other rucksack."

Rose was dragged over to the short set of steps in the side of the fuselage and shoved up.

"Get in a seat!" she was ordered.

She saw that there were two rows of single seats with an aisle between them. There were six in all, the front two were obviously for the pilot and co-pilot. The co-pilot's seat was empty. She was shoved into the first seat on the left inside the door by Cousin James who then dumped the rucksack on the seat diagonally behind the pilot. Lucas climbed up and made his way past her to sit just behind the pilot.

The pilot made his away forward to his seat and buckled in. He looked very unhappy. Cousin James went back to the door, his right hand with the pistol behind his back. Rose wasn't yet in her seatbelt so was able to twist around, wondering if she could somehow get out at the last moment. She feared that once that door was shut and the aircraft was airborne, she was doomed. That notion made her desperate.

Thus she saw what happened next. Just as the pilot started the engines Marvin came back from the ute carrying a rucksack., the one that was handed over at Dobbyn Rose presumed. He reached the bottom of the steps and was met by Cousin James who held out his left hand for the rucksack. Without thinking, Marvin handed it up to him and then found himself staring into the muzzle of Cousin James' pistol!

Rose's emotions barely had time to get past the stab of alarm stage before both men acted. Marvin shouted in fear and jumped back as Cousin James fired. Rose heard Marvin cry out in pain even over the revving of the engines. The pilot stopped testing his engines and turned to lookback in alarm.

"What the bloody hell!" he called.

Cousin James tossed the second rucksack onto the floor at the back of the fuselage and reached out to pull the door shut. He then turned and waved the pistol at the pilot.

"Just fly this thing like we agreed and you will get well paid," he shouted above the roar of the engines.

*Yeah, paid like Marvin just was!* Rose thought, and by the look that crossed the scared pilot's face she thought that was what he was thinking too.

But he did not have much choice in the circumstances so turned to the front and continued with his cockpit drill. Cousin James sat down opposite Rose and put on his seat belt. He did not tell her to put hers on, which worried her and gave her plenty of room for speculation.

Rose was very experienced in aircraft so none of the procedures were of any novelty or concern to her, just Cousin James with his gun. She felt sure he was going to take revenge on her by either shooting her or throwing her out of the aircraft. She began to tremble as fear built up.

The pilot tested the engines with the brakes on and then started his take-off. The engines roared until at full power and then he released the brakes. Just as he did there was peculiar 'whack' noise. Rose heard it but could not place what caused it. Then it came again and it was Lucas who recognised it. He pointed to a small hole that had just appeared in the skin of the fuselage. It was just near his head. He turned and ducked down and peered back out through the nearest window.

"Marvin! He's got a rifle and he's shooting at us!" Lucas called.

"Go! Get this thing up!" Cousin James shouted at the pilot.

There was another whack and then a distinct metallic *ting!* The aircraft began moving forward. Rose crouched low in her seat, terrified of being hit by a bullet.

As the speed increased Rose began to relax, or as much as she could in such a terrifying situation, but she distinctly heard another metallic *whang!* and several thumps as the aircraft raced along the runway. And then they were up. The pilot pulled the stick back and the aircraft lifted off under full power.

But not for long! A few seconds after take-off and while they were still only a few hundred feet up, the port motor gave a distinct cough and started missing. Suddenly, the whole aircraft shuddered. The pilot cried out on alarm and swore, and Rose saw his hands working frantically at the controls. Then the port motor began shuddering and a horrible grinding noise sounded. Smoke began to billow from the engine. Rose gulped and went dry in the throat. Normally she was quite at ease flying but she had never been in this sort of situation.

The aircraft suddenly banked to port as they climbed, and Rose glimpsed the huge mine pit and the mountain out to starboard before it was lost to view. Sky appeared in its place, so she looked out her window to port. Fear of the aircraft crashing became her dominant emotion. She looked out and saw they were now swinging round to the west. The nose of the aircraft suddenly went down.

Cousin James was out of his seat in a moment and moved to stand over the pilot, the pistol pointed at his head.

"What are you doing? Where are you going?" he shouted.

"I am going around to do an emergency landing," the pilot replied. "I can't climb on one engine with this much load on board."

"You can't go back to that airfield," Cousin James screamed. "Marvin is there, and he's got a rifle!"

The pilot shook his head and leaned over to switch off the port engine. But he kept banking to port.

"Then I will land on the Barkly Highway," he said.

Rose looked out and clearly saw the highway coming in to view as the aircraft came round.

*Good idea,* she thought. She could see a long straight stretch of several kilometres.

Lucas thought so too. "Just don't hit one of those bloody road trains," he said in a sarcastic drawl.

Cousin James moved to look over the pilot's shoulder and then yelled. "Don't land there! That's a cop car!"

Rose lifted herself to look through the front and sure enough, there were the red and blue flashing lights of a police car coming from the direction of Cloncurry! She smiled and thought, *Saved!*

But Cousin James had other ideas. "Just keep flying," he ordered.

"Or what? You'll shoot me and you will all die in the crash?" the pilot retorted in a sarcastic tone. "Listen buster, I ain't going to try to fly across the Coral Sea on one engine. We have to land."

"Then go south. Land on that gravel road there. But get as far along it as you can," Cousin James ordered, again waving the pistol in a threatening way.

The pilot shrugged and began turning the aircraft to starboard. Rose had a brief glimpse of the gravel road and thought, *Is that the road to Ballara or to the Wee MacGregor?*

And suddenly she didn't care. It was all familiar territory to her! She smiled at the memory of crossing all that country while evading the crooks.

Cousin James saw that smile and it infuriated him. Satisfied the pilot was obeying orders he strode aft and stood over her.

"What are you grinning at bitch?" he snarled. "You have wrecked everything! It is all your fault!"

His face contorted by rage he suddenly lifted the pistol and aimed it at Rose's face. She blanched and then tensed ready to die while deeply regretting it, but not as frightened as she thought she would be. But Lucas acted. His hand shot out and knocked the gun aside, just as Cousin James pulled the trigger.

"Don't be stupid boss!" he shouted.

Rose flinched and felt the blast but was not hit.

"Bastard! Mongrel!" Cousin James shouted, turning to point the pistol at Lucas.

The hand holding the gun was just in front of Rose. Instinctively she punched at it. The gun went off again, but this time went flying out of Cousin James' hand to clatter across the floor and under the seats. The pilot shouted in fright and Lucas came out of his seat like an enraged tiger. He grappled with Cousin James and the pair fell to the floor, both trying to strangle or pummel the other.

The pilot took one terrified look over his shoulder and put the nose down. His hands went to work on the control levers. Rose heard hydraulics at work and a glance showed flaps being lowered.

*And wheels, I hope!*

Looking out she saw they were low over a stretch of gravel road about a kilometre long with trees and low rocky hills on either side. The aircraft swooped in the midday heated air and the pilot wrestled with the controls.

Rose braced for a crash.

# Chapter 38

## COUSIN JAMES

The aircraft flared as the pilot flattened out just above the gravel road. Rose tensed and tried to find her seat belt. She glimpsed a white-trunked gum tree flash past close to the port wing. Lucas and Cousin James were still struggling, punching, gouging, and swearing on the floor between the seats.

Wheels crunched on gravel. The aircraft bounced and then came down with a bump. Brakes squealed and the remaining engine was switched off. Rose stayed braced in case they hit something or went into a ditch. But the pilot had done his job well and they rolled safely to a stop.

The moment they did, the pilot was out of his seat and came scrambling aft, clambering over the two struggling men.

"Get out!" he yelled, "Get out in case she burns!"

A moment later he was at the door, scrabbling to find the handle. It swung open. Blinding glare flooded in, mixed with dust. Galvanized by fear of fire Rose was out of her seat but could not get out without stepping on the men. But they had also stopped fighting and Cousin James scrambled to his feet and rushed to the door. He shoved her hard in the face as he clawed his way through the open door. The pilot was already gone. Then Cousin James was out, and Rose was able to step down between Lucas's limbs.

He looked up, his face bruised and bleeding. "You get out, Miss. I'll follow you," he said.

Rose did. In two bounds she was through that doorway and standing on the gravel road. She ran away from the aircraft for at least twenty paces before slowing and looking back. Aware that her life might still be in danger she looked around to see what Cousin James was doing, ready to bolt into the bush away from him.

But it was he who was running! She saw him looking wildly in all directions as he ran. He saw her but the gaze did not seem to focus. He raced off up a long slope through spinifex, falling several times as he went. She saw that the pilot was standing beside the port engine using a small fire extinguisher on it. He was obviously no threat to her. She began to relax. Then she saw Lucas climbing awkwardly down the steps, and in his left hand was the pistol!

*The pistol! Oh you dumb bum!* she castigated herself.

She had forgotten it in the panic to get out. She turned to run, estimating that it would be a long shot for Lucas with a pistol. She thought she could outrun him as he obviously had something wrong with his left leg.

But as she did, Lucas called out. "Miss MacGregor! Miss MacGregor! Don't run. You come and get this pistol." With that he placed it on the ground and then went limping away from it.

At first Rose thought it must be a trick or a trap, but Lucas went on limping until he was in the shade of some trees and there he lowered himself to sit and lean back on one. Estimating that she could get to the pistol before he could Rose first looked around to check where Cousin James was and then hurried back across to pick it up. She had never held a pistol so was very careful with it.

*Where is the safety catch?* she wondered.

Then she remembered watching Cousin James take the magazine out and she looked until she found a catch on the side of the hand grip. She pressed it and the magazine fell out into her other hand.

"Well done! That's right," Lucas called.

Rose moved out of the blazing sun into the shade of a nearby tree. The pilot moved to stand near Lucas. Rose looked at Lucas curiously.

"Thank you for saving my life," she said gesturing with the pistol.

Lucas shrugged. "That's okay. You're a good kid. I hope my kids turn out as good. Besides, I will do enough time in jail for the kidnapping and shooting without having your murder on the charge sheet."

"Why didn't you try to get away?" Rose asked, indicating the vast area bush and stony hills around them.

Lucas made a face and shook his head. "No good. I tripped and busted me knee when that bloke was shooting at me. And besides, you have my wallet and all my ID so the cops will have no trouble rounding me up."

The pilot now asked, "Are you really Rod MacGregor's daughter?" Rose nodded. "Oh my gawd! What have I gotten myself into? That mongrel," and he gestured toward Cousin James who was now hundreds of metres away and near the top of the first ridge, "he told me it was just smuggling gold and a couple of people who needed to leave the country."

Lucas laughed. "No, abduction and ransom is his game."

Rose saw Cousin James vanish over the skyline. "Have either of you got a mobile phone?"

They both had, so she said, "You'd better call for the police and an ambulance."

"Yeah, but I don't know where we are," the pilot said.

Lucas pointed. "You can get back in that thing and activate your emergency GPS gadget."

"Not on your nelly! Not until that engine is cold and I am sure there isn't going to be a fire," the pilot replied.

Rose shook her head. "You are on the road to Ballara. Just tell them that," she said. She turned and started walking back across the road, meaning to chase Cousin James.

"Where are you going?" Lucas called after her.

"To keep tabs on Cousin James," she said.

The pilot looked very concerned. "You can't just go walking off into those hills. You could get lost."

At which Rose just laughed. "Not me! These hills and I are old friends. Just tell the police which way I have gone," she said. She resumed walking, stepping off the road and into the spinifex with practised ease.

As she did, she heard Lucas say to the pilot. "You better believe her. She gave us the slip in those hills for a whole week, and she was carrying her baby sister. She'll be alright."

And that compliment from her most feared enemy glowed in her very being. *I'll be alright! I know what I am doing, and poor Cousin James has no idea.*

She smiled at that and then realised she had the pistol in one hand and the magazine in the other. She slipped the magazine back into the pistol as she detoured around a sticky bush. She realised she was now subconsciously avoiding such things.

Now she started worrying about what she would do when she caught up with Cousin James (She was absolutely certain he would not escape). She looked at the pistol and worried about how to use it. She had never been trained to use one. She knew her father owned one but he kept it locked up somewhere.

*And all his security men have them,* she thought, sadly aware that those people might figure a lot more in her life from now on.

"I will get dad to get them to train me," she said, thinking it might be a useful skill.

Then it dawned on her that it did not matter that she wasn't trained. *All I have to do is lie and tell Cousin James I can use it,* she reasoned.

She reached the crest of the first rise and paused to look around. She took a deep breath and stretched in the sunshine, enjoying the wonderful vista under that huge sky. Off to the south she could see a rugged range of mountains.

*I think they are the ones the tunnel goes through, over on the other side. To the Wee MacGregor Mine.*

She smiled and looked around, noting those seemingly endless ranges and stony knolls in every direction and even a few big mountains in the distance, a real wilderness but she did not feel in the least daunted by it.

And there was Cousin James, struggling through the spinifex and sticky bushes on the other side of a small dry creek. He was heading roughly west and that made Rose smile again.

*He has no idea where he is or where he is heading,* she thought.

But she had so she began to stride confidently down the slope in pursuit. Cousin James looked back and though the distance was too great for her to see his facial expression Rose was sure it included dismay and fear.

As she walked down the slope, weaving through the scattered spinifex clumps and bunches of sticky plants and the odd tree, Rose thought about the whole week. She sensed that it would possibly be the defining event of her life.

*But not the most important or satisfying thing I do*, she mused.

In her mind she ticked off a list of possible achievements in the future. As she did, she remembered another of Captain Ross's sayings, this one during a leadership lesson.

"Don't aim at happiness," he had said. "At the end of your life, hopefully ninety odd years away, when you are on your deathbed you want to be satisfied that you have done the best that you could with what God gave you. And with few regrets. Be honest and do honourable things you are proud of. So aim for respect and satisfaction. You can make yourself happy in your own mind."

"I will," Rose vowed, and it came to her that possibly the greatest thing she might do was raise a family of good kids that she was proud of.

*When I'm older and after I've met Mr Right!* she thought, with an embarrassed blush at what might be involved in that process.

While crossing the creek she considered what the immediate future might bring. From her reading and overhearing things at home she understood there would be a lot of legal trouble and publicity.

*Captain Ross and Ma'am will be in trouble for wearing their uniforms and him for shooting at Lucas,* she reasoned.

And when it came to the publicity and the court cases, she made a firm decision to continually point out that she was able to do all that she had done because she had been trained as a cadet. Which led to her to deciding to make sure her father looked after the Rosses.

*He will hire the best lawyers in the country, or he will have a very angry daughter to deal with,* she told herself.

She sensed that she was no longer in the 'Daddy's Little Girl' position where all she had to do was look innocent and flutter her eyelashes. That post had been taken by Little Miss Ball of Mischief. But Rose found she did not resent that. She loved Belinda too and knew they would always share a special bond. What she did know was that she now had a different relationship with her father, one based solidly on love and respect. It was, she realised, a more mature, and special bond with him. She relished those thoughts as she started up the next slope.

And there was Cousin James, trying to run in the spinifex. Twice he tripped but Rose did not bother to run. She knew that the heat and thirst and general panic of being lost in this vast landscape would bring him to a halt. It did. She topped the next rise and found him trying to hide in the spinifex. He stood up and looked frantically around. Rose saw that he had run through some spiky bush or other that had scratched his face and arms and torn his clothes and he was sweating and gasping. The sight gave her a spurt of malicious pleasure.

*Serves you right, you mongrel! Now you know how we felt!*

She did not go near him, just held up the pistol and pointed back the way they had come. Cousin James swore and cursed and then began to weep, which cut no ice with Rose.

*You tried to kill us, you bastard!* she thought.

So she shepherded him back to the road, arriving there just as the first police car came racing into view.

# Enjoy more C.R. Cummings stories

## The Cadet Series

www.ingramcontent.com/pod-product-compliance
Lightning Source LLC
Chambersburg PA
CBHW050545260626
47157CB00002B/439